ALSO BY FREDERICK FORSYTH

THE
AFGHAN

Frederick Forsyth

A SIGNET BOOK

SIGNET
Published by New American Library, a division of
Penguin Group (USA) Inc., 375 Hudson Street,
New York, New York 10014, USA
Penguin Group (Canada), 90 Eglinton Avenue East, Suite 700, Toronto,
Ontario M4P 2Y3, Canada (a division of Pearson Penguin Canada Inc.)
Penguin Books Ltd., 80 Strand, London WC2R 0RL, England
Penguin Ireland, 25 St. Stephen's Green, Dublin 2,
Ireland (a division of Penguin Books Ltd.)
Penguin Group (Australia), 250 Camberwell Road, Camberwell, Victoria 3124,
Australia (a division of Pearson Australia Group Pty. Ltd.)
Penguin Books India Pvt. Ltd., 11 Community Centre, Panchsheel Park,
New Delhi - 110 017, India
Penguin Group (NZ), 67 Apollo Drive, Rosedale, North Shore 0745,
Auckland, New Zealand (a division of Pearson New Zealand Ltd.)
Penguin Books (South Africa) (Pty.) Ltd., 24 Sturdee Avenue,
Rosebank, Johannesburg 2196, South Africa

Penguin Books Ltd., Registered Offices:
80 Strand, London WC2R 0RL, England

Published by Signet, an imprint of New American Library, a division of
Penguin Group (USA) Inc. Previously published in a G. P. Putnam's Sons edition.

First Signet Printing, August 2007
10 9 8 7 6 5 4 3 2 1

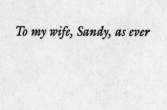

To my wife, Sandy, as ever

PART ONE
STINGRAY

CHAPTER 1

IF THE YOUNG TALIB bodyguard had known that making the cell phone call would kill him, he would not have done it. But he did not know, so he did, and it did.

On the seventh of July 2005, four suicide bombers let off their haversack bombs in Central London. They killed fifty-two commuters and injured about seven hundred, at least one hundred crippled for life.

Three of the four were British born and raised but of Pakistani immigrant parentage. The fourth was a Jamaican by birth, British by naturalization, and had converted to Islam. He and one other were still teenagers; the third was twenty-two and the group leader thirty. All had been radicalized, or brainwashed, into extreme fanaticism, not abroad but right in the heart of England after attending extremist mosques and listening to similar preachers.

Within twenty-four hours of the explosion, they had been identified and traced to various residences in and around the northern city of Leeds; indeed, all had spoken with varying strengths of Yorkshire accent. The leader was a special-needs teacher called Mohammad Siddique Khan.

During the scouring of their homes and possessions, the police discovered a small treasure trove that they chose not to reveal. There were four receipts showing that one of the senior two had bought cell phones of the buy-use-and-throw variety, tri-band versions usable almost anywhere in the world, and each containing a prepaid SIM card worth about twenty pounds sterling. The phones had all been bought for cash and all were missing. But the police traced their numbers and "red-flagged" them all in case they ever came onstream.

It was also discovered that Siddique Khan and his closest intimate in the group, a young Punjabi called Shehzad Tanweer, had visited Pakistan the previous November and spent three months there. No trace was found of whom they had seen, but weeks after the explosions the Arab TV station Al Jazeera broadcast a defiant video made by Siddique Khan as he planned his death, and it was clear this video had been made during that visit to Islamabad.

It was not until late 2006 that it also became clear that one of the bombers took one of the "lily-white" untraceable cell phones with him and presented it to his Al

Qaeda organizer/instructor. (The British police had already established that none of the bombers had the technical skill to create the bombs themselves without instruction and help.)

Whoever this AQ higher-up was, he seems to have passed on the gift as a token of respect to a member of the elite inner committee grouped around the person of Osama bin Laden in his invisible hideaway in the bleak mountains of South Waziristan that run along the Pakistani/Afghan border west of Peshawar. It would have been given for emergency purposes only, because all AQ operatives are extremely wary of cell phones, but the donor could not have known at the time that the British fanatic would be stupid enough to leave the receipt lying around his desk in Leeds.

There are four divisions to bin Laden's inner committee. They deal with operations, financing, propaganda and doctrine. Each branch has a chieftain, and only bin Laden and his coleader, Ayman al-Zawahiri, outrank them. By September 2006, the chief organizer of finance for the entire terror group was al-Zawahiri's fellow Egyptian, Tewfik al-Qur.

For reasons which became plain later, he was under deep disguise in the Pakistani city of Peshawar on September 15, not departing on an extensive and dangerous tour outside the mount redoubt but returning from one. He was waiting for the arrival of the guide who would take him back into the Waziri peaks and into the presence of the Sheikh himself.

To protect him in his brief stay in Peshawar, he had

been assigned four local zealots belonging to the Taliban movement. As befits men who originate in the north-western mountains, the chain of fierce tribal districts that runs along this ungovernable frontier, they were techni-cally Pakistanis but tribally Waziris. They spoke Pashto rather than Urdu, and their loyalties were to the Pashtun people, of whom the Waziris are a subbranch.

All were raised from the gutter in a *madrassah,* or Ko-ranic boarding school, of extreme orientation, adhering to the Wahhabi sect of Islam, the harshest and most in-tolerant of all. They had no knowledge of, or skill in, anything other than reciting the Koran, and were thus, like teeming millions of *madrassah*-raised youths, virtu-ally unemployable. But, given a task to do by their clan chief, they would die for it. That September, they had been charged with protecting the middle-aged Egyptian, who spoke Nilotic Arabic but had enough Pashto to get by. One of the four youths was Abdelahi, and his pride and joy was his cell phone. Unfortunately, its battery was flat because he had forgotten to recharge it.

It was after the midday hour. Too dangerous to emerge to go to the local mosque for prayers; al-Qur had said his orisons along with his bodyguards in their top-floor apartment. Then he had eaten sparingly and retired for a short rest.

Abdelahi's brother lived several hundred miles to the west in the equally fundamentalist city of Quetta, and their mother had been ill. He wished to inquire after her, so he tried to get through on his cell phone. Whatever he wished to say would be unremarkable, just part of the trillions of words of "chatter" that pass through the ether of all five continents every day. But his phone would not work. One of his companions pointed out the absence of black bars in the battery window and explained about charging. Then Abdelahi saw the spare phone lying on the Egyptian's attaché case in the sitting room.

It was fully charged. Seeing no harm, he dialed his brother's number and heard the rhythmic ringing tone far away in Quetta. And in an underground rabbit warren of connecting rooms in Islamabad that constitute the listening department of Pakistan's Counter-Terrorism Center, a small red light began to pulse.

Many who live in it regard Hampshire as England's prettiest county. On its south coast, facing the waters of the Channel, it includes the huge maritime port of Southampton and the naval dockyard of Portsmouth. Its administrative center is the historic city of Winchester, dominated by its cathedral, almost a thousand years old.

At the very heart of the county, away from all the motorways and even the main roads, lies the quiet valley of the River Meon, a gentle chalk stream along whose banks lie villages and townlets that go back to the Saxons.

One single A-class road runs through from south to north, but the rest of the valley is a network of winding lanes edged with overhanging trees, hedges and meadows. This is farm country the way it used to be, with few fields larger than ten acres, and even fewer farms larger than five hundred. Most of the farmhouses are of ancient beam, brick and tile, and some of these are served by clusters of barns of great size, antiquity and beauty.

The man who perched at the apex of one such barn had a panorama of the Meon Valley and a bird's-eye view of the nearest village, Meonstoke, barely a mile away. At the time, several zones to the east, that Abdelahi made the last phone call of his life, the roof climber wiped some sweat off his forehead and resumed his task of carefully removing the clay peg tiles that had been placed there hundreds of years earlier.

He should have had a team of expert roofers, and they should have clad the whole barn in scaffolding. It would have been faster and safer to do the job that way, but much more expensive. And that was the problem. The man with the claw hammer was an ex-soldier, retired after his twenty-five-year career, and he had used up most of his bounty to buy his dream: a place in the country to call home at last. Hence the barn with ten acres, and a track to the nearest lane and then to the village.

But soldiers are not always shrewd with money, and the conversion of the medieval barn into a country house and a snug home had produced estimates from professional companies that specialize in such conversions that took his breath away. Hence the decision that, whatever time it took, he would do it himself.

The spot was idyllic enough. In his mind's eye he could see the roof restored to its former leakproof glory, with nine-tenths of the original and unbroken tiles retained and the other ten percent bought from a yard selling the artifacts of old demolished buildings. The rafters of the hammer beam roof were still sound as the day they were hacked from the oak tree, but the cross-battens would have to come off, to be replaced over good, modern roofing felt.

He could imagine the sitting room, kitchen, study and hall he would make far below him where dust now smothered the last old hay bales. He knew he would need professionals for the electrics and the plumbing, but he had already signed on at Southampton Technical College for night courses in bricklaying, plastering, carpentry and glazing.

One day, there would be a flagstone patio and a kitchen garden; the track would be a graveled drive, and sheep would graze the old orchard. Each night, camping in the paddock as nature favored him with a balmy late-summer heat wave, he went over the figures and reckoned that with patience and a lot of hard work he could just survive on his modest budget.

He was forty-four, olive-skinned, black-haired and -eyed, lean and very hard of physique. And he had had enough. Enough of deserts and jungles, enough of malaria and leeches, enough of freezing cold and shivering nights, enough of garbage food and pain-racked limbs. He would get a job locally, find a Labrador or a couple of Jack Russells and maybe even a woman to share his life.

The man on the roof removed another dozen tiles, kept the ten whole ones, threw down the fragments of the broken ones, and in Islamabad the red light pulsed.

*   *   *

Many think that with a prepaid SIM card in a cell phone all future billing is canceled out. That is true for the purchaser and user but not for the service provider. Unless the phone is used only within the parameters of the transmitting area where it was bought, there is still a settling up to be accomplished, but between the cell phone companies, and their computers do it.

As Abdelahi's call was taken by his brother in Quetta, he began to use time on the radio mast situated just outside Peshawar. This belongs to Paktel. So the Paktel computer began to search for the original vendor of the cell phone in England with the intent of saying, electronically, "One of your customers is using my time and airspace, so you owe me." But the Pakistani CTC had for years required both Paktel and its rival Mobitel to patch through every call sent or received by their networks to the CTC listening room. And, alerted by the British, the CTC had inserted British software into its eavesdropping computers, with an intercept program for certain numbers. One of these had suddenly gone active.

The young Pashto-speaking Pakistani Army sergeant monitoring the console hit a button and his superior officer came on the line. The officer listened for several seconds, then asked, "What is he saying?"

The sergeant listened, and replied, "Something about the speaker's mother. He seems to be speaking to his brother."

"From where?"

Another check. "The Peshawar transmitter."

There was no need to tell the sergeant any more. The entire call would automatically be recorded for later study. The immediate task was to locate the sender. The CTC major on duty that day had little doubt this would not be possible in one short phone call. Surely the fool would not spend long on the line?

From his desk high above the cellars, the major pressed three buttons, and by speed dial a phone trilled in the office of the CTC head of station in Peshawar.

Years earlier, and certainly before the event now known as 9/11, the destruction of the World Trade Center, on 11 September 2001, the Pakistani Inter-Services Intelligence Department, always known as the ISI, had been deeply infiltrated by fundamentalist Muslims of the Pakistani Army. That was its problem, and the reason for its complete unreliability in the struggle against the Taliban and their guests, Al Qaeda.

But Pakistan's president General Musharraf had had little choice but to listen to the USA's strongly worded "advice" to clean house. Part of that program has been the steady transfer of extremist officers out of ISI and back to normal military duties; the other part had been the creation inside ISI of the elite Counter-Terrorism Center, staffed by a new breed of young officers who had no truck with Islamist terrorism, no matter how devout the terrorists might be. Colonel Abdul Razak, formerly a tank commander, was one. He commanded the CTC in Peshawar, and he took the call at half past two.

He listened attentively to his colleague in the national capital, then asked, "How long?"

"About three minutes, so far."

Colonel Razak had the good fortune to have an office just eight hundred yards from the Paktel mast, within the thousand-yard-or-less radius normally needed for his direction finder to work efficiently. With two technicians, he raced to the flat roof of the office block to start the D/F sweeps of the city that would seek to pin the source of the signal to a smaller and ever-smaller area.

In Islamabad, the listening sergeant told his superior, "The conversation has finished."

"Damn," said the major. "Three minutes and forty-four seconds. Still, one could hardly have expected more."

"But he doesn't appear to have switched off," said the sergeant.

In a top-floor apartment in the Old Town of Peshawar, Abdelahi had made his second mistake. Hearing the Egyptian emerging from his private room, he had hastily ended his call to his brother and shoved the cell phone under a nearby cushion. But he forgot to turn it off. Half a mile away, Colonel Razak's sweepers came closer and closer.

Both Britain's Secret Intelligence Service (SIS) and America's Central Intelligence Agency (CIA) have big operations in Pakistan for obvious reasons. It is one of the principal war zones in the struggle against the present terrorism. Part of the strength of the Western alliance, right back to 1945, has been the ability of the two agencies to work together.

There have been spats, especially over the rash of British traitors starting with Philby, Burgess and Maclean in 1951. Then the Americans became aware they, too, had a whole rogues' gallery of traitors working for Moscow, and the interagency sniping stopped. The end of the Cold War in 1991 led to the asinine presumption among politicians on both sides of the Atlantic that peace had come at last and come to stay. That was precisely the moment that the new Cold War, silent and hidden in the depths of Islam, was experiencing birth pangs.

After 9/11, there was no more rivalry, and even the traditional horse trading ended. The rule became: If we have it, you guys had better share it. And vice versa. Contributions come into the common struggle from a patchwork quilt of other foreign agencies, but nothing matches the closeness of the Anglosphere information gatherers.

Colonel Razak knew both the heads of station in his own city. On personal terms, he was closer to the SIS man, Brian O'Dowd, and the rogue cell phone was originally a British discovery. So it was O'Dowd he rang with the news when he came down from the roof.

At that moment, Mr. al-Qur went to the bathroom, and Abdelahi reached under the cushion for the cell phone to put it back on top of the attaché case where he had found it. With a start of guilt, he realized it was still on, so he switched it off at once. He was thinking of battery wastage, not interception. Anyway, he was too late by eight seconds. The direction finder had done its job.

"What do you mean you've found it?" asked O'Dowd. His day had suddenly become Christmas and several birthdays rolled into one.

"No question, Brian. The call came from a top-floor apartment of a five-story building in the Old Quarter. Two of my undercover people are slipping down there to have a look and work out the approaches."

"When are you going in?"

"Just after dark. I'd like to make it three a.m., but the risk is too big. They might fly the coop . . ."

Colonel Razak had been to Camberley Staff College in England on a one-year, Commonwealth-sponsored course, and was proud of his command of idiom.

"Can I come?"

"Would you like to?"

"Is the pope Catholic?" said the Irishman.

Razak laughed out loud. He enjoyed the banter.

"As a believer in the one true God, I wouldn't know," he said. "All right. My office at six. But it is mufti. And I mean our mufti."

He meant there would not only be no uniforms but no Western suits, either. In the Old Town, and especially in the Qissa Khawani Bazaar, only the *shalwar kameez* assembly of loose trousers and long shirt would pass unnoticed. Or the robes and turbans of the mountain clans. And that also applied to O'Dowd.

The British agent was there just before six, with his black-painted, black-windowed Toyota Land Cruiser. A British Land Rover might have been more patriotic, but the Toyota was the preferred vehicle of local fundamentalists and would pass unnoticed. He also brought a bottle of the single-malt whiskey known as Chivas Regal. It was Abdul Razak's favorite tipple. He had once chided his Pakistani friend on his taste for the alcoholic tincture from Scotland.

"I regard myself as a good Muslim, but not an obsessive one," said Razak. "I do not touch pork, but see no harm in dancing, or a good cigar. To ban these is Taliban fanaticism, which I do not share. As for the grape, or even grain, wine was widely drunk during the first four caliphates, and if one day in paradise I am chided by a higher authority than you then I shall beg the all-merciful Allah for forgiveness. In the meantime, give me a top-up."

It was perhaps strange that a tank corps officer should have made such an excellent policeman, but such was Abdul Razak. He was thirty-six, married with two children and educated. He also embodied a capacity for lateral thought, for quiet subtlety and the tactics of the mongoose facing the cobra rather than the charging elephant. He wanted to take the apartment at the top of the block flats without a raging firefight, if he could. Hence his approach was quiet and stealthy.

Peshawar is a most ancient city, and no part older than the Qissa Khawani Bazaar. Here caravans traveling the Great Trunk Road through the towering and intimidating Khyber Pass into Afghanistan have paused to refresh men and camels for many centuries. And, like any good bazaar, the Qissa Khawani has always provided for man's basic needs—blankets, shawls, carpets, brass artifacts, copper bowls, food and drink. It still does.

It is multiethnic and multilingual. The accustomed eye can spot the turbans of Afridis, Waziris, Ghilzai and Pakistani from nearby, contrasting with the Chitrali caps from farther north and the fur-trimmed winter hats of Tajiks and Uzbeks.

In this maze of narrow streets and lanes where a man can lose any pursuer are the shops and food stalls of the clock bazaar, basket bazaar, money changers, bird market and the bazaar of the storytellers. In imperial days, the British called Peshawar the Piccadilly of Central Asia.

The apartment identified by the D/F sweeper as the source of the phone call was in one of those tall, narrow buildings with intricately carved balconies and shutters; it was four floors above a carpet warehouse on a lane wide enough for only one car. Because of the heat in the summer, all these buildings have flat roofs where tenants can catch a breath of cool night air, and open stairwells leading up from the street below. Colonel Razak led his team quietly and on foot.

He sent four men, all in tribal clothes, up to the roof of a building four houses down the street from the target. They emerged on the roof, and calmly walked from roof to roof until they reached the final building. Here, they waited for their signal. The colonel led six men up the stairs from the street. All had machine pistols under their robes save the point man, a heavily muscled Punjabi, who bore the rammer.

When they were all lined up in the stairwell, the colonel nodded to the point man, who drew back the rammer and shattered the lock. The door sprang inward, and the team went inside at the run. Three of the men on the roof came straight down the access stairs; the fourth remained above in case anyone tried to escape.

When Brian O'Dowd tried to recall later, it all seemed extremely fast and blurred. That was the impression the occupants got as well.

The attack squad had no idea how many men would be inside or what they would find. It could have been a small army; it could have been a family sipping tea. They did not even know the layout of the apartment; architect's plans may be filed in London or New York but not in the Qissa Khawani Bazaar. All they knew was that a call had been made from a red-flagged cell phone.

In fact, they found four young men watching TV. For two seconds, the attack group feared they might have raided a perfectly innocent household. Then they registered that all the young men were heavily bearded, all were mountain men, and one, the fastest to react, was reaching beneath his robes for a gun. His name was Abdelahi, and he died with four bullets from a Heckler & Koch MP5 in the chest. The other three were smothered and held down before they could fight. Colonel Razak had been very clear: He wanted them alive, if possible.

The presence of the fifth man was announced by a crash in the bedroom. The Punjabi had dropped his rammer, but his shoulder was enough. The door came down, and two CTC hard men went in, followed by Colonel Razak. In the middle of the room, they found a middle-aged Arab, his eyes wide and round with fear or hatred. He stooped to try to gather up the laptop computer he had hurled to the terra-cotta tiles in an effort to destroy it.

Then he realized there was no time, turned and ran for the window, which was wide-open. Colonel Razak screamed, "Grab him," but the Pakistani missed. The Egyptian had been caught naked to the waist because of the heat, and his skin was slick with sweat. He did not even pause for the banister but went straight over and crashed on the cobbles forty feet below. Bystanders gathered round the body within seconds, but the AQ financier gurgled twice and died.

The building and street had become a chaos of shouting and running figures. Using his mobile phone, the colonel called up the fifty uniformed soldiers he had positioned in the black-windowed vans four streets away. They came racing down the alley to restore order, if that is what even more chaos can be called. But they served their purpose; they sealed the apartment block. In time, Abdul Razak would want to interview every neighbor, and, above all, the landlord, the carpet seller at street level.

The corpse on the street was surrounded by the army and blanketed. A stretcher would appear. The dead man would be carried away to the morgue of Peshawar General Hospital. No one still had the faintest idea who he was. All that was clear was that he had preferred death to the tender attention of the Americans at Bagram Camp up in Afghanistan, where he would surely have been horse-traded by Islamabad with the CIA station chief in Pakistan.

Colonel Razak turned back from the balcony. The three prisoners were handcuffed and hooded. There would have to be an armed escort to get them out of here; this was "fundo" territory. The tribal street would not be on his side. With the prisoners and the body gone, he would spend hours scouring the flat for every last clue about the man with the red-flagged cell phone.

Brian O'Dowd had been asked to wait on the stairs during the raid. He was now in the bedroom holding the damaged Toshiba laptop. Both knew this would almost certainly be the crown jewel. All the passports, all the cell phones, any scrap of paper however insignificant, all the prisoners and all the neighbors—the lot would be taken to a safe place and wrung dry for anything they could yield. But first the laptop . . .

The dead Egyptian had been optimistic if he thought denting the frame of the Toshiba would destroy its golden harvest. Even seeking to erase the files within it would not work. There were wizards over in Britain and the USA who would painstakingly strip out the hard drive and peel away the subterfuge chatter to uncover every word the Toshiba had ever ingested.

"Pity about whoever-he-was," said the SIS agent.

Razak grunted. The choice he had made was logical. Hang on for days and the man could have disappeared. Spend hours snooping around the building and his agents would have been spotted; the bird would still have flown. So he had gone in hard and fast, and with five extra seconds he would have had the mysterious suicide in handcuffs. He would prepare a statement for the public that an unknown criminal had died in a fall while resisting arrest. Until the corpse was identified. If he turned out to be an AQ higher-up, the Americans would insist on an all-singing, all-dancing press conference to claim the triumph. He still had no idea how high up Tewfik al-Qur had really been.

"You'll be pinned down here for a while," said O'Dowd. "Can I do you the favor of seeing the laptop safely back to your HQ?"

Fortunately, Abdul Razak possessed a wry humor. In his work, it was a saving grace. In the covert world, only humor keeps a man sane. It was the word "safely" that he enjoyed.

"That would be most kind of you," he said. "I'll give you a four-man escort back to your vehicle. Just in case. When this is all over, we must share the immoral bottle you brought over this evening."

Clutching the precious cargo to his chest, flanked fore and aft and on each side by Pakistani soldiers, the SIS man was brought back to his Land Cruiser. The technology he needed was already in the rear, and at the wheel, protecting machinery and vehicle, was his driver, a fiercely loyal Sikh.

They drove to a spot outside Peshawar, where O'Dowd hooked up the Toshiba to his own bigger and more powerful Tecra; and the Tecra opened a line in cyberspace to the British government communication HQ at Cheltenham, deep in the Cotswold Hills of England.

O'Dowd knew how to work it, but he was still hazy about the sheer magic—at least to a layman—of cybertechnology. Within a few seconds, across thousands of miles of space, Cheltenham had acquired the entire image of the Toshiba's hard drive. It had gutted the laptop as efficiently as a spider drains the juices from a captured fly.

The head of station drove the laptop to CTC headquarters and delivered it into safe hands. Before he reached the CTC office block Cheltenham had shared the treasure with America's National Security Agency at Fort Meade, Maryland. It was pitch-black in Peshawar, dusk in the Cotswolds and midafternoon in Maryland. It mattered not. Inside GCHQ and NSA, the sun never shines; there is no night and no day.

In both sprawling complexes of buildings set in rustic countryside, the listening goes on from pole to pole and all points between. The trillions of words spoken by the human race every day, in five hundred languages and more than a thousand dialects, are heard, culled, winnowed, sorted, rejected, retained and, if interesting, studied and traced.

Even that is just the start. Both agencies encode and decrypt in hundreds of codes, and each has special divisions dedicated to file recovery and the unearthing of cybercrime. As the planet rolled through another day and another night, two agencies began to strip down the measures al-Qur thought had obliterated his private files. The experts found the limbo files and exposed the slack spaces.

The process has been compared to the work of a skilled restorer of paintings. With immense care, the outer layers of grime or later paint are eased off the original canvas to reveal the hidden work beneath. Mr.

al-Qur's Toshiba began to reveal document after document that he thought had been wiped away or over-painted.

Brian O'Dowd had of course alerted his own colleague and superior, the head of station in Islamabad, even before accompanying Colonel Razak on the raid. The senior SIS man had informed his "cousin," the CIA station chief. Both men were avidly waiting for news. In Peshawar, there would be no sleep.

Colonel Razak returned from the bazaar at midnight with his treasure trove in several bags. The three surviving bodyguards were lodged in cells in the basement of his own building. He would certainly not entrust them to the common jail. Escape or assisted suicide would be almost a formality. Islamabad now had their names and was no doubt haggling with the U.S. Embassy, which contained the CIA station. The colonel suspected they would end up in Bagram for months of interrogation, even though he suspected they did not even know the name of the man they were guarding.

The telltale cell phone from Leeds, England, had been found and identified. It was slowly becoming clear the foolish Abdelahi had only borrowed it without permission. He was on a slab in the morgue with four bullets in the chest but an untouched face. The man next door had a smashed head, but the city's best facial surgeon was trying to put it back together. When he had done his best, a photo was taken. An hour later, Colonel Razak rang O'Dowd with ill-concealed excitement. Like all counterterrorist agencies collaborating on the struggle against Islamist terror groups, the CTC of Pakistan has a huge gallery of photos of suspects.

Simply because Pakistan is a long way from Morocco means nothing. AQ terrorists stem from at least forty nationalities and double that number of ethnic groups. And they travel. Razak had spent the night flashing his gallery of faces from his computer to a big plasma screen in his office, and he kept coming back to one face.

It was already plain from the captured passports—eleven of them, all forged and all of superb quality—that the Egyptian had been traveling, and for this he had clearly changed his appearance. And yet the face of the man who could pass unnoticed in a bank's boardroom in the West, and who was yet consumed by hatred for everything and everyone not of his own twisted faith, seemed to have something in common with the shattered head on the marble slab.

He caught O'Dowd over breakfast, which he was sharing with his American CIA colleague in Peshawar. Both men left their scrambled eggs and raced over to CTC headquarters. They too stared at the face and compared it with the photo from the morgue. If only it could be true . . . And both men had one priority: to tell Head Office about the stunning discovery, that the body on the slab was none other than Tewfik al-Qur, Al Qaeda's senior banker himself.

Midmorning, a Pakistani Army helicopter came to take it all away. The prisoners, shackled and hooded; two dead bodies; and the boxes of evidence recovered from the apartment. Thanks were profuse, but Peshawar is an outstation; the center of gravity was moving, and moving fast. In fact, it had already arrived in Maryland.

In the aftermath of the disaster now known simply as 9/11, one thing became clear, and no one seriously denied it. The evidence not simply that something was going on, but pretty much that what was going on had been there all the time. It was there as intelligence is almost always there; not in one beautiful, gift-wrapped package, but in dribs and drabs, scattered all over. Seven or eight of the USA's nineteen primary intel-gathering or law enforcement agencies had their bits. But they never talked to each other.

Since 9/11, there has been a huge shake-up. There are now the six principals to whom everything has to be revealed at an early stage. Four are politicians: the president, vice president and the secretaries for defense and state. The two professionals are the National Security Adviser, Stephen Hadley, overseeing the Department of Homeland Security and the nineteen agencies—and, on top of the pile, the director of national intelligence, John Negroponte.

The CIA is still the primary outside-the-USA intel-gathering body, but the director of central intelligence is no longer the lone ranger he used to be. Everyone reports upward, and the three watchwords are: collate, collate, collate. Among the giants, the National Security Agency at Fort Meade is still the biggest, in budget and personnel, and the most secret. It alone retains no links to the public or media. It works in darkness, but it listens to everything, decrypts everything, translates everything and analyzes everything. Yet so impenetrable is some of the stuff overheard, recorded, downloaded, translated and studied that it also uses "out-of-house" committees of experts. One of these is the Koran Committee.

As the treasure from Peshawar came in, electronically or physically, other agencies also went to work. Identification of the dead man was vital and the task went to the FBI. Within twenty-four hours, the Bureau reported it was certain. The man who went over the Peshawar balcony was indeed the principal finance gatherer for Al Qaeda, and one of the rare intimates of OBL himself. The connection had been through Ayman al-Zawahiri, his fellow Egyptian. It was he who had spotted and headhunted the fanatical banker.

The State Department took the passports. There were a stunning eleven of them. Two had never been used but now showed entry and exit stamps all over Europe and the Middle East. To no one's surprise, six of them were Belgian, all in different names and all completely genuine, except the details inside.

For the global intelligence community, Belgium has long been the leaky bucket. Since 1990, a staggering nineteen thousand Belgian "blank" passports have been reported stolen—and that is according to the Belgian government itself. In fact, they were simply sold by civil servants on the take. Forty-five were from the Belgian consulate in Strasbourg, France, and twenty from the Belgian Embassy at The Hague, Holland. The two used by the Moroccan assassins of anti-Taliban resistance fighter Ahmad Shah Massoud were from the latter. So was one of the six used by al-Qur. The other five were assumed to be from the still-missing 18,935.

The Federal Aviation Administration, using its contracts and huge leverage across the world of international aviation, checked out plane tickets and passenger lists. It was tiresome, but entry and exit stamps pretty much pinpointed the flights to be checked.

Slowly but surely, it began to come together. Tewfik al-Qur had seemingly been charged to raise large sums of untraceable money to make unexplained purchases. There was no evidence he had made any himself, so the only logical deduction was that he had put others in funds to make the purchases themselves. The U.S. authorities would have given their eyeteeth to learn precisely whom he had seen. These names, they guessed, would have rolled up an entire covert network across Europe and the Middle East. The one notable target country the Egyptian had not visited was the USA.

It was finally at Fort Meade that the trail of revelation hit the buffer. Seventy-three documents had been downloaded from the Toshiba recovered in the apartment at Peshawar. Some were mere airline timetables, and the flights listed on them that al-Qur had actually taken were now known. Some were public domain financial reports that had seemingly interested the financier so that he had noted them for later perusal. But they gave nothing away.

Most were in English, some in French or German. It was known al-Qur spoke all three languages fluently, apart from his native Arabic. The captured bodyguards, up in Bagram Camp and singing happily, had revealed the man spoke halting Pashto, indicating he must have spent some time in Afghanistan, though the West had no trace of when or where.

It was the Arabic texts that caused the unease. Because Fort Meade is basically a vast Army base, it comes under the Department of Defense. The commanding officer of NSA is always a four-star general. It was in the office of this soldier that the chief of the Arabic Translation Department asked for an interview.

The absorption of NSA with Arabic had been increasing steadily over the nineties as Islamist terrorism, apart from the constant interest evoked by the Israel-Palestine situation, began to grow. It leapt to prominence with the attempt by Ramzi Yousef on the World Trade Towers with a truck bomb in 1993. But after 9/11, it became a question of: "Every single word in that language, we want to know." So the Arabic department is huge and involves thousands of translators, most of them Arabs by birth and education, with a smattering of non-Arab scholars.

Arabic is not just one language. Apart from the classical Arabic of the Koran and academia, it is spoken by half a billion people but in at least fifty different dialects and accents. If the speech is fast, accented, using local idiom and the quality is bad, it will usually need a translator from the same area as the speaker to be relied on to catch every meaning and nuance.

More, it is often a flowery language, using much imagery, flattery, exaggeration, simile and metaphor. Add to that, it can be very elliptical, with meanings inferred rather than openly said. It is quite different from one-meaning-only English.

"We are down to two last documents," said the head of Arabic translation. "They seem to be from different hands. We believe one may well be from Ayman al-Zawahiri himself and the other from al-Qur. The first seems to have the word patterns of al-Zawahiri as taken from his previous speeches and videos. Of course, with sound we could be positive to one hundred percent.

"The reply seems to be from al-Qur, but we have no text on record of what he writes like in Arabic. As a banker, he mainly spoke and wrote in English.

"But both documents have repeated references to the Koran and passages therein. They are invoking Allah's blessing on something. Now, I have many scholars of Arabic, but the language and subtle meanings contained in the Koran are special. Written fourteen hundred years ago. I think we should call on the Koran Committee to take a look."

The commanding general nodded.

"Okay, Professor, you got it." He glanced up at his ADC. "Get hold of our Koran scholars, Harry. Fly them in. No delays, no excuses."

CHAPTER 2

THERE WERE FOUR MEN in the Koran Committee, three Americans and a British academic. All were professors, none were Arabs, but all had spent their lives steeped in the study of the Koran and its thousands of attendant scholarly commentaries.

One was resident at Columbia University, New York, and following the order from Fort Meade a military helicopter was dispatched to bring him to the NSA. Two were respectively with the RAND Corporation and the Brookings Institution, both in Washington. Army staff cars were detached to collect them.

The fourth and youngest was Dr. Terry Martin, on secondment to Georgetown University, Washington, from the School of Oriental and African Studies, London. Part of the University of London, SOAS manages to enjoy a worldwide reputation for Arabic scholarship.

In terms of the study of matters Arabic, the Englishman had had a head start. He had been born and raised in Iraq, the son of an accountant with a major oil company operating there. His father had deliberately not sent him to the Anglo-American school but to a private academy that schooled the sons of the elite of Iraqi society. By the time he was ten, he could, linguistically at least, pass for an Arab boy among the others. Only his pink face and tufty ginger hair made plain that he could never completely pass for an Arab.

Born in 1965, he was in his eleventh year when Mr. Martin Senior decided to leave Iraq and return to the safety of the UK. The Ba'ath Party was back in power, but that power truly resided not with President Bakr but with his vice president, who was carrying out a ruthless pogrom of his political enemies, real and imagined.

The Martins had already lived through the tumultuous times since the balmy days of the fifties when the boy king Feisal was on the throne. They had seen the massacre of the young king and his pro-Western premier, Nuri Said, the equally gory murder on camera in the TV studio of his successor General Kassem, and the first arrival of the equally brutal Ba'ath Party. That in turn had been toppled, then returned to power in 1968. For seven years, Martin Senior watched the growing power of the psychotic Vice President Saddam Hussein and in 1975 decided it was time to leave.

His elder son, Mike, was thirteen and ready for a British boarding school. Martin Senior had obtained a good post with Burmah Oil in London, thanks to a kind word from a certain Denis Thatcher, whose wife, Margaret, had just become leader of the Conservative Party. All four of them—the father, Mrs. Martin, Mike and Terry—were back in the UK by Christmas.

Terry's brilliant brain had already been noted. He walked through exams for boys two and even three years his senior as a knife through butter. It was presumed, as it turned out almost rightly, that a series of scholarships and bursaries would carry him through senior school and Oxford or Cambridge. But he wanted to continue with Arabic studies. While still at school, he had applied to the SOAS, attending the spring interview in 1983, joining as an undergraduate that same autumn, studying the history of the Middle East.

He walked through a First-Class degree in three years, and then put in two more for his doctorate, specializing in the Koran and the first four caliphates. He took a sabbatical year to continue Koranic studies at the famed Al-Azhar Institute in Cairo and on his return was offered a lectureship at the young age of twenty-seven, a signal honor because when it comes to matters Arabic SOAS is one of the toughest schools in the world. He was promoted to a readership at the age of thirty-four, earmarked for a professorship by forty. He was forty-one the afternoon the NSA came seeking his advice, spending a year as a visiting professor at Georgetown because that same spring of 2006 his life had fallen apart.

The emissary from Fort Meade found him in a lecture hall, concluding a talk on the teachings of the Koran as relevant to the contemporary age.

It was plain from the wings of the stage that his students liked him. The hall was packed. He made his lectures have the feeling of a long and civilized conversation among equals, seldom referring to notes, jacket off, pacing up and down, his short, plump body radiating enthusiasm to impart and share, to give serious attention to a point raised from the floor, never putting a student down for lack of knowledge, talking in layman's language, keeping the body of the lecture short with plenty of time for student questions. He had reached that point when the spook from Fort Meade appeared in the wings.

A red-plaid shirt from the fifth row raised a hand. "You said you disagreed with the use of the term 'fundamentalist' to refer to the philosophy of the terrorists. Why?"

Given the blizzard of publicity concerning matters Arabic, Islamic and Koranic that had swept across America since 9/11, every question session swerved quickly from theoretical scholarship to the onslaught on the West that had occupied so much of the previous ten years.

"Because it is a misnomer," said the professor.

"The very word implies 'back to basics.' But the planters of bombs in trains, buses and malls are not going back to the basics of Islam. They are writing their own new script, then arguing retroactively, seeking to find Koranic passages that justify their war.

"There are fundamentalists in all religions. Christian monks in a closed order, sworn to poverty, self-denial, chastity, obedience—these are fundamentalists. Ascetics exist in all religions, but they do not advocate indiscriminate mass murder of men, women and children. That is the key phrase. Judge all religions and all sects within those religions by that phrase and you will see that to wish to return to the basic teachings is not terrorism, for in no religion, including Islam, do the basic teachings advocate mass murder."

In the wings, the man from Fort Meade tried to attract Dr. Martin's attention. The professor glanced sideways and noted the young man with the short-barbered hair, button-down shirt and dark suit. He had government written all over him. He tapped the watch on his wrist. Martin nodded.

"Then what would you call the terrorists of today? Jihadists?"

It was an earnest young woman farther back. From her face, Dr. Martin judged her parents must have come from the Mideast: India, Pakistan, Iran perhaps. But she did not wear the hijab scarf over the head to indicate strict Muslim.

"Even 'jihad' is the wrong word. Of course jihad exists, but it has rules. Either it is a personal struggle within oneself to become a better Muslim, but in that case it is completely nonaggressive. Or it means true holy war, armed struggle in the defense of Islam. That's what the terrorists claim they are about. But they choose to airbrush the rules out of the text.

"For one thing, true jihad can only be declared by a legitimate Koranic authority of proven and accepted repute. Bin Laden and his acolytes are notorious for their lack of scholarship. Even if the West had indeed attacked, hurt, damaged, humiliated and demeaned Islam and thus all Muslims, there are still rules, and the Koran is absolutely specific on these.

"It is forbidden to attack and kill those who have offered no offense and done nothing to hurt you. It is forbidden to kill women and children. It is forbidden to take hostages, and it is forbidden to mistreat, torture or kill prisoners. The AQ terrorists and their followers do all four on a daily basis. And let us not forget that they have killed far more fellow Muslims than Christians or Jews."

"Then what do you call their campaign?"

The man in the wings was becoming agitated. A full general had given him an order. He did not wish to be the last to report back.

"I would term them 'the New Jihadis,' because they have invented an unholy war outside the laws of the holy Koran and thus of true Islam. True jihad is not savage, but what they practice is. Last question, I am afraid."

There was a gathering of books and notes. A hand shot up from the front. Freckles, white T-shirt advertising a student rock group.

"All the bombers claim to be martyrs. How do they justify this?"

"Badly," said Dr. Martin, "because they have been duped, well educated though some of them are. It is perfectly feasible to die a *shahid*, or martyr, fighting for Islam in a truly declared jihad. But again there are rules and these are quite specific in the Koran. The warrior must not die by his own hand even though he has volunteered for a no-return mission. He must not know the time and place of his own death.

"Suicides do exactly that. Yet suicide is specifically forbidden. In his lifetime, Muhammad absolutely refused to bless the body of a suicide even though the man had ended his own life to avoid the crippling agony of disease. Those who commit mass murder of innocents and commit suicide are destined for hell, not paradise. The false preachers and imams who trick them down this road will join them there. And now, I fear, we must rejoin the world of Georgetown and hamburgers. Thank you for your attention."

They gave him a standing ovation, and, pink with embarrassment, he took his jacket and walked into the wings.

"Sorry to interrupt, Professor," said the man from Fort Meade. "But the brass need the Koran Committee back at the fort. The car is outside."

"In a hurry?"

"Yesterday, sir. There's a flap."

"Any ideas?" asked Martin.

"No, sir."

Of course. "Need to know." The unshakable rule. If you do not need to know to do your job, they are not going to tell you. Martin's curiosity would have to wait. The car was the usual dark sedan with telltale aerial on the roof. It needed to be in touch with base all the time. The driver was a corporal, but even though Fort Meade is an Army base the man was in plain clothes, not uniform. No need to advertise, either.

Dr. Martin climbed into the back while the driver held the door open. His escort took the front passenger's seat, and they began to drive through the traffic out to the Baltimore highway.

Far to the east, the man converting his own barn into a retirement home stretched out by the campfire in the orchard. He was perfectly happy like that. If he could sleep in rocks and snowdrifts, he could certainly sleep on the soft grass beneath the apple trees.

Campfire fuel was absolutely no problem. He had enough rotten old planks to last a lifetime. His billycan sizzled above the red embers, and he prepared a welcome mug of steaming tea. Fancy drinks are fine in their way, but after a hard day's work a soldier's reward is a mug of piping tea.

He had in fact taken the afternoon off from his lofty task up on the roof and walked into Meonstoke to visit the general store and buy provisions for the weekend.

It was clear everyone knew that he had bought the barn and was trying to restore it himself. That went down well. Rich Londoners with a checkbook to flash and a lust to play the squire were greeted with politeness up front but a shrug behind their back. But the dark-haired single man who lived in a tent in his own orchard while he did the manual work himself was, so ran the growing belief in the village, a good sort.

According to the postman, he seemed to receive little mail save a few official-looking, buff envelopes, and even these he asked to be delivered to the Buck's Head public house to save the postman the haul up the long, muddy track—a gesture appreciated by the postman. The letters were addressed to "Colonel," but he never mentioned that when he bought a drink at the bar or a newspaper or food at the store. Just smiled and was very polite. The local and growing appreciation of the man was tinged with curiosity. So many "incomers" were brash and forward. Who was he, and where had he come from, and why had he chosen to settle in Meonstoke?

That afternoon, on his ramble through the village, he had visited the ancient church of St. Andrew's, and met and fallen into conversation with the rector, Reverend Jim Foley.

The ex-soldier was beginning to think he would enjoy life where he had decided to settle. He could pedal his rugged mountain bike down to Droxford on the Southampton road to buy straight-from-the-garden food in the produce market. He could explore myriad lanes he could see from his roof and sample ale in the old beamed pubs they would reveal.

But in two days, he would attend Sunday matins at St. Andrew's in the quiet gloom of the ancient stone and he would pray, as he often did.

He would ask for forgiveness of the God in whom he devoutly believed for all the men he had killed and for the rest of their immortal souls. He would ask for eternal rest for all the comrades he had seen die beside him, he would give thanks that he had never killed women or children nor any who came in peace and he would pray that one day he too could expiate his sins and enter into the kingdom.

Then he would come back to the hillside and resume his labors. There were only another thousand tiles to go.

Vast as is the National Security Agency complex of buildings, it is only a tiny fraction of Fort Meade, one of the largest military bases in the USA. Situated four miles east of Interstate 95 and halfway between Washington and Baltimore, the base is home to around ten thousand military staff and twenty-five thousand civilian employees. It is a city in itself, and has all the habitual facilities of a small city. The "spook" part is tucked away in one corner, inside a rigidly guarded security zone that Dr. Martin had never visited before.

The sedan bearing him glided through the sprawling base with no let or hindrance until it came to the zone. At the main gate, passes were examined, and faces peered through the windows at the British academic as his escort vouched for him. Half a mile later, the car drew up at a side door of the huge main block, and Dr. Martin and his escort entered. There was a desk guarded by Army personnel. More checks, some phoning, thumbs placed on pads, iris recognition, final admission.

After what seemed like another marathon of corridors, they came to an anonymous door. The escort knocked and went in. Martin found himself at last among faces he knew, and recognized friends, colleagues and fellow members of the Koran Committee.

Like so many government service conference rooms, it

was anonymous and functional. There were no windows, but air-conditioning kept the air fresh. A circular table and padded upright chairs. On one wall, a screen, presumably for displays and graphics, should it be needed. Side tables with coffee and trays of food for the insatiable American stomach.

The hosts were clearly two nonacademic intelligence officers who introduced themselves with give-nothing-away courtesy. One was the deputy director of the NSA, sent to attend by the general himself. The other was a senior officer from Homeland Security in Washington.

And there were the four academics, including Dr. Martin. They all knew each other. Before agreeing to be co-opted onto the no-name, no-publicity committee of experts steeped in one book and one religion, they'd known each other vicariously from their published works and personally from seminars, lectures and conferences. The world of such intense Koranic study is not large.

Terry Martin greeted Drs. Ludwig Schramme from Columbia University, Ben Jolley from RAND, and "Harry" Harrison from Brookings, who certainly had a different first name but was always known as Harry. The oldest and therefore the presumed senior was Ben Jolley, a great bearded bear of a man who, promptly and despite pursed lips from the deputy director, drew out and lit up a fearsome briar pipe from which he drew happily, once it got going like an autumn bonfire. The Westinghouse extraction technology overhead did its best and almost succeeded, but was clearly going to need a complete servicing.

The deputy director cut straight to the heart of the reason for the convocation of the scholars. He distributed copies of two documents, one file to each. There were the Arabic originals as teased out of the AQ financier's laptop, and translations by the in-house Arabic division. The four men went straight to the Arabic versions and read in silence. Dr. Jolley puffed; the man from Homeland Security winced. The four finished more or less at the same time.

Then they read the English translations to see what had been missed and why. Jolley looked up at the two intelligence officers. "Well?"

"Well . . . what, Professor?"

"What," asked the Arabist, "is the problem that has brought us all here?"

The deputy director leaned over and tapped a portion of the English translation. "The problem is that. There. What does it mean? What are they talking about?"

All four of them had spotted the Koranic reference in the Arabic text. They had no need of translation. Each had seen the phrase many times and studied its possible various meanings. But that had been in scholarly texts. This was in modern letters. Three references in one of the letters, a single reference in the other.

"Al-Isra? It must be a code of some kind. It refers to an episode in the life of the Prophet Muhammad."

"Then forgive our ignorance," said the man from Homeland. "What is al-Isra?"

"You explain, Terry," said Dr. Jolley.

"Well, gentlemen," said Terry Martin, "it refers to a

revelation in the life of the prophet. To this day, scholars argue as to whether he experienced a genuinely divine miracle or whether it was simply an out-of-body experience.

"Briefly, he was asleep one night, a year before his emigration from his birthplace of Mecca to Medina, when he had a dream. Or a hallucination. Or a divine miracle. For brevity, let me say dream and stick with it.

"In his dream, he was transported from the depths of modern Saudi Arabia across deserts and mountains to the city of Jerusalem, then a city holy to only Christians and Jews."

"Date? On our calendar?"

"Around 622 A.D."

"Then what happened?"

"He found a tethered horse, a horse with wings. He was bidden to mount it. The horse flew up to heaven, and the prophet confronted Almighty God Himself, who instructed him in all the prayer rituals required of a true believer. These he memorized and later dictated to a scribe as what became an integral part of the 6666. These verses became and remain the basis of Islam."

The other three professors nodded in agreement.

"And they believe that?" asked the deputy director.

"Let us not be too patronizing," Harry Harrison interrupted sharply. "In the New Testament, we are told that Jesus Christ fasted in the wilderness for forty days and forty nights and then confronted and rebuffed the Devil himself. After that period alone with no food, a man would surely be hallucinating. But for Christian true believers, it is Holy Scripture, and not to be doubted."

"All right, my apologies. So al-Isra is the meeting with the archangel?"

"No way," said Jolley. "Al-Isra is the journey itself. A magical journey. A divine journey, undertaken on the instructions of Allah Himself."

"It has been called," Dr. Schramme cut in, "a journey through the darkness to great enlightenment . . ."

He was quoting from an ancient commentary. The other three knew it well and nodded.

"So what would a modern Muslim and a senior operative in Al Qaeda mean by it?"

This was the first time the academics had been given an inkling as to the source of the documents. Not an intercept but a capture.

"Was it fiercely guarded?" asked Harrison.

"Two men died trying to prevent us seeing it."

"Ah, well, yes. Understandable." Dr. Jolley was studying his pipe with great attention. The other three looked down. "I fear it can be nothing but a reference to some kind of project, some operation. And not a small one."

"Something big?" asked the man from Homeland Security.

"Gentlemen, devout Muslims—not to say fanatical ones—do not regard al-Isra lightly. For them, it was something that changed the world. If they have code-named something al-Isra, they intend that it should be huge."

"And no indication what it might be?"

Dr. Jolley looked round the table. His three colleagues shrugged.

"Not a hint. Both the writers call down divine blessings on their project, but that is all. That said, I think I can speak for us all in suggesting you find out what it refers to. Whatever else, they would never give the title al-Isra to a mere satchel bomb, a devastated nightclub, a wrecked commuter bus."

No one had been taking notes. There was no need. Every word had been recorded. This was, after all, the building known in the trade as "the Puzzle Palace."

Both professional intelligence officers would have the transcripts within an hour, and would spend the night preparing their joint report. That report would leave the building before dawn, sealed and couriered with armed guard, and it would go high. Very high. As high as it gets in the USA, which is the White House.

Terry Martin shared a limousine with Ben Jolley on the ride back to Washington. It was bigger than the sedan in which he had come, with a partition between front and rear compartments. Through the glass, they could see the backs of two heads: the driver and their youthful escorting officer.

The gruff old American thoughtfully kept his pipe in his pocket and stared out at the passing scenery, a sea of the russet and gold of autumn leaves. The younger Britisher stared the other way, and also lapsed into reverie.

In all his life, he had only really loved four people,

and he had lost three of them in the past ten months. At the start of the year, his parents, who had had their two sons in their thirties and were both over seventy, had died almost together. Prostate cancer had taken his father, and his mother had simply been too broken-hearted to want to go on. She wrote a moving letter to each of her sons, took a bottle of sleeping pills in a piping hot bath, fell asleep and, in her own words, "went to join Daddy."

Terry Martin was devastated but survived by leaning on two strong men, the only two he loved more than himself. One was his partner of fourteen years, the tall, handsome stockbroker with whom he shared his life. And then, one wild March night, there had been the drunken driver, going crazily fast, and the crunch of metal hitting a human body, and that body on a slab, and the awful funeral, with Gordon's parents stiffly disapproving of his open tears.

He had seriously contemplated ending his own by-now-miserable life, but his elder brother, Mike, seemed to sense his thoughts, moved in with him for a week and talked him through the crisis.

He'd hero-worshipped his brother since they were boys in Iraq, and through their years at the British public school at Haileybury, outside the market town of Hertford.

Mike had always been everything he was not. Dark to his fair, lean to his plump, hard to his soft, fast to his slow, brave to his frightened. Sitting in the limousine, gliding through Maryland, he let his thoughts return to that final rugby match against Tonbridge, with which Mike had ended his five years at Haileybury.

When the two teams came off the field, Terry had been standing by the roped passageway, grinning. Mike had reached out and ruffled his hair.

"Well," he said, "we did it, Bro."

Terry had been seized by gut-wrenching fear when the moment had come to tell his brother that he now knew he was gay. The older man, by then an officer in the Paras and just back from combat in the Falklands, had thought about it for a moment, cracked his mocking grin and handed back the final line given by Joe E. Brown in *Some Like It Hot*: "Well, nobody's perfect."

From that moment, Terry's hero worship of his elder brother knew no limits.

In Maryland, the sun set. In the same time zone, it was setting over Cuba, and on the southwestern peninsula known as Guantánamo a man spread his prayer mat, turned to the east, knelt and began his prayers. Outside the cell, a GI watched impassively. He had seen it all before, many times, but his instructions were never, ever to let his watchfulness slip.

The man who prayed had been in the jail, formerly Camp X-Ray, now Camp Delta, and in the media usually "Gitmo," short for Guantánamo Bay, for nearly five years. He had been through the early brutalities and privations without a cry or a scream. He had tolerated the scores of humiliations of his body and his faith without a sound, but when he stared at his tormentors even they could read the implacable hatred in the black eyes above the black beard so he was beaten the more. But he never broke.

In the "stick and carrot" days when inmates were encouraged to denounce their fellows in exchange for favors, he'd remained silent and earned no better treatment. Seeing this, others had denounced him in exchange for concessions, but as the denunciations were complete inventions he had neither confirmed nor denied them.

In the room full of files kept by the interrogator as proof of their expertise, there was much about the man who prayed that night, but almost nothing from him. He had civilly answered questions put to him years earlier by one of the interrogators who had decided on a humane approach. That was how a passable record of his life existed at all.

But the problem was still the same. None of the interrogators had ever understood a word of his native language and had always relied on the interpreters, or "'terps," who accompanied them everywhere. But the 'terps had an agenda, too. They also received favors for interesting revelations, so they had a motive to make them up.

After four years, the man at prayer was dubbed "noncooperative," which simply meant unbreakable. In 2004, he had been transferred across the Gulf to the new Camp Echo, a locked-down, permanent-isolation unit. Here, the cells were smaller, with white walls, and exercise was allowed only at night. For a year, the man had not seen the sun.

No family clamored for him, no government sought news of him, no lawyer filed papers for him. Detainees round him became deranged and were taken away for therapy. He just stayed silent and read his Koran. Outside, the guards changed while he prayed.

"Goddamn Arab," said the man coming off duty. His replacement shook his head.

"He's not Arab," he said. "He's an Afghan."

"So, what do you think of our problem, Terry?"

It was Ben Jolley, out of his daydream, staring at Martin across the rear of the limo.

"Doesn't sound good, does it?" Terry Martin replied. "Did you see the faces of our two spook friends? They knew we were only confirming what they had suspected, but they were definitely not happy when we left."

"No other verdict, though. They have to discover what it is, this al-Isra operation."

"But how?"

"Well, I've been around spooks for a long time. Been advising as best I can on matters of the Mideast since the Six-Day War. They have a lot of ways: sources on the inside, turned agents, eavesdropping, file recovery, overflying; and the computers help a lot, cross-referencing data in minutes that used to take weeks. I guess they'll figure it out and stop it somehow. Don't forget we have come one hell of a long way since Gary Powers was shot down over Sverdlovsk in 'sixty, or the U2 took those photos of the Cuban missiles in 'sixty-two. Guess before you were born, right?"

He chuckled chestily at his own antiquity as Terry Martin nodded.

"Maybe they have someone right inside Al Qaeda," he suggested.

"Doubt it," said the older man. "Anyone that high up would have given us the location of the leadership by now, and we'd have taken them down with smart bombs."

"Well, maybe they could slip someone inside Al Qaeda to find out and report back."

Again, the older man shook his head, this time with total conviction.

"Come on, Terry, we both know that's impossible. A native-born Arab would quite possibly be turned and work against us. As for a non-Arab, forget it. We both know all Arabs come from extended families, clans, tribes. One inquiry of the family or clan and the impostor would be exposed.

"So he would have to be CV perfect. Add to that, he would have to look the part, speak the part and, most important, play the part. One syllable wrong in all those prayers and the fanatics would hear it. They recite five times a day, and never miss a beat."

"True," said Martin, knowing his case was hopeless but enjoying the fantasy. "But one could learn the Koranic passages, and invent an untraceable family."

"Forget it, Terry. No Westerner can pass for an Arab among Arabs."

"My brother can," said Dr. Martin. In seconds, if he could have bitten off his own tongue he would have.

But it was all right. Dr. Jolley grunted, dropped the subject and studied the outskirts of Washington. Neither head in the front, beyond the glass, moved an inch. He let out a sigh of relief. Any mike in the car must be turned off.

He was wrong.

CHAPTER 3

THE FORT MEADE REPORT on the deliberations of the Koran Committee was ready by dawn that Saturday and destroyed several planned weekends. One of those roused Saturday night at his home in Old Alexandria was Marek Gumienny, deputy director of operations at the CIA. He was bidden to report straight to his office without being told why.

The "why" was on his desk when he got there. It was not even dawn over Washington, but the first indications of the coming sun pinked the distant hills of Prince George's County, where the Patuxent River flows down to join the Chesapeake.

Marek Gumienny's office was one of the few on the sixth and top floor of the big, oblong building among the cluster that forms the headquarters of the CIA and is known simply as "Langley." It had recently been redubbed "the Old Building," to distinguish it from the mirror-image New Building that housed the expanding agency since 9/11.

In the hierarchy of the CIA, the director of Central Intelligence has traditionally been a political appointment, but the real muscle is habitually the two deputy directors. Ops handles the actual intelligence gathering, while the DD Intelligence covers the collation and analysis of the incoming harvest to turn raw information into a meaningful picture.

Just below these two are Counter-Intelligence (to keep the agency free from penetration and in-house traitors) and Counter-Terrorism (increasingly becoming the boiler room as the agency's war swerved from the old USSR to the new threats out of the Mideast).

DDOs, back to the start of the Cold War around 1945, had always been Soviet experts with the Soviet Division and SE (Satellites and East Europe) making the running for an ambitious career officer. Marek Gumienny was the first Arabist to be appointed DDO. As a young agent, he had spent years in the Middle East, mastered two of its languages (Arabic and Farsi, the language of Iran) and knew its culture.

Even in this twenty-four-hour-a-day building, predawn on a Saturday is not an easy time to rustle up piping hot, aromatic black coffee the way he liked it, so he brewed his own. While it perked, Gumienny started on the package on his desk containing the slim, wax-sealed file.

He knew what to expect. Fort Meade may have handled the file recovery, translation and analysis, but it was CIA in collaboration with the British and Pakistan's CTC over in Peshawar who had made the capture. CIA's stations in Peshawar and Islamabad had filed copious reports simply to keep their boss in the picture.

The file contained all the documents downloaded from the AQ financier's computer, but the two letters—taking up three pages—were the stars. The DDO spoke fast and fluent street Arabic, but reading script is always harder so he repeatedly referred to the translations.

He read the report of the Koran Committee, prepared jointly by the two intelligence officers at the meeting, but it offered him no surprises. To him, it was clear the references to al-Isra, the magical journey of the prophet through the night, could only be the code for some kind of important project.

That project now had to have a name in-house for the American intelligence community. It could not be al-Isra; that alone would betray to others what they had found out. He checked with file cryptography for a name to describe, in the future, how he and all his colleagues would call the Al Qaeda project, whatever it was.

Code names come out of a computer by a process known as random selection, the aim being to give nothing away. The CIA naming process that month was using fish; the computer chose "Stingray," so "Project Stingray" it became.

The last sheet in the file had been added Saturday night. It was brief and short. It came from the hand of a man who disliked wasting words, one of the six principals, the director of national intelligence. Clearly, the file out of Fort Meade had gone straight to the National Security committee (Steve Hadley), to the DNI and to the White House. Marek Gumienny imagined there would have been lights burning late in the Oval Office.

The final sheet was on the DNI-headed paper. It said in capital letters:

WHAT IS AL-ISRA

IS IT NUCLEAR, BIOLOGICAL, CHEMICAL,
   CONVENTIONAL?

FIND OUT WHAT, WHEN AND WHERE.

TIMESCALE: NOW

RESTRAINTS: NONE

POWERS: ABSOLUTE

JOHN NEGROPONTE

There was a scrawled signature. There are nineteen primary intelligence-gathering and archive-storing agencies in the USA. The letter in Marek Gumienny's hand gave him authority over them all. He ran his eye back to the top of the sheet. It was addressed to him personally. There was a tap on the door.

A young GS15 stood there with yet another delivery. General Service is simply a salary scale; a "15" means a very junior staffer. Gumienny gave the young man an encouraging smile; he had clearly never been this high up the building before. Gumienny held out his hand, signed the clipboard to confirm receipt and waited until he was alone again.

The new file was a courtesy from the colleagues at Fort Meade. It was a transcript of a conversation held by two of the Koran eggheads in the car on the way back to Washington. One of them was British. It was his last line that someone at Fort Meade had underlined with a brace of question marks in red ink.

During his time in the Middle East, Marek Gumienny had had much to do with the British, and, unlike some of his fellow countrymen who had been trying to cope with the hellhole of Iraq for three years, he was not too proud to admit that the CIA's closest allies, in what Kipling once called "the Great Game," were a repository of much arcane knowledge about the badlands between the Jordan River and the Hindu Kush.

For a century and a half, either as soldiers or administrations of the old empire, or as eccentric explorers, the British had been trudging over desert, mountain range and goat pen in the zone that had now become the intelligence time bomb of the world. The British codenamed the CIA "the Cousins" or "the Company," and the Americans called the London-based Secret Intelligence Service "the Friends" or "the Firm." For Marek Gumienny, one of those friends was a man with whom he had shared good times, not-so-good times and downright dangerous times when they were both field agents. Now he was pinned to a desk in Langley, and Steve Hill had been pulled out of the field and elevated to controller Middle East at the Firm's Vauxhall Cross headquarters.

Gumienny decided a conference would do no harm

and might yield some good. There was no security problem. The Brits, he knew, would have just about everything he had. They, too, had transmitted the guts of the laptop from Peshawar to their own listening and cryptography HQ at Cheltenham. They, too, would have gutted the laptop and printed out its contents. They, too, would have analyzed the strange references to the Koran contained in the coded letters.

What Marek Gumienny had that was probably not with London was the bizarre remark by a British academic in the back of a car in the middle of Maryland. He punched up a number on the console on his desk. Central switchboards are fine up to a point, but modern technology has meant that any senior executive can be connected faster by speed dial on his personal satellite telephone.

A number rang in a modest commuter house in Surrey, just outside London. Eight a.m. in Langley, one p.m. in London, the house about to sit down to a roast beef lunch. A voice answered on the third ring. Steve Hill had enjoyed his golf and was about to enjoy his beef.

"Hallo?"

"Steve? Marek."

"My dear chap, where are you? Over here, by any chance?"

"No, I'm at my desk. Can we go to secure?"

"Sure. Give me two minutes"—and, in the background—"Darling, hold the roast." The phone went down.

With the next call, the voice from England was slightly tinny but uninterceptable.

"Am I to understand that something has hit the ventilation system close to your ear?" asked Hill.

"All over my nice clean shirt," admitted Gumienny. "I guess you have much the same stuff as I have out of Peshawar?"

"I expect so. I finished reading it yesterday. I was wondering when you would call."

"I have something you may not have, Steve. We have a visiting professor over here from London. He made a chance remark Friday evening. I'll cut to the chase. Do you know a man called Martin?"

"Martin who?"

"No, that's his surname. His brother over here is called Dr. Terry Martin. Does it ring a bell?"

Steve Hill had dropped all banter. He sat holding the phone and staring into space. Oh, yes, he knew the Martin brother. Back in the first Gulf War of 1990–91, he had been one of the control team in Saudi Arabia when the academic's brother had slipped into Baghdad and lived there as a humble gardener under the noses of Saddam's secret police while transmitting back priceless intelligence from a source inside the dictator's cabinet.

"Could be," he conceded. "Why?"

"I think we should talk," said the American. "Face-to-face. I could fly over. I have the Grumman."

"When do you want to come over?"

"Tonight. I can sleep on the plane. Be in London for breakfast."

"Okay. I'll arrange it with Northolt."

"Oh, and Steve, while I'm flying could you get out the full file on this man Martin? I'll explain when I see you."

West of London, on the road to Oxford, lies the Royal Air Force base of Northolt. For a couple of years after World War II, it was actually London's civil airport as Heathrow was hastily constructed. Then it relapsed to a secondary airfield, and finally to a field for private and executive jets. But because it remains an RAF property, flights in and out can be fixed to take place in complete security without the usual formalities.

The CIA has its own very private airfield near Langley and a small fleet of executive jets. Marek Gumienny's all-powerful piece of authority paper secured him the Grumman V, aboard which he slept in perfect comfort on the flight over. Steve Hill was at Northolt to meet him.

He took his guest not to the green-and-sandstone ziggurat at Vauxhall Cross on the south bank of the Thames by Vauxhall Bridge, home of the SIS, but to the much quieter Cliveden Hotel, formerly a private mansion, set inside its own estate not thirty miles from the airport. He had reserved a small conference suite with room service and privacy.

There he read the analysis of the American Koran Committee, remarkably similar to the analysis from Cheltenham, and the transcript of the conversation in the back of the car.

"Damn fool," he muttered when he reached the end. "The other Arabist was right. It can't be done. It's not just the lingo, it's all the other tests. No stranger, no foreigner, could ever pass them."

"So, given my orders from the All-High, what would you suggest?"

"Pick up an AQ insider and sweat it out of him," said Hill.

"Steve, if we had the faintest idea of the location of anyone that high in Al Qaeda, we'd take them as a matter of course. We don't have any such target in our sights as of now."

"Wait and watch. Someone will use the phrase again."

"My people have to presume that if al-Isra is to be the next spectacular, it will be the USA that is the target. Waiting for a miracle that may not happen will not pacify Washington. Besides, AQ must know by now we got the laptop. Chances are, they will never use that phrase again, except person to person."

"Well," said Hill, "we could put it about in places they would hear it, that we have it all and are closing in. They would discontinue, cut and run."

"Maybe, maybe not. But we'd never know. We'd still be in limbo, never knowing whether Project Stingray had been terminated or not. And if not? And if it works? Like my boss says: Is it nuclear, biochemical, conventional? Where and when? Can your man Martin really pass for an Arab among Arabs? Is he really that good?"

"He used to be," grunted Hill, and passed over a file. "See for yourself."

The file was an inch thick, standard buff manila, labeled simply with a name: COLONEL MIKE MARTIN.

The Martin boys' maternal grandfather had been a tea planter at Darjeeling, India, between the two world wars.

While there, he had done something almost unheard of. He had married an Indian girl.

The world of the British tea planters was small, remote and snooty. Brides were brought out from England or found among the daughters of the officer class of the Raj. The boys had seen pictures of their grandfather Terence Granger, tall, pink-faced, blond-mustached, pipe in mouth and gun in hand, standing over a shot tiger.

And there were pictures of Miss Indira Bohse, gentle, loving and very beautiful. When Terence Granger would not be dissuaded, the tea company, rather than create an alternative scandal by firing him, hit on a solution. They posted the young couple to the wilds of Assam, up on the Burmese border.

If it was supposed to be a punishment, it did not work. Granger and his new bride loved the life up there—a wild, ravined countryside teeming with game and tigers. And there Susan was born in 1930. By 1943, war had rolled toward Assam, the Japanese advancing through Burma to the border. Terence Granger, though old enough to avoid the Army, insisted on volunteering, and in 1945 died crossing the river Irrawaddy.

With a tiny widow's pension from the company, Indira Granger went to the only place she could, back into her own culture. Two years later came more trouble: India was being partitioned for independence. Ali Jinnah insisted on his Muslim Pakistan to the north; Pandit Nehru settled for mainly Hindu India to the south. Waves of refugees rolled north and south and violent fighting broke out.

Fearing for her daughter's safety, Mrs. Granger sent Susan to stay with her late husband's younger brother, a very proper architect, in Haslemere, Surrey. Six months later, the mother died in the rioting.

Susan Granger came at the age of seventeen to the land of her fathers, which she had never seen. She spent a year at a girls' school, and three as a nurse at Farnham General Hospital. At twenty-one, the youngest age allowed, she applied as a stewardess with the British Overseas Airways Corporation. She was drop-dead beautiful, with tumbling chestnut hair, her father's blue eyes and a skin of an English girl with a honey gold suntan.

BOAC put her on the London–Bombay route because of her fluent Hindi. The route then was long and slow: London–Rome–Cairo–Basra–Bahrain–Karachi–Bombay. No crew could make it all the way; the first crew change and stopover was at Basra, southern Iraq. There, at the country club in 1951, she met oil company accountant Nigel Martin. They married in 1952.

There was a ten-year wait until the birth of the first son, Michael, and three more years to the second son, Terry. But they were like chalk and cheese.

Marek Gumienny stared at the photo in the file. Not a suntan but a naturally saturnine complexion, black hair and dark eyes. He realized the genes of the grandmother had jumped a generation to the grandson; he was nothing remotely like his brother, the academic, in Georgetown, whose pink face and ginger hair came from his father.

He recalled the objections of Dr. Ben Jolley. Any infiltrator with a chance of getting away with it inside Al

Qaeda would have to look the part and speak the part. Gumienny skipped through the rest of the boyhood.

They had both gone in succession to the Anglo-Iraqi school, and learned also from their dad, or their nanny, the gentle plum Fatima from up-country, who would go back to the tribe with enough saved wages to find a proper young man for a husband.

There was a reference which could only have come from an interview with Terry Martin; the older boy in his white Iraqi dishdasha, racing about the lawn of the house in the Saadun suburb of Baghdad, and his father's delighted guests laughing with pleasure and shouting. "But Nigel, he's more like one of us."

More like one of us, thought Marek Gumienny, more like one of them. Two points down of Ben Jolley's four; he looked the part and could pass for an Arab in Arabic. Surely, with intensive schooling, he could master the prayer rituals?

The CIA man read a bit more. As Vice President Saddam Hussein had started nationalizing the foreign-owned oil companies, and that included Anglo-Iraqi in 1972. Nigel Martin had stuck it out three more years before bringing the whole family home in 1975. The boy Mike was thirteen, ready to go to senior school at Haileybury. Marek Gumienny needed a break and coffee.

"He could do it, you know," he said when he came back from the restroom. "With enough training and backup, he really could. Where is he now?"

"Apart from two stints working for us when we borrowed him, he spent his military career between the

Paras and the Special Forces. Retired last year after completing his twenty-five. And no, it wouldn't work."

"Why not, Steve? He has it all."

"Except the background. The parentage, the extended family, the birthplace. You don't just walk into Al Qaeda except as a youthful volunteer for a suicide mission; a low-level lowlife, a gofer. Anyone who would have the trust to get near the gold-standard project in preparation would have to have years behind him. That's the killer, Marek, and it remains the killer. Unless . . ."

He drifted off into a reverie, then shook his head.

"Unless what?" asked the American.

"No, it's not on the table," said Hill.

"Indulge me."

"I was thinking of a ringer. A man whose place he could take. A doppelgänger. But that's flawed, too. If the real object were still alive, AQ would have him in their ranks. If he were dead, they'd know that, too. So, no dice."

"It's a long file," said Marek Gumienny. "Can I take it with me?"

"It's a copy, of course. Eyes only?"

"You have my word, ol' buddy. My eyes only. And my personal safe. Or the incinerator."

The DD Ops flew back to Langley, but a week later he phoned again. Steve Hill took the call at his desk in Vauxhall Cross.

"I think I should fly back," the DDO said without preamble. Both men knew that by then the British prime minister in Downing Street had given his friend in the

White House his word on total cooperation from the British side on tracking down Project Stingray.

"No problem, Marek. Do you have a breakthrough?" Privately, Steve Hill was intrigued. With modern technology, there is nothing that cannot be passed from CIA to SIS in complete secrecy, and in a matter of seconds. So why fly?

"The ringer," said Gumienny. "I think I have him. Ten years younger but looks older. Height and build. Same dark face. An AQ veteran."

"Sounds fine. But how come he's not with the bad guys?"

"Because he's with us. He's in Guantánamo. Has been for five years."

"He's an Arab?" Hill was surprised; he ought to have known about a high-ranking AQ Arab in Gitmo these past five years.

"No, he's an Afghan. Name of Izmat Khan. I'm on my way."

Terry Martin was still sleepless a week later. That stupid remark. Why could he not keep his mouth shut? Why did he have to brag about his brother? Supposing Ben Jolley had said something? Washington was one big, gossiping village, after all. Seven days after the remark in the back of the limousine, he rang his brother.

Mike Martin was lifting the last clutch of unbroken tiles off his precious roof. At last, he could start on the laying of the roofing felt and the battens to keep it down. Within a week, he could be waterproof. He heard the tinkling notes of "Lillibolero" from his mobile. It was in the pocket of his jacket, which was hanging from a nail nearby. He inched across the dangerously frail rafters to reach it. The screen announced it was his brother in Washington.

"Hi, Terry."

"Mike, it's me." He still could not work out how people he was ringing knew already. "I've done something stupid, and I want to ask your pardon. About a week ago, I shot my mouth off."

"Great. What did you say?"

"Never mind. Look, if ever you get a visitation from any men in suits—you know who I mean—you are to tell them to piss off. What I said was stupid. If anyone visits . . ."

From his eagle's nest, Mike Martin could see the charcoal gray Jaguar nosing slowly up the track that led from the lane to the barn.

"It's okay, Bro," he said gently. "I think they're here."

The two spymasters sat on folding camp chairs, and Mike Martin on the bole of a tree that was about to be chainsawed into bits for campfire timber. Martin listened to the "pitch" from the American, and cocked an eyebrow at Steve Hill.

"Your call, Mike. Our government has pledged the White House total cooperation on whatever they want or need, but that stops short of pressuring anyone to go on a no-return mission."

"And would this one fit that category?"

"We don't think so," Marek Gumienny interjected. "If we could even discover the name and whereabouts of one single AQ operative who would know what is going down here, we'd pull you out and do the rest. Just listening to the scuttlebutt might do the trick . . ."

"But passing off . . . I don't think I could pass for an Arab anymore. In Baghdad fifteen years ago, I made myself invisible by being a humble gardener living in a shack. There was no question of surviving an interrogation by the moukhabarat. This time, you'd be looking at intensive questioning. Why would someone who has been in American hands for five years not have become a turncoat?"

"Sure, we figure they would question you. But with luck the questioner would be a high-ranker brought in for the job. At which point, you break out and finger the man for us. We'll be standing by, barely yards away."

"This," said Martin, tapping the file about the man in the Guantánamo cell, "is an Afghan. Ex-Taliban. That means Pashtun. I never got to be fluent in Pashto. I'd be spotted by the first Afghan on the plot."

"There would be months of tutorials, Mike," said Steve Hill. "No way you go until you feel you are ready. Not even then if you don't think it will work. And you would be staying well away from Afghanistan. The good news about Afghan fundos is that they hardly ever appear outside their own manor."

"Do you think you could talk poor Arabic with the accent of a Pashtun of limited education?"

Mike Martin nodded. "Possibly. And if the towelheads bring in an Afghan, who really knew this guy?"

There was silence from the other two men. If that happened, everyone round the fire knew it would be the end.

As the two spymasters stared at their feet rather than explain what would happen to an agent unmasked at the heart of Al Qaeda, Martin flipped open the file on his lap. What he saw caused him to freeze.

The face was five years older, lined by suffering, and ten years more than his calendar age. But it was still the boy from the mountains, the near corpse at Qala-i-Jangi.

"I know this man," he said quietly. "His name is Izmat Khan."

The American stared at him openmouthed.

"How the hell can you know him? He's been cooped up at Gitmo since he was captured five years ago."

"I know, but many years before that we fought the Russians in the Tora Bora."

The men from London and Washington recalled the Martin file. Of course, that year in Afghanistan helping the muj in their struggle against Soviet occupation. It was a long shot, but not unfeasible that the men had met. For ten minutes, they asked him about Izmat Khan, to see what else he could add. Martin handed the file back.

"What is he like now, Izmat Khan? How has he changed in five years with your people at Camp Delta?"

The American from Langley shrugged. "He's tough, Mike. Very, very hard. He arrived with a bad head wound and double concussion. Injured during capture. At first, our medics thought he was maybe . . . well . . . a bit simple. Backward. Turned out he was just totally disoriented. The concussion, and the journey. This was early December 2001, just after 9/11. Treatment was . . . how shall I put it? . . . not gentle. Then it seemed nature took its course, and he recovered enough for questioning."

"And what did he tell you?"

"Not very much. Just his résumé. Resisted all third degree, and all offers. Just stares at us, and what the grunts see in those black eyes is not brotherly love. That is why he is in lockdown. But, from others, we understand he has passable Arabic, learned inside Afghanistan, and before that from years in a *madrassah* rote-learning the Koran. And two British-born AQ volunteers who were in there with him, and have now been released, say he now has some halting English that they taught him."

Martin glanced sharply at Steve Hill. "They'd have to be picked up and kept in quarantine," he said.

Hill nodded. "Of course. It can be arranged."

Marek Gumienny rose and wandered round the barn while Martin studied the file. He stared into the fire, and deep in the embers saw a bleak and bare hillside far away. Two men, a cluster of rocks and the Soviet Hind helicopter gunship swinging to the attack. A whisper from the turbaned boy: "Are we going to die, Angleez?" Gumienny came back, squatted on the ground and poked the fire. The image went up in a cloud of sparks.

"Quite a project you have taken on here, Mike. I'd have thought this was a job for a crew of professionals. You doing it all yourself?"

"As much as I can. For the first time in twenty-five years, I have the time."

"But not the dough, eh?"

Martin shrugged. "There are scores of security companies out there, if I want a job. Iraq alone has spawned more professional bodyguards than one can count, and still more are wanted. They make more in a week working for your guys in the Sunni Triangle than they made in half a year as soldiers."

"But that would mean back to the dust, the sand, the danger, the too-early death. Didn't you retire from that?"

"And what are you offering? A vacation with AQ in the Florida Keys?"

Marek Gumienny had the grace to laugh. "Americans are accused of many things, Mike, but not often of being ungenerous to those who have helped them. I am thinking of a consultancy at, say, two hundred thousand dollars a year for five years. Paid abroad; no need to disturb the tax man. No need actually to show up for work. No need to go into harm's way ever again."

Mike Martin's thoughts flitted to a scene in his all-time-favorite film. T. E. Lawrence has offered Auda abu Tayi money to join him in the attack on Aqaba. He recalled the great reply: Auda will not ride to Aqaba for the British gold, he will ride to Aqaba because it pleases him. He stood up.

"Steve, I want my home shrouded in tarpaulins from top to bottom. When I come back, I want it just the way I left it."

The controller Middle East nodded. "Done," he said.

"I'll get my kit. There's not much of it. Enough to fill the boot, no more."

And so the Western strike-back against Project Stingray was agreed upon under apple trees in a Hampshire orchard. Two days later, by random selection, a computer dubbed it "Operation Crowbar."

If challenged, Mike Martin would never have been able to defend himself. But in all the briefings he later gave them about the Afghan who had once been his friend, there was one detail he kept to himself.

Perhaps he thought that "need to know" was a two-way street. Perhaps he thought the detail too unimportant. It had to do with a muttered conversation in the shadows of a cave hospital run by Arabs in a place called Jaji.

PART TWO
WARRIORS

CHAPTER 4

THE DECISION in the Hampshire orchard led to a blizzard of decision making from the two spymasters. To start with, sanction and approval had to be sought from both men's political masters.

This was easier said than done, because Mike Martin's first condition was that no more than a dozen people should ever know what Operation Crowbar was about. His concern was completely understood.

If fifty people know anything that interesting, one will eventually spill the beans. Not intentionally, not viciously, not even mischievously, but inevitably.

Those who have ever been in deep cover in a lethal situation know that it is nerve-racking enough to trust in one's own tradecraft never to make a mistake and be caught. To hope that one will never be given away by some utterly unforeseeable fluke is constantly stressful.

But the ultimate nightmare is to know that the capture and the long, agonizing death to follow happened because some fool in a bar boasted to his girlfriend and was overheard—that is the worst fear of all. So Martin's condition was acceded to at once.

In Washington, John Negroponte agreed that he alone would be the repository and gave the go-ahead. Steve Hill dined at his club with a man in the British government and secured the same result. That made four.

But each man knew he personally could not be on the case twenty-four hours a day. Each needed an executive officer to run things day to day. Marek Gumienny appointed a rising Arabist in the CIA's Counter-Terrorism division; Michael McDonald dropped everything, explained to his family that he had to work in the UK for a while and flew east as Marek Gumienny returned home.

Steve Hill picked his own deputy on the Middle East Desk, Gordon Phillips. Before they parted company, the two principals agreed that every aspect of Crowbar would have a plausible cover story so that no one lower than the top ten would really know that a Western agent was going to be slipped inside Al Qaeda.

Both Langley and Vauxhall Cross were told that the two men about to go missing were simply on a career-improving, academic-study sabbatical and would be away from their desks for about six months.

Steve Hill introduced the two men who would now be working together, and told them what Crowbar was going to try to do. Both McDonald and Phillips went very silent. Hill had installed them both not in offices in the headquarters building by the Thames but in a safe house, one of several retained by the Firm, out in the countryside.

When they had unpacked and convened in the drawing room, he tossed them both a thick file.

"Finding an Ops HQ starts tomorrow," he said. "You have twenty-four hours to commit this to memory. This is the man who is going to go in. You will work with him until that day, and for him after that. This"—he tossed a thinner file on the coffee table—"is the man he is going to replace. Clearly, we know much less. But that is everything the U.S. interrogators have been able to secure from him in hundreds of hours of interrogations at Gitmo. Learn this also."

When he was gone, the two younger men asked for a large pot of coffee from the household staff and started to read.

It was during a visit to the Farnborough Airshow in the summer of 1977, when he was fifteen, that the schoolboy Martin fell in love. His father and younger brother were with him, fascinated by the fighters and bombers, aerobatic fliers and first-viewing prototypes. For Mike, the high point was the visit of the Red Devils, the stunt team from the Parachute Regiment, free-falling, from tiny specs in the sky to swooping to earth in their harnesses right in the heart of the tiny landing zone. That was when he knew what it was he wanted to do.

He wrote a personal letter to the Paras during his last summer term at Haileybury, in 1980, and was offered an interview at the Regimental Depot at Aldershot for that same September. He arrived, and stared at the old Dakota, out of which his predecessors had once dropped to try to capture the bridge at Arnhem, until the sergeant escorting the group of five ex-schoolboys led them to the interview room.

He was regarded by his school—and the Paras always checked—as a moderate scholar but a superb athlete. That suited the Paras just fine. He was accepted, and began training at the end of the month, a grueling twenty-two weeks that would bring the survivors to April 1981.

There were four weeks of square bashing, basic weapons handling, field craft and physical fitness; then two more weeks of the same, plus signals, first aid and precautions against NBC—nuclear, bacteriological and chemical—warfare.

The seventh week was for more witness training, getting harder all the time; but not as bad as weeks eight and nine—endurance marches through the Brecon range in Wales in midwinter, where fit men have died of exposure, hypothermia and exhaustion. The numbers began to thin out.

Week ten saw the course at Hythe, Kent, for shooting on the range where Martin, just turned nineteen, was rated a marksman. Eleven and twelve were "test" weeks—just running up and down sandy hills carrying tree trunks in the mud, rain and hail.

"Test weeks?" muttered Martin. "What the hell has the rest been?"

After test weeks, the remaining young men got their coveted red beret, and then three more weeks in the Brecons for defense exercises, patrolling and "live firing." By then, late January, the Brecons were utterly bleak and freezing. The men slept, rough and wet, without fires.

Sixteen to nineteen covered what Mike Martin had come for: the parachute course at RAF Abingdon, where a few more dropped out, and not just from the aircraft. At the end came the "wings parade," when the wings of a paratrooper were finally pinned on. That night, the old 101 club at Aldershot saw another riotous party.

There were two more weeks devoted to a field exercise called "last fence," and some polishing up of parade ground skills; week twenty-two saw the "Pass Out Parade," when proud parents could finally view their spotty youths amazingly transformed into soldiers.

Private Mike Martin had long been earmarked as POM—potential officer material—and in April 1981 went to join the new short course at the Royal Military Academy Sandhurst, passing out in December as a second lieutenant. If he thought glory awaited him, he was entirely mistaken.

There are three battalions in the Parachute Regiment, and Martin was assigned to 3 Para, which happened to be Aldershot in penguin mode.

For three years out of every nine, or one tour out of three, each battalion is off of parachuting and used as ordinary truck-borne infantry. Paras hate penguin mode.

Martin, as a platoon commander, was assigned to Recruit Platoon, putting newcomers through the same miseries he had endured. He might have remained there for the rest of 3 Para's tour as penguins but for a faraway gentleman called Leopoldo Galtieri. On 1 April 1982, the Argentine dictator invaded the Falkland Islands. Three Para was told to kit up and get ready to move out.

Within a week, driven by the implacable Margaret Thatcher, a British task force was steaming south in a collection of vessels, bound for the far end of the Atlantic, where southern winter, with its roaring seas and driving rain, was waiting for them.

The journey south was on the liner *Canberra*, with a first stop at Ascension Island, a bleak button of a place lashed by constant wind. Here there was a pause as, far away, the last diplomatic efforts were pursued to persuade Galtieri to evacuate or Margaret Thatcher to back off. Neither could dream of agreeing and surviving in office. The *Canberra* sailed on, shadowing the expedition's only carrier, the *Ark Royal*.

When it became clear that invasion was inevitable, Martin and his team were "cross-decked" by helicopter from *Canberra* to a landing craft. Gone were the civilized conditions of the liner. The same wild and stormy night that Martin and his men cross-decked in Sea King helicopters, another Sea King went down and sank, taking with her nineteen of the Special Air Service Regiment, the biggest one-night loss the SAS has ever sustained.

Martin took his thirty men ashore with the rest of 3

Para, landing at San Carlos Water. It was miles from the main island's capital at Port Stanley, but for that reason it was unopposed. Without a pause, the Paras and the Marines began the grueling forced march through the mud and rain east to the capital.

They carried everything in Bergen rucksacks so heavy it was like carrying another man. The appearance of an Argentine Skyhawk meant diving into the slime, but, in the main, the "Argies" were after the ships offshore, not the men in the mud below. If the ships could be sunk, the onshore men were finished.

The real enemy was the cold, the constant freezing rain, the exhausting "tab" across a landscape that could not support a single tree. Until Mount Longdon.

Pausing below the hills, 3 Para set themselves up in a lonely farm called Estancia House, and prepared to do what their country had sent them seven thousand miles to do. It was the night of 11–12 June.

It was supposed to be a silent night attack, and remained so until Corporal Milne stepped on a mine. After that, it became noisy. The Argie machine guns opened up, and flares lit the hills and the valley like daylight. Three Para could either run back to cover or run into the fire and take Longdon. They took Longdon, with twenty-three dead and over forty injured.

It was the first time, as bullets tore the air around his head and men fell beside him, that Mike Martin experienced that strange, brassy taste on the tongue that is the taste of fear.

But nothing touched him. Of his own platoon of

thirty, including one sergeant and three corporals, six were dead and nine injured.

The Argentine soldiers who had held the ridge were forced recruits, lads from the sunny pampas—the sons of the well-off could avoid military service—and wanted to go home, out of the rain, cold and mud. They had quit their bunkers and foxholes and were heading back to shelter in Port Stanley.

At dawn, Mike Martin stood atop Wireless Ridge, looked east to the town and rising sun, and rediscovered the God of his fathers, whom he had neglected for many years. He prayed his thanks, and vowed never to forget again.

At the time the ten-year-old Mike Martin was capering round his father's garden at Saadun, Baghdad, to the delight of the Iraqi guests, a boy was being born a thousand miles away.

West of the road from Pakistani Peshawar to Afghan Jalalabad lies the range of the Spin Gahr, the White Mountains, dominated by the towering Tora Bora.

These mountains, seen from afar, are like a great barrier between the two countries, bleak and cold, always tipped with snow, and in winter wholly covered.

The Spin Gahr lies inside Afghanistan, with the Safed range on the Pakistani side. Running down to the rich plains around Jalalabad are myriad streams that carry the snowmelt and rain off the Spin Gahr, and these form many upland valleys where small patches of land may be planted, orchards raised and flocks of sheep and goats grazed.

Life is harsh, and with the life-support system being so sparse the communities of the valleys are small and scattered. The people bred up here are the ones the old British Empire knew and feared, calling them the Pathans, now Pashtun. Back then they fought from behind their rocky fastness with long, brass-bound muskets called the "jezail," with which each man was accurate as a modern sniper.

Rudyard Kipling, the poet of the old Raj, evoked the deadliness of the mountain men against subalterns expensively educated in England in just four lines:

A scrimmage in a Border Station—
A canter down some dark defile—
Two thousand pounds of education
Drops to a ten-rupee jezail—

In 1972, there was a hamlet in one of these upland valleys called Maloko-zai—like all these hamlets, named after a long-dead warrior founder. There were five walled compounds in the settlement, each the home of one extended family of about twenty persons. The village headman was Nuri Khan, and it was in his compound and round his fire that the men gathered on a summer evening to sip hot, unmilked, sugarless tea.

As with all the compounds, the walls were where the residences and livestock pens were built, so that all faced inward. The fire of mulberry logs blazed as the sun dropped far to the west and darkness clothed the mountains, bringing chill even in high summer.

From the women's quarters, the cries were muted, but if one was especially loud the men would cease their jovial conversation and wait to see if news would arrive. The wife of Nuri Khan was bearing her fourth child, and her husband prayed that Allah would grant him a second son. It was only right that a man should have sons to take care of the flocks when young and defend the compound when he had become a man. Nuri Khan had a boy of eight and two daughters.

The darkness was complete and only the flames lit the hawk-nosed faces and black beards when a midwife came scurrying from the shadows. She whispered in the ear of the father, and his mahogany face broke into a flashing smile.

"*Inshallah,* I have a son," he cried. His male relatives and neighbors rose as one, and the air crackled and roared with the sound of their rifles exploding upward into the night sky. There was much embracing and congratulations and thanks to all-merciful Allah, who had granted His servant a son.

"How will you call him?" asked a herdsman from a nearby compound.

"I shall call him Izmat after my own grandfather, may his soul rest in eternal peace," said Nuri Khan. And so it was when an imam came to the hamlet a few days later for the naming and the circumcision.

There was nothing unusual about the raising of the child. When he could toddle, he toddled, and when he could run he ran furiously. Like farm boys, he wanted to do the things the older boys did, and by five was entrusted to help drive the flocks up to the high pastures in summer and watch over them while the women cut forage for the winter.

He yearned to be out of the house of the women, and on the proudest day of his life so far was at last allowed to join the men round the fire and listen to stories of how the Pashtun had defeated the red-coated Angleez in these mountains only a hundred and fifty years ago, as if it was yesterday.

His father was the richest man in the village in the only way a man could be rich—in cows, sheep and goats. These, along with relentless caring and hard work, provided meat, milk and hides. Patches of corn yielded porridge and bread; fruit and nut oil came from the prolific mulberry and walnut orchards.

There was no need to leave the village, so for the first eight years of his life Izmat Khan did not. The five families shared the small mosque, and joined each other for communal worship on Fridays. Izmat's father was devout but not fundamentalist, and certainly not fanatical.

Beyond this mountain existence, Afghanistan called itself the Democratic Republic, or DRA, but as was so often the case this was a misnomer. The government was communist, and heavily supported by the USSR. In terms of religion, this was an oddity, because the people of the wild interior were traditionally devout Muslims for whom atheism was godlessness and therefore unacceptable.

But equally traditionally, the Afghans of the cities were moderate and tolerant—the fanaticism would be imposed on them later. Women were educated, few covered their faces, singing and dancing was not only allowed but commonplace, and the feared secret police pursued those suspected of political opposition, not religious laxity.

Of the two links the hamlet of Maloko-zai had with the outside world, one was the occasional party of Kuchi nomads passing through with a mule train of contraband, avoiding the Great Trunk Road through the Khyber Pass, with its patrols and border guards, seeking the track to the town of Parachinar across in Pakistan.

They would have news of the plains and the cities, of the government in faraway Kabul and the world beyond the valleys. And there was the radio, a treasured relic that squawked and screeched but then uttered words they could understand. This was the BBC's Pashto service, bringing the Pashtun a noncommunist version of the world. It was a peaceful boyhood. Then came the Russians.

It mattered little to the village of Maloko-zai who was right or wrong. They neither knew nor cared that their communist president had displeased his mentors in Moscow because he could not control his bailiwick. It mattered only that an entire Soviet Army had rolled across the Amu Darya River from Soviet Uzbekistan, roared through the Salang Pass and taken Kabul. It was not yet about Islam versus atheism; it was an insult.

Izmat Khan's education had been very basic. He had learned the Koranic verses necessary for prayer, even though they were in a language called Arabic and he could not understand them. The local imam was not resident; indeed, it was Nuri Khan who led the prayers—yet he had taught the boys of the village the rudiments of reading and writing, but only in Pashto. It was his father who had taught him the rules of the Pukhtunwali, the code by which a Pashtun must live. Honor, hospitality, the necessity of vendetta to avenge insult—these were the rules of the code. And Moscow had insulted them.

It was in the mountains that the resistance began, and they called themselves "Warriors of God," Mujaheddin. But first the mountain men needed a conference, a *shura,* to decide what to do and who would lead them.

They knew nothing of the Cold War, but they were told they now had powerful friends, the enemies of the USSR. That made perfect sense. He who is the enemy of my enemy . . . First among these were Pakistan, lying right next door, and ruled by a fundamentalist dictator, General Zia-ul-Haq. Despite the religious difference, he was allied with the Christian power called America, and her friends, the Angleez, the onetime enemy.

Mike Martin had tasted action and knew he enjoyed it. He did a tour in Northern Ireland, operating against the IRA, but the conditions were miserable, and though the danger of a sniper's bullet in the back was constant the patrols were boring. He looked around, and in the spring of 1986 applied for the SAS.

Quite a proportion of the SAS comes from the Paras because their training and combat roles are similar, but the SAS claims their tests are harder. Martin's papers went through the regiment's records office at Hereford, where his fluent Arabic was noted with interest, and he was invited to a selection course.

The SAS claims they take very fit men and then start to work on them. Martin did the standard "initial" course of six weeks among others drawn from the Paras, infantry, cavalry, armor, artillery and even engineers. Of the other "crack" units, the Special Boat Squadron draws their recruits exclusively from the Marines.

It is a simple course based on a single precept. On the first day, a smiling sergeant instructor told them all: "On this course, we don't try to train you. We try to kill you."

They did, too. Only ten percent of applicants pass the initial. It saves time later. Martin passed. Then came continuation training: jungle training in Belize, and an extra month back in England devoted to interrogation resistance. "Resistance" means trying to stay silent while some extremely unpleasant practices are being inflicted. The good news is that both the regiment and the volunteer have the right every hour to insist on an RTU—return to unit.

Martin started in the late summer of 1986, with twenty-two SAS, as a troop commander with the rank of captain. He opted for "A" Squadron, the free-fallers, a natural choice for a Para.

If the Paras had no use for his Arabic, the SAS did, for it has a long and intimate relationship with the Arab world. It was formed in the Western Desert in 1941, and its empathy with the sands of Arabia has never left it.

It had the jokey reputation of being the only Army

unit that actually makes a profit—not quite true but close. SAS men are the world's most sought-after body-guards and trainers of bodyguards. Throughout Arabia, the sultans and emirs have always sought out the SAS to train their own personal guards, and they pay hand-somely for it. Martin's first assignment was with the Saudi National Guard in Riyadh, when, in the summer of 1987, he was called home.

"I don't like this sort of thing," said the CO in his office at Sterling Lines, the regiment's Hereford HQ. "No, I bloody well don't. But the green slime wants to borrow you. It's the Arabic thing."

He had used the occasionally friendly phrase reserved by fighting soldiers for intelligence people. He meant the SIS—the Firm.

"Haven't they got their own Arabic speakers?" asked Martin.

"Oh, yes, desks full of them. But this isn't just a ques-tion of speaking it. And it's not really Arabia. They want someone to go behind the Soviet lines in Afghanistan and work with the resistance, the Mujaheddin."

The military dictator of Pakistan had decreed that no serving soldier of a Western power was to be allowed to penetrate into Afghanistan via Pakistan. He did not say so, but his own ISI military intelligence much enjoyed administering the American aid pouring in the direction of the muj, and he further had no wish to see a serving American or British soldier, infiltrated via Pakistan, cap-tured by the Russians and paraded around.

But halfway through the Soviet occupation, the British

had decided the man to back was not the Pakistani choice Hekmatyar, but the Tajik named Shah Massoud, who, rather than skulking in Europe or Pakistan, was doing real damage to the occupiers. The trouble was in bringing that aid to him. His territory was up in the north.

Securing good guides from the muj units near the Khyber Pass was not a problem. As in the time of the Raj, a few pieces of gold go a long way. There is an aphorism that you cannot buy the loyalty of an Afghan, but you can always rent it.

"The key word at every stage, Captain," they told him at SIS headquarters, which back then was at Century House near the Elephant and Castle, "is 'deniability.' That is why you actually have to—just a technicality—resign from the Army. Of course, the moment you come back"—he was nice enough to say when, not if—"you will be completely reinstated."

Mike Martin knew perfectly well that within its ranks the SAS already had the ultrasecret Revolutionary Warfare Wing, whose task was to stir up as much trouble for communist regimes worldwide as they could handle. He mentioned this.

"This is even more covert," said the mandarin. "We call this unit Unicorn—because it doesn't exist. There are never more than twelve, and at the moment only four men, in it. We really need someone to slip into Afghanistan through the Khyber Pass, secure a local guide and be brought north to the Panjshir Valley where Shah Massoud operates."

"Bringing gifts?" asked Martin. The smooth one made a helpless gesture.

"Only tokens, I am afraid. A question of what a man can carry. But later, we might move to mule trains and a lot more kit, if Massoud will send his own guides south to the border. It's a question of first contact, don't you see."

"And the gift?"

"Snuff. He likes our snuff. Oh, and two Blowpipe surface-to-air tubes with missiles. He is much troubled by air attacks. You'd have to teach his people how to use them. I reckon you'd be away six months. How do you feel about it?"

Before the invasion was half a year old, it was clear that the Afghans would still not do one thing that had always been impossible for them: unite. After weeks of arguing in Peshawar and Islamabad, with the Pakistani Army insisting it would not distribute American funds and weapons to any but the resisters accredited to them, the number of rival resistance groups was reduced to seven. Each had a political leader and a war commander. These were the Peshawar 7.

Only one was not Pashtun: Professor Rabbani, as well as his charismatic war leader, Ahmad Shah Massoud, both Tajiks from the far north. Of the other six, three were soon nicknamed the "Gucci commanders," because they rarely—if ever—entered occupied Afghanistan, preferring to wear Western dress in safety abroad.

Of the other three, two—Sayyaf and Hekmatyar—

were fanatical supporters of the Muslim Brotherhood of ultra-Islam, the latter being so cruel and vindictive that by the end he had executed more Afghans than he had killed Russians.

The one who tribally controlled the province of Nangarhar where Izmat Khan had been born was the mullah Maulvi Younis Khalis. He was a scholar and preacher, but he had a twinkle in his eye that spoke of kindness, as opposed to the cruelty of Hekmatyar, who loathed him.

Although the oldest of the seven and over sixty, for much of the next ten years Younis Khalis made forays into occupied Afghanistan to lead his men personally. When he was not there, his war commander was Abdul Haq.

By 1980, the war had come to the valleys of the Spin Gahr. The Soviets were teeming through Jalalabad below the mountains, and their air force had started punitive raids on mountain villages. Nuri Khan had sworn allegiance to Younis Khalis as his warlord, and been granted the right to form his own *lashkar,* or fighting yeomanry.

He could shelter much of the animal wealth of his village in the natural caves that riddled the White Mountains, and his people could shelter in them, too, when the air raids came. But he decided it was time for the women and children to cross the border to seek refuge in Pakistan.

The small convoy would of course need a male chaperone for the journey and the stay at Peshawar, however long that would last. As *mahram,* he appointed his own father, over sixty and stiff of limb. Donkeys and mules were secured for the journey.

Fighting back his tears at the shame of being sent out like a child, eight-year-old Izmat Khan was embraced by his father and brother, took the bridle of the mule bearing his mother and turned toward the high peaks and Pakistan. It would be seven years before he returned from exile, and when he came it would be to fight the Russians with cold ferocity.

To legitimize themselves in the eyes of the world, it had been agreed the warlords would each form a political party. That of Younis Khalis was called Hizb Islami, and everyone under his rule had to join it. Outside Peshawar, a rash of tented cities had sprung up under the auspices of something called the United Nations, though Izmat Khan had never heard of it. The UN had agreed that each warlord, now masquerading as political parties, should have his separate refugee camp, and no one should be admitted who was not a member of the appropriate party.

There was another organization handing out food and blankets. Its insignia was a stumpy red cross. Izmat Kahn had never seen one of those, either, but he knew hot soup, and after the arduous crossing of the mountains he drank his fill. There was one more condition required of inhabitants of the camps and those benefiting from the largesse of the West, funneled through United Nations and General Zia-ul-Haq: Boys needed to be educated at a Koranic school, or *madrassah,* in each refugee camp. This would be their only education. They would not learn about math or science, history or geography. They would just learn endlessly to recite the verses of the Koran. For the rest, they would only learn about war.

The imams of these *madrassahs* were, in the main, donated, salaried and funded by Saudi Arabia, and many were Saudis. They brought with them the only version of Islam permitted in Saudia Arabia: Wahhabism, the harshest and most intolerant creed within Islam. Thus, within sight of the sign of the cross dispensing food and medications, a whole generation of young Afghans was about to be brainwashed into fanaticism.

Nuri Khan visited his family as often as he could, two or three times a year, leaving his *lashkar* in the hands of his elder son. But it was a harsh journey, and Nuri Khan looked older each time. In 1987, when he arrived, he looked lined and drawn. Izmat's elder brother had been killed in a bombing raid while ushering others toward the safety of the caves. Izmat was fifteen, and his chest nearly burst with pride when his father bade him return, join the resistance and become Mujahid.

There was much weeping from the women, of course, and mumbling from Grandfather, who would not survive another winter on the plain outside Peshawar. Then Nuri Khan, his remaining son and the eight men he had brought with him to see their families turned west to cross the peaks into Nangarhar Province and the war.

The boy who came back was different, and the landscape he found was shattered. In all the valleys, hardly a stone bothy was standing. The Sukhoi fighter-bombers and the Hind helicopter gunships had devastated the valleys in the mountains from the Panjshir to the north, where Shah Massoud had his fighting zone, down to Paktia and the Shinkay range. The people of the plains could be controlled or intimidated by the Afghan Army or by the KHAD, the secret police taught and stiffened by the Soviet KGB.

But the people of the mountains, and those from the plains and cities who chose to join them, were intractable, and, as it later turned out, unconquerable. Despite air cover, which the British had never had, the Soviets were experiencing something like the fate of the British column cut to pieces on the suicidal march from Kabul to Jalalabad.

The roads were unsafe from ambush, the mountain unapproachable save by air. And the deployment in muj hands of the American Stinger missile since September 1986 had forced the Soviets to fly higher—too high to be accurate—or risk being hit. The Soviet losses were mounting relentlessly, with further manpower reductions due to wounds and disease, and even in a controlled society like the USSR the morale was dropping like a falcon on the swoop.

It was a savagely cruel war. Few prisoners were ever taken, and the quickly dead were the lucky ones. The mountain clans especially hated the Russian fliers, and, if taken alive, they could be pegged out in the sun with a small cut in the stomach wall so the entrails would burst forth and fry in the sun until death brought release. Or they could be given over to the women and their skinning knives.

The Soviet response was to bomb, rocket and strafe

anything that moved: man, woman, child or animal. They seeded the mountains with untold millions of air-dropped mines, which eventually created a nation of crutches and prosthetic limbs. Before it was over, there would be a million Afghans dead, a million crippled and five million refugees.

Izmat Khan knew all about guns from his time in the refugee camp, and the favorite was, of course, the Kalashnikov AK-47. It was a supreme irony that this Soviet weapon, the preferred assault rifle of every dissident movement and terrorist in the world, was now being used against them. But the Americans were providing them for a reason: Every Afghan could replenish his ammunition from the packs of a dead Russian, which saved carrying time across the mountains if the ammunition had been noncompatible.

Assault rifle apart, the weapon of choice was the rocket-propelled grenade, the RPG—simple, easy to use, easy to reload and deadly at short-to-medium range. This, too, was provided by the West.

Izmat Khan was big for fifteen, desperately trying to grow a fuzz round the chin, and the mountains soon made him as hard as he had ever been. Witnesses have seen the Pashtun mountain men moving like mountain goats through their own terrain, legs seemingly immune to exhaustion, breathing unlabored when others are gasping for breath.

He had been back home for a year when his father summoned him. There was a stranger with him; face burned dark from the sun, black-bearded, wearing a gray woolen *shalwar kameez* over stout hiking boots and a sleeveless jerkin. On the ground behind him stood the biggest backpack the boy had ever seen, and two tubes wrapped in sheepskin. On his head was a Pashtun turban.

"This man is a guest and a friend," said Nuri Khan. "He has come to help us and fight with us. He has to take his tubes to Shah Massoud in the Panjshir, and you will guide him there."

CHAPTER 5

THE YOUNG PASHTUN stared at the stranger. He did not seem to have understood what Nuri Khan had said.

"Is he Afghan?" he asked.

"No, he is Angleez."

Izmat Khan was staggered. This was the old enemy. More, he was what the imam in the *madrassah* had condemned with constant venom. He must be *kafir*, an unbeliever, a Nasrani, a Christian, destined to burn for all eternity in hell. And he was to escort this man over a hundred miles of mountainside to a great valley in the north? To spend days and nights in his company? Yet his father was a good man, a good Muslim, and he had called him friend. How could this be?

The Englishman tapped his forefingers lightly on his chest near the heart.

"*Salaam aleikhem*, Izmat Khan," he said. The father

spoke no Arabic, even though there were now many Arab volunteers farther down the mountain range. The Arabs kept themselves to themselves, always digging, so there was no cause to mix with them and learn some of their language. But Izmat had read the Koran over and over again; it was written in Arabic only, and his imam had spoken only his native Saudi Arabic. Izmat had a good working knowledge.

"*Aleikhem as-salaam,*" he acknowledged. "How do you call yourself?"

"Mike," said the man.

"Ma-ick." Izmat tried it. Strange name.

"Good, let us take tea," said his father. They were sheltering in a cave mouth about ten miles from the wreckage of their hamlet. Farther inside the cave, a small fire glowed, too far inside to let a visible plume of smoke emerge to attract a Soviet aircraft.

"We will sleep here tonight. In the morning, you will go north. I go south to join Abdul Haq. There will be another operation against the Jalalabad-to-Kandahar road."

They chewed on goat and nibbled rice cakes. Then they slept. Before dawn, the two heading north were roused, and left. Their journey led them through a maze of linking valleys where there would be some shelter. But between the valleys were mountain ridges, and the sides of the mountains had steep slopes covered in rock and shale but with little or no cover. It would be wise to scale these by moonlight and stay in the valleys by day.

Bad luck struck them on the second day out. To speed

the rate of march, they had left night camp before dawn, and just after first light they found themselves forced to cross a large expanse of rock and shale to find cover on the next spine of hills. To wait would have meant hiding all day until nightfall. Izmat Khan urged that they cross in daylight. Halfway across the mountainside, they heard the growl of the gunship engines.

Both man and boy dived for the ground and lay motionless, but not in time. Over the crest ahead, menacing as a deadly dragonfly, came the Soviet Mi-24 D, known simply as the Hind. One of the pilots must have seen a flicker of movement or perhaps the glint of metal down there on the rock field, for the Hind turned from its course and headed toward them. The roar of the two Isotov engines grew in their ears, as did the unmistakable *tacka-tacka-tacka* of the main rotor blades.

With his head buried in his forearms, Mike Martin risked a quick glance. There was no doubt they had been spotted. The two Soviet pilots, sitting in their tandem seats, with the second above and behind the first, were staring straight at him as the Hind went into attack mode. To be caught in the open without cover by a helicopter gunship is every foot soldier's nightmare. He glanced round. One hundred yards away was a single group of boulders; not as high as a man's head, but just enough to shelter behind. With a yell to the Afghan boy, he was up and running, leaving his hundred-pound Bergen rucksack where it was but carrying one of the two tubes that had so intrigued his guide.

He heard the running feet of the boy behind him, the

roaring of his own blood in his ears and the matching snarl of the diving Hind. He would never have made the dash had he not seen something about the gunship that gave a flicker of hope. Its rocket pods were empty, and it carried no underslung bombs. He gulped at the thin air, and hoped his guess was right. It was.

Pilot Simonov and his copilot Grigoriev had been on a dawn patrol to harass a narrow valley where agents had reported that muj were hiding out. They had dropped their bombs from a higher altitude, then gone in lower to blast the rocky cleft with rockets. A number of goats had pelted from the crack in the mountains, indicating there had indeed been human life sheltering in there. Simonov had shredded the beasts with his 30mm cannon, using up most of the shells.

He had gone back to a safe altitude and was heading home to the Soviet base outside Jalalabad when Grigoriev had spotted a tiny movement on the mountainside below and to the port side. When he saw the figures start to run, he flicked his cannon to FIRE mode and dived. The two running figures far below were heading for a cluster of rocks. Simonov steadied the Hind at two thousand feet, watched the two figures hurl themselves into the rock cluster and fired. The twin barrels of the GSH cannon shuddered as the shells poured out, then stopped. Simonov swore as his ammunition ran out. He had used his cannon shells on goats, and here were muj to kill and he had none left. He lifted the nose and turned in a wide arc to avoid the mountain crest and the Hind clattered out over the valley.

Martin and Izmat Khan crouched behind their pitiable cluster of rocks. The Afghan boy watched as the Angleez rapidly opened his sheepskin case and extracted a short tube. He was vaguely aware that someone had punched him in the right thigh, but there was no pain. Just numbness.

What the SAS man was assembling as fast as his fingers would work was one of the two Blowpipe missiles he was trying to bring to Shah Massoud in the Panjshir. It was not as good as the American Stinger, but more basic, lighter and simpler.

Some surface-to-air missiles are guided to target by a ground-based radar "fix." Others carry their own tiny radar set in the nose. Others emit their own infrared beam. These are the beam-riders. Others are heatseekers, whose nose cones "smell" the heat of the airplane's own engines and home toward it. Blowpipe was much more basic than that; it was styled command to line of sight, or CLOS; and it meant the firer had to stand there and guide the rocket all the way to target by sending radio signals from a tiny control stick to the movable fins in the rocket's head.

The disadvantage of the Blowpipe was always that to ask a man to stay still in the face of an attacking gunship was to secure a lot of dead operators. Martin pushed the two-stage missile into the launching tube, fired up the battery and the gyro, squinted through the sight and found the Hind coming straight back at him. He steadied the image in the sights and fired. With a whoosh of blazing gases, the rocket left the tube on his shoulder and headed blindly into the sky. Being completely nonautomatic, it now required his control to rise or drop, turn left or right. He estimated the range at fourteen hundred yards and closing fast. Simonov opened fire with his chain gun.

In the nose of the Hind, the four barrels hurling out a curtain of finger-sized machine-gun bullets began to turn. Then the Soviet pilot saw the tiny flickering flame of the Blowpipe coming toward him. It became a question of nerve.

Bullets tore into the rocks, blowing away chunks of stone in all directions. It lasted two seconds, but at two thousand rounds per minute some seventy bullets hit the rocks before Simonov tried to evade and the bullet stream swept to one side.

It is proven that in a no-thought instinctive emergency a man will normally pull left. That is why driving on the left of the highway, though confined to very few countries, is actually safer. A panicking driver pulls off the road into the meadow rather than into a head-on collision. Simonov panicked and slewed the Hind to its left.

The Blowpipe had lost its first stage and was going supersonic. Martin tweaked the trajectory to his right just before Simonov swerved. It was a good guess. As it turned out, the Hind exposed its belly, and the warhead slammed into it. It was only just under five pounds weight, and the Hind is immensely strong. But even that size of warhead at a thousand miles per hour is a terrific punch. It cracked the base armor, entered and exploded.

Drenched with sweat on the icy mountainside, Martin

saw the beast lurch with the impact, start to stream smoke and plunge toward the valley floor far below.

When it impacted in the riverbed, the noise stopped. There was a silent peony of flame as the two Russians died, then a plume of dark smoke. That alone would bring attention from the Russians at Jalalabad. Harsh and long though the journey might be overland, it was only a few minutes for a Sukhoi ground-attack fighter.

"Let's go," he said in Arabic to his guide. The boy tried to rise but could not. Then Marin saw the smudge of blood on the side of his thigh. Without a word, he put down the reusable Blowpipe launch tube, went for his Bergen and brought it back.

He used his Ka-bar knife to slit the trouser leg of the *shalwar kameez*. The hole was neat and small, but it looked deep. If it came from one of the cannon shells, then it was only a fragment of casing, or maybe a splinter of rock, but he did not know how near the femoral artery it might be. He had trained at Hereford Accident and Emergency Ward, and his first-aid knowledge was good; but the side of an Afghan mountain with the Russians coming was no place for complex surgery.

"Are we going to die, Angleez?" asked the boy.

"*Inshallah,* not today, Izmat Khan. Not today," he said. He faced a bad quandary. He needed his Bergen and everything in it. He could carry either the Bergen or the boy, not both.

"Do you know this mountain?" he asked as he rummaged for shell dressings.

"Of course," said the Afghan.

"Then I must come back with another guide. You must tell him where to come. I will bury the bag and the rockets."

He opened a flat steel box and took out a hypodermic syringe. The white-faced boy watched him.

So be it, thought Izmat Khan. If the infidel wishes to torture me, let him. I will utter no sound.

The Angleez pushed the needle into his thigh. He made no sound. Seconds later, as the morphine took effect, the agony in his thigh began to diminish. Encouraged, he tried to rise. The Englishman had produced a small, foldable trenching tool and was digging a furrow in the shale among the rocks. When he had done, he covered his Bergen and the two rocket tubes with stones until nothing could be seen. But he had memorized the shape of the cairn. If he could only be brought back to this mountainside, he could recover all his kit.

The boy protested that he could walk, but Martin simply hoisted him over one shoulder and began to march. Being all skin and bone, muscle and sinew, the Afghan weighed no more than the Bergen at about a hundred pounds. Still, heading upward into ever-thinner air and against gravity was not an option. He made course sideways across the scree and slowly downward to the valley. It turned out to be a wise choice.

Downed Soviet airplanes always attracted Pashtun eager to strip the wreck for whatever might be of use or value. The plume of smoke had not yet been spotted by the Soviets, and Simonov's last transmission had been a final scream on which no one could get a bearing. But

the smoke had attracted a small party of muj from an·
other valley. They saw each other a thousand feet about
the valley floor.

Izmat Khan explained what had happened. The mountain men broke into delighted grins and started slapping
the SAS man on the back. He insisted his guide needed
help and not just a bowl of tea in some *chaikhana* in the
hills. He needed transportation and a surgical hospital.
One of the muj knew a man with a mule, only two valleys
away. He went to get him. It took until nightfall. Martin
administered a second shot of morphine.

With a fresh guide and Izmat Khan on a mule at last,
they marched through the night, just three of them,
until in the dawn they came to the southern side of the
Spin Gahr and the guide stopped. He pointed ahead.

"Jaji," he said. "Arabs."

He also wanted his mule back. Martin carried the boy
the last two miles. Jaji was a complex of five hundred
caves, and the so-called Afghan-Arabs had been working
on them for three years, broadening, deepening, excavat-
ing and equipping them into a major guerrilla base.
Though Martin did not know it, inside the complex
were barracks, a mosque, a library of religious texts,
kitchens, stores and a fully equipped surgical hospital.

As he approached, Martin was intercepted by the
outer ring of guards. It was clear what he was doing: He
had a wounded man on his back. The guards discussed
among themselves what to do with the pair, and Martin
recognized the Arabic of North Africa. They were interrupted by the arrival of a senior man who spoke like a

Saudi. Martin understood everything but thought it unwise to utter a word. With sign language, he indicated his friend needed emergency surgery. The Saudi nodded, beckoned and led the way.

Izmat Khan was operated on within an hour. A vicious fragment of cannon casing was extracted from the leg.

Martin waited until the lad woke up. He squatted, local style, in the shadows at the corner of the ward, and no one took him for anything other than a Pashtun mountain man who had brought in his friend.

An hour later, two men entered the ward. One was very tall, youthful, bearded. He wore a camouflage combat jacket over Arab robes and a white headdress. The other was short, tubby, also no more than midthirties, with a button nose and round glasses perched on the end of it. He wore a surgical smock. After examining two of their own number, the pair came to the Afghan. The tall man spoke in Saudi Arabic.

"And how is our young Afghan fighter feeling?"

"*Inshallah,* I am much better, Sheikh." Izmat spoke back in Arabic, and gave the older man a title of reverence. The tall man was pleased.

"Ah, you speak Arabic, and still so young." He smiled.

"I was seven years in a *madrassah* at Peshawar. I returned last year to fight."

"And who do you fight for, my son?"

"I fight for Afghanistan," said the boy.

Something like a cloud passed across the features of the Saudi. The Afghan realized he might not have said what was wanted.

"And I also fight for Allah, Sheikh," he added.

The cloud cleared, and the gentle smile came back. The Saudi leaned forward and patted the youth on the shoulder.

"The day will come when Afghanistan will no longer have need of you, but the all-merciful Allah will always have need of a warrior like you. Now, how is our young friend's wound healing?" He addressed the question to the Pickwickian doctor.

"Let us see," said the doctor, and peeled back the dressing.

The wound was clean, bruised round the edges but closed by six stitches and not infected. He tutted his satisfaction and redressed the suture.

"You will be walking in a week," said Dr. Ayman al-Zawahiri.

Then he and Osama bin Laden left the ward. No one took any notice of the sweat-stained muj squatting in the corner with his head on his knees as if asleep.

Martin rose and crossed to the youth on the bed. "I must go," he said. "The Arabs will look after you. I will seek to find your father and ask for a fresh guide. Go with Allah, my friend."

"Be careful, Ma-ick," said the boy. "These Arabs are not like us. You are *kafir*, unbeliever. They are like the Imam in my *madrassah*. They hate all infidel."

"Then I would be grateful if you would not tell them who I was," said the Englishman.

Izmat Khan closed his eyes. He would die under torment rather than betray his new friend. It was the code.

When he opened his eyes, the Angleez was gone. He heard later the man had reached Shah Massoud in the Panjshir, but he never saw him again.

After his six months behind the Soviet lines in Afghanistan, Mike Martin made it home via Pakistan, unspotted and with fluent Pashto added to his armory. He was sent on leave, remustered into the Army and, being still in service with the SAS, posted to Northern Ireland again. But this time it was different.

The SAS were the men who really terrified the IRA, and to kill, or, better still, capture alive, torture and kill what they called a Sassman, was the IRA's greatest dream. Mike Martin found himself working with the 14th Intelligence Company, known as "the Detachment," or "the Det."

These were the watchers, the trackers, the eavesdroppers. Their job was to be so stealthy as never to be seen, but to find out where the IRA killers would strike next. To do this, they performed some remarkable feats.

IRA leaders' houses were penetrated via the roof tiles and bugged from the attic downward. Bugs were placed in dead IRA men's coffins, for it was the habit of the godfathers to hold conferences while pretending to pay their respects to the casket. Long-range cameras caught images of moving mouths, and lip-readers deciphered the words. Rifle-mikes recorded conversations through closed windows. When the Det had a real gem, they passed it to the hard men.

The rules of engagement were strict. The IRA men

had to fire first, and they had to fire at the SAS. If they threw down their guns at the challenge, they had to be taken prisoner. Before firing, both SAS and Paras had to be immensely careful. It is a recent tradition of British politicians and lawyers that Britain's enemies have civil rights but her soldiers do not.

Notwithstanding, in the eighteen months Martin spent as an SAS captain in Ulster he participated in the dark-of-night ambushes. In each, a party of armed IRA men was caught by surprise and challenged. Each time they were foolish enough to draw and point weapons. Each time, it was the Royal Ulster Constabulary that found the bodies in the morning.

But it was in the second shoot-out that Martin took his bullet. He was lucky. It was a flesh wound in the left bicep, but enough to see him flown home and sent for convalescence at Headley Court, Leatherhead. That was where he met the nurse, Lucinda, who was to become his wife after a brief courtship.

Reverting to the Paras in the spring of 1990, Mike Martin was posted to the Ministry of Defence in Whitehall, London. Having set up home in a rented cottage near Chobham so that Lucinda could continue her career, Martin found himself for the first time a commuter in a dark suit on the morning train to London. He ranked as a Staff Officer 3, and worked in the office of MOSP, the Military Operations, Special Projects Unit. Once again, it was to be a foreign aggressor who would get him out of there.

On August 2 that year, Saddam Hussein of Iraq invaded neighboring Kuwait. Once again, Margaret Thatcher would have none of it, and U.S. president George H. W. Bush concurred. Within a week, plans were in furious preparation to create a multinational coalition to counterinvade and free the oil-rich ministate.

Even though the MOSP office was at full stretch, the reach and influence of the Secret Intelligence Service was enough to trace him and "suggest" he join a few of the "friends" for lunch.

It was a discreet club on St. James's Street, and his hosts were two senior men from the Firm. Also at the table was a Jordanian-born, British-naturalized analyst brought in from GCQH at Cheltenham. His job there was to listen to and analyze eavesdropped radio chatter inside the Arab world. But his role at the lunch table was different.

He conversed with Mike Martin in rapid Arabic, and Martin replied. Finally, he nodded at the two spooks from Century House. "I've never heard anything like it," he remarked. "With that face and voice, he can pass."

With that, the man left the table, clearly having performed his function.

"We would be so damnably grateful," said the senior mandarin, "if you would go into Kuwait and see what is going on there."

"What about the Army?" asked Martin.

"I think they will see our point of view," murmured the other.

The Army grumbled again but let him go. Weeks later, passing himself as a Bedouin camel drover, Martin slipped over the Saudi border into Iraqi-occupied Kuwait. On the plod north to Kuwait City, he passed several Iraqi patrols but they took no notice of the bearded nomad leading two camels to market. The Bedouin are so determinedly nonpolitical that they have for millennia watched the invaders sweep hither and thither through Arabia and never intervened. So the invaders have mostly let them be.

In several weeks inside Kuwait, Martin contacted and assisted the fledgling Kuwaiti resistance, taught them the tricks of the trade, plotted the Iraqi positions, strong points and weaknesses, and then came out again.

His second incursion during the Gulf War was into Iraq itself. He went over the Saudi border in the west and simply caught an Iraqi bus heading for Baghdad. His cover was a simple peasant clutching a wicker basket of hens.

Back in a city he knew intimately, he took a position as a gardener in a wealthy villa, living in a shack at the end of the garden. His mission was to act as message collector and passer; for this, he had a small, foldable, parabolic dish aerial whose "blitz" messages were uninterceptable by the Iraqi secret police but which could reach Riyadh.

One of the best-kept secrets of that war was that the Firm had a source, an "asset" high in Saddam's government. Martin never met him; he just picked up the messages at preagreed dead-letter boxes, or "drops," and sent them to Saudi Arabia, where the American-led Coalition HQ was both appreciative and mystified. Saddam capitulated on 28 February 1991, and Mike Martin came out, only to be very nearly shot by the French Foreign Legion as he came through the border in the dark.

On the morning of 15 February 1989, General Boris Gromov, commander of the Soviet 40th Army, the army of occupation in Afghanistan, walked alone back across the Friendship Bridge over the Amu Darya River into Soviet Uzbekistan. His entire army had preceded him. The war was over.

The euphoria did not last long. The USSR's own Vietnam had ended in disaster. Her restive European satellites were becoming openly mutinous, and her economy was disintegrating. By November, the Berliners had torn down the wall, and the Soviet empire simply fell apart.

In Afghanistan, the Soviets had left behind a government that most analysts predicted would last no time as the victorious warlords formed a stable government and took over. But the pundits were wrong. The government of President Najibullah, the whiskey-appreciating Afghan the Soviets had abandoned in Kabul, hung on for two reasons. One was that the Afghan Army was simply stronger than any other force in the country, backed as it was by the KHAD secret police, and was able to control the cities and thus the bulk of the population.

More to the point, the warlords simply disintegrated into a patchwork quilt of snarling, grabbing, feuding, self-serving opportunists who, far from uniting to form a stable government, did the reverse: They created a civil war.

None of this affected Izmat Khan. With his father still head of the family, although stiff and old before his time, and with the help of neighbors, he helped rebuild the hamlet of Maloko-zai. Stone by stone and rock by rock, they cleared the rubble left by the bombs and rockets and remade the family compound next to the mulberry and pomegranate trees.

With his leg fully healed, he had returned to the war and taken command of his father's *lashkar* in all but name, and the men had followed him, for he had been blooded. When peace came, his guerrilla group seized a huge cache of weapons the Soviets could not be bothered to carry home.

These they took over the Spin Gahr to Parachinar in Pakistan, a town that is virtually nothing but an arms bazaar. There they traded the Soviet leftovers for cows, goats and sheep to restart the flocks.

If life had been hard before, starting over was even harder, but he enjoyed the labor, and the sense of triumph that Maloko-zai would live again. A man must have roots, and his were here. At twenty, he both uttered the call and led the prayers at the village mosque on a Friday.

The Kuchi nomads passing through brought grim tales from the plains. The Army of the DRA, loyal to Najibullah, still held the cities, but the warlords infested the countryside and they and their men behaved liked brigands. Tolls were arbitrarily set up on main roads, and travelers were stripped of their money and goods or badly beaten.

Pakistan, in the form of its ISI Directorate, was backing Hekmatyar to become controller of all Afghanistan, and in areas he ruled utter terror existed. All who had formed the Peshawar 7 to fight the Soviets were now at each other's throats, and the people groaned. From heroes, the muj were now seen as tyrants. Izmat Khan thanked the merciful Allah that he was spared the misery of the plains.

With the end of the war, the Arabs had almost all gone from the mountains and their precious caves. The one who by the end had become their uncrowned leader, the tall Saudi from the cave hospital, was also gone. Some five hundred Arabs had stayed behind, but they were not popular, were scattered far and wide and living like beggars.

When he was twenty, Izmat Khan was visiting a neighboring valley when he saw a girl washing the family clothes in the stream. She failed to hear his horse because of the sound of the running water, and before she could draw the end of her hejab across her face he had made eye contact. She fled in alarm and embarrassment. But he had seen that she was beautiful.

Izmat did what any young man would have. He consulted his mother. She was delighted, and soon two aunts had joined with her in happy conspiracy to find the girl and persuade Nuri Khan to contact the father to arrange a union. Her name was Maryam, and the wedding took place in the late spring of 1993.

Of course, it was in the open air, full of blossoms being blown off the walnut trees. There was a feast, and the bride came from her village on a decorated horse. There was playing of the flutes and attan dancing under the trees, but of course only for the men. With his *madrassah* training, Izmat protested at the singing and dancing, but his father was rejuvenated and overruled him. So for a day, Izmat rejected his strict Wahhabi training, and he, too, danced in the meadow, and the eyes of his bride followed him everywhere.

The delay between the first glimpse by the stream and the marriage was necessary, both to arrange the details of the dowry and to build a new house for the newlyweds inside the Khan compound. It was here that he took his bride when night had fallen and the exhausted villagers returned home, and his mother forty yards away nodded in satisfaction when a single girl's cry in the night told her that her daughter-in-law had become a woman. Three months later, it was clear she would bear a child in the snows of February.

As Maryam carried Izmat's child, the Arabs came back. The tall Saudi who led them was not among them; he was somewhere far away called Sudan. But he sent much money, and by paying tribute to the warlords was able to set up training camps. Here, at Khalid ibn Walid, Al Farouk, Sadeek, Khaldan, Jihad Wai and Darunta, the thousands of new volunteers from across the Arabic-speaking world came to train for war.

But what war? So far as Izmat Khan could see, they took no sides in the civil war among the tribal satraps, so who were they training to fight? He learned that it was all because the tall one, whom his followers called the Emir, had declared jihad against his own government in Saudi Arabia and against the West.

But Izmat Khan had no quarrel with the West. The West had helped with arms and money to defeat the Soviets, and the only *kafir* he had ever met had saved his life. It was not his holy war, not his jihad, he decided. His concern was for his country whose situation was devolving into madness.

CHAPTER 6

THE PARACHUTE REGIMENT accepted him back and asked no questions, because that was what it was told to do, but he was already acquiring a reputation as a bit of an oddity. Two unexplained absences from duty, each for six months, inside four years, causes raised eyebrows over breakfast in any military unit. For 1992, he was sent to the Staff College at Camberley, and thence back to the ministry, but as a major.

This time, it was to the Directorate of Military Operations again, but as a Staff Officer 2 in Department 3, the Balkans. The war was still raging, the Serbs under Milošević were dominant, and the world was sickened by the massacres known as "ethnic cleansing." Chafing at the lack of any chance of action, he spent two years commuting in a dark suit from the suburbs to London.

Officers who have served in the SAS can return for a

second tour, but only by invitation. Mike Martin got his call from Hereford at the end of 1994. It was the Christmas present he had been hoping for. But it did not please Lucinda.

There had been no baby; there were two careers heading in different directions. Lucinda had been offered a big promotion. She called it "the chance of a lifetime," but it meant going to work in the Midlands. The marriage was under strain, and Mike Martin's orders were to command B Squadron, twenty-two SAS, and take them covertly to Bosnia. Ostensibly, they would be part of the United Nations' UNPROFOR peacekeeping mission. In fact, they would hunt down and snatch war criminals. He was not allowed to tell Lucinda the details, only that he was leaving again.

It was the last straw. She presumed it was a transfer back to Arabia, and she quite properly put to him an ultimatum: You can have the Paras, the SAS and your bloody desert or you can come to Birmingham and have a marriage. He thought it over and chose the desert.

Outside the seclusion of the high valleys of the White Mountains, his old party leader, Younis Khalis, died, and the Hizb Islami Party was then wholly in the control of Hekmatyar, whose reputation for cruelty Izmat loathed.

By the time Izmat's baby was born in February 1994, President Najibullah had fallen but was alive, confined to a UN guesthouse in Kabul. He had supposedly been succeeded by Professor Rabbani, but he was a Tajik and so not acceptable to the Pashtun. Outside Kabul, only the warlords ruled their domains, but the real master was chaos and anarchy.

But something else was also happening. After the Soviet war, thousands of young Afghans had gone back to the Pakistani *madrassah*s to complete their educations. Others, too young to have fought at all, went over the border to achieve an education—any education. What they got was years of Wahhabi brainwashing. Now they were coming back, but they were different from Izmat Khan.

Because the old Younis Khalis, though ultradevout, had possessed some residual moderation in him, his *madrassah*s in the refugee camps had taught Islam with a hint of temperance. Others concentrated only on the ultra-aggressive passages from the Sword Verses to be found in holy Koran. And old Nuri Khan, though devout also, was humane, and saw no harm in singing, dancing, sports and some tolerance of others.

The returnees were ill educated, having been taught by barely literate imams. They knew nothing of life, of women—most lived and died virgins—or even of their own tribal cultures, as Izmat had learned from his father. Apart from the Koran, they knew only one other thing: war. Most came from the deep south, where Islam had always been the most strict in all of Afghanistan.

In the summer of 1994, Izmat Khan and a cousin left the upland valley for Jalalabad. It was a short visit, but long enough to witness the savage massacre inflicted by the followers of Hekmatyar on a village that had finally refused to pay him any more tribute money. The two travelers found the menfolk tortured and slain, the women beaten, the village torched. Izmat Khan was disgusted. In Jalalabad, he learned what he had seen was quite commonplace.

Then something happened in the deep south. Since the fall of any semblance of a central government, the old official Afghan Army had simply reassigned itself to the local warlord who paid the best. Outside Kandahar, some soldiers took two teenage girls back to their camp and gang-raped them.

The local preacher in the village where they came, who also ran his own religious school, went to the Army camp with thirty students and sixteen rifles. Against the odds, they trounced the soldiers, and hanged the commandant from the barrel of a tank gun. The priest was called Mohammad Omar, or Mullah Omar. He had lost his right eye in battle.

The news spread. Others appealed to him for help. He and his group swelled in numbers, and responded to the appeals. They took no money, they raped no women, they stole no crops, they asked no reward. They became local heroes. By December 1994, twelve thousand had joined them, adopting this mullah's black turban. They called themselves the students. In Pashto, "student" is *talib,* and the plural is *taliban.* From village vigilantes, they became a movement, and when they captured the city of Kandahar, an alternative government.

Pakistan, through its forever-plotting ISI, had been trying to topple the Tajik in Kabul by backing Hekmatyar, but he had failed repeatedly. As the ISI was deeply infiltrated by ultraorthodox Muslims, Pakistan switched support to the Taliban. With Kandahar, the new movement inherited a huge cache of arms, plus tanks, armored cars, trucks, guns, six MiG-21 ex–Soviet fighters and six heavy helicopters. They began to sweep north. In 1995, Izmat Khan embraced his wife, kissed his baby farewell and then came down from the mountains to join them.

Later, on the floor of a cell in Cuba, he would recall that the days on the upland farm with his wife and child had been the happiest days of his life. He was twenty-three.

Too late, he learned there was a dark side to the Taliban. In Kandahar, even though the Pashtun had been devout before, they were subjected to the harshest regimen the world of Islam has ever seen.

All girls' schools were closed at once. Women were forbidden to leave the house save in company of a male relative. The all-enveloping burqa robe was decreed at all times; the clacking of female sandals on tiles was decreed forbidden as being too sexy.

All singing, dancing, the playing of music, sports and kite flying—a national pastime—was forbidden. Prayers were to be said the required five times a day. Beards on men were compulsory. The enforcers were often teenage fanatics in their black turbans, taught only the Sword Verses, cruelty and war. From liberators they became the new tyrants, but the advance became unstoppable. Their mission was to destroy the rule of the warlords, and as these were well hated by the people, the people acquiesced to the new strictness. At least there was law, order, no more corruption, no more rape, no more crime; just fanatic orthodoxy.

Mullah Omar was a warrior-priest but nothing more. Having started his revolution by hanging a rapist from a gun barrel, he withdrew into seclusion in his southern fortress, Kandahar. His followers were like something out of the Middle Ages, and among the many things they could not recognize was fear. They worshipped the one-eyed mullah behind his walls, and before the Taliban fell eighty thousand would die for him. Far away in Sudan, the tall Saudi who controlled the twenty thousand Arabs now based in Afghanistan watched and waited.

Izmat Khan joined a *lashkar* of men drawn from his own province, Nangarhar. He was quickly respected because he was mature, had fought the Russians and been wounded.

The Taliban army was no real army; it had no commanding general, no general staff, no officer corps, no ranks and no infrastructure. Each *lashkar* was semi-independent under its tribal leader, who often held sway through personality and courage in combat, plus religious devotion. Like the original Muslim warriors of the first caliphates, they swept their enemies aside by fanatical courage, which gave rise to a reputation for invincibility—so much so that opponents often capitulated without a shot fired. When they finally ran into real soldiers, the forces of the charismatic Tajik Shah Massoud, they took unspeakable losses. They had no medical corps, so their wounded just died by the roadside. But still, they came on.

At the gates of Kabul, they negotiated with Massoud, but he refused to accept their terms and withdrew to his own northern mountains, whence he had fought and defied the Russians. So began the next civil war, between the Taliban and the Northern Alliance of Massoud, the Tajik, and Rashid Dostum, the Uzbek. It was 1996. Only Pakistan, who had organized it, and Saudi Arabia, who paid for it, recognized the new, weird government of Afghanistan.

For Izmat Khan, the die was cast. His old ally Shah Massoud was now his enemy. Far to the south, an airplane landed. It brought back the tall Saudi who had spoken to him eight years earlier in a cave at Jaji and the chubby doctor who had pulled a chunk of Soviet steel from his leg. Both men paid immediate obeisance to Mullah Omar, paying huge tribute in money and equipment, and thus securing his lifelong loyalty.

After Kabul, there was a pause in the war. Almost the first act of the Taliban in Kabul was to drag the toppled ex-president Najibullah from his house arrest, torture, mutilate and execute him, hanging his corpse from a lamppost. That set the tenor of the rule to come. Izmat Khan had no taste for cruelty for its own sake. He had fought hard enough in the conquest of his country to rise from volunteer to commander of his own *lashkar*, and this, in turn, grew, as word of his leadership spread, until it became one of the four divisions in the Taliban army. Then he asked to be allowed to go back to his native Nangarhar, and was made provincial governor. Based in Jalalabad, he could visit his family, wife and baby.

He had never heard of Nairobi or Dar es Salaam. He had never heard of anyone called William Jefferson Clinton. He had indeed heard much of a group now based in his country called Al Qaeda, and knew that its adherents had declared global jihad against all unbelievers, especially the West, and most of all against a place called America. But it was not his jihad.

He was fighting the Northern Alliance to unite his homeland once and for all, and the alliance had been beaten back to two small and obscure enclaves. One was a group of Hazara resistants, bottled up in the mountains of Dara-i-Suf, and the other was Massoud himself, in the impregnable Panjshir Valley and the northeastern corner called Badakhshan.

On August 7, bombs exploded outside the American embassies in two African capitals. He knew nothing of this. Listening to foreign radio was now banned, and he obeyed. On August 21, America launched seventy Tomahawk cruise missiles at Afghanistan. They came from the two missile cruisers *Cowpen* and *Shiloh* in the Red Sea, and from the destroyers *Briscoe, Elliot, Hayler, Milius* and the submarine *Columbia,* all in the Arabian Gulf south of Pakistan.

They were aimed at the training camps of Al Qaeda, and the caves of the Tora Bora. Among those that went astray was one that entered the mouth of an empty, natural cave high in the mountain above Maloko-zai. The detonation deep inside the cave split the mountain, and an entire face peeled away. Ten million tons of rock crashed into the valley below.

When he reached the mountain, there was nothing to recognize. The entire valley had been buried. There was no stream anymore, no farm, no orchards, no stock pens, no stables, no compounds, no mosque. His entire family and all his neighbors were gone. His parents, uncles, aunts, sisters, wife and child were dead beneath millions of tons of granite rubble. There was nowhere to dig and nothing to dig for. He had become a man with no roots, no relatives, no clan.

In the dying August sun, he knelt on the shale high above where his dead family lay, turned west toward Mecca, bowed his head to the ground and prayed. But it was a different prayer this time; it was a mighty oath, a sworn vendetta, a personal jihad unto death, and it was against the people who had done this. He declared war on America.

A week later, he had resigned his governorship and gone back to the front. For two years, he fought the Northern Alliance. While he was away, the tactically brilliant Massoud had counterattacked and again caused huge losses to the less competent Taliban. There had been massacres at Mazar-e-Sharif, where first the native Hazara had risen in revolt and killed six hundred Taliban; the avenging Taliban had gone back and butchered over two thousand civilians.

The Dayton Agreement had been signed; technically, the Bosnian war was over. But what had been left behind was nightmarish. Muslim Bosnia had been the main theater of war, even though the Bosnians, Serbs and Croats had all been involved. It had been the bloodiest conflict in Europe since World War II.

The Croats and the Serbs, far and away the better armed, had inflicted most of the brutalities. A thoroughly and rightly ashamed Europe set up a war crimes tribunal at The Hague in Holland and waited for the first indictments. The problem was, the guilty ones were not about to come forward with their hands up. Milošević would offer no help at all; indeed, he was preparing fresh miseries for another Muslim province, Kosovo.

Part of Bosnia, the exclusively Serbian third, had declared itself the Serb Republic, and most of the war criminals were hiding there. This was the task: Find them, identify them, snatch them and bring them out to stand trial. Living mainly in the fields and forests, the SAS spent 1997 hunting down what they called the "PIFWICs"—persons indicted for war crimes.

By 1998, he was back in the UK, and back in the Paras, a lieutenant colonel and instructor at Camberley Staff College. The following year, he was made commanding officer, First Battalion, known as 1 Para. The NATO allies had again intervened in the Balkans, this time a little more speedily than before, and again to prevent a massacre big enough to cause the media to use the overemployed term "genocide."

Intelligence had convinced both the British and American governments that Milošević intended to "cleanse" the rebellious province of Kosovo, and to do so thoroughly. The medium would be the expulsion of most of its 1.8 million citizens westward into neighboring Albania. Under the NATO banner, the Allies gave Milošević an ultimatum. He ignored it, and columns of weeping and destitute Kosovans were driven through the mountain passes into Albania.

The NATO response was no invasion on the ground but bombing raids instead, which lasted seventy-eight days and wrecked both Kosovo and Serbian Yugoslavia itself. With his country in ruins, Milošević finally conceded, and NATO moved into Kosovo to try to govern the wreckage. The man in charge was a lifelong Para, General Mike Jackson, and 1 Para went with him.

That would probably have been Mike Martin's last "action" posting had it not been for the West Side Boys.

On the ninth of September 2001, news flashed through the Taliban army that had the soldiers roaring *"Allahu-akhbar,"* Allah is great, over and over again. The air above Izmat Khan's camp outside Bamiyan crackled with the shots fired in a delirium of joy. Someone had assassinated Ahmad Shah Massoud. Their enemy was dead. The man whose charisma had held together the cause of the useless Rabbani, whose cleverness as a guerrilla fighter had caused the Soviets to revere him and whose generalship had carved Taliban forces to pieces, was no more.

In fact, he had been assassinated by two suicide bombers, ultrafanatical Moroccans with stolen Belgian passports pretending to be journalists, and sent by

Osama bin Laden as a favor to his friend Mullah Omar. The Saudi had not thought of the ploy; it was the far cleverer Egyptian Ayman al-Zawahiri who realized that if Al Qaeda did this favor for Omar, the one-eyed mullah could never expel them for what was going to happen next.

On the eleventh, four airliners were hijacked over the American east coast. Within ninety minutes, two had destroyed the World Trade Center in Manhattan, one had devastated the Pentagon, and the fourth, as its rebellious passengers invaded the flight deck to rip the hijackers from the controls, had crashed in a field.

Within days, the identity and inspiration of the nineteen hijackers had been established; within a few more days, the new American president had given Mullah Omar a flat ultimatum: Yield up the ringleaders or take the consequences. Because of Massoud, Omar could not capitulate. It was the code.

In the West African hellhole of Sierra Leone, years of civil war and barbarism had left the once-rich former British colony a vista of chaos, banditry, filth, disease, poverty and hacked-off limbs. Years earlier, the British had decided to intervene, and the UN had been prevailed upon to ship in fifteen thousand troops, who, broadly, just sat in their barracks in the capital, Freetown. The jungle beyond the city limits was regarded as simply too dangerous. But the UN force included an element of the British Army, and they at least patrolled the backcountry.

In late August, a patrol of eleven men from the Royal Irish Rangers was lured off the main road and down a track to the village which acted as the headquarters of a rebel band calling themselves the West Side Boys. They were, in effect, out-of-control psychopaths—they were relentlessly drunk on pure alcohol native hooch; they rubbed their gums with cocaine, or cut their arms to rub the dope into the cuts to get a faster "hit." The horrors they had inflicted on the peasantry over a wide range were unspeakable; but there were four hundred of them, and they were armed to the teeth. The rangers were quickly captured and held hostage.

Mike Martin, after a stint in Kosovo, had brought 1 Para to Freetown, where they were based at Waterloo Camp. After complex negotiations, five of the rangers were ransomed, but the remaining six seemed destined to be chopped up. In London, the chief of Defence staff, Sir Charles Guthrie, gave the word: Go in there and get them out by force.

The task force was forty-eight SAS men, twenty-four from the SBS and ninety from 1 Para. Ten SAS men in jungle camouflage were dropped in a week before the attack and lived unseen in the jungle round the bandit village, watching, listening and reporting back. Everything the West Side Boys said and did was overheard by the SAS men in the bush a few yards away and transmitted. That was how the British knew there was no further hope of a peaceful exfiltration.

Mike Martin went in with the second wave after an unlucky rebel mortar had injured six, including the commander of the first wave, who had to be evacuated without ceremony.

The village—or, in fact, the twin villages of Gberi Bana and Magbeni—straddled a slimy and stinking river called Rokel Creek. The seventy SAS took Gberi Bana, where the hostages were located, rescued them all and fought off a series of manic counterattacks. The ninety Paras took Magbeni. There were, at dawn, about two hundred West Side Boys in each.

Six prisoners were taken, trussed and brought back to Freetown. A few of them escaped into the jungle. No attempt was made to count the bodies, either in the wreckage of the two villages or the surrounding jungle, but no one ever disputed the figure of three hundred dead.

The SAS and the Paras took twelve injured, and one SAS man, Brad Tinnion, died of his wounds. Mike Martin, having lost the CO of his first wave, arrived in the second Chinook, and led the final wipeout of Magbeni. It was old-fashioned fighting, point-blank range and hand-to-hand. On the south side of the Rokel Creek, the Paras had lost their radio to the same mortar blast that hit the attack leader. So the circling helicopters overhead could not report on the fall of their own mortar shells, and the jungle was too thick to see them drop.

Eventually, the Paras just charged, blood pumping, screaming and swearing, until the West Side Boys, happy to torture peasants and prisoners, fled, died, fled again and died, until there were none left.

It was six months almost to the day that Martin was back in London when breakfast was interrupted by those unbelievable images on the TV screen of fully loaded and fueled airliners flying straight into the twin towers. A week later, it was plain the USA would have to go into Afghanistan in pursuit of those responsible, with or without the agreement of the Kabul government.

London at once agreed that it would provide whatever was needed from its own resources, and the immediate requirements were air-to-air refueling tankers and Special Forces. The SIS head of station in Islamabad said he would also need all the help he could get.

That was a matter for Vauxhall Cross, but the Defence attaché in Islamabad also asked for help. Mike Martin was taken from his desk at Para HQ, Aldershot, and found himself on the next flight to Islamabad as Special Forces liaison officer.

He arrived two weeks to the day after the destruction of the World Trade Center, and the day the first allied attacks went in.

CHAPTER 7

IZMAT KHAN WAS STILL commanding in the north, on the Badakhshan front, when the bombs rained on Kabul. As the world studied Kabul and diversionary tactics in the south, the U.S. Special Forces slipped into Badakhshan to help General Fahim, who had taken over Massoud's army. This was where the real fighting would be; the rest was window dressing for the media. The key would be Northern Alliance ground forces and American air-power.

Without ever taking off, Afghanistan's puny air force was vaporized. Its tanks and artillery, if they could be spotted, were "taken out." The Uzbek, Rashid Dostum, who had spent years in safety across the border, was persuaded to come back and open a second front in the northwest to match Fahim's front in the northeast. And in November, the great breakout began. The key was target marking, the technology that has quietly revolutionized warfare since the first Gulf War of 1991.

Hidden invisible among the allied forces, Special Forces personnel squint through long-range binoculars to identify the enemy's dug-in positions, guns, tanks, ammunition dumps, reserves, supplies and command bunkers. Each is marked, or "painted," with an infrared dot from a shoulder-held projector. Via radio, an air strike is called up.

In the destruction of the Taliban army facing the Northern Alliance, these strikes either came from far away in the south, where U.S. Navy carriers hovered off the coast, or with A-10 tank busters flying out of well-rewarded Uzbekistan. Unit by unit, with bombs and rockets that could not miss as they followed the infrared beam, the Taliban army was blown away and the Tajiks charged in in triumph.

Izmat Khan retreated and retreated as position after position was devastated and lost. The Taliban army of the north started at over thirty thousand soldiers, but were losing a thousand a day. There was no medication, no evacuation, no doctors. The wounded said their prayers and died like flies. They screamed *"Allahu-akhbar"* and charged into walls of bullets.

The original volunteers for the Taliban army had long been used up. Few were left. Taliban recruiting squads had pressed tens of thousands more into the ranks, but many did not want to fight. The true fanatics were dwindling away. And still Izmat Khan had to pull them back, each time convinced that, being in the front of every combat, he could not last another day. By November 18, they had reached the town of Kunduz.

By a fluke of history, Kunduz is a small enclave of Gilzai southerners, all Pashtun, in a sea of Tajiks and Hazaras. Thus, the Taliban army could take refuge there. And it was there they agreed to surrender.

Among Afghans there is nothing dishonorable in a negotiated surrender, and, once agreed, its terms are always honored. The entire Taliban army surrendered to General Fahim, and Fahim accepted.

Inside the Taliban were two non-Afghan groups. There were six hundred Arabs, all devoted to Osama bin Laden, who had sent them there. Well over three thousand Arabs had already died, and the American attitude was that they would not weep salt tears if the rest went to Allah as well.

There were also about two thousand Pakistanis who were clearly going to be a thundering embarrassment to Islamabad if they were discovered. The Pakistani ruler, General Musharraf, had been left in not a shred of doubt after 9/11 that he had a choice: become a dedicated ally of the USA, with billions and billions of dollars in aid; or continue to support, via the ISI, the Taliban, and thus bin Laden, and pay the direct consequences. He chose the USA.

But the ISI still had a small army of agents inside Afghanistan, and the Pakistani volunteers fighting with the Taliban would not stint from revealing the encouragement they had once been given to go north. Over three nights, a secret air bridge exfiltrated most of them back to Pakistan.

In another covert deal, some four thousand prisoners were sold for varying sums, according to desirability, to the USA and Russia. The Russians wanted any Chechens, and, as a favor to Tashkent, any anti-Tashkent Uzbeks.

The original army that surrendered was over fourteen thousand, but their numbers were coming down. Finally, the Northern Alliance announced to the world media, streaming north to cover the real war story, that it had only eight thousand prisoners.

Then it was decided to hand over a further five thousand to the Uzbek commander, General Dostum. He wished to take them far to the west, to Sheberghan, inside his own territory. They were packed into steel freight containers without food or water, and so compressed they could only stand, straining upward for the air pocket above their heads. Somewhere on the road west, it was agreed to give them airholes. This was done with heavy machine guns that went on firing until the screaming stopped.

Of the remaining 3,015, the Arabs were selected out. They came from every part of the Muslim world; there were Saudis, Yemenis, Moroccans, Algerians, Egyptians, Jordanians and Syrians. The ultraradical Uzbeks had been shipped back to the tender mercies of Tashkent, and most of the Chechen also, but a few had managed to remain. Through the campaign, the Chechens had earned the reputation of the most ferocious, cruel and suicidal of all.

The balance of twenty-four hundred remained behind

in Tajik hands, and have not been heard of since. Izmat Khan was spoken to by one of the selectors in Arabic. He replied in Arabic, and was thought to be an Arab for that reason. He bore no badges of rank, was filthy, matted, hungry and exhausted. When he was pushed in a certain direction, he was too tired to protest. Thus, he ended up one of the six Afghans in the group destined to be sent west to Mazar-e-Sharif and into the hands of Dostum and his Uzbeks. By this time, the Western media were watching, and the prisoners were given a guarantee of safe conduct by the newly arrived United Nations.

Trucks were found from somewhere, and the six hundred were loaded abroad for the journey west along the pitted track to Mazar. But their final destination would not be the city itself but a huge prison fortress ten miles farther west.

So they came to the mouth of hell, but it was called the fort of Qala-i-Jangi.

The conquest of Afghanistan, if measured from the first bomb to the fall of Kabul to the Northern Alliance, was about fifty days, but Special Forces from both allied countries were operational inside Afghanistan well before that. Mike Martin yearned to go with them, but the British High Commission in Islamabad was adamant it needed him on the spot to liaise with the Pakistani Army brass.

Until Bagram. This vast ex-Soviet air base north of Kabul was clearly going to be a major allied base during the eventual occupation. Taliban aircraft based there were gutted wrecks, and the control tower was a ruin. But the sheer size of the runway, the numerous huge hangars and the living quarters where the Soviet garrison had once lived were all restorable with time and money.

It was captured in the third week of November and a team of Special Boat Squadron men moved in to stake the British claim. Mike Martin used the news as a first-rate excuse to hitch a lift from the Americans at Rawalpindi airfield to go and have a look at the place, as he put it.

It was bleak and comfortless, but the SBS had "liberated" a hangar all of their own before the Americans took the lot and were hunkered down at the back, as far from the icy wind as possible.

Soldiers have a remarkable talent for making a kind of home out of the weirdest places, and the Special Forces are the aces because they seem to find themselves in places weirder than most. The SBS unit of twenty had gone foraging with their long-base Land Rovers and seized a series of steel freight containers, which had been dragged inside.

With drums, planks and a bit of ingenuity, these were being turned into billets with beds, sofas, tables, electric lights and—supremely important—a power point to plug in the kettle and brew up mugs of tea.

It was on the morning of November 26 that the unit CO told his men: "There seems to be something going on at a place called Qala-i-Jangi, west of Mazar. Some prisoners appear to have risen in revolt, taken their guards' weapons and are putting up a fight. I think we should have a look."

Six Marines were chosen, and two Land Rovers allocated and fueled. As they were about to leave, Martin asked, "Mind if I tag along? You might be able to use an interpreter."

The CO of the small SBS unit was a Marine captain. Martin was a Para colonel. There was no objection. Martin boarded the second vehicle beside the driver. Behind him, two Marines crouched over the .30 calibre machine gun. They headed north on the six-hour drive, through the Salang Pass, to the northern plains and the city of Mazar and the fort of Qala-i-Jangi.

The exact incident that triggered the massacre of the prisoners at Qala-i-Jangi was disputed at the time, and will remain so. But there are compelling clues.

The Western media, never shy of getting something completely wrong, persistently called the prisoners "Taliban." They were the opposite. They were, in fact, with the exception of the six Afghans included by accident, the defeated army of Al Qaeda. As such, they had come to Afghanistan specifically to pursue jihad—to fight and to die. What were trucked west from Kunduz were the six hundred most dangerous men in Asia.

What met them at Qala were one hundred partly trained Uzbeks under a desperately incompetent commander. Rashid Dostum himself was away; in charge was his deputy, Sayid Kamel.

Among the six hundred were about sixty of three non-Arab categories. There were Chechens, who, suspecting back at Kunduz that being selected for shipment to the Russians was a recipe for death, avoided the cull. There were anti-Tashkent Uzbeks who had also figured out that only a miserable death awaited them back in Uzbekistan and hid themselves. And there were Pakistanis who wrongly avoided repatriation to Pakistan, where they would have been set free.

The rest were Arabs. They were, unlike many of the Taliban left behind at Kunduz, volunteers, not pressed men. They were all ultrafanatical. They had all been through the AQ training camps; they knew how to fight with ferocity and skill. And they had little desire to live. All they asked of Allah was the chance to take a few Westerners or friends of Westerners with them and thus die a *shahid*, a martyr.

The fort of Qala is not constructed like a Western fort. It is a huge, ten-acre compound with open spaces, trees and one-story buildings. The whole area is enclosed by a fifty-foot wall, but each side is sloped so that a climber can scramble up the ramp and peer over the parapet at the top.

This thick wall plays host to a labyrinth of barracks, stores and passages, with another maze of tunnels and cellars beneath them. The Uzbeks had only captured it ten days earlier and seemed not to know that there was a Taliban armory and magazine stored at the southern end. That was where they shooed the prisoners.

At Kunduz, the captives had been relieved of their rifles and RPGs, but no one had done a body search. Had the prisoners been frisked, the captors would have realized almost every man had a grenade or two hidden inside his robes. That was how they arrived in the motorcade at Qala-i-Jangi.

The first hint came on the Saturday night of their arrival. Izmat Khan was in the fifth truck, and heard the boom from a hundred yards away. One of the Arabs, gathering several Uzbeks around him, detonated his grenade, blowing himself and five Uzbeks to pemmican. Night was coming on. There were no lights. Dostum's men decided to do body searches the next morning. They herded the prisoners into the compound without food or water and left them, squatting on the ground, surrounded by armed, already-nervous guards.

At dawn, the searches began. The prisoners, still docile in their battle fatigue, allowed their hands to be tied behind them. As there were no ropes, the Uzbeks used the prisoners' turbans. But turbans are not ropes.

One by one the prisoners were hauled upright to be frisked. Out came handguns, grenades—and money. As the money piled up, it was taken away to a side room by Sayid Kamel and his deputy. An Uzbek soldier, peering through the window a little later, saw the two men pocketing the lot. The soldier entered to protest, and was told in no uncertain terms to get lost. But he came back with a rifle.

There were two prisoners who saw this and had worked their hands free. They entered the room after the soldier, seized the rifle and used its butt to beat all three Uzbeks to death. As there had been no shooting, nothing was noticed, but the compound was becoming a powder keg.

The Americans from the CIA, Johnny "Mike" Spann and Dave Tyson, had entered the area, and Spann began a series of interrogations right out in the open. He was surrounded by six hundred fanatics whose only ambition before going to Allah was to kill an American. Then some Uzbek guard saw the armed Arab and yelled a warning. The Arab fired and killed him. The powder keg went off.

Izmat Khan was squatting on the dirt waiting for his turn. Like the others, he had worked his hands free. As the shot Uzbek soldier fell, others atop the walls opened up with machine guns. The slaughter had begun.

Over a hundred prisoners died in the dirt with bound hands, and were found that way when it was finally safe for the UN observers to enter. Others untied their neighbors' hands so that they could fight. Izmat Khan led a group of others, including his five fellow Afghans, in a dodging, weaving run through the trees to the south wall, where he knew the armory was from a previous visit when the fort was in Taliban hands.

Twenty Arabs nearest to Mike Spann fell on him and beat him to death with fists and feet. Dave Tyson emptied his handgun into the mob, killed three, heard the click of hammer on empty chamber and was lucky to make the main gate just in time.

Within ten minutes, the open compound was empty except for the corpses, or the wounded who cried out until they died. The Uzbeks were now outside the wall, the main gate was slammed and the prisoners were inside. The siege had begun; it would last six days, and no one was even interested in taking prisoners. Each side was convinced the other had broken the terms of surrender, but by then it did not matter anymore.

The armory door was quickly shattered and the treasure trove distributed. There was enough for a small army and masses of resupply for only five hundred men. They had rifles, grenades, launchers, RPGs and mortars. Taking what they could, they fanned out through the tunnels and passages until they owned the fortress. Every time an Uzbek outside put his head over the parapet, an Arab, firing through a slit from across the compound, took a shot.

Dostum's men had no choice but to call for help, urgently. It came in the form of hundreds more Uzbeks sent by General Dostum, who hurried toward Qala-i-Jangi. Also on their way were American Green Berets, four men from Fort Campbell, Kentucky, one U.S. Air Force man to assist in air coordination and six from the 10th Mountain Division. Basically, their job was to observe, report and call in air strikes to break the resistance.

By midmorning, coming up from Bagram base north of the recently captured capital of Kabul were two long-base Land Rovers bearing six British Special Forces from the Special Boat Squadron (SBS) and an interpreter, Lieutenant Colonel Mike Martin of the SAS.

Tuesday saw the Uzbek counterattack taking shape. Shielded by their simple tank, they reentered the compound and began to pound the rebel positions. Izmat

Khan had been recognized as a senior commander and given charge of one wing of the south face. When the tank opened up, he ordered his men into the cellars. When the bombardment stopped, they came back up again.

He knew it was only a matter of time. There was no way out, and no chance for mercy. Not that he wanted it. He had finally, at the age of twenty-nine, found the place he was going to die, and it was as good as any other.

Tuesday also saw the arrival of the U.S. strike aircraft. The four Green Berets and the airman were lying just outside the parapet at the top of the external ramp, plotting targets for the fighter-bombers. Thirty strikes took place that day, and twenty-eight of them slammed into the masonry inside which the rebels were hiding, killing about a hundred of them, largely by rockfalls. Two bombs were not so good.

Mike Martin was down the wall from the Green Berets, about a hundred yards from them, when the first bomb went amiss. It landed right in the middle of the circle formed by the five Americans. If it had been a contact-fused antipersonnel bomb, they would have been shredded. The fact that all survived with shattered eardrums and some bone breaks was in itself a miracle.

The bomb was a J-DAM, a bunker buster, designed to penetrate deep into masonry before exploding. Landing nose down in gravel, it shot forty feet down before going off. The Americans found themselves on top of an earthquake, were hurled around, but survived.

The second mishit was even more unfortunate. It took out the Uzbek tank, and their command post behind it.

By Wednesday, the Western media had arrived and were swarming all over the fort, or at least the outside of it. They may not have realized it, but their presence was the only factor that would eventually inhibit the Uzbeks from achieving a total wipeout of the rebels to the last man.

In the course of the six days, twenty rebels tried to take their chances by escaping under cover of night cross-country. Every one of them was caught by the peasantry and lynched. These were the Hazaras, who recalled the Taliban butchery of their people three years before.

Mike Martin lay on top of the ramp, peering through the parapet and down into the open compound. The bodies from the first days still lay there, and the stench was appalling. The Americans, with their black woolly hats, had uncovered faces and had already been well photographed by cameramen and TV filmmakers. The seven British preferred anonymity. All wore the *shemagh,* the cotton wraparound headdress that keeps out sand, dust, flies and gawkers. By Wednesday, it served another purpose: to filter the stink.

Just before sundown, the surviving CIA man, Dave Tyson, who had come back after a day in Mazar-e-Sharif, was bold enough to enter the compound with a TV crew desperate for an award-winning movie. Martin watched them creeping along the far wall. Marine J was lying beside him. As they watched, a snatch squad of rebels came out of an unseen door in the wall, seized the four Westerners and dragged them inside.

"Someone ought to get them out of there," remarked Marine J in a conversational tone. He looked round. Six pairs of eyes were staring at him without a sound.

He uttered two intensely sincere words—"Oh, shit"— vaulted the wall, went down the inner ramp and raced across the open space. Three SBS men went with him. The other two and Martin provided sniper cover. The rebels were by now confined to the south wall only. The sheer daftness of what the four Marines had done caught the rebels by surprise. There were no shots until they reached the door in the far wall.

Marine J was first in. Hostage recovery is practiced and practiced by both SAS and SBS until it is second nature. At Hereford, the SAS have "the death house" for little else; at their Poole HQ, the SBS have the same.

The four SBS men came through the door without ceremony, identified the three rebels by their clothes and beards and fired. The procedure is called "double tap": two bullets straight in the face. The three Arabs did not get off a shot; anyway, they were facing in the wrong direction. David Tyson and the British TV crew agreed then and there never to mention the incident, and they never have.

By Wednesday evening, Izmat Khan realized he and his men could not stay aboveground any longer. Artillery had arrived, and down the length of the compound it was beginning to reduce the south face to rubble. The cellars were the last resort. The surviving rebels were down to under three hundred.

Some of these decided not to go belowground but to die under the sky. They staged a suicidal counterattack that succeeded for a hundred yards, killing a number of unwary Uzbeks with short reaction times. But then the machine gun on the Uzbeks' replacement tank opened up and cut the Arabs to pieces. They were mostly Yemenis with some Chechens.

On Thursday, on American advice, the Uzbeks took barrels of diesel fuel brought for their tank and poured it down conduits into the cellars below. Then they set fire to it.

Izmat Khan was not in that section of the cellars, and the stench of the bodies overrode the smell of the diesel, but he heard the *whoomf* and felt the heat. More died, but the survivors came staggering out of the smoke toward him. They were all choking and gagging. In the last cellar, with about a hundred and fifty men around him, Izmat Khan slammed and bolted the door to keep out the smoke. Beyond the door, the hammering of the dying became fainter and finally stopped. Above them, the shells slammed into the empty rooms.

The last cellar led to a passage and at the far end the men could smell fresh air. They tried to see if there was a way out, but it was only a gutter from above. That night, the new Uzbek commander, Din Muhammad, hit upon the idea of diverting an irrigation ditch into that pipe. After the November rains, the ditch was full and the water in it icy.

By midnight, the remaining men were waist-deep in water. Weakened by hunger and exhaustion, they began to slip beneath the surface and drown.

Up on the surface, the United Nations was in charge, surrounded by media, and their instructions were to take prisoners. Through the rubble of the collapsed buildings above them, the last rebels could hear the bullhorn ordering them to come out, unarmed and with hands up. After twenty hours, the first began to stagger toward the stairs. Others followed. Defeated at last, Izmat Khan, the last Afghan left alive, went with them.

Up on the surface, stumbling over the broken stone blocks that had once been the south face, the last eighty-six rebels found themselves facing a forest of pointed guns and rockets. In the daylight of Saturday dawn, they looked like scarecrows from a horror film. Filthy, stinking, black from cordite soot, ragged, matted, bearded and hypothermic, they tottered and some fell. One of these was Izmat Khan.

Coming down a rock pile, he slipped, reached out to steady himself and grabbed a rock. A chunk came away in his hand. Thinking he was being attacked, a nervous young Uzbek fired his RPG.

The fiery grenade went past the Afghan's ear into a boulder behind him. The stone splintered, and a piece the size of a baseball hit him with devastating force in the back of the head.

He was wearing no turban. It had been used to bind his hands six days earlier and never recovered. The rock would have pulped the skull if it had hit at ninety degrees. But it ricocheted off, slicing the scalp and knocking him into a near coma. He fell in the rubble, blood gushing from the gash. The rest were marched away to trucks waiting outside.

An hour later, the seven British soldiers were moving through the compound, taking notes. Mike Martin, as senior officer, although technically the unit interpreter, would have a long report to make. He was counting the dead, though he knew there were scores—maybe up to two hundred—still underground. One body interested him. It was still bleeding. Corpses don't bleed.

He turned the scarecrow over. The clothing was wrong. This was Pashtun dress. There were not supposed to be any Pashtun present. He took his *shebagh* from his head and wiped the grime-smeared face. Something vaguely familiar.

When he took out his Ka-bar, a watching Uzbek grinned. If the foreigner wanted to have some fun, why not? Martin cut into the pant leg of the right thigh.

It was still there, puckered with the six stitches, the scar where the Soviet shell fragment had gone in over thirteen years before. For the second time in his life, he hoisted Izmat Khan over one shoulder in a fireman's lift and carried him. At the main gate, he found a white Land Rover with a United Nations insignia on it.

"This man is alive but injured," he said. "He has a bad head wound."

Duty done, he boarded the SBS Land Rover for the drive back to Bagram.

The American trawl team found the Afghan in Mazar Hospital three days later and claimed him for interrogation. They trucked him to Bagram, but to their own side of this vast air base, and there he came to two days after that, slowly and groggily, on the floor of a makeshift cell, cold and shackled but just alive.

On the fourteenth of January 2002, the first detainees arrived at Guantánamo Bay, Cuba, from Kandahar. They were blindfolded, shackled, hungry, thirsty and soiled. Izmat Khan was one of them.

Colonel Mike Martin returned to London in the spring of 2002 to spend three years as deputy chief of staff, HQ Directorate of Special Forces, Duke of York Barracks, Chelsea. He retired in December 2005 after a party at which a group of friends including Jonathan Shaw, Mark Carleton-Smith, Jim Davidson and Mike Jackson tried—and failed—to drink him under the table. In January 2006, he bought a listed barn in the Meon Valley, Hampshire, and started in the late summer to restore it into a country home.

United Nations records later showed that 514 Al Qaeda fanatics died at Qala-i-Jangi and eighty-six survived, all injured. All went to Guantánamo Bay. Sixty Uzbek guards also died. General Rashid Dostum became defense minister in the new Afghan government.

PART THREE
CROWBAR

CHAPTER 8

OPERATION CROWBAR'S FIRST TASK was to choose its cover story so that even those working inside it would not know anything about Mike Martin or even the concept of infiltrating a ring inside Al Qaeda.

The "legend" chosen was that it would be an Anglo-American joint venture against a steadily growing opium threat coming out of the poppies of Afghanistan, to the refinery/kitchens of the Middle East. Thence, the refined heroin was infiltrating the West, destroying lives and generating funds for further terrorism.

The "script" continued to the effect that Western efforts to shut off terrorism's supply of funds at the level of the world's banks had driven the fanatics to lean to drugs—a cash-only crime method.

And finally, even though the West already had powerful agencies like the U.S. DEA and British customs engaged in the fight against narcotics, Crowbar had been agreed upon by both governments to be a specific, one-target operation prepared to use covert forces outside the niceties of diplomatic courtesy to raid and destroy any factories found in any foreign country turning a blind eye to the trade.

The modus operandi, Crowbar staff would be told as they were reassigned, involved using the highest tech known to man, both to listen and to watch, in order to identify high-ranking criminals, routes, storage facilities, refineries, ships and aircraft that might be involved. As it happened, none of the new staff doubted a word of it.

This was just the cover story, and it would remain in place until there was simply no further use for it, when-ever that would be. But after the Fort Meade conference, there was no way Western intelligence was going to place all its eggs in the Crowbar basket. Frantic, though ultra-discreet, efforts would continue elsewhere to discover what al-Isra could possibly refer to.

But the intelligence agencies were in a quandary. Be-tween them, they had scores of informants inside the world of Islamic fundamentalism, some willing, some under duress.

The question was: How far can we go before the real leaders realize that we know about al-Isra? There were clear advantages to letting Al Qaeda believe that nothing had been harvested from the laptop of the dead banker at Peshawar.

This was confirmed when the first mentions of the phrase in general conversation with Koranic scholars known to be sympathetic to extremism drew only courteous but blank responses.

Whoever knew about the real significance of the phrase, AQ had kept that circle extremely tight, and it was quickly clear it did not include any Western informants. So the decision was taken to match secrecy with secrecy. The West's countermeasure would be Crowbar—and only Crowbar.

The project's second chore was to find and establish a new and remote headquarters. Both Marek Gumienny and Steve Hill agreed to get well away from London and Washington. Their second agreement was to base Crowbar somewhere in the British Isles.

After analysis of what would be needed in terms of size, lodgings, space and access, the consensus came down firmly on the side of a decommissioned air base. Such places are usually well away from cities, contain mess halls, canteens, kitchens, and accommodation aplenty. Add to that hangars for storage and a runway for the landing and departure of covert visitors. Unless the decommissioning had been too long ago, refurbishment back to operational requirements could be quickly accomplished by the property-maintenance division of one of the armed services—in this case, the Royal Air Force.

When it came to which base, the choice fell on a former American base, which the Cold War had planted several dozen of on British soil. Fifteen were listed and examined, including Chicksands, Alconbury, Lakenheath, Fairford, Molesworth, Bentwaters, Upper Heyford and Greenham Common. All were vetoed.

Some were operational, and service personnel still chatter. Others were in the hands of property developers; some had had their runways plowed up and returned to agriculture. Two are still training sites for the intelligence services. Crowbar wanted a virgin site all to itself. Phillips and McDonald settled upon RAF Edzell, and secured the approval of their respective superiors.

Although the sovereign ownership of Edzell base never left the RAF, it was for years leased to the U.S. Navy, even though it is miles from the sea. It is actually situated in the Scottish county of Angus, due north of Brechin and northwest of Montrose, on the southern threshold of the Highlands.

It lies well off the main A90 highway from Forfar to Stonehaven. The village itself is one of a thinly scattered number spread over a large area of forest and heather, with the North Esk flowing through it.

The base, when the two executive officers went up to visit it, served all their purposes. It was as remote from prying eyes as one could wish; it contained two good runways with control tower, and all the buildings they needed for the resident staff. All that would be added would be the golf-ball-shaped white domes hiding listening antennas that could hear the click of a beetle half a world away, and the conversion of the former USN Ops block into the new communications, or comms, center.

Into this complex would be diverted links to GCHQ Cheltenham and NSA Maryland; direct and secure lines to Vauxhall Cross and Langley to permit instant access to Marek Gumienny and Steve Hill; and a permanent "feed" from eight more intel-gathering agencies from both nations, prime among them the yield from America's space satellites, run by the National Reconnaissance Office in Washington.

With permission granted, the "works and bricks" people from the Royal Air Force went on a "blitz" assignment to bring Edzell back into commission. The good folk of Edzell village noticed that something was afoot, but, with much winking and tapping of the sides of noses, accepted that once again it would be hush-hush, just like the good old days. The local landlord laid in some extra supplies of ale and whiskey, hoping that custom might revert to the way it used to be before decommissioning. Otherwise, nobody said a thing.

While the painters were running their paintbrushes over the walls of the officers' quarters of a Scottish air base, the office of Siebart and Abercrombie, on a modest City of London street called Crutched Friars, received a visit.

Mr. Ahmed Lampong had arrived by appointment following an exchange of e-mails between London and Jakarta, and was shown into the office of Mr. Siebart, son of the founder. Had the London-based shipping broker known it, Lampong is simply one of the minor languages of the island of Sumatra, whence his Indonesian visitor originally came. And it was an alias, though his passport would confirm the name and his passport was flawless.

So also was his English, and in response to Alex Siebart's compliments he admitted that he had perfected it while studying for his master's degree at the London

School of Economics. He was fluent, urbane and charming; more to the point, he brought the prospect of business. There was nothing to suggest he was a fanatical member of the Islamist terrorist organization Jemaat Islamiyah, responsible for a wave of bombings in Bali.

His credentials as senior partner in Sumatra Trading International were in order, as were his bank references. When he asked permission to outline his problem, Mr. Siebart was all ears. As a preamble, Mr. Lampong solemnly laid a sheet of paper in front of the British ship broker.

The sheet had a long list. It began with Alderney, one of the British Channel Islands, and continued through Anguilla, Antigua and Aruba. Those were just the *As*. There were forty-three names, ending with Uruguay, Vanuatu and Western Samoa.

"These are all tax-haven countries, Mr. Siebart," said the Indonesian, "and all practice banking secrecy. Like it or not, some extremely dubious businesses, including criminal enterprises, shelter their financial secrets in places like these. And these"—he produced a second sheet—"are just as dubious in their way. These are merchant shipping flags of convenience."

Antigua was again up front, with Barbuda, Bahamas, Barbados, Belize, Bermuda, Bolivia and Burma to follow. There were twenty-seven in this list, ending with St. Vincent, Sri Lanka, Tonga and Vanuatu.

There were African hellholes like Equatorial Guinea, flyspecks on the world map like São Tomé and Principe, the Comoros and the coral atoll Vanuatu. Among the more enchanting were Luxembourg, Mongolia and Cambodia, which have no coast at all. Mr. Siebart was perplexed, though nothing he had seen was news to him.

"Put the two together and what do you come up with?" asked Mr. Lampong in triumph. "Fraud, my dear sir, fraud on a massive and increasing scale. And, alas, most prevalent of all in the part of the world where I and my partners trade. That is why we have decided only in future to deal with the institution renowned for its integrity. The City of London."

"Very kind of you," murmured Mr. Siebart. "Coffee?"

"Cargo theft, Mr. Siebart. Constant and increasing. Thank you, no, I have just had breakfast. Cargoes are assigned—valuable cargoes—and then vanish. No trace of the ship, the charterers, the brokers, the crew, the cargo—and, least of all, the owners. All hiding among this forest of different flags and banks. And far too many of them highly corrupt."

"Dreadful," agreed Siebart. "How can I help?"

"My partners and I have agreed we will have no more of it. True, it will cost a bit more. But we wish to deal in future only and solely with ships of the British merchant fleet flying the Red Ensign, out of British ports under a British skipper and vouched for by a London broker."

"Excellent." Siebart beamed. "A wise choice, and of course we must not forget full insurance coverage for vessel and cargo by Lloyd's of London. What cargoes do you want shipped?"

Matching freighters to cargoes and cargoes to freighters is precisely what a shipping broker does, and

Siebart and Abercrombie were long-standing pillars of the City of London's ancient partnership, the Baltic Exchange.

"I have done my research well," said Mr. Lampong, producing more letters of recommendation. "We have been in discussion with this company; importers of high-value British limousines and sports cars into Singapore. For our part, we ship fine furniture timbers like rosewood, tulipwood and padauk from Indonesia to the USA. This comes from North Borneo, but would be a part cargo, with the remainder being sea containers on deck with embroidered silks from Surabaya, Java, also bound for the USA. Here"—he laid down a final letter—"are the details of our friends in Surabaya. We all agree we wish to trade British. Clearly, this would be a triangular voyage for any British freighter. Could you find us a suitable UK-registered freighter for this task? I have in mind a regular and ongoing partnership."

Alex Siebart was confident he could find a dozen suitable Red Ensign vessels to pick up the charter. He would need to know vessel size, price and desired dates.

It was finally agreed that he would supply Mr. Lampong with a "menu" of vessels of the needed tonnage for the double cargo and the charter price. Mr. Lampong, when he had consulted his partners, would provide desired collection dates at the two Far Eastern ports and the U.S. delivery port. They parted with mutual expressions of confidence and goodwill.

"How nice," sighed Alex Siebart's father when he

told him over lunch at Rules, "to be dealing with old-fashioned and civilized gentlemen."

If there was one place that Mike Martin could not show his face, it was Edzell air base. Steve Hill was able to call into play that array of contacts that exists in every business, "the old boys' network."

"I won't be at home most of this winter," said his guest at lunch in the Special Forces Club. "I'm going to try to see a bit more of the Caribbean sun. So I suppose you could borrow the place."

"There will be a rent, of course," said Hill. "As much as my modest budget can afford."

"And you won't knock it about?" asked the guest. "All right, then. When can I have it back?"

"We hope to be there no longer than mid-February. It's just for some seminars. Tutors coming and going, that sort of thing. Nothing . . . physical."

Martin flew from London to Aberdeen, and was met by a former SAS sergeant whom he knew well. He was a tough Scot who clearly had returned to his native heather in his retirement.

"How are you keeping, boss?" he asked, employing the old jargon for SAS men talking to an officer. He hefted Martin's kit bag into the rear, and eased out of the airport car park. He turned north at the outskirts of Aberdeen, and took the A96 road in the direction of Inverness. The mountains of the Scottish Highlands enveloped them within a few miles. Seven miles after the turn, he pulled left off the main road.

The signpost said simply: KEMNAY. They went through the village of Monymusk and hit the Aberdeen–Alford road. Three miles later, the Land Rover turned right, ran through Whitehouse and headed for Keig. There was a river beside the road; Martin wondered whether it contained salmon or trout, or neither.

Just before Keig, a side road turned across the river and up a long, winding private drive. Round two bends, the stone bulk of an ancient castle sat on a slight eminence looking out over a stunning vista of wild hills and glens.

Two men emerged from the main entrance, came forward and introduced themselves.

"Gordon Phillips. Michael McDonald. Welcome to Castle Forbes, family seat of Lord Forbes. Good trip, Colonel?"

"It's Mike, and you were expecting me. How? Angus here made no phone call."

"Well, actually, we had a man on the airplane. Just to be on the safe side," said Phillips.

Mike Martin grunted. He had not spotted the tail, He was clearly out of practice.

"Not a problem, Mike," said the CIA man McDonald. "You're here. Now a range of tutors have your undivided attention for eighteen weeks. Why not freshen up, and after lunch we'll start the first briefing."

During the Cold War, the CIA maintained a chain of safe houses right across the USA. Some were inner-city apartments for the holding of discreet conferences whose participants were better not seen at the head office. Others were rural retreats such as renovated farmhouses, where agents back from a stressful mission could have a relaxed vacation while also being debriefed, detail by detail, on their time abroad.

And there were some chosen for their obscurity, where a Soviet defector could be held in the kindliest of detention while checks were made on his authenticity, and where a vengeful KGB, working out of the Soviet Embassy or consulate, could not get at him.

Agency veterans still wince at the memory of Colonel Yurchenko, who defected in Rome, and was amazingly allowed to dine out in Georgetown with his debriefing officer. He went to the men's room and never came back. In fact, he had been contacted by the KGB, who reminded him of his family back in Moscow. Full of remorse, he was daft enough to believe the promises of amnesty and redefected. He was never heard of again.

Marek Gumienny had one simple question for the small office inside Langley that runs and maintains the safe houses: What is the most remote, obscure and hard to get into or out of facility that we have?

The answer came from his real estate colleague in no time at all. "We call it 'the Cabin.' It is lost to the human race, somewhere up in the Pasayten Wilderness of the Cascade range."

Gumienny asked for every detail and every picture available. Within thirty minutes of receiving the file, he had made his choice and given his orders.

East of Seattle, in the wilds of Washington State, is the

range of steep, forested and, in the winter, snow-clothed mountains known as the Cascades. Inside the borders of the Cascades are three zones: the National Park, the logging forest and the Pasayten Wilderness. The first two have access roads and some habitations.

Hundreds of thousands of visitors go to the park every year while it is open, and it is riddled with tracks and trails, the former viable for rugged vehicles, the latter for hikers or horses. And the wardens know every inch of it.

The logging forest is off-limits to the public for safety reasons, but it, too, has a network of tracks along which snarling trucks habitually haul the felled tree trunks to the delivery points for the sawmills. In deep winter, both have to close down because the snow makes most movement almost impossible.

But east of them both, running up to the Canadian border, is the wilderness. Here, there are no tracks, one or two trails, and only in the far south of the terrain, near Hart's Pass, a few log cabins.

Winter and summer, the wilderness teems with wildlife and game; the few cabin owners tend to summer in the wilderness, then disconnect all systems, lock up and withdraw to their city mansions. There is probably nowhere in the USA as bleak or remote in winter, with the possible exception of the area of northern Vermont known simply as "the Kingdom," where a man may vanish and be found rock solid in the spring thaw.

Years earlier, a remote log cabin had come up for sale, and the CIA bought it. It was an impulse purchase, later regretted, but occasionally used by senior officers for summer vacations. In October, when Marek Gumienny made his inquiry, it was closed and locked. Despite the looming winter and the costs, he demanded it be reopened, and that its transformation begin.

"If that's what you want," said the head of the real estate office, "why not use the Northwest Detention Center in Seattle?"

Despite the fact he was talking to a colleague, Gumienny had no choice but to lie.

"It is not just a question of keeping an ultra-high-value asset away from prying eyes, nor of preventing him from escape. I have to consider his own safety. Even in supermax jails, there have been fatalities."

The head of safe houses got the point. At least, he thought he had. Utterly and completely invisible, utterly and completely escape-proof. Totally self-contained for at least a six-month period. It was not really his specialty. He brought in the team who had devised the security at the fearsome Pelican Bay supermax in California.

The Cabin was almost inaccessible to start with. A very basic road went a few miles north of the tiny town of Mazama and then ran out, still ten miles short. There was nothing for it but to use skyhooks and use them extensively. With the power invested in him, Marek Gumienny commandeered a Chinook heavy-lift helicopter from McChord Air Force Base south of Seattle to be used as a cart horse.

The build team was from Army Engineers; raw materials were purchased locally with state police advice. Everyone was on a need-to-know basis, and the legend was that the Cabin was being converted into an ultra-high-security research center. In truth, it was to become a one-man jail.

At Castle Forbes, the regime started intensively, and became more so. Mike Martin was required to change out of Western clothes into the robes and turban of a Pashtun tribesman. His beard and hair were to grow as long as the time allowed.

The housekeeper was allowed to stay on; she had not the slightest interest in the laird's guests, nor did Hector, the gardener. The third remaining resident was Angus, the former SAS sergeant who had become Lord Forbes's estate manager, or "factor." Even if an interloper had wished to penetrate the estate, he would have been most unwise with Angus on the prowl.

For the rest, "guests" came and went, save two whose residence had to be permanent. One was Najib Qureshi, a native Afghan, former teacher in Kandahar, refugee given asylum in Britain, naturalized citizen and translator at GCHQ Cheltenham. He had been detached from his duties and transferred to Castle Forbes. He was the language tutor and coach in all forms of behavior that would be expected of a Pashtun. He taught body language, gestures, how to squat on the heels, how to eat, how to walk and the postures for prayer.

The other was Dr. Tamian Godfrey; midsixties, iron gray hair in a bun at the back, she had been married for years to a senior officer in the Security Service, MI5, until his death two years earlier. Being "one of us," as

Steve Hill put it, she was no stranger to security procedures, the cult of need to know, and had not the slightest intention of mentioning her presence in Scotland to
anyone ever.

Moreover, she could work without being told that the
man she was here to tutor would be going into harm's
way, and became determined he would never slip up because of something she had forgotten. Her expertise was
the Koran; her knowledge of it was encyclopedic, and
her Arabic impeccable.

"Have you heard of Muhammad Asad?" she asked
Martin. He admitted he had not.

"Then we shall start with him. Born Leopold Weiss, a
German Jew, he converted to Islam and became one of
its greatest scholars. He wrote probably the best commentary ever on al-Isra, the journey from Arabia to
Jerusalem and thence to heaven. This was the experience
that instituted the five daily prayers, keystone of the
faith. You would have had this at your *madrassah* as a
boy, and your imam, being a Wahhabi, would have believed totally that it was a real, physical journey and not
just a vision in a dream. So you believe the same. And
now, the daily prayers. Say after me . . ."

Najib Qureshi was impressed. She knows more about
the Koran than I do, he mused.

For exercise, they wrapped up warmly and went walking the hills, shadowed by Angus, quite legally equipped
with his hunting rifle.

Even though he knew Arabic, Mike Martin realized
what a staggering amount he had to learn. Najib Qureshi

taught him to speak Arabic with a Pashtun accent, for Izmat Khan's voice, speaking Arabic to fellow prisoners in Camp Delta, had been recorded secretly in case he had secrets to divulge. He did not, but for Mr. Qureshi the accent was invaluable because he could teach his pupil to imitate it.

Although Mike Martin had spent six months with the muj in the mountains during the Soviet occupation, that was seventeen years earlier, and he had forgotten much. Qureshi coached him in Pashto, even though it had been agreed from the start that Martin could never pass as a Pashtun among other Pashtun.

But mostly, it was two things: the prayers, and what had happened to him in Guantánamo Bay. The CIA was the principal provider of interrogators in Camp Delta; Marek Gumienny had discovered three or four who had dealt with Izmat Khan from the moment of his arrival onward.

Michael McDonald flew back to Langley to spend days with these men, draining them dry of every detail they could recall, plus the notes and tapes they had made. The cover story was that Izmat Khan was being considered for release under the NFD rules—no further danger—and Langley wanted to be sure.

All the interrogators were adamant that the Pashtun mountain warrior and Taliban commander was the hardest man in detention. He had vouchsafed very little, complained not at all, cooperated to the minimum, accepted all the privations and punishments with stoicism. But, they agree, when you looked into those black eyes you just knew he would love to tear your head off.

When he had it all, he flew back in the CIA Grumman and landed right at Edzell air base. Thence, a car took him north to Forbes Castle, and he briefed Mike Martin.

Tamian Godfrey and Najib Qureshi concentrated on the daily prayers. Martin would have to say them in front of others, and he had better get them right. There was one ray of hope, according to Najib. He was not a born Arab; the Koran was only in classical Arabic and no other language. A one-word slip could be put down to mispronunciation. But for a boy who had spent seven years in a *madrassah,* one entire phrase was too much. So with Najib rising and bowing, forehead to the carpet, beside him, and Tamian Godfrey, due to her stiff knees, in a chair, they recited and recited and recited.

There was progress also at Edzell air base where an Anglo-American technical team was installing and linking all the British intelligence services and those of the USA into one nexus. The accommodation and facilities were up and running. When the U.S. Navy was in residence, the base had had, apart from housing and workstations, a bowling alley, beauty salon, delicatessen, post office, basketball court, gym and theater. Gordon Phillips, aware of his budget, and with Steve Hill breathing down his neck, left the fripperies much as they were—defunct.

The RAF shipped in catering staff, and the RAF regiment took over perimeter security. No one doubted the base was becoming a listening post for opium traffickers.

From the USA, giant Galaxies and Starlifters flew in with listening monitors that could and would scan the world. Arabic translations were not imported, because this would be handled by GCHQ Cheltenham and Fort Meade, both of whom would be in constant secure contact with Crowbar, as the new listening post had been coded.

Before Christmas, the twelve computer workstations were established and brought onstream. These would be the nerve center, and six operators would hover over them day and night.

Crowbar Center was never devised as a new intelligence agency of its own, but simply a short-term, "dedicated"—that is, single-purpose—operation, with whom all British and U.S. agencies would, thanks to John Negroponte's blanket authority, cooperate without stint or delay.

To assist in this effort, Crowbar's computers were fitted with ultrasecure ISDN BRENT lines, with two BRENT keys for each station. Each had its own removable hard drive that would be taken out when not in use and stored in a guarded safe.

Crowbar's computers were then linked directly into the communications systems of the head office, or HO, the term for SIS headquarters at Vauxhall Cross, and Grosvenor, the term employed for the CIA station at the U.S. Embassy in Grosvenor Square, London.

To seal the operation from any unwanted interference, the Crowbar address for its communications was hidden under a STRAP3 access code, with a bigot list limiting those in the know to a very few senior officers indeed.

Then Crowbar began to listen to every word spoken in the Middle East, in the Arabic language and in the world of Islam. It was only doing what was already being done by others, but the pretense had to be maintained.

When Crowbar went operational, it had one other access. Apart from sound, it was interested in vision. Also piped into the obscure Scottish air base were the images the National Reconnaissance Office was picking up from its KH-11 "Keyhole" satellites over the Arab world, and the yield of the increasingly popular Predator drones, whose high-definition images from twenty thousand feet went back to the American Army Central Command, or CENTCOM, headquarters at Tampa, Florida.

Some of the more penetrating minds at Edzell realized that Crowbar was ready and waiting for something, but they were not quite sure what.

Shortly before Christmas 2006, Mr. Alex Siebart recontacted Mr. Lampong at his Indonesian company office to propose one of the two general cargo freighters registered in Liverpool as suitable for his purpose. By chance, both were owned by the same small shipping company, and Siebart and Abercrombie had chartered them before on behalf of clients who had been amply satisfied. McKendrick Shipping was a family business; it had been in the merchant marine for a century. The company chief was also the family patriarch, Liam McKendrick, who captained the *Countess of Richmond,* and his son, Sean, captained the other.

The *Countess of Richmond* was eight thousand tons, flew the Red Ensign, was moderately priced and would be available for a fresh cargo out of a British port by March 1.

What Alex Siebart did not add was that he had warmly recommended the contract to Liam McKendrick if it came their way, and the old skipper had concurred. If Siebart and Abercrombie could find him a cargo from the USA back to the UK, it would make a very nice and profitable triangular voyage for the spring.

Unbeknownst to either man, Mr. Lampong contacted someone in the British city of Birmingham, an academic at Aston University, who drove himself to Liverpool. With high-powered binoculars, the *Countess of Richmond* was examined in detail, and a long-range lens took over a hundred pictures of her from different angles. A week later, Mr. Lampong e-mailed back. He apologized for the delay, explaining that he had been up-country examining his sawmills, but that the *Countess of Richmond* sounded exactly right. His friends in Singapore would be in touch with details of the cargo of limousines to be brought from the UK to the Far East.

In truth, the friends in Singapore were not Chinese but Malaysian; and not simply Muslims but ultrafanatical Islamists. They had been put in funds out of a new account created in Bermuda by the late Mr. Tewfik al-Qur, who had deposited the original monies, before

transfer with a small private bank in Vienna that suspected nothing. They did not even intend to take a
loss on the limousines, but to recoup their investment
by selling them once their purpose had been served.

Marek Gumienny's explanation to the CIA interrogators
that Izmat Khan might be coming up for trial was not un-
true. He intended to arrange exactly that, and to secure
an acquittal and release.

In 2005, a U.S. Appeals Court had decreed that the
rights of prisoners of war did not apply to members of
Al Qaeda. The Federal Court had upheld President
Bush's intention to order the trials of terrorist suspects
by special military tribunals. That, for the first time in
four years, gave the detainees the chance of a defense
attorney. Gumienny intended that Izmat Khan's defense would be that he had never been in Al Qaeda, but
a serving Afghan Army officer, albeit under the Taliban,
and had nothing whatever to do with 9/11 or Islamist
terrorism. And he intended that the court should accept that.

It would require John Negroponte, as director of National Intelligence, to request his colleague Donald
Rumsfeld, as secretary of defense, to "have a word" with
the military judges of the case.

Mike Martin's leg was healing nicely. He had noted
when he read Izmat Khan's slim file after the concordat
in the orchard that the man had never described how he
had acquired the scar on the right thigh. Martin saw no

reason to mention it either. But when Michael McDonald arrived back from Langley with the more copious notes over Izmat Khan's numerous interrogations, he had been concerned that the questioners had pressed the Afghan for an explanation of the scar and never received one. If the existence of the scar was by any chance known to anyone inside Al Qaeda and Mike Martin bore no such scar, his cover would be "blown."

Martin had no objection, for he had something in mind. A surgeon was flown from London to Edzell, and then by the newly acquired Bell JetRanger helicopter to the lawn of Forbes Castle. He was the Harley Street surgeon with full security clearance who could be relied on to remove the occasional bullet and say nothing more about it.

It was all done with a local anesthetic. The incision was easy, for there was no bullet or fragment to be extracted. The problem was, make it heal in a few weeks but look much older than that.

The surgeon, James Newton, excised a quantity of tissue beneath and around the incision to make it deeper, as if something had come out, and created a concavity in the flesh. His sutures were large, clumsy, unstraight stitches, drawing the edges of the wound together so that they would pucker as they healed. He sought to make it look like the work done in a field hospital in a cave, and there were six stitches.

"You must understand," he said as he left, "if a surgeon looks at that, he will probably spot that it cannot be fifteen years old. A nonmedical man should accept it.

But it needs twelve weeks to settle down."

That was in early November. By Christmas, nature and the body of a very fit forty-four-year-old had done an excellent job. The puffiness and redness were gone.

CHAPTER 9

"IF YOU ARE GOING where I think you are going, young Mike," said Tamian Godfrey on one of their daily hikes, "you will have to master the various levels of aggressiveness and fanaticism that you will be likely to encounter. At the core is self-arrogated jihad, or holy war, but various factions arrive at this via various routes and behave in various ways. They are not all the same by a long chalk."

"It seems to start with Wahhabism," said Martin.

"In a way, but let us not forget that Wahhabism is the state religion of Saudi Arabia, and Osama bin Laden has declared war on the Saudi establishment for being heretics. There are many groups way out on the extremist wing beyond the teachings of Muhammad al-Wahhab.

"He was an eighteenth-century preacher who came

out of the Nejd, the bleakest and harshest part of the interior of the Saudi peninsula. He left behind him the harshest and most intolerant of all the many, many interpretations of the Koran. That was then; this is now. He has been superseded. Saudi Wahhabism has not declared war on the West, or on Christianity; nor does it propose indiscriminate mass murder of anyone, let alone women and children. What Wahhab did was leave behind the seedbed of total intolerance in which today's terror masters could plant the young seedlings before turning them into killers."

"Then how come they are not still confined to the Arabian peninsula?" asked Martin.

"Because," cut in Najib Qureshi, "for thirty years Saudi Arabia has used its petrodollars to fund the internationalization of its state creed, and that includes every Muslim country in the world, including the place of my birth. There is no reason to think any of them realized what a monster was being set free or how it would be diverted to mass murder. Indeed, there is ample reason to believe now, a bit late in the day, that Saudi Arabia is terrified of the creature it has funded for three decades."

"Then why has Al Qaeda declared war on the source of its creed and its funding?"

"Because other prophets have arisen, even more intolerant, even more extreme. These have preached the creed not simply of intolerance of anything not Islamic, but of the duty of attack and destruction. The Saudi government is denounced for dealing with the West, permitting U.S. troops on its holy soil. And that applies to every secular Muslim government as well. For the fanatics they are all as guilty as Christians and Jews."

"So who do you think I shall be meeting in my travels, Tamian?" asked Martin. The scholar found a stone the size of a chair and sat down to rest her legs.

"There are numerous groups, but two are at the core. Do you know the word *salafi?*"

"I have heard of it," admitted Martin.

"These are the back-to-the-beginning brigade. They really want to restore the great golden age of Islam. Back to the first four caliphates, over a thousand years ago. Wild beards, sandals, robes, rigorous Sharia'ah legal code, rejection of modernity and the West that brought it. There is no such earthly paradise, of course, but fanatics were never deterred by unreality. In pursuit of their manic dream Nazis, communists, Maoists, followers of Pol Pot, have slaughtered hundreds of millions, half of them their own kith and kin, for not being extreme enough. Think of Stalin's and Mao's purges—all fellow communists, but butchered for being backsliders."

"When you described the *salafis*, you were describing the Taliban," said Martin.

"Among others. These are the suicide bombers, the simple believers; trusting their masters, following their spiritual guides; not very bright but completely obedient, and believing that all their deranged hatred is going to please the mighty Allah."

"There are worse?" asked Martin.

"Oh, yes," said Tamian Godfrey, resuming her walk

but directing the party firmly back toward the castle, whose tower could just be seen two short valleys away.

"The ultras—the real ultras—I would designate with one word: *takfir*. Whatever it meant in Wahhab's day, it has changed. The true *salafi* will not smoke, gamble, dance, accept music in his presence, drink alcohol or consort with Western women. With his dress, appearance and religious devotion, he is immediately identifiable for what he is. From an internal security point of view, identifiability is half the battle.

"But some will adopt every single custom of the West, however much they may loathe them, in order to pass as fully Westernized and therefore harmless. All nineteen of the 9/11 bombers slipped through because they looked and acted the part. The same with the four London bombers; apparently normal young men, going to the gym, playing cricket, polite, helpful, one of them a special needs teacher, smiling constantly and planning mass murder. These are the ones to watch.

"Many are clean-shaven, barbered, groomed, dressed in suits, educated, with a good degree. These are the ultimate; prepared to become chameleons against their faith to achieve mass murder for their faith. Thank heavens, here we are; my old legs are giving out. Time for the midday prayers. Mike, you will utter the call and then lead us in prayer. You may be asked to later. It is a great privilege."

Just after the New Year, an e-mail was sent from the office of Siebart and Abercrombie to Jakarta. The

Countess of Richmond, with a full cargo of crated Jaguar
sedans for Singapore, would sail from Liverpool on the
first of March. After unloading at Singapore, she would
proceed in ballast to North Borneo to take aboard the
hold cargo of timber before turning for Surabaya for the
deck cargo of crated silks.

The construction crew working inside the Pasayten
Wilderness was finally and deeply grateful when the job
was done by the end of January. To keep up the work rate,
the men had chosen to overnight right on the site, and
until the central heating came onstream they had been extremely cold. But the bonus was large and tempting. They
took the discomfort and completed on schedule.

To the naked eye, the Cabin looked much the same but
larger. In fact, it had been transformed. To cope with a
staff of two officers, the bedrooms would suffice; for the
extra eight guards to accomplish twenty-four-hour-a-day
surveillance, an extra bunkhouse had been added, and a
dining hall beside it.

The spacious sitting room was retained, but a recre-
ation room, with pool table, library, plasma TV and
ample DVD selection, had created yet another extension.
Both were built of insulated pine logs.

The third extension appeared to be built with the
usual uninsulated, rustic logs. Its exterior walls were, in
fact, clad only with split tree trunks; inside, the walls
were reinforced concrete. The whole penitentiary wing
was impregnable from without and escape-proof from
within.

It was reached from the guards' quarters through a single steel door, with food service hatch and spy hole. Beyond this door was a single but spacious room. It contained a steel bed frame deeply embedded in the concrete floor; it could never be moved by bare hands. Nor could the wall shelving, also embedded in the concrete.

There were, however, carpets on the floor, and heat came from baseboard-level grilles that could never be opened. The room also had a door opposite the spy hole, and the detainee could open or close it at will. It led only to the exercise yard.

The yard was bare save for a concrete bench in the center away from the walls. The walls were ten feet tall and as smooth as a pool table. No man could get anywhere near the top; nor was there anything that could be propped against the wall or stood on.

For sanitation, there was a recessed area off the sitting room/bedroom containing a single hole in the floor for bodily functions and a shower whose controls were in the hands of the guards outside.

Because all the new materials had come in by helicopter, the only visible exterior addition was a landing pad under the snow. Otherwise, the Cabin stood in its five-hundred-acre plot, surrounded on all sides by the pine, larch and spruce, even though the trees had been cut back to a hundred yards in every direction.

When they came, the ten guardians of probably the country's most expensive and exclusive prison were two middle-grade CIA men from Langley and eight junior staffers who had completed all the mental and physical tests at the Farm training school and were hoping for an exciting first assignment. Instead, they got a forest in the snow. But they were all fit and eager to impress.

The military trial at Guantánamo Bay began just before the end of January and was held in one of the larger rooms in the interrogation block, decked out now for its judicial purpose. Anyone hoping for a half-mad Colonel Jessup or any of the histrionics portrayed in *A Few Good Men* would have been sorely disappointed. The proceedings were low-tone and orderly.

There were eight detainees being considered for release as of "no further danger," and seven were vociferous in stating their harmlessness. Only one maintained a scornful silence. His case was heard last.

"Prisoner Khan, into what language would you like these proceedings to be translated?" asked the colonel, flanked by a male major and a female captain, presiding on the dais at the end of the room under the seal of the United States of America. All three were from the U.S. Marines legal branch.

The prisoner was facing them, hauled to his feet by the Marine guards flanking him. Desks set facing each other had been allocated to prosecuting and defending attorneys—the former military, the latter civilian. The prisoner shrugged gently, and stared at the female Marine captain for several seconds; then he let his gaze come to rest on the wall above the judges.

"This court is aware that the prisoner understands

Arabic, so that is the language the court chooses. Any objection, Counselor?"

The question was to the defending attorney, who shook his head. He had been warned about his client when he took the case. From all he had heard, he was convinced he had no chance. It was a civil rights–based appearance, and he knew what the surrounding Marines thought of white knights from the civil rights movement. A helpful client would have been nice. Still, he reasoned, the Afghan's attitude at least got the attorney off the hook. He shook his head. No objection. Arabic would do.

The Arabic 'terp advanced and positioned himself close to the Marine guards. It was a wise choice; there was only one Pashtun interpreter, and he had had a rough time with the Americans because he had coaxed nothing out of his fellow Afghan. Now he had nothing to do, and saw the approaching end of a quite comfortable lifestyle.

There had only ever been seven Pashtun at Gitmo, the seven wrongly included among the foreign fighters at Kunduz five years earlier. Four had gone back, simple farm boys who had renounced all Muslim extremism with considerable enthusiasm; and the other two had had mental breakdowns so complete that they were still under psychiatric care. The Taliban commander was the last one.

The prosecuting counsel began, and the 'terp uttered a stream of sibilant Arabic. The gist was that the Yankees are going to send you back to the slammer and throw away the keys, you arrogant Taliban shit. Izmat Khan slowly lowered his gaze and fixed on the 'terp. The eyes said it all. The Lebanon-born American reverted to literal translation. The man might be dressed in a ludicrous orange jumpsuit, shackled hand and foot, but you never knew with this bastard.

The prosecutor did not take long. He stressed five years of virtual silence, a refusal to name collaborators in the war of terror against the USA, and the fact the prisoner had been caught in a jail uprising in which an American had been brutally stomped to death. Then he sat down. He had no doubt of the outcome. The man would have to remain in custody for years to come.

The civil rights attorney took a little longer. He was pleased that as an Afghan the prisoner had absolutely nothing to do with the atrocity of 9/11. He had been fighting in an all-Afghan civil war at the time, and had nothing to do with the Arabs behind Al Qaeda. As for Mullah Omar and the Afghan government sheltering bin Laden and his cronies, that was a dictatorship of which Mr. Khan was a serving officer but not a part.

"I really must urge this court to admit the reality," he wound up. "If this man is a problem, he is an Afghan problem. There is a new and democratically elected government there now. We should ship him back for them to deal with."

The three judges withdrew. They were away for thirty minutes. When they returned, the captain was pink with anger. She still could not believe what she had heard. Only the colonel and the major had had the interview with the chairman of the Joints Chiefs of Staff and knew his orders.

"Prisoner Khan, be upstanding. This court has been made aware that the government of President Karzai has agreed that if you are returned to your native land, you will be sentenced to life imprisonment over there. That being so, this court intends to burden the American taxpayer with you no longer. Arrangements will therefore be made to ship you back to Kabul. You will return as you arrived: in shackles. That is all. Court rises."

The captain was not the only one in shock. The prosecuting attorney wondered how this would look on his career prospects. The defending counsel was feeling slightly light-headed. The 'terp for one panicking moment had thought the mad colonel would order the cuffs taken off, in which case he, the good son of Beirut, was going straight out of the window.

The British Foreign Office is situated in King Charles Street, just off Whitehall, and within easy glancing distance of the window across Parliament Square outside of which King Charles I was decapitated. As the New Year's holiday slipped into memory, the small protocol team that had been set up the previous summer resumed its task.

This was to coordinate with the Americans the ever more complex details of the forthcoming 2007 G8 conference. The 2005 meeting of the governments of the eight richest states in the world had been at Gleneagles Hotel in Scotland, and it had been a success up to a point. The point however had been, as always, the roaring crowds of protesters that presented problems which each year got steadily worse and worse. At Gleneagles, the Perthshire landscape had been disfigured by miles and miles of chain-link fencing to create a complete cordon sanitaire round the entire estate. The access road had been fenced and guarded.

Led by two fading pop stars, the call had gone out for a million protesters at world poverty to march though Edinburgh close by. That was just the antipoverty brigade. Then the antiglobalization cohorts had thrown their flour bombs and waved their placards.

"Don't these yo-yos realize that global trade generates the wealth with which to fight poverty?" asked one angry diplomat. The answer: Apparently not.

Genoa was remembered with a shudder. That was why the idea out of the White House, who would be hosting 2007, was acclaimed: simple, elegant, brilliant. A location sumptuous but utterly isolated: immune, unreachable, secure, totally under control. It was the mass of detail that concerned the protocol team—that, and the advancement to mid-April. Something about the U.S. midterm elections. So the British team accepted what had been agreed and announced, and got on with their administrational task.

Far away to the southeast, two huge USAF Starlifters began to drop toward the sultanate of Oman. They came from the East Coast of the USA, with one midair refueling by a tanker out of the Azores. The two aerial juggernauts came out of the sunset on the Dhofari hills, heading east, and asking for landing instructions at the Anglo-American desert air base of Thumrait.

In their cavernous hulls, the two giants contained an entire military unit. One had the living accommodations, from flat-pack, skilled-assembly hutments to generators, air-conditioning, refrigeration plants, TV aerials and even corkscrews for the fifteen-person technical team.

The other cargo aircraft carried what is called "the sharp end." Two pilotless reconnaissance drones, Predators, along with their guidance and imaging kit and the men and women who would operate them.

A week later, they were set up. On the far side of the air base, out of bounds to nonunit personnel, the bungalows were up, the air conditioners hummed, the latrines were dug, the kitchen cooked; and under their hooped shelters, the two Predators waited until their mission should be given to them. The aerial surveillance unit was also patched through to Tampa, Florida, and Edzell, Scotland. Someday, they would be told what they had to watch—day and night, rain and shine—photograph and transmit back. Until then, men and machines waited in the heat.

Mike Martin's final briefing took a full three days, and it was important enough that Marek Gumienny flew over in the agency Grumman. Steve Hill came up from London, and the two spymasters joined their executive officers, McDonald and Phillips.

There were only five of them in the room, for Gordon Phillips operated what he called "the slide show" himself. Rather more developed than the slide projectors of yesteryear, this projector threw up picture after picture on a high-definition plasma screen in perfect color and detail. At a touch on the remote, it could close in on any detail, and bring that detail up in magnification to fill the screen.

The point of the briefing was to show Mike Martin every last piece of information in the possession of the entire gamut of Western agencies concerning faces he might meet.

The sources were not just the Anglo-American agencies. Over forty nations' agencies were pouring their discoveries into central databases. Apart from the rogue states—Iran, Syria and the failed states like Somalia—governments across the planet were sharing information on terrorists of the ultra-aggressive Islamist creed.

Rabat was invaluable in targeting its own Moroccans; Aden fed in names and faces from South Yemen; Riyadh had swallowed its embarrassment and provided columns of faces from its own Saudi list.

Martin stared at them all as they all flashed up. Some were face-on portraits taken in a police station; others were snatched with long lenses on streets or in hotels. The faces' possible variants were shown: with or without beard; in Arab or Western dress; long hair, short hair or shaven.

There were mullahs and imams from various extremist mosques; youths believed to be simple message carriers; faces of those known to help with support services like funds, transport, safe houses.

And there were the big players, the ones who controlled the various global divisions and had access to the very top.

Some were dead, like Mohammed Atef, first director of operations, killed by an African bomb in Afghanistan; his successor, serving life without parole; his successor, also dead; and the believed present one.

Somewhere in there was the doctorly face of Tewfik al-Qur, who dove over a balcony in Peshawar five months earlier. A few faces down the line was Saud Hamud al-Utaibi, new head of AQ in Saudi Arabia, and believed very much alive.

And there were the blanks, the outline of a head, black on white. These included the AQ chief from Southeast Asia, successor to al-Hanbali, and probably the man behind the latest bombings of tourist resorts in the Far East. And, surprisingly, the AQ chief for the United Kingdom.

"We knew who he was until about six months ago," said Gordon Phillips. "Then he quit just in time. He is back in Pakistan, hunted day and night. The ISI will get him eventually . . ."

"And ship him up to us in Bagram," grunted Marek Gumienny. They all knew that inside the U.S. base north of Kabul was a very special facility where everyone "sang" eventually.

"You will certainly seek out this one," said Steve Hill, as a grim-faced imam flashed on the screen. It was a snatched shot and came from Pakistan. "And this one."

It was an elderly man, looking mild and courtly; also a

snatched shot, on a quayside somewhere, with bright blue water in the background; it came from the Special Forces of the United Arab Emirates in Dubai.

They broke, ate, resumed, slept and started again. Only when the housekeeper was in the room with trays of food did Phillips switch off the TV screen. Tamian Godfrey and Najib Qureshi stayed in their rooms or walked the hills together. Finally, it was over.

"Tomorrow, we fly," said Marek Gumienny.

Mrs. Godfrey and the Afghan analyst came to the helipad to see him off. He was young enough to be the Koranic scholar's son.

"Take care of yourself, Mike," she said, then swore. "Damn, stupid me, I'm choking up. God go with you, lad."

"And if all else fails, may Allah keep you in His care," said Qureshi.

The JetRanger could only take the two senior controllers and Martin. The two executive officers would drive down to Edzell and resume their mission.

The Bell landed well away from prying eyes and the group of three ran across to the CIA Grumman V. A Scottish snow squall caused them all to shelter under waterproofs held over their heads, so no one saw that one of the men was not in Western dress.

The crew of the Grumman had tended to some strange-looking passengers, and knew better than to raise even an eyebrow at the heavily bearded Afghan whom the deputy director of operations was escorting across the Atlantic with a British guest.

They did not fly to Washington but to a remote peninsula on the southeast coast of Cuba. Just after dawn, on February 14, they touched down at Guantánamo and taxied straight into a hangar whose doors closed at once.

"I'm afraid you have to remain on the plane, Mike," said Marek Gumienny. "We'll get you out of here under cover of dark."

Night comes fast in the tropics, and it was pitch-black by seven p.m. That was when four CIA men from "special tasks" entered the cell of Izmat Khan. He rose, sensing something wrong. The regular guards had quit the corridor outside his cell half an hour earlier. That had never happened before.

The four men were not brutal, but they were not taking no for an answer, either. Two grabbed the Afghan, one round the torso with arms pinioned, the other round the thighs. The chloroform pad took only twenty seconds to work. The writhing stopped, and the prisoner went limp.

He went onto a stretcher and thence to a wheeled gurney. A cotton sheet was placed over the body and he was wheeled outside. A crate was waiting. The entire cell block was devoid of guard staff. No one saw a thing. A few seconds after the abduction, the Afghan was inside the crate.

It was not badly equipped, as crates go. From the outside, it was just a large timber box such as are used for general freight purposes. Even the markings were totally authentic.

Inside, it was insulated against any sound emerging. In the roof was a small, removable panel to replenish fresh air, but that would not be taken down until the crate was safely airborne. There were two comfortable armchairs welded to the floor, and a low-wattage, amber light.

The recumbent Izmat Khan was placed in the chair that already had restrainer straps fitted to it. Without cutting off circulation to the limbs, they secured so that he could relax but not leave the chair. He was still asleep.

Finally satisfied, the fifth CIA man—the one who would travel in the crate—nodded to his colleagues, and the end of it was closed off. A forklift hoisted the crate a foot off the ground and ran it out to the airfield, where the Hercules was waiting. It was an AC-130 Talon from Special Forces, fitted with extra-range tanks, and could make its destination easily.

Unexplained flights into and out of Gitmo are regular as clockwork. The tower gave a quick "Clear to take off" in response to the staccato request, and the Hercules was airborne for McChord base, Washington State.

An hour later, a closed car drove up to the Camp Echo block and another small group got out. Inside the empty cell, a man was garbed in orange jumpsuit and soft slippers. The unconscious Afghan had been photographed before being covered and removed. With the use of the Polaroid print, a few minor snips were made to the beard and hair of the replacement. Every fallen tuft was collected and removed.

When it was over, there were a few gruff farewells, and the party left, locking the cell door behind them. Twenty minutes later, the soldiers were back, mystified but incurious. The poet Tennyson had got it right: Theirs not to reason why.

They checked the familiar figure of their prize prisoner, and waited for the dawn.

The morning sun was tipping the pinnacles of the Cascades when the AC-130 drifted down to its home base at McChord. The base commander had been told this was a CIA shipment, a last consignment for their new research facility up in the forests of the wilderness. Even with his rank, he needed to know no more, so he asked no more. The paperwork was in order, and the Chinook stood by.

In flight, the Afghan had come round. The roof panel was open, and the air inside the hull of the Hercules fully pressurized and fresh. The escort smiled encouragingly, and offered food and drink. The prisoner settled for soda through a straw.

To the escort's surprise, the prisoner had a few phrases in English, clearly gleaned over five years' listening in Guantánamo. He asked the time only twice in the journey, and once bowed his face as far as it would go and murmured his prayers. Otherwise, he said nothing.

Just before touchdown, the roof panel was replaced, and the waiting forklift driver had not the slightest suspicion he was not lifting an ordinary load of freight from the rear ramp of the Hercules across to the Chinook.

Again, the ramp doors closed. The small, battery-powered pilot light inside the crate remained on, but invisible from outside, just as all sounds were inaudible.

But the prisoner was, as his escort would later report to Marek Gumienny, like a pussycat. No trouble at all, sir.

Given that it was mid-February, they were lucky with the weather. The skies were clear but freezing cold. At the helipad outside the Cabin, the great twin-rotored Chinook landed and opened its rear doors. But the crate stayed inside. It was easier to disembark the two passengers straight from the crate to the snow.

Both men shivered as the rear wall of the crate came off. The snatch team from Guantánamo had flown with the Hercules and up front in the Chinook. They were waiting for the last formality.

The prisoner's hands and feet were shackled before the restraining straps were removed. Then he was bidden to rise and shuffled down the ramp into the snow. The resident staff, all ten of them, stood round in a semicircle, guns pointing.

With an escort so heavy they could hardly get through the doors, the Taliban commander was walked across the helipad, through the cabin and into his own quarters. As the door closed, shutting out the bitter air, he stopped shivering.

Six guards stood round him in his large cell as the manacles were finally removed. Shuffling backward, they left the cell, and the steel door slammed shut. He looked round. It was a better cell, but it was still a cell. He recalled the courtroom. The colonel had told him he would return to Afghanistan. They had lied again.

*   *   *

It was midmorning, and the sun was blazing down on the Cuban landscape, when another Hercules rolled in to land. This also was equipped for long-distance flying, but, unlike the Talon, it was not armed to the teeth, and did not belong to Special Forces. It came from MATS, the Air Force transport division. It was to carry one single passenger across the globe.

The cell door swung open.

"Prisoner Khan, stand up. Face the wall. Adopt the position."

The belt went round the midriff; chains fell from it to the ankle cuffs, and another set to the wrists, held together in front of the waist. The position permitted a shuffling walk, no more.

There was a short walk to the end of the block with six armed guards. The high-security truck had steps at the back, a mesh screen between the prisoners and the driver, and black windows.

When he was ordered out at the airfield, the prisoner blinked in the harsh sunlight.

He shook his shaggy head and looked bewildered. As his eyes became accustomed to the glare, he gazed round and saw the waiting Hercules, and a group of American officers staring at him. One of them advanced and beckoned.

Meekly, he followed across the scorching tarmac. Shackled though he was, six armed grunts surrounded him all the way. He turned to have one last look at the place that had held him for five miserable years. Then he shuffled up into the hull of the aircraft.

In a room one flight below the operations deck of the control tower, two men stood and watched him.

"There goes your man," said Marek Gumienny.

"If they ever find out who he really is," replied Steve Hill, "may Allah have mercy on him."

PART FOUR
JOURNEY

CHAPTER 10

IT WAS A LONG and wearisome flight. There were no in-flight refueling facilities, which are expensive. This Hercules was just a prison ship, doing a favor for the Afghan government, which ought to have picked up their man in Cuba but had no aircraft for the job.

They flew via American bases in the Azores and Ramstein, Germany, and it was late afternoon of the following day that the AC-130 dropped toward the great air base of Bagram at the southern edge of the bleak Shomali Plain.

The flight crew had changed twice, but the escort squad had stayed the course, reading, playing cards, catnapping, as the four sets of whirling blades outside the portholes drove them east, ever east. The prisoner remained shackled. He, too, slept as best he could.

As the Hercules taxied onto the apron beside the

huge hangars that dominate the American zone within Bagram base, the reception group was waiting. The U.S. provost major heading the escort party was gratified to see the Afghans were taking no chances. Apart from the prison van, there were twenty Afghan Special Forces soldiers, headed by the unit commander, Brigadier Yusef.

The major trotted down the ramp to clear the paperwork before handing over his charge. This took a few seconds. Then he nodded to his colleagues. They unchained the Afghan from the fuselage rib and led him shuffling out into a freezing Afghan winter.

The troops enveloped him, dragged him to the prison van and threw him inside. The door slammed shut. The U.S. major decided he absolutely would not want to change places. He threw up a salute to the brigadier, who responded.

"You take good care of him, sir," said the American. "That is one very hard man."

"Do not worry, Major," said the Afghan officer. "He is going to Pul-i-Charki jail for the rest of his days."

Minutes later, the prison van drove off, followed by the truck with the Afghan SF soldiers. They took the road south to Kabul. It was not until complete darkness that the van and the truck became separated in what would later be officially described as an unfortunate accident. The van proceeded alone.

Pul-i-Charki is a fearsome, brooding block of a place to the east of Kabul, near the gorge at the eastern end of the Kabul plain. Under the Soviet occupation, it was controlled by the KHAD secret police, and constantly rang with the screams of the tortured.

During the civil war, several tens of thousands never left alive. Conditions had improved since the creation of the new, elected Republic of Afghanistan, but its stone battlements, corridors and dungeons still seem to echo with the shrieks of its ghosts. Fortunately, the prison van never made it.

Ten miles after losing the military escort, a pickup truck came out of a side road and took up station behind the van. When the truck flashed its lights, the van driver pulled over at the prereconnoitered flat area off the road and behind a clump of stunted trees. There, the "escape" took place.

The prisoner had been uncuffed as soon as the van left the last security check at Bagram's perimeter. Even as the van rolled, he had changed into the warm, gray, woolen *shalwar kameez* and boots provided. Just before the pullover, he had wound round his head the feared black turban of the Talib.

Brigadier Yusef, who had descended from the cabin of the truck to be taken on board by the pickup, now took charge. There were four bodies in the open back of the utility.

All had come fresh from the city mortuary. Two were bearded, and they had been dressed in Talib clothing. They were actually construction workers who had been atop some very insecure scaffolding when it collapsed and killed them both.

The other two derived from separate car accidents.

Afghan roads are so potholed that the smoothest place to drive is the crown at the center. As it is considered rather effeminate to pull over just because someone is coming the other way, the harvest in fatalities is impressive. The two smooth-shaven bodies were in prison service uniform.

The prison officers would be found with handguns drawn, but dead; the bullets were fired into the bodies there and then. The ambushing Taliban were scattered at the roadside, also shot with slugs from the pistols of the guards. The van door was savaged with a pickax and left swinging open. That was how the van would be found sometime the next day.

When the theater had been accomplished, Brigadier Yusef took the front seat of the pickup beside the drive. The former prisoner climbed in the back with the two Special Forces men he had brought with him. All three wrapped the trailing end of their turbans round their faces to shelter from the cold.

The pickup skirted Kabul, and cut across country until it intercepted the highway south to Ghazni and Kandahar. There waited, as each night, the long column of what all Asia knows as the "jingly" trucks.

They all seem to have been built about a century ago. They snort and snarl along every road of the Middle and Far East, emitting their columns of choking black smoke. Often, they are seen broken down by the roadside, the driver being prepared to trudge many miles to find and buy the needed part.

They seem to find their way over impossible mountain

passes, along the sides of bare hillsides on crumbling tracks. Sometimes, the gutted skeleton of one can be seen in the defile below the road. But they are the commercial lifeblood of a continent, carrying an amazing variety of supplies to the tiniest and most isolated settlements and the people who live in them.

The British named them jingle trucks many years ago because of their decorations. They are carefully painted on every available surface with scenes from religion and history. There are representations from Christianity, Islam, Hinduism, Sikhism and Buddhism, often gloriously mixed up. They are decorated and caparisoned with ribbons, tinsel and even bells. Hence they jingle.

The line on the highway south of Kabul contained several hundred, their drivers sleeping in their cabs, waiting for the dawn. The pickup slewed to a halt beside the line. Mike Martin jumped from the back and walked to the cab. The shrouded figure behind the wheel had his face hidden by a *shemagh* of checkered cloth.

On the other side, Brigadier Yusef nodded but said nothing. End of the road. Start of the journey. As he turned away, he heard the driver speak.

"Good luck, boss."

That term again. Only the SAS called their officers "boss." What the American provost major at Bagram had not known as he made the handover was not only who his prisoner was, but that since the installation of President Hamid Karzai the Afghan Special Forces had been created and trained at his request by the SAS.

Martin turned away, and started to walk down the line

of trucks. Behind him, the taillights of the pickup faded as it headed back to Kabul. In the cab, the SAS sergeant made a cell phone call to a number in Kabul. It was taken by the head of station. The sergeant uttered two words and terminated.

The SIS chief for all Afghanistan also made a call on a secure line. It was four in the morning in Kabul, eleven at night in Scotland. A one-line message came up on one of the screens. Phillips and McDonald were already in the room, hoping to see what they then saw. "Crowbar is running."

On a freezing, pitted highway, Mike Martin permitted himself one last glance behind him. The red lights of the pickup were gone. He turned and walked on. Within a hundred yards, he had become the Afghan.

He knew what he was looking for, but he was a hundred trucks down the line until he found it. A license plate from Karachi, Pakistan. The driver of such a truck would be unlikely to be Pashtun and so would not notice his imperfect command of Pashto. He would be likely to be a Baluchi, heading home to Pakistan's Baluchistan Province.

It was too early for the drivers to be rising, and unwise to rouse the driver of the chosen truck; tired men woken suddenly are not in the best of tempers, and Martin needed him in a generous mood. For two hours, he curled up beneath the truck and shivered.

Around six, there was a stirring, and a hint of pink in the east. By the roadside, someone started a fire and set a billy on it to boil. In central Asia, much of life is lived in and around the teahouse, the *chaikhana*, which can be created even with a fire, a brew of tea and a group of men. Martin rose, walked over to the fire and warmed his hands.

The tea brewer was Pashtun but taciturn, which suited Martin fine. He had taken off his turban, unwound it and stowed it in the tote bag hanging from his shoulder. It would be unwise to advertise being Talib until one knew the company was sympathetic. With a fistful of his Afghanis, he bought a steaming cup and sipped gratefully. Minutes later, the Baluchi clambered sleepily out of his cab and came over for tea.

Dawn broke. Some of the trucks began to kick to life, with plumes of black smoke. The Baluchi walked back to his cab. Martin followed.

"Greetings, my brother."

The Baluchi responded, but with some suspicion.

"Do you by any chance head south to the border and Spin Boldak?"

If the man was heading back to Pakistan, the small border town south of Kandahar would be where he would cross. By then, Martin knew, there would be a price on his head. He would have to skirt the border controls on foot.

"If it pleases Allah," said the Baluchi.

"Then in the name of the All-Merciful, would you let a poor man trying to get home to his family ride with you?"

The Baluchi thought. His cousin normally came with him on these long hauls to Kabul, but he was sick in

Karachi. This trip he had driven alone, and it was exhausting.

"Can you drive one of these?" he asked.

"In truth, I am a driver of many years."

They drove south in companionable silence, listening to
the Eastern pop music on the old plastic radio propped
above the dash. It screeched and whistled, but Martin
was not sure whether this was just the static or the tune.

The day wore on, and they chugged through Ghazni
and on toward Kandahar. On the road, they paused for
tea and food—the usual goat and rice—and filled the
tank. Martin helped with the cost from his bundle of
Afghanis, and the Baluchi became much more friendly.

Though Martin spoke neither Urdu nor the Baluchi
dialect, and the man from Karachi spoke only a smattering of Pashto, with sign language and some Arabic from
the Koran they got along well.

There was a further overnight stop north of Kandahar,
for the Baluchi would not drive in the dark. This was
Zabol Province, wild country, and peopled by wild men.
It was safer to drive in the daylight with hundreds of
other trucks in front, behind and yet more heading
north. Bandits prefer the night.

At the northern outskirts of Kandahar, Martin claimed
he needed a nap, and curled up along the bench behind
the seats that the Baluchi used as his bed. Kandahar had
been the headquarters and stronghold of the Taliban,
and Martin wanted no reformed Talib to think he saw an
old friend in a passing truck.

South of Kandahar, he again spelled the Baluchi at the

wheel. It was still midafternoon when they came to Spin Boldak; Martin claimed he lived in the northern outskirts, bade his host a grateful farewell and was dropped off miles before the border checkpoint.

Because the Baluchi spoke no Pashto, he had kept his radio tuned to a pop station and Martin never heard the news. At the border, the lines were longer even than usual, and when he finally rolled to the barrier he was shown a picture. A black-bearded Talib face stared at him.

He was an honest and hardworking man. He wanted to get home to his wife and four children. Life was hard enough. Why spend days—even weeks—in an Afghan jail trying to explain that he had been totally ignorant?

"By the prophet, I have never seen him," he swore, and they let him go.

Never again, he thought as he trundled south on the Quetta road. He might hail from the most corrupt city in Asia, but at least you knew where you were in your own hometown. Afghans were not his people. Why get involved? He wondered what the talib had done.

Martin had been warned that the hijack of the prison van, the murder of its two warders and the escape of a returnee from Guantánamo Bay could not be covered up. To start with, the U.S. Embassy would make a fuss.

The "murder" scene had been discovered by patrols sent up the Bagram road when the prison van failed to arrive at the jail. The separation of the van from its military escort was put down to incompetence. But the freeing of the prisoner was clearly by a criminal gang of Taliban leftovers. A hunt was mounted for them.

Unfortunately, the U.S. Embassy offered the Karzai government a photograph, which could not be refused. The CIA and SIS heads of station tried to slow things down, but there was only so much they could do. By the time all border posts received a faxed photograph, Martin was still north of Spin Boldak.

Though he knew nothing of this, Martin was determined there would be no chances taken at border crossings. In the hills above Spin Boldak, he hunkered down and waited for night. From the position he had climbed to, he could see the lie of the land, and the route he would take on the march to come.

The small town was five miles ahead and half a mile below him. He could see the road snaking in and the trucks on it. He could see the massive old fort that had once been a stronghold of the British Army.

He knew the capture of that fort in 1919 had been the last time the British Army used medieval scaling ladders. They had approached secretly by night, and, apart from the bellowing of the mules, the clang of ladles on cauldrons and the swearing of the soldiers when they stubbed their toes, were silent as the grave so as not to wake the defenders.

The ladders had been ten feet too short, so they'd crashed into the dry moat with a hundred soldiers on them. Happily, the Pashtun defenders, crouching behind the walls, presumed the force attacking them must be enormous, so they'd quit through the back door and run for the hills. The fort fell without a shot.

Before midnight, Martin stole quietly past its walls,

through the town and into Pakistan. Sunrise found him ten miles down the Quetta road. Here he found a *chaikhana* and waited until a truck that accepted paying passengers came along and gave him passage to Quetta. At last, the black Talib turban, instantly recognizable in those parts, became an asset and not a liability. So on it went.

If Peshawar is a fairly extreme Islamist city, Quetta is more so, only exceeded in its ferocity of sympathy for Al Qaeda by Miram Shah. These are within the Northwest Frontier provinces, where local tribal law prevails. Though technically across the border from Afghanistan, the Pashtun people still prevail, as does the Pashto language, and extreme devotion to ultratraditional Islam. A Talib turban is the mark of a man to be reckoned with.

Though the main road south from Quetta heads for Karachi, Martin had been advised to take the smaller highway southwest to the wretched port of Gwadar.

This lies almost on the Iranian border at the extreme western end of Baluchistan. Once a sleepy and malodorous fishing village, it has developed into a major harbor and entrepôt, contentedly devoted to smuggling, especially opium. Islam may denounce the use of narcotics, but that is for Muslims. If the infidels of the West wish to poison themselves and pay handsomely for the privilege, that has nothing to do with true servants and followers of the prophet.

Thus, the poppies are grown in Iran, Pakistan and, most of all, Afghanistan, refined to base morphine locally and hence smuggled farther west to become heroin, and death. In this holy trade, Gwadar plays its part.

In Quetta, seeking to avoid conversation with Pashto speakers who might unmask him, Martin had found another Baluchi truck driver heading for Gwadar. It was only in Quetta that he learned there was a five-million-afghani price on his head—but only in Afghanistan.

It was on the third morning after he heard the words "Good luck, boss" that he dropped off the truck and settled gratefully for a cup of sweet green tea at a sidewalk café. He was expected, but not by locals.

The first of the two Predators had taken off from Thumrait twenty-four hours earlier. Flying in rotation, the UAVs would keep up a constant day-and-night patrol over their assigned surveillance area.

A product of General Atomics, the Predator UAV RQ-1 is not much to look at. It resembles something that might have come from the airplane modeler's doodling pad.

It is only twenty-seven feet long and pencil slim. Its tapered seagull wings have a span of forty-eight feet. Right at the rear a single 113-horsepower Rotax engine drives the propellers that push it along, and the Rotax just sips petrol from its hundred-gallon fuel tank.

Yet from this puny impulsion, it can speed up to 117 knots, or loiter along at seventy-three. Its maximum endurance aloft is forty hours, but its more normal mission would be to fly up to four hundred nautical miles radius from home base, spend twenty-four hours on the job and fly home again.

Being a rear-engined "pusher" device, its directional controls are up front. They can be operated by its controller manually, or switched to remote control from a computerized program to do what is wanted and keep doing it until given fresh instructions.

The Predator's true genius lies in its bulbous nose, the detachable Skyball avionics pod.

All of the communications kit faces upward, to talk to and listen to the satellites up there in space. These receive all its photo images and overheard conversations and pass them back to base.

What faces downward is the Lynx synthetic-aperture radar and the L-3 Wescam photographic unit. More modern versions, such as the two used over Oman, can overcome night, clouds, rain, hail and snow with the multispectral targeting system.

After the invasion of Afghanistan, when the juiciest of targets were spotted but could not be attacked in time, the Predator went back to the makers, and a new version emerged. It carried the Hellfire missile, giving the eye in the sky a weaponized variant.

Two years later, the head of Al Qaeda from Yemen left his compound far in the invisible interior with four chums in a Land Cruiser. He did not know it, but several pairs of American eyes were watching him on a screen in Tampa.

On the word of command, the Hellfire left the belly of the Predator, and seconds later the Land Cruiser and its occupants simply vaporized. It was all witnessed in full color on a plasma screen in Florida.

The two Predators out of Thurait were not weaponized. Their whole task was to patrol at twenty thousand feet—out of sight, inaudible, radar immune—and watch the ground and sea below.

There were four mosques in Gwadar, but discreet British inquiries of the Pakistani ISI extracted the information that the fourth and smallest was flagged as a hotbed of fundamentalist agitation. Like most of the smaller mosques in Islam, it was a one-imam place of worship, surviving on donations from the faithful. This one had been created and was run by imam Abdullah Halabi.

He knew his congregation well, and from his raised chair as he led the prayers he could spot a visiting newcomer at a glance. Even at the back, the black Talib turban caught his eye.

Later, before the black-bearded stranger could replace his sandals and lose himself in the crowds of the street, the imam tugged at his sleeve.

"Greeting of our all-merciful Lord be upon you," he murmured. He used the Arabic phrase, not Urdu.

"And upon you, Imam," said the stranger. He, too, spoke Arabic, but the imam noticed the Pashto accent. Suspicion confirmed; the man was from the tribal Territories.

"My friends and I are adjourning to the *madafa*," he said. "Would you join us and take tea?"

The Pashtun considered for a second, then gravely inclined his head. Most mosques have a *madafa* attached, a more relaxed and private social club for prayers, gossip and religious schooling. In the West, the indoctrination of the teenagers into ultra-extremism is often accomplished there.

"I am Imam Halabi. Does our new worshipper have a name?" he asked.

Without hesitation, Martin produced the first name of the Afghan president and the second of the Special Forces brigadier.

"I am Hamid Yusuf," he said.

"Then, welcome, Hamid Yusuf," said the imam. "I notice you dare to wear the turban of the Taliban. Were you one of them?"

"Since I joined Mullah Omar at Kandahar in 1994."

There were a dozen in the *madafa*, a shabby shack behind the mosque. Tea was served. Martin noticed one of the men staring at him. The same man then excitedly drew the imam aside and whispered frantically. He would not, he explained, ever dream of watching television and its filthy images, but he had been past a TV shop and there was a set in the window.

"I am sure it is the man," he hissed. "He escaped from Kabul but three days ago."

Martin did not understand Urdu, least of all in the Baluchi accent, but he knew he was being talked about. The imam may have deplored all things Western and modern, but, like most, he found the cell phone damnably convenient, even if it was made by Nokia in Christian Finland. He asked three friends to engage the stranger in talk and not to let him leave. Then he retired to his own humble quarters and made several calls. He returned much impressed.

To have been a Talib from the start, to have lost his entire family and clan to the Americans, to have commanded half the northern front in the Yankee invasion, to have broken open the armory at Qala-i-Jangi, to have survived five years in the American hellhole, to have escaped the clutches of the Washington-loving Kabul *refime*—this man was not a refugee; he was a hero.

Imam Halabi may have been a Pakistani, but he had a passionate loathing of the government of Islamabad for its collaboration with America. His sympathies were wholly with Al Qaeda. To be fair to him, the five-million-afghani reward that would make him rich for life did not tempt him in the slightest.

He returned to the hall and beckoned the stranger to him.

"I know who you are," he hissed. "You are the one they call the Afghan. You are safe with me, but not in Gwadar. Agents of the ISI are everywhere, and you have a price on your head. Where are your lodgings?"

"I have none. I have only just arrived from the north," said Martin.

"I know where you have come from; it is all over the news. You must stay here, but not for long. Somehow, you must leave Gwadar. You will need papers, a new identity, safe passage away from here. Perhaps I know a man."

He sent a small boy from his *madrassah* running to the harbor. The boat he sought was not in port. It arrived twenty-four hours later. The boy was still patiently waiting at the berth where it always docked.

Faisal bin Selim was a Qatari by birth. He had been born to poor fishermen in a shack on the edge of a muddy creek near a village that eventually became the bustling capital of Doha. But that was after the discovery of oil, the creation of the United Arab Emirates out of the Trucial States, the departure of the British, the arrival of the Americans and long before the money poured in like a roaring tide.

In his boyhood, he had known poverty, and automatic deference to the lordly white-skinned foreigners. But from his first days, bin Selim had determined he would rise in the world. The path he chose was what he knew: the sea. He became a deckhand on a coastal freighter, and as his ship plied the coast from Masirah Island and Sallah in the Dhofari Province of Oman round to the ports of Kuwait and Bahrain at the head of the Persian Gulf he learned many things with his agile mind.

He learned that there was always someone with something to sell, and prepared to sell it cheap. And there was someone else, somewhere, prepared to buy that something and pay more. Between the two stood the institution called customs. Faisal bin Selim made himself prosperous by smuggling.

In his travels, he saw many things that he came to admire: fine cloth and tapestries, Islamic art, ancient Korans, precious manuscripts and the beauty of the great mosques. And he saw other things he came to despise: rich Westerners, porcine faces lobster pink in the sun, disgusting women in tiny bikinis, drunken slobs, all that undeserved money.

The fact that the rulers of the Gulf States also benefited from money that simply poured in black streams from the desert sands did not escape him. As they, too, flaunted their Western habits, drank the imported alcohol, slept with the golden whores, he came to despise them, too.

By his midforties, twenty years before a small Baluchi boy waited for him at the dock in Gwadar, two things had happened to Faisal bin Selim.

He had earned and saved enough money to commission, buy and own outright a superb timber-trading dhow, constructed by the finest craftsmen at Sur in Oman, and called *Rasha,* the pearl. And he had become a fervent Wahhabi.

When the new prophets arose to follow the teachings of Maududi and Sayyid Qutb, they declared jihad against the forces of heresy and degeneracy, and he was with them. When young men went to fight the godless Soviets in Afghanistan, his prayers went with them; when others flew airliners into the towers of the Western god of money, he knelt and prayed that they would indeed enter the gardens of Allah.

To the world, he remained the courteous, fastidious, frugal-living, devout master and owner of the *Rasha.* He plied his trade along the entire Gulf coast and round into the Arabian Sea. He did not seek trouble, but if a true believer sought his help, whether in alms or a passage to safety, he would do what he could.

He had come to the attention of Western security forces because a Saudi AQ activist, captured in the Hadramaut and confessing all in a cell in Riyadh, let slip that messages of the utmost secrecy destined for bin Laden himself, so secret that they could only be confided verbally to a messenger who would memorize them verbatim and take his own life before capture, would occasionally leave the Saudi peninsula by boat. The emissary would be deposited on the Baluchi coast, whence he would take his message north to the unknown caves of Waziristan where the sheikh resided. The boat was the *Rasha*. With the agreement and assistance of the ISI, it was not intercepted, just watched.

Faisal bin Selim arrived in Gwadar with a cargo of white goods from the duty-free entrepôt of Dubai. Here, the refrigerators, washing machines, microwave cookers and televisions were sold at a fraction of their retail price outside the Freeport warehouses.

He was commissioned to take back with him to the Gulf a cargo of Pakistani carpets, knotted by the thin fingers of little-boy slaves, destined for the feet of the rich Westerners buying luxury villas on the sea island being built off Dubai and Qatar.

He listened gravely to the small boy with the message, nodded, and two hours later, with his cargo safely inland without disturbing Pakistani customs, left the *Rasha* in the charge of his Omani deckhand and walked sedately through Gwadar to the mosque.

From years of trading with Pakistan, the courtly Arab spoke good Urdu, and he and the imam conversed in that language. He sipped his tea, took sweet cakes and wiped his fingers on a small cambric handkerchief. All the while, he nodded and glanced at the Afghan. When he heard of the breakout from the prison van, he smiled in approval. Then he broke into Arabic.

"And you wish to leave Pakistan, my brother?"

"There is no place for me here," said Martin. "The imam is right. The secret police will find me and hand me back to the dogs of Kabul. I will end my life before that."

"Such a pity," murmured the Qatari. "So far . . . such a life. And if I take you to the Gulf States, what will you do?"

"I will try to find other true believers and offer what I can."

"And what would that be? What can you do?"

"I can fight. And I am prepared to die in Allah's holy war."

The courtly captain thought for a while.

"The loading of the carpets takes place at dawn," he said. "It will take several hours. They must be well below-decks, lest the sea spray touch them. Then I shall depart, sails down. I shall cruise close past the end of the harbor mole. If a man were to leap from the concrete to the deck, no one would notice."

After the ritual salutations, he left. In the darkness, Martin was led by the boy to the dock. Here he studied the *Rasha* so that he would recognize her in the morning. She came past the mole just before eleven. The gap was eight feet, and Martin made it with inches to spare, after a short run.

The Omani had the helm. Faisal bin Selim greeted Martin with a gentle smile. He offered his guest fresh water to wash his hands and delicious dates from the palms of Muscat.

At noon, the elderly man spread two mats on the broad coaming round the cargo hold. Side by side, the two men knelt for the midday prayers. For Martin, it was the first occasion of prayer other than in a crowd where a single voice can be drowned by all the others. He was word-perfect.

When an agent is way out there in the cold, on a "black" and dangerous job, his controllers at home are avid for some sign that he is all right: still alive, still at liberty, still functioning. This indication may come from the agent himself, by phone call, a message in the classified ads of a paper or a chalk mark on a wall, a preagreed "drop." It may come from a watcher who makes no contact but observes and reports back. It is called a "sign of life." After days of silence, controllers become very twitchy waiting for some sign of life.

It was midday in Thumrait, early breakfast time in Scotland, the wee small hours in Tampa. The first and the third could see what the Predator could see, but did not know its significance. Need to know; they had not been told. But Edzell air base knew.

Clear as crystal, alternately lowering the forehead to

the deck and raising the face to the sky, the Afghan was saying his prayers on the deck of the *Rasha*. There was a roar from the terminal operators in the ops room. Seconds later, Steve Hill took a call at his breakfast table, and gave his wife a passionate and unexpected kiss.

Two minutes later, Marek Gumienny took a call in bed in Old Alexandria. He woke up, listened, smiled, murmured, "Way to go," and went back to sleep. The Afghan was still on course.

CHAPTER II

WITH A GOOD WIND off the south, the *Rasha* hoisted sail, closed down her engine, and the rumbling below was replaced by the calm sounds of the sea: the lapping of the water under the bow, the sigh of the wind in the sails, the creak of block and tackle.

The dhow, shadowed by the invisible Predator four miles above her, crept along the coast of southern Iran and into the Gulf of Oman. Here, she turned half to starboard, trimmed her sail as the wind took her full astern and headed for the narrow gap between Iran and Arabia called the Straits of Hormuz.

Through this narrow gap, where the tip of Oman's Musandam Peninsula is only eight miles from the Persian shore, a constant stream of mighty tankers went past: some low in the water, full of crude oil for the energy-hungry West; others riding high, going up-gulf to fill with Saudi or Kuwaiti crude.

The smaller boats like the dhow stayed closer to the shore to allow the leviathans the freedom of the deep channel. Supertankers, if there is something in their way, simply cannot stop.

The *Rasha*, being in no hurry, spent one night hove to amid the islands east of the Omani naval base at Kumzar. Sitting on the raised poop deck in the balmy night, still clearly visible on a plasma screen at a Scottish air base, Martin caught sight of two "cigarette boats" by the light of the moon and heard the roar of their huge outboards as they sped out of Omani waters to make the crossing to southern Iran.

These were the smugglers he had heard about; owing allegiance to no country, they ran the smuggling trade. On some empty Iranian or Baluchi beach, they would rendezvous at dawn with the receivers, off-load their cargo of cheap cigarettes and take on board, surprisingly, angora goats so valued in Oman.

On a flat sea, their pencil-slim aluminum boats, with the cargo lashed midships and the crew hanging on for dear life, would be powered by two immense 250-horsepower outboards at over fifty knots. They are virtually uncatchable, know every creek and inlet, and are accustomed to driving without lights in complete darkness right across the paths of the tankers to the shelter of the other side.

Faisal bin Selim smiled tolerantly. He, too, was a smuggler, but rather more dignified than these vagabonds of the Gulf he could hear in the distance.

"And when I have brought you to Arabia, my friend, what will you do?" he asked quietly. The Omani deckhand was at the forepeak, handline over the side, trying for a fine fish for breakfast. He had joined the other two for evening prayers. Now was the hour of pleasant conversation.

"I do not know," admitted the Afghan. "I know only that I am a dead man in my own country; Pakistan is closed to me, for they are running dogs of the Yankees. I hope to find other true believers, and ask to fight with them."

"Fight? But there is no fighting in the United Arab Emirates. They, too, are wholly allied to the West. The interior is Saudi Arabia, where you will be found immediately and sent back. So . . ."

The Afghan shrugged. "I only ask to serve Allah. I have lived my life. I will leave my fate in His care."

"And you say you are prepared to die for Him," said the courtly Qatari.

Mike Martin thought back to his boyhood and his prep school in Baghdad. Most of the pupils were Iraqi boys, but they were the sons of the cream of society, and their fathers were keen that they would speak perfect English and rise to rule great corporations dealing with London and New York. The curriculum was in English, and that included the learning of traditional English poetry.

Martin had always had one favorite: the story of how Horatius of Rome defended the last bridge before the invading army of the House of Tarquin as the Romans hacked down the bridge behind him. There was a verse the boys used to chant together:

> To every man upon this earth,
> Death cometh soon or late.
> And how can man die better
> Than facing fearful odds,
> For the ashes of his fathers,
> And the temples of his gods.

"If I can die *shahid*—in the service of His jihad, of course," he replied.

The dhow master considered for a while, and changed the subject.

"You are wearing the clothes of Afghanistan," he said. "You will be spotted in minutes. Wait."

He went below and came back with a freshly laundered dishdasha, the white cotton robe that falls from shoulders to ankles in an unbroken line.

"Change," he ordered. "Drop the *shalwar kameez* and the Talib turban over the side."

When Martin was changed, bin Selim handed him a new headdress, the red-flecked *keffiyeh* of a Gulf Arab, and the black cord circlet to hold it in place.

"Better," said the old man when his guest had completed the transformation. "You will pass for a Gulf Arab, save when you speak. But there is a colony of Afghans in the area of Jeddah. They have been in Saudi Arabia for generations, but they speak like you. Say that is where you come from and strangers will believe you.

Now let us sleep. We rise at dawn for the last day of cruising."

The Predator saw them weigh anchor and leave the islands, sailing gently round the rocky tip of Al Ghanam and turning southwest down the coast of the United Arab Emirates.

There are seven in the UAE, but only the names of the biggest and richest—Dubai, Abu Dhabi and Sharjah—spring to mind. The other four are much smaller, much poorer and almost anonymous. Two of these, Ajman and Umm al-Qaiwain, are cheek by jowl alongside Dubai, whose oil riches have made it the most developed of the seven.

Fujairah alone lies on the other side of the peninsula, facing east onto the Gulf of Oman. The seventh is Ras al-Khaimah.

It lies on the same coast as Dubai, but far up along the shore toward the Straits of Hormuz. It is dirt-poor and ultratraditional. For that reason, it has eagerly accepted the gifts of Saudi Arabia, including heavily financed mosques and schools—but all teaching Wahhabism. Ras al-K, as Westerners know it, is the local home of fundamentalism and sympathy for Al Qaeda and jihad. On the port side of the slowly cruising dhow, it would be the first to be reached. This occurred at sundown.

"You have no papers," said the captain to his guest. "And I cannot provide them. No matter, they have always been a Western impertinence. More important is money. Take these."

He thrust a wad of UAE dirhams into Martin's hand.

They were cruising in the fading light past the town, a mile away on the shore. The first lights began to flicker among the buildings.

"I will put you ashore farther down the coast," said bin Selim. "You will find the coast road and walk back. I know a small guesthouse in the Old Town. It is cheap, clean and discreet. Take lodgings there. Do not go out. You will be safe, and, *inshallah,* I may have friends who can help you."

It was fully dark when Martin saw the lights of the hotel and the *Rasha* slipped toward the shore. Bin Selim knew it well; the converted Hamra Fort, which had a beach club for its foreign guests, and the club had a jetty. After dark, it would be abandoned.

"He's leaving the dhow," said a voice in the ops room at Edzell air base. Despite the darkness, the thermal imager of the Predator at twenty thousand feet saw the agile figure leap from the dhow to the jetty, and the dhow reverse her engine and pull back to the deeper water and the sea.

"Never mind the boat; stay with the moving figure," said Gordon Phillips, leaning over the console operator's shoulder. The instructions went to Thumrait, and the Predator was instructed to follow the thermal image of a man walking along the coast road back toward Ras al-K.

It was a five-mile hike, but Martin reached the Old Town section round midnight. He asked twice, and was directed to the address of the guesthouse. It was five hundred yards from the family home of the al-Shehhi, whence had come Marwan al-Shehhi, who flew the airliner into the south tower of the World Trade Center on 9/11. He was still a local hero.

The proprietor was surly and suspicious until Martin mentioned Faisal bin Selim. That and the sight of a wad of dirhams cleared the air. He was bidden to enter, and shown to a simple room. There were seemingly just two other paying guests, and they had retired.

Unbending his attitude, the room keeper invited Martin to join him for a cup of tea before turning in. Over tea, Martin had to explain that he was from Jeddah, but of Pashtun extraction.

With his dark looks, full black beard and the repeated references to Allah of the truly devout, Martin convinced his host that he also was a true believer. They parted with mutual wishes for a good night's sleep.

The dhow master sailed on through the night. His destination was on the harbor, known as "the Creek," in the heart of Dubai. Once simply that—a muddy creek, smelling of dead fish, where men mended their nets in the heat of the day—it has become the last "picturesque" sight in the bustling capital, opposite the gold soukh, beneath the windows of the towering Western hotels. Here, the trading dhows are berthed side by side, and the tourists come to stare at the last portion of "Old Arabia."

Bin Selim hailed a taxi, and instructed the driver to take him three miles up the coast to the Sultanate of Ajman, smallest and second poorest of the seven. There, he dismissed the taxi, ducked into a covered soukh of twisting alleys and clamoring stalls and lost himself to any following "tail," should there have been one.

There was not. The Predator was concentrating on a guesthouse in the heart of Ras al-Khaimah. The dhow master slipped from the soukh into a small mosque, and made a request of the imam. A boy was sent scurrying through the town and came back with a young man who genuinely was a student in the local technical college. He was also a graduate of the Darunta training camp owned and run by Al Qaeda outside Jalalabad until 2001.

The old man whispered in the ear of the younger, who nodded and thanked him. Then the dhow master went back through the covered market, emerged, hailed a taxi and returned to his freighter in the Creek. He had done all he could. It was up to the younger men now. *Inshallah.*

That same morning, but later due to the time difference, the *Countess of Richmond* eased out of the estuary of the Mersey and into the Irish Sea. Captain McKendrick had the conn, and took his freighter south. In time, she would, keeping Wales to her left, clear the Irish Sea and Lizard Point, to meet the Channel and the eastern Atlantic. Then her course lay south, past Portugal, through the Mediterranean to the Suez Canal, and thence to the Indian Ocean.

Belowdecks, as the cold March seas flew up over the bow of the *Countess,* was a cargo of carefully protected and crated Jaguar sedans, destined for the showrooms of Singapore.

Four days passed before the Afghan sheltering in Ras al-Khaimah received his visitors. Following his instructions, he had not gone out, or at least not as far as the street. But he had taken the air in the closed courtyard at the rear of the house, screened from the streets by double gates eight feet high. Here various delivery vans came and went.

While in the courtyard he was seen by the Predator, and his controllers in Scotland noted his change of dress.

His visitors, when they came, did not arrive to deliver food, drink or laundry, but to make a collection. They backed the van close to the rear door of the building. The driver stayed at the wheel; the other three entered the house.

The lodgers were both away at work, the room keeper by agreement out at the shops. The team of three had their directions. They went swiftly to the appropriate door and entered without knocking. The seated figure, reading his Koran, rose to find himself facing a handgun in the grip of a man trained in Afghanistan. All three were hooded.

They were quiet and efficient. Martin knew enough of fighting men to recognize his visitors knew their business. The hood went over his head and fell to his shoulders. His hands came behind his back, and the plastic cuffs went on. Then he was marching—or being marched—out the door, down the tiled corridor and into the back of the van. He lay on his side, heard the door slam, felt the van lurch out of the gate and into the street.

The Predator saw it, but the controllers thought it was another laundry delivery. In minutes, the van was out of sight. There are many miracles that modern spy technology can accomplish, but controllers and machines can still be fooled. The snatch squad had no idea there was a Predator above them, but their shrewdly choosing mid-morning for the snatch rather than midnight fooled the watchers at Edzell.

It took three more days before they realized that their man no longer appeared daily in the courtyard to give the "sign of life." In short, he had disappeared. They were watching an empty house. And they had no idea which of the several vans had taken him.

In fact, the van had not gone far. The hinterland behind the port and city of Ras al-K is wild and rocky desert rising to the mountains of Ras al-Jibal. Nothing can live here but goats and salamanders.

Just in case the man they had snatched was under surveillance, with or without his knowledge, the kidnappers were taking no chances. There were tracks leading up into the hills, and they took one. In the rear, Martin felt the vehicle leave the tarred road and start to jolt over pitted track.

Had there been a tailing vehicle, it could not have avoided detection. Even staying out of sight, its plume of rising desert dust would have given it away. A surveillance helicopter would have been even more obvious.

The van stopped five miles up the track into the hills. The leader—the one with the handgun—took powerful binoculars and surveyed the valley and the coast, right back to the Old Town, whence they had come. Nothing came toward them.

When he was satisfied, the van turned and went back down the hills. Its real destination was a villa standing in a walled compound in the outer suburbs of the town. With the gates relocked, the van reversed up to an open door, and Martin was marched back out and down another tiled passage.

The plastic ties came off his wrists, and a cool metal shackle went on the left one. There would be a chain, he knew, and a bolt in the wall that could not be ripped free. When his hood came off, it was the kidnappers who had their heads covered. They withdrew backward, and the door slammed. He heard bolts go into sockets.

The cell was not a cell in the true meaning. It was a ground-floor room that had been fortified. The window had been bricked up, and though Martin could not see it, a painting of a window adorned the outside to fool even those with binoculars peering over the compound wall.

Considering what he had undergone years before in the SAS program of "interrogation resistance," it was even comfortable. There was a single bulb in the ceiling protected against thrown objects by a wire cage. The light was subdued but adequate.

There was a camp bed, and just enough slack in his chain to allow him to lie on it to sleep. The room also had an upright chair that he could reach, and a chemical toilet. All were within reach but in different directions.

His left wrist, however, was in a stainless-steel shackle that linked to a chain, and the chain went to a wall bracket. He could not begin to reach the door, through which his interrogators would enter—if at all—with food and water, and a spy hole in the door meant they could check on him any time and he would neither hear nor see them.

At Castle Forbes, there had been lengthy and passionate discussions over one problem: Should he carry any tracking device on him?

There are now tracker transmitters so tiny they can be injected under the skin without cutting the epidermis at all. This is pinhead-sized. Warmed by blood, they need no power source. But their range is limited. Worse, there are ultrasensitive detectors that can spot them.

"These people are absolutely not stupid," Phillips had stressed. His colleague from CIA Counter-Terrorism agreed.

"Among the best educated of them," said McDonald, "their mastery of very high technology, and especially the computer sciences, is awesome."

No one at Forbes doubted that if Martin was subjected to a hypertech body search and something were discovered, he would be dead within minutes.

Eventually, the decision was no planted bleeper. No signal sender. The kidnappers came for him an hour later. They were hooded again.

The body search was lengthy and thorough. The clothes went first, until he was naked, and they were taken away for searching in another room.

They did not even employ invasive throat and anal search. The scanner did it all. Inch by inch, it was run over his body in case it bleeped, meaning it had discovered a non-body-tissue substance. Only his mouth caused it to bleep. They forced his mouth open and examined every filling. Otherwise—nothing.

They returned his clothing, and prepared to leave.

"I left my Koran at the guesthouse," said the prisoner. "I have no watch or mat, but it must be the hour of prayer."

The leader stared at him through the spy hole. He said nothing, but two minutes later he returned with mat and Koran. Martin thanked him gravely.

Food and water were brought regularly. Each time, he was waved back with the handgun as the tray was deposited where he could reach it. The chemical lavatory was emptied in the same way.

It was three days before his interrogation began, and for this he was masked, lest he look out the windows, and led down two corridors. When his mask was removed, he was astonished. The man in front of him, sitting calmly behind a carved refectory table, for all the world like a potential employer interviewing an applicant, was youthful, elegant, civilized, urbane and uncovered. He spoke in perfect Gulf Arabic.

"I see no point in masks," he said, "nor silly names. Mine, by the way, is Dr. al-Khattab. There is no mystery here. If I am satisfied you are who you say you are, you will be welcome to join us. In which case, you will not betray us. If not, then I am afraid you will be killed at once. So let us not pretend, Mr. Izmat Khan. Are you really the one they call 'the Afghan'?"

"They will be concerned about two things," Gordon Phillips warned him during one of their interminable briefings at Forbes Castle. "Are you truly Izmat Khan, and are you the same Izmat Khan who fought at Qala-i-Jangi? Or have five years in Guantánamo turned you into something else?"

Martin stared back at the smiling Arab. He recalled the warnings of Tamian Godfrey. Never mind the wild-bearded screamers; watch out for the one who will be smooth-shaven; who will smoke, drink, consort with girls; who will pass for one of us. Wholly Westernized. A human chameleon, hiding the hatred. Totally deadly. There was a word . . . *takfir*.

"There are many Afghans," he said. "Who calls me 'the Afghan'?"

"Ah, you have been incommunicado for five years. After Qala-i-Jangi, word spread about you. You do not know about me, but I know much about you. Some of our people have been released from Camp Delta. They spoke highly of you. They claim you never broke. True?"

"They asked me about myself. I told them that."

"But you never denounced others? You mentioned no names? That is what the others say of you."

"They wiped out my family. Most of me died then. How do you punish a man who is dead?"

"A good answer, my friend. So, let us talk about Guantánamo. Tell me about Gitmo."

Martin had been briefed hour after hour about what had happened to him on the Cuban peninsula. The arrival on 14 January 2002—hungry, thirsty, soiled with

urine, blindfolded, shackled so tightly the hands were
numb for weeks. Beards and heads shaved, clothed in orange coveralls, stumbling and tripping in the darkness of
the hoods . . .

Dr. al-Khattab took copious notes, writing on yellow
legal notepaper with an old-fashioned fountain pen.
When a passage was reached where he knew all the answers, he ceased, and contemplated his prisoner with a
gentle smile.

In the late afternoon, he offered a photograph.

"Do you know this man?" he asked. "Did you ever
see him?"

Martin shook his head. The face looking up from the
photograph was General Geoffrey D. Miller, successor as
camp commandant to General Rick Baccus. The latter
had sat in on interrogations, but General Miller left it to
the CIA teams.

"Quite right," said al-Khattab. "He saw you, according to one of our released friends, but you were always
hooded as a punishment for noncooperation. And when
did the conditions start to improve?"

They talked until sundown, then the Arab rose.

"I have much to check on," he said. "If you are telling
the truth, we will continue in a few days. If not, I'm
afraid I shall have to issue Suleiman with the appropriate
instructions."

Martin went back to his cell. Dr. al-Khattab issued
rapid orders to the guard team and left. He drove a modest rented car, and he returned to the Hilton Hotel in
Ras al-Khaimah town, elegantly dominating the Al Saqr

deepwater harbor. He spent the night and left the next day. By then, he was wearing a well-cut cream tropical suit. When he checked in with British Airways at Dubai International Airport, his English was impeccable.

In fact, Ali Aziz al-Khattab had been born a Kuwaiti, the son of a senior bank official. By Gulf standards, that meant that his upbringing had been effortless and privileged. In 1989, his father had been posted to London as deputy manager of the Bank of Kuwait. The family had gone with him, and avoided the invasion of their homeland by Saddam Hussein in 1990.

Ali Aziz, already a good English speaker, was enrolled in a British school at age fifteen and emerged three years later with accentless English and excellent grades. When his family returned home, he elected to stay on and go for a degree at Loughborough Technical College. Four years later, he emerged with a science degree in chemical engineering, and proceeded on to a doctorate.

It was not in the Arabian Gulf but in London that he began to attend the mosque run by a firebrand preacher of anti-Western hatred and became what the media like to call "radicalized." In truth, by twenty-one he was fully brainwashed, and a fanatical supporter of Al Qaeda.

A "talent spotter" suggested he might like to visit Pakistan; he accepted, and then went on, through the Khyber Pass, to spend six months at an Al Qaeda terrorist training camp. He had already been marked out as a "sleeper" who should lie low in England and never come to the attention of the authorities.

Back in London, he did what they all do: He reported

to his embassy that he had lost his passport and was issued a new one, which did not carry the telltale Pakistan entry stamp. As far as anyone who asked was concerned, he had been visiting family and friends in the Gulf and had never been near Pakistan, let alone Afghanistan. He secured a post as lecturer at Aston University, Birmingham, in 1999. Two years later, Anglo-American forces invaded Afghanistan.

There were several weeks of panic in case any trace of him in the terror camps had been left lying round, but, in his case, AQ's head of personnel, Abu Zubaydah, had done his job. No traces were found of any al-Khattab ever having been there. So he remained undiscovered, and rose to be AQ's commanding agent in the UK.

As Dr. al-Khattab's London-bound airliner was taking off, the *Java Star* eased away from her berth in the Sultanate of Brunei on the coast of Indonesian North Borneo and headed for the open sea.

Her destination was the West Australian port of Fremantle, as usual, and her Norwegian skipper, Knut Herrmann, had no inkling his journey would be anything other than usual, routine and eventless.

He knew that the seas in those parts remain the most dangerous waters in the world, but not because of shoals, riptides, rocks, tempests, reefs or tsunamis. The danger here is pirate attacks.

Every year, between the Straits of Malacca to the west and the Celebes Sea to the east, there are over five hundred pirate attacks on merchant shipping, and up to a hundred hijackings. Occasionally, the crew are ransomed back to the shipowners. Sometimes they are all killed and never heard of again; in those cases, the cargo is stolen and sold on the black market.

If Captain Herrmann sailed with an easy mind on the "milk run" to Fremantle, it was because he was convinced his cargo was useless to the dacoits of the sea. But on this trip, he was wrong.

The first leg of his course lay north, away from his eventual destination. It took him six hours to pass the ramshackle town of Kudat and come round the northernmost tip of Sabah and the island of Borneo. Only then could he run southeast for the Sulu Archipelago.

He intended to move through the coral-and-jungle islands by taking the deepwater strait between Tawitawi and Jolo islands. South of the islands, it was a clear run down the Celebes Sea to the south and eventually Australia.

His departure from Brunei had been watched, and a cell phone call made. Even if it had been intercepted, the call referred only to the recovery of a sick uncle who would be out of the hospital in twelve days. That meant: twelve hours to intercept.

The call was taken on a creek on Jolo Island, and the man who took it would have been recognized by Mr. Alex Siebart, of Crutched Friars, City of London. It was Mr. Lampong, who no longer affected being a businessman from Sumatra.

The twelve men he commanded in the velvety tropical night were cutthroats, but they were well paid and would stay obedient. Criminality apart, they were also

Muslim extremists. The Abu Sayyaf movement of the southern Philippines, whose last peninsula is only a few miles from Indonesia on the Sulu Sea, has the reputation not only for religious extremism but also of being killers for hire. The offer Mr. Lampong had put to them enabled them to fulfill both functions.

The two speedboats they occupied put to sea at dawn, took up position between the two islands and waited. An hour later, the *Java Star* bore down on them, passing from the Sulu Sea into the Celebes. Taking her over was a simple task, and the gangsters were well practiced.

Captain Herrmann had taken the helm through the night, and as dawn came up over the Pacific, away to his left, he handed over to his Indonesian first officer and went below. His crew of ten *lashkars* were also in their bunks in the fo'c'sle.

The first thing the Indonesian officer saw was a pair of speedboats racing up astern, one on each side. Dark, barefoot, agile men leapt effortlessly from speedboat to deck and ran after toward the superstructure and bridge where he stood. He had just time to press the emergency buzzer to his captain's cabin, and the men were bursting through the door from the flybridge. Then there was a knife at his throat, and a voice screaming, *"Capitán, capitán . . ."*

There was no need. A tired Knut Herrmann was coming topside to see what was going on. He and Mr. Lampong arrived on the bridge together. Lampong held a mini Uzi. The Norwegian knew better than to begin to resist. The ransom would have to be sorted out between the pirates and his employer company HQ in Fremantle.

"Captain Herrmann . . ."

The bastard knew his name. This had been prepared.

"Please ask your first officer, did he in any circumstances make a radio transmission in the past five minutes?"

There was no need to ask. Lampong was speaking in English. For the Norwegian and his Indonesian officer, it was the common language. The first officer screamed that he had not touched the radio's transmit button.

"Excellent," said Lampong, and issued a stream of orders in the local dialect. This the first officer understood, and opened his mouth to scream. The Norwegian understood not a word, but he understood everything when the dacoit holding his number two jerked the seaman's head back and sliced his throat open with a single cut. The first officer kicked, jerked, slumped and died. Captain Herrmann had not been sick in forty years at sea, but he leaned against the wheel and emptied his stomach.

"Two pools of mess to be cleaned up," said Lampong. "Now, Captain, for every minute you refuse to obey my orders, that will happen to one of your men. Am I clear?"

The Norwegian was escorted to the tiny radio shack behind the bridge, where he selected channel 16, international distress frequency. Lampong produced a written sheet.

"You will not just read this in a calm voice, Captain. When I press TRANSMIT and nod, you will shout this message with panic in your voice. Or your men die, one by one. Are you ready?"

Captain Herrmann nodded. He would not even have to act in order to affect extreme distress.

"Mayday, Mayday, Mayday. *Java Star, Java Star* . . . catastrophic fire in engine room . . . I cannot save her . . . my position . . ."

He knew the position was wrong even as he read it out. It was a hundred miles south into the Celebes Sea. But he was not about to argue. Lampong cut the transmission. He brought the Norwegian at gunpoint back to the bridge.

Two of his own seamen had been put to work frenziedly scrubbing up the blood and the vomit on the floor of the bridge. The other eight he could see marshaled in a terrified group out on the hatch covers with six dacoits to watch them.

Two more of the hijackers stayed on the bridge. The other four were tossing life rafts, life belts and a pair of inflatable jackets down into one of the speedboats. It was the one with the extra fuel tanks stored amidships.

When they were ready, the speedboat left the side of the *Java Star* and went south. On a calm, tropical sea, at an easy fifteen knots, they would be a hundred miles south in seven hours, and back in their pirate creeks in ten after that.

"A new course, Captain," said Lampong civilly. His tone was gentle, but the implacable hatred in his eyes gave the lie to any humanity toward the Norwegian.

The new course was back toward the northeast, out of the cluster of islands that make up the Sulu Archipelago, and across the national line into Filipino waters.

The southern province of Mindanao Island is Zamboanga, and parts of it are simply no-go areas for Filipino government forces. This is the terrain of Abu Sayyaf. Here they are safe to recruit, train and bring their booty. The *Java Star* was certainly booty, albeit unmarketable. Lampong conferred in the local lingo to the senior among the pirates. The man pointed ahead to the entrance to a narrow creek flanked by impenetrable jungle.

What he asked was: "Can your men manage her from here?" The pirate nodded. Lampong called his orders to the group round the *lashkar* seamen at the bow. Without even replying, they herded the sailors to the rail and opened fire. The men screamed and toppled into the warm sea. Somewhere below, sharks turned to the blood smell.

Captain Herrmann was so taken by surprise he would have needed two or three seconds to react. He never got them. Lampong's bullet took him full in the chest, and he, too, toppled back from the flybridge into the sea. Half an hour later, towed by two small tugs that had been stolen weeks earlier, and with much screaming and shouting, the *Java Star* was at her new berth beside a stout teak jetty.

The jungle concealed her from all sides and from above. Also hidden were the two long, low, tin-roofed workshops that housed the steel plates, cutters, welders, power generator and paint.

The last, despairing cry from the *Java Star* on channel 16 had been heard by a dozen vessels, but the nearest to the spot given as her position was a refrigerator ship loaded with fresh and highly perishable fruit for the American market across the Pacific. She was commanded by a Finnish skipper, who diverted at once to the spot. There he found the bobbing life rafts, small tents on the ocean swell that had opened and inflated automatically as designed. He circled once and spotted the life belts and two inflated jackets. All were marked with the name: MV *Java Star*. According to the law of the sea, which he respected, Captain Raikkonen cut power and lowered a pinnace to look inside the rafts. They were empty, so he ordered them sunk. He had lost several hours and could stay no longer. There was no point.

With a heavy heart, he reported by radio that the *Java Star* was lost with all hands. Far away in London, the news was noted by insurers Lloyd's International, and at Ipswich, UK, Lloyd's shipping list logged the loss. For the world, the *Java Star* had simply ceased to exist.

CHAPTER 12

IN FACT, the interrogator was gone for a week. Martin remained in his cell with only the Koran for company. He would, he felt, soon be among that revered company who had memorized every one of the 6,666 verses in it. But years in Special Forces had finally given him a rare gift among humans: the ability to remain motionless for exceptionally long periods and defy boredom and the urge to fidget.

So he schooled himself again to adapt to the inner contemplative life that alone can stop a man in solitary confinement from going mad.

This talent did not prevent the operations room at Edzell air base from becoming very tense. They had lost their man, and the inquiries from Marek Gumienny in Langley and Steve Hill in London became more pressing. The Predator was double-assigned: to look down on

Ras al-Khaimah in case Crowbar appeared again, and to monitor the dhow *Rasha* when it appeared in the Gulf and docked somewhere in the UAE.

Dr. al-Khattab returned when he had confirmed every aspect of the story as it concerned Guantánamo Bay. It had not been easy. He had not the slightest intention of betraying himself to any of the four British inmates who had been sent home. They had all declared repeatedly that they were not extremists and had been swept up in the American net by accident. Whatever the Americans thought, Al Qaeda could confirm it was all true.

To make it harder, Izmat Khan had spent so long in solitary for noncooperation that no other detainee had got to know him well. He admitted he had picked up fragmentary English, but that was from the endless interrogations when he had listened to the CIA man and then the translation by the one Pashto-speaking 'terp.

From what al-Khattab could discover, his prisoner had not slipped up once. What little could be gleaned from Afghanistan indicated that the breakout from the prison van between Bagram and Pul-i-Charki jail had indeed been genuine. What he could not know was that this episode had been accomplished by the very able head of station of the SIS office inside the British Embassy. Brigadier Yusef had acted out his rage most convincingly, and the agents of the by-now-resurgent Taliban were convinced. And they said so to Al Qaeda inquiries.

"Let us go back to your early days in the Tora Bora," he proposed when the interrogation resumed. "Tell me about your boyhood."

Al-Khattab was a clever man, but he also could not know that, even though the man in front of him was a ringer, Martin knew the mountains of Afghanistan better than he. The Kuwaiti's six months in the terrorist training camps had been exclusively among fellow Arabs, not Pashtun mountain men. He noted copiously even the names of the fruits in the orchards of Maloko-zai. His hand sped across the legal pad, covering page after page.

On the third day of the second session, the narrative had reached the day that proved a crucial hinge in the life of Izmat Khan: August 21, 1998, the day the Tomahawk cruise missiles crashed in the mountains.

"Ah, yes, truly tragic," he murmured. "And strange, for you must be the only Afghan for whom no family member remains alive to vouch for you. It is a remarkable coincidence, and as a scientist I hate coincidences. What was the effect on you?"

In fact, Izmat Khan, at Guantánamo, had refused to talk about why he hated Americans with such a passion. It was information from the other fighters who had survived Qala-i-Jangi and reached Camp Delta that filled the gap. In the Taliban army, Izmat Khan had become an iconic figure, and his story was whispered round the campfires as the man immune to fear. The other survivors had told the interrogators the story of the annihilated family.

Al-Khattab paused and gazed at his prisoner. He still had grave reservations, but of one thing he had become certain. The man truly was Izmat Khan; his doubts were over the second question: Had he been "turned" by the Americans?

"So you claim you declared a sort of private war? A very personal jihad? And you have never relented? But what did you actually do about it?"

"I fought against the Northern Alliance, the allies of the Americans."

"But not until October and November 2001," said al-Khattab.

"There were no Americans in Afghanistan until then," said Martin.

"True. So you fought for Afghanistan . . . and lost. Now you wish to fight for Allah."

Martin nodded. "As the sheikh predicted," he said.

For the first time, Dr. al-Khattab's urbanity completely forsook him. He stared at the black-bearded face across the table for a full thirty seconds, mouth agape, pen poised but unmoving. Finally, he spoke, in a whisper, "You . . . have actually met the sheikh?"

In all his weeks in the camp, al-Khattab had never actually met Osama bin Laden. Just once, he had seen a black-windowed Land Cruiser passing by, but it had not stopped. But he would, quite literally, have taken a meat cleaver and severed his left wrist for the chance of meeting, let alone conversing with, the man he venerated more than any other on earth. Martin met his gaze and nodded. Al-Khattab recovered his poise.

"You will start at the beginning of this episode and describe exactly what happened. Leave out nothing, no tiny detail."

So Martin told him. He told him of serving in his father's *lashkar* as a teenager freshly back from the *madrassah* outside Peshawar. He told of the patrol with others, and how they had been caught on a mountain-side with only a group of boulders to shelter in.

He made no mention of any British officer, nor any Blowpipe missile, nor the destruction of the Hind gun-ship. He told only of the roaring chain gun in the nose; the fragments of bullet and rock flying around until the Hind—eternal praise be to Allah—ran out of ammunition and flew away.

He told of feeling a blow like a punch or a hit from a hammer in the thigh, and being carried by his comrades across the valleys until they found a man with a mule and took it from him.

And he told of being carried to a complex of caves at Jaji and being handed over to Saudis who lived and worked there.

"But the sheikh, tell me of the sheikh," insisted al-Khattab. So Martin told him. The Kuwaiti took down the dialogue word for word.

"Say that again, please."

"He said to me: 'The day will come when Afghanistan will no longer have need of you, but the all-merciful Allah will always have need of a warrior like you.'"

"Then what happened?"

"He changed the dressing on the leg."

"The sheikh did that?"

"No, the doctor who was with him. The Egyptian."

Dr. al-Khattab sat back and let out a long breath. Of course, the doctor, Ayman al-Zawahiri, companion and confidant, the man who had brought Egyptian Islamic

Jihad to join the sheikh to create Al Qaeda. He began to tidy up his papers.

"I have to leave you again. It will take a week, maybe more. You will have to stay here. Chained, I am afraid. You have seen too much, you know too much. But if you are indeed a true believer, and truly 'the Afghan,' you will join us as an honored recruit. If not . . ."

Martin was back in his cell when the Kuwaiti left. This time, al-Khattab did not return straight to London. He went to the Hilton, and wrote steadily and carefully for a day and a night. When he was done, he made several calls on a new and "lily-white" cell phone that then went into the deepwater harbor. In fact, he was not being listened to, but even if he had been his words would have meant little. But Dr. al-Khattab was still in freedom because he was a very careful man.

The calls he made arranged a meeting with Faisal bin Selim, master of the *Rasha,* which was moored in Dubai. That afternoon, he drove his cheap rental car to Dubai and conversed with the elderly captain, who took a long personal letter and hid it deep in his robes. And the Predator kept circling at twenty thousand feet.

Islamist terror groups have already lost far too many senior operatives not to have realized that for them, however careful they are, cell phone and sat phone calls are dangerous. The West's interception, eavesdrop and decryption technology is simply too good. Their other weakness is the transferring of sums of money through the normal banking system.

To overcome the latter danger, they use the *hundi* system, which, with variations, is as old as the first caliphate. *Hundi* is based on the total-trust concept, which any lawyer will advise against. But it works because any money launderer who cheated his customer would soon be out of business or worse.

The payer hands over his money in cash to the *hundi* man in place A and asks that his friend in place B shall receive the equivalent minus the *hundi* man's cut.

The *hundi* man has a trusted partner, usually a relative, in place B. He informs his partner, and instructs him to make the money available—all in cash—to the payer's friend who will identify himself thus.

Given the tens of millions of Muslims who send money back to families in the home country, and given that there are neither computers nor even checkable dockets, and given that it is all in cash and both payers and receivers can use pseudonyms, the money movements are virtually impossible to intercept or trace.

For communications, the solution lies in hiding the terrorist messages in three-figure codes which can be e-mailed or texted round the world. Only the recipient, with a decipher list of up to three hundred such number groups, can work out the message. This works for brief instructions and warnings. Occasionally, a lengthy and exact text must travel halfway round the world.

Only the West is always in a hurry. The East has patience. If it takes so long, then it takes that long. The *Rasha* sailed that night and made her way back to Gwadar. There, a loyal emissary, alerted in Karachi down the coast by a text message, had arrived on his motorcy-

cle. He took the letter and rode north across Pakistan to
the small but fanatic town of Miram Shah.

There, the man trusted enough to go into the high
peaks of South Waziristan was waiting at the named
chaikhana and the sealed package changed hands again.
The reply came back the same way. It took ten days.

But Dr. al-Khattab did not stay in the Arabian Gulf.
He flew to Cairo, and then due west to Morocco. There,
he interviewed and selected the four North Africans who
would become part of the second crew. Because he was
still not under surveillance, his journey appeared on no
one's radar.

When the handsome cards were dealt, Mr. Wei Wing Li received a pair of twos. Short, squat and toadlike, his shoulders were surmounted by a football of a head and a face
deeply pitted with smallpox. But he was good at his job.

He and his crew had arrived at the hidden creek on the
Zamboanga peninsula two days before the *Java Star*.
Their journey from China, where they featured in the
criminal underworld of Guangdong, had not involved
the inconvenience of passports or visas. They had simply
boarded a freighter whose captain had been amply re-
warded, and had thus arrived off Jolo Island, where two
speedboats out of the Filipino creeks had taken them off.

Mr. Wei had greeted his host, Mr. Lampong, and
the local Abu Sayyaf chieftain who had recommended
him, inspected the living quarters for his dozen crewmen, taken the fifty percent of his fee "up front" and
asked to see the workshops. After a lengthy inspec-

tion, he counted the tanks of oxygen and acetylene, and pronounced himself satisfied. Then he studied the photos taken in Liverpool. When the *Java Star* was finally in the creek, he knew what had to be done and set about it.

Ship transformation was his specialty, and over fifty cargo vessels plying the seas of Southeast Asia with false names and papers also had false shapes thanks to Mr. Wei. He had said he needed two weeks and had been given three, but not an hour longer. In that time, the *Java Star* was going to become the *Countess of Richmond*. Mr. Wei did not know that. He did not need to know.

In the photos he studied, the name of the vessel had been airbrushed out. Mr. Wei was not bothered with names or papers. It was shapes that concerned him.

There would be parts of the *Java Star* to cut out and others to cut off. There would be features to be fashioned from welded steel. But most of all, he would create six long, steel sea containers that would occupy the deck from below the bridge to the forepeak in three pairs.

Yet they would not be real. From all sides, and from above, they would appear authentic down to the Hapag-Lloyd's markings. They would pass inspection at a range of a few feet. Yet inside, they would have no interior walls; they would constitute a long gallery with a hinged, removable roof, and access through a new door, to be cut in the bulkhead below the bridge and then disguised to be invisible unless one knew the location of the release catch.

What Mr. Wei and his team would not do was the

painting. The Filipino terrorists would do that, and the ship's new name would be applied after he had left.

The day he fired up his oxyacetylene cutters, the *Countess of Richmond* was passing through the Suez Canal.

When Ali Aziz al-Khattab returned to the villa, he was a changed man. He ordered the shackles removed from his prisoner, and invited him to share his table at lunch. His eyes glittered with a deep excitement.

"I have communicated with the sheikh himself," he purred. Clearly, the honor consumed him. The reply was not written. It had been confided in the mountains to the messenger verbally, and he had memorized it. This is also a common practice in the higher reaches of Al Qaeda.

The messenger had been brought all the way to the Arabian Gulf, and when the *Rasha* docked the message had been given word for word to Dr. al-Khattab.

"There is one last formality," he said. "Would you please raise the hem of your dishdasha to the midthigh?"

Martin did so. He knew nothing of al-Khattab's scientific discipline, only that he had a doctorate. He prayed it was not in dermatology. The Kuwaiti examined the puckered scar with keen attention. It was exactly where he was told it would be. It had the six stitches sutured into place in a Jaji cave eighteen years earlier by a man he revered.

"Thank you, my friend. The sheikh himself sends his personal greetings. What an incredible honor. He and the doctor remembered the young warrior and the words spoken.

"He has authorized me to include you in a mission that will inflict on the Great Satan a blow so terrible that even the destruction of the towers will seem minor.

"You have offered your life to Allah. The offer is accepted. You will die gloriously, a true *shahid*. You and your fellow martyrs will be spoken of a thousand years from now."

After three weeks of wasted time, Dr. al-Khattab was now in a hurry. The resources of Al Qaeda down the entire coasts were called upon. A barber came to trim the shaggy mane to a Western-style haircut. He also prepared to shave off the beard. Martin protested. As a Muslim and as an Afghan, he wanted his beard. Al-Khattab conceded it could be clipped to a neat Vandyke around the point of the chin, but no longer.

Suleiman himself took full-face photos, and twenty-four hours later appeared with a perfect passport, showing the bearer to be a marine engineer from Bahrain, known to be a staunchly pro-Western sultanate.

A tailor came, took measurements and reappeared with shoes, socks, shirt, tie and dark gray suit, along with a small valise to carry them.

The traveling party prepared to leave the next day. Suleiman, who turned out to be from Abu Dhabi, would be going all the way, accompanying the Afghan. The other two were "muscle," locally produced, locally recruited and dispensable. The villa, having served its purpose, would be scoured and abandoned.

As he prepared to leave before them, Dr. al-Khattab turned to Martin.

"I envy you, Afghan. You can never know how much. You have fought for Allah, bled for Him, taken pain and the foulness of the infidel for Him. And now you will die for Him. If only I could be with you."

He held out his hand, English style, then recalled that he was an Arab and embraced the Afghan. At the door, he turned one final time.

"You will be in paradise before me, Afghan. Save a place for me there. *Inshallah*."

Then he was gone. He always parked his hired car several hundred yards away and round two corners. Outside the villa gates, she crouched, as always, adjusting a shoe and glancing up and down the road. There was nothing but some chit of a girl two hundred yards up, trying to start a scooter that refused to fire. But she was local, in *jilbab*, covering the hair and half the face. Still, it offended him that a woman would have any motorized vehicle at all.

He turned and walked away toward his car. The girl with the spluttering engine leaned forward and spoke into something inside the basket above the front mudguard. Her clipped English spoke of Cheltenham Ladies' College.

"Mongoose 1, on the move," she said.

Anyone who has ever been involved in what Kipling called "the Great Game," and what James Jesus Angleton of the CIA referred to as the "wilderness of mirrors," will surely agree the greatest enemy is the UCU.

The Unforeseen Cock-Up has probably wrecked more covert missions than treachery or brilliant counterintelligence by the other side. It almost put an end to Operation Crowbar. And it all started because everyone consumed by the new atmosphere of cooperation was trying to be helpful.

The pictures from the two Predators that were "spelling" each other over the UAE and the Arabian Sea were going back from Thumrait to Edzell air base, which knew exactly why, and American Army CENTCOM at Tampa, Florida, which thought the British had simply asked for some routine aerial surveillance. Martin had insisted that no more than twelve should ever know he was out in the cold, and the number was still only at ten. And they were not in Tampa.

Whenever the Predators were over the Emirates, their images contained a teeming mass of Arabs, non-Arabs, cars, cabs, docks and houses. There were far too many to begin checking out every one. But the dhow called the *Rasha,* and her elderly master, *were* known about. So when she was docked, anyone visiting her was also of possible interest.

But there were scores. She had to be loaded and unloaded, refueled and reprovisioned. The Omani crewman scrubbing her down exchanged pleasantries with passersby on the quayside. Tourists wandered by to gawk at a real trading dhow of traditional teak. Her skipper was visited onboard by his local agents and personal friends. When a single, clean-shaven young Gulf Arab in white dishdasha and white, filigreed *thub* skullcap conferred with Faisal bin Selim, he was just one of many.

Edzell operations room had a menu of a thousand faces of confirmed and suspected AQ members and sympathizers, and every image from the Predators was electronically compared. Dr. al-Khattab did not trigger red flags because he was not known. So Edzell missed him. These things happen.

The slim young Arab visiting the *Rasha* rang no bells in Tampa either, but the Army sent the images as a courtesy to the National Security Agency at Fort Meade, Maryland, and the National Reconnaissance Office—spy satellites—in Washington. The NSA provided them as a service to their British partners at GCHQ Cheltenham, who had a good, long look, missed al-Khattab and sent the images to the British Security Service—counterintelligence—more commonly known as MI5, at Thames House, just down the embankment from the Houses of Parliament.

Here, a young probationer, keen to impress, ran the faces of all the visitors to the *Rasha* through the Face Recognition database.

It is not all that long ago that the recognition of human faces relied on talented agents who worked in half darkness, poring over grainy images with magnifying glasses trying to answer two questions: Who is the man/woman in this photo, and have we ever seen them before? It was always a lonely quest, and took years before a dedicated scrutineer developed the sixth sense that could recall that the "chummy" in the photo had been at a Vietnamese diplomatic cocktail party in Delhi five years earlier and was certainly for that reason from the KGCB.

Then came the computer. Software was prepared that reduced the human face to over six hundred tiny measurements and stored them. It seems every human face in the world can be broken down into measurements. It may be the exact distance to the micron between the pupils of the eyes, the width of the nose at seven points between eyebrows and tip, twenty-two measurements for the lips alone, and the ears . . .

Ah, the ears. Face analysts love the ears. Every crease and furrow, wrinkle and curve, fold and lobe, is different. They are like fingerprints. Even the ones on the left and right side of the head are not quite the same. Plastic surgeons ignore them, but give a skilled facewatcher both ears in good definition and he will get his "match."

The computer software had a memory bank far bigger than a thousand faces stored at Edzell. It had convicted criminals of apparently no political persuasion at all, because even they can work for terrorists if the price is right. It had immigrants, legal and illegal, and not necessarily Muslim converts. It had thousands and thousands of faces taken from demonstrations, as the protesters rolled by the hidden cameras, waving their placards and chanting their slogans. And it did not confine its database to the United Kingdom. In short, it had over three million human faces from all over the world.

The computer broke down the face talking to the master of the *Rasha,* compensated for the oblique angle of the shot by picking the single image where the man raised his head to look at a jet taking off from Abu Dhabi airport, secured its six hundred measurements and began to compare. It could even adjust for added or shaved facial hair.

Fast though it was, the computer still took an hour to do its work. But it found him.

He was a face in a crowd outside a mosque just after 9/11 cheering enthusiastically whatever the orator was saying. This orator was known as Abu Qatada, fanatical Al Qaeda supporter in Britain, and the crowd he was addressing that late September day of 2001 was from al-Muhajiroun, a jihad-supporting extremist group.

Abstracting the face of the student from the file, the probationer took it to his superior. From there, it went up to the formidable lady running MI5, Eliza Manningham-Buller. She ordered that the man be traced. No one then knew the probationer had uncovered the chieftain of Al Qaeda in Britain.

It took a bit more time, but another match came up; he was receiving his doctorate at an academic ceremony. His name was Ali Aziz al-Khattab, a highly Anglicized academic with a post at Aston University, Birmingham.

With what the authorities had, he was either a highly successful, long-term sleeper or a foolish man who in his student days had dabbled with extreme politics. If every citizen in the second category were arrested, there would be more detainees than police.

For sure, he had apparently never been anywhere near extremists since that day outside the mosque. But a fully reformed foolish boy is not spotted conferring with the captain of the *Rasha* in Abu Dhabi port. So . . . he was in the first category: an AQ sleeper, until proven otherwise.

Further discreet checks revealed he was back in Britain, resuming his laboratory work at Aston. The question was: Arrest him or watch him? The problem was, a single aerial photograph that could not be revealed would not secure a conviction. It was decided to put the academic under surveillance, costly though it was.

The quandary was solved a week later when Dr. al-Khattab booked a flight back to the Arabian Gulf. That was when the SRR was brought in.

Britain has for years possessed one of the best "tracker" units in the world. It was known as the 14th Intelligence Company, or the Detachment, or, more simply, the Det. And it was extremely covert. Unlike the SAS and the SBS, it was not designed as a unit of ultra-hard fighters. Its talents were extreme stealth and skill at planting bugs, taking long-range photos, eavesdropping and tracking. It was particularly effective against the IRA in Northern Ireland.

In several cases, it was the information provided by the Det that enabled the SAS to set an ambush for a terrorist attack unit and wipe them out. Unlike the hard units, the Det used women extensively. As trackers, they were more likely to pass as harmless and not to be feared. The information they were able to bring back was indeed very much to be feared.

In 2005, the British government decided to expand and upgrade the Det. It became "the Special Reconnaissance Regiment." It had an inaugural parade in which everyone, including the presiding general, was photographed only from the waist down. Its headquarters remain secret, and if the SAS and SBS are discreet the SRR is invisible. But Dame Eliza asked for them and got them.

When Dr. al-Khattab boarded the airliner from Heathrow to Dubai, there were six from the SRR on board, scattered invisibly among three hundred passengers. One was the young accountant in the row behind the Kuwaiti.

Because this was just a shadowing operation, no reason could be seen not to ask the Special Forces of the UAE for cooperation. Ever since World Trade Center terrorist Marwan al-Shehhi was discovered to have come from the UAE, and even more since the leak that the White House was tempted to bomb the Al Jazeera TV station at Qatar, the UAE had been extremely sensitive about Islamist extremism—and nowhere more than in Dubai, headquarters of the Special Forces.

Thus, two hired cars and two rented scooters were available for the SRR team when it landed, just in case Dr. al-Khattab was being picked up. It was noted he had carry-on baggage only. They need not have bothered; he rented a small Japanese compact, which gave them time to move into position.

He was tailed first from the airport to the Creek in Dubai, where once again the *Rasha* was moored after her return from Gwadar. This time, he did not approach the vessel, but stood by his car a hundred yards away until bin Selim spotted him.

Minutes later, a young man known to no one emerged from belowdecks on the *Rasha,* moved through the crowd and whispered in the ear of the Kuwaiti. It was the answer from the man in the mountains of Waziristan coming back. Al-Khattab's face registered amazement.

He then drove along the traffic-teeming road up the coast, through Ajman and Umm al-Qaiwain and into Ras al-Khaimah. There, he went to the Hilton to check in and change. It was considerate of him, because the three young women in the SRR team could use the female washroom to change into the all-covering *jilbab* and get back to their vehicles.

Dr. al-Khattab emerged in his white dishdasha and drove away through the town. He adopted several maneuvers designed to shake off a "tail," but he had no chance. In the Arabian Gulf, the motor scooter is everywhere, ridden by both sexes, and, the clothes being the same, one rider is much like another. Since being assigned to the job, the team had been studying road maps of all seven emirates until they had memorized every highway. That was how he was tailed to the villa.

If ever there had been any residual doubt that he was up to no good, his tail-shaking antics dispelled it. Innocent men do not behave like that. He never spent the night at the villa, and the SRR woman followed him back to the Hilton. The three men found a position on a hilltop that commanded a view of the target villa and kept vigil through the night. No one came or went.

The second day was different. There were visitors. The watchers could not know it, but they brought the new passport and the new clothes. Their car numbers were noted, and one would be traced and arrests made later. The third was the barber, also later traced.

At the end of the second day, al-Khattab emerged for the last item. That was when Katy Sexton, tinkering with her scooter up the road, alerted her colleagues that the target was on the move.

At the Hilton, the Kuwaiti academic revealed his plans, when, speaking from his room, which had been bugged in his absence, he booked passage on the morning flight out of Dubai for London. He was escorted all the way home to Birmingham and never saw a thing.

MI5 had done a cracking job and knew it. The coup was circulated on a "for your eyes only" basis to just four men in the British intelligence community. One of them was Steve Hill. He nearly went into orbit.

The Predator was reassigned to survey the villa in the far desert-side suburbs of Ras al-Khaimah. But it was midmorning in London, afternoon in the Gulf. All the bird saw were the cleaners going in. And the raid.

It was too late to stop the Special Forces of the UAE from sending in their closedown squad, commanded by a former British officer, Dave De Forest. The SIS head of station in Dubai—a personal friend, anyway—was onto him like a shot. Word was immediately put out on the jungle telegraph that the "hit" had stemmed from an anonymous tip from a neighbor with a grudge.

The two cleaners knew nothing; they came from an agency, they had been prepaid and the keys had been delivered to them. However, they had not finished, and swept up in a pile was a quantity of black hair, evidently from a scalp, and from a beard—the texture is different. Other than that, there were no traces of the men who had lived there.

Neighbors reported a closed van, but no one could recall the number. It was eventually discovered abandoned, and revealed to have been stolen, but much too late to be of help.

The tailor and the barber were a better harvest. They did not hesitate to talk, but they could describe only the five men in the house. Al-Khattab was already known. Suleiman was described and then identified from mug shots, because he was on a suspect list locally. The two underlings were described, but the descriptions rang no bells of recognition.

It was the fifth man that De Forest, with his perfect Arabic, concentrated on. The SIS station chief sat in. The two Gulf Arabs who had done the tailoring and the barbering came from Ajman, and were simply workers at their trade.

No one in that room knew about any Afghan; they simply took a complete description and passed it to London. No one knew about any passport because Suleiman had done it all himself. No one knew why London was becoming hysterical about a big man with shaggy black hair and a full beard. All they could report was that he was now neatly barbered, and possibly in a dark two-piece mohair suit.

But it was the final snippet that came from the barber and the tailor that delighted Steve Hill, Marek Gumienny and the team at Edzell.

The Gulf Arabs had been treating their man like an honored guest. He was clearly being prepared for departure. He was not a dead body on a tiled floor in the Arabian Gulf.

At Edzell, Michael McDonald and Gordon Phillips shared the same joy, but a puzzle. They knew their agent had passed all the tests and been accepted as a true Jihadi. After weeks of worry, they had had their second sign of life.

But had their agent discovered a single thing about Stingray, the object of the whole exercise? Where had he gone? Was there any way he could contact them?

Even if they could have spoken to their agent, he could not have helped. He did not know, either.

And no one knew that the *Countess of Richmond* was unloading her Jaguars at Singapore.

CHAPTER 13

EVEN THOUGH THE TRAVELING party could not know there were pursuers a few hours behind them, their escape was, for them, a lucky chance.

Had they turned toward the coast housing the six emirates, they would probably have been caught. In fact, they headed east, over the mountainous isthmus, toward the seventh emirate, Fujairah, on the Gulf of Oman.

They soon left the last paved road and took to rutted tracks, and lost themselves among the baking brown hills of Jabal Yibir. From the col at the height of the range, they descended toward the small port of Dibbah.

Well to the south on the same coast, the police at Fujairah City received a request and a full description from Dubai and mounted a roadblock at the entrance to their town on the mountain road. Many vans were stopped, but none contained the four terrorists.

There is not much to Dibbah, just a cluster of white houses, a green-domed mosque, a small port for fishing vessels and the occasional charger boat for Western scuba divers. Two creeks away, an aluminum boat waited, drawn up on the shingle, its huge outboards out of the water. Its cargo space amidships was occupied by chained-down tanks of extra fuel. Its two-man crew was sheltering in the shade of a single camel thorn among the rocks.

For the two local youths, this was the end of their road. They would take the stolen van high into the hills and abandon it. Then they would simply disappear into the same streets that had produced Marwan al-Shehhi. Suleiman and the Afghan, their Western clothes still in bags to shield them from the flying salt water, helped push the cigarette boat backward into waist-deep water.

With both passengers and the crew aboard, the smuggler craft idled its way up the coast almost to the tip of the Musandam Peninsula. The smugglers would only make the high-speed dash across the strait in darkness.

Within twenty minutes of the sun's setting, the helmsman bade his passengers hold on and opened up the power. The smuggler erupted out of the rocky waters of the last tip of Arabia and hurled itself toward Iran. With five hundred horsepower behind it, the nose rose, and the craft began to skim. Martin judged they were covering the water at almost fifty knots. The slightest ripple on the sea was like hitting a log, and the spray flayed them. All four, who had wrapped their *keffiyeh*s round their faces as a shield from the sun, now kept them there to protect from the spray.

In less than thirty minutes, the first scattered lights of the Persian coast were visible to port, and the smuggler raced east toward Gwadar and Pakistan. This was the route Martin had covered under the sedate sails of the *Rasha* a month before. Now he was returning at ten times her speed.

Opposite the lights of Gwadar, the crew slowed and stopped. It was a welcome relief. With funnels and muscles, they hoisted the drums to the stern and refilled each engine to the brim. Where they were going to fill up again for the return journey was their business.

Faisal bin Selim had told Martin these smugglers could get from Omani waters to Gwadar in a single night and be back with a fresh cargo by dawn. This time, they were clearly going farther, and would have to travel in daylight as well.

Dawn found them well inside Pakistani waters, but close enough to shore to be taken for a fishing boat going about its business, save that no fish can swim that fast. However, there was no sign of officialdom, and the bare, brown coast sped past. By midday, Martin realized the destination must be Karachi. As to why, he had no idea.

They refueled at sea one more time, and, as the sun dipped to the west behind them, were deposited at a reeking fishing village outside the sprawl of Pakistan's biggest port and harbor.

Suleiman may not have been there before, but his

briefing must have been by someone who had done a recce. Martin knew that Al Qaeda did meticulous research, regardless of time and expense; it was one of the few things he could admire.

The Gulf Arab sought out the only vehicle for hire in the village and negotiated a price. The fact two strangers had come ashore from a smuggler craft with no suggestion of legality raised not an eyebrow. This was Baluchistan; the rules of Karachi were for idiots.

The interior stank of fish and body odor, and the misfiring engine could manage no more than forty miles per hour. Neither could the roads. But they found the highway, and reached the airport with time to spare.

The Afghan was appropriately bewildered and clumsy. He had only twice traveled by air, each time in an American AC-130 Hercules, and each time as a prisoner in shackles. He knew nothing of check-in desks, flight tickets, passport controls. With a mocking smile, Suleiman showed him.

Somewhere in the vast sprawling mass of pushing and shoving humanity that comprises the main concourse of Karachi International Airport, the Gulf Arab found the ticket desk of Malaysia Airlines and bought two single tickets in economy class to Kuala Lumpur. There were lengthy visa application forms to fill out, which Suleiman did, in English. He paid in cash American dollars, the world's common currency.

The flight was on a European Airbus A330, and took six hours, plus two for time zone change. It landed at half past eight, after the serving of a snack breakfast. For the second time, Martin offered his new Bahraini passport, and wondered if it would pass muster. It did; it was perfect.

From international arrivals, Suleiman led the way to domestic departures and bought two single tickets. Only when Martin had to proffer his boarding pass did he see where they were heading—the island of Labuan.

He had heard of Labuan, but only vaguely. Situated off the northern coast of Borneo, it belonged to Malaysia. Though its tourist publicity spoke of a bustling cosmopolitan island with stunning coral in the surrounding waters, Western briefings on the criminal underworld mentioned another, darker reputation.

It was once part of the Sultanate of Brunei, twenty miles across the water on the Borneo coast. The British took it in 1846 and kept it for 115 years, barring three years under Japanese occupation during World War II. Labuan was handed by the British to the state of Sabah in 1963 as part of decolonization, then ceded to Malaysia in 1984.

It is one of those oddities that has no visible economy within its fifty-square-mile oval territory, so it has created one. With a status of international offshore financial center, no-tax free port, flag of convenience and smuggling mecca, Labuan has attracted some extremely dubious clientele.

Martin realized he was being flown into the heart of the world's most ferocious ship-hijacking, cargo-stealing, crew-murdering industry. He needed to make contact with base to give a sign of life, and he needed to work out how. Fast.

There was a brief stopover at Kuching, first port of call on the island of Borneo, but nonalighting travelers did not leave the airplane.

Forty minutes later, it took off to the west, circled over the sea and turned northeast for Labuan. Far below the turning aircraft, the *Countess of Richmond*, in ballast, was steaming for Kota Kinabalu, to pick up her cargo of padauk and rosewood.

After takeoff, the stewardess distributed landing cards. Suleiman took them both and began to fill them in. Martin had to pretend he neither understood nor wrote written English, and could speak it only haltingly. He could hear it all round him. Besides, though he and Suleiman had changed into shirts and suits at Kuala Lumpur, he had no pen, and no excuse for asking for the loan of one. Ostensibly, they were a Bahraini engineer and an Omani accountant heading for Labuan on contract to the natural gas industry, and that was what Suleiman was filling in.

Martin muttered that he needed to go to the lavatory. He rose and went after where there were two. One was vacant, but he pretended both were in use, turned and went forward. There was a point. The Boeing 737 had a two-cabin service: economy and business. Dividing the two was a curtain, and Martin needed to get beyond it.

Standing outside the door of the business-class toilet, he beamed at the stewardess who had distributed the landing cards, uttered an apology and plucked from her top pocket a fresh landing card and her pen. The lavatory door clicked open, and he went in. There was only time to scrawl a brief message on the reverse of the landing card, fold it into his breast pocket, emerge and return the pen. Then he went back to his seat.

Suleiman may have been told the Afghan was trustworthy, but he stuck like a clam. Perhaps he wanted his charge to avoid making any mistakes through naïveté or inexperience; perhaps it was the years of training in the ways of Al Qaeda, but his watchfulness never faltered, even during prayers.

Labuan airport was a contrast to Karachi: small and trim. Martin still had no idea exactly where they were headed, but suspected the airport might be the last chance to get rid of his message, and hoped for a stroke of luck.

It was only a fleeting moment, and it came on the pavement outside the concourse. Suleiman's memorized instructions must have been extraordinarily precise. He had brought them halfway across the world, and was clearly a seasoned traveler. Martin could not know that the Gulf Arab had been with Al Qaeda for ten years, and had served the movement in Iraq and the Far East, notably Indonesia. Nor could he know what Suleiman's specialty was.

Suleiman was scouring the access road to the concourse building that served both arrivals and departures on one level, and he was looking for a taxi when one appeared heading toward them. It was occupied, but clearly about to deposit its cargo on the pavement.

There were two men, and Martin caught the English accent immediately. Both were big and muscular; both wore khaki shorts and flowered beach shirts. Both were damp in the blazing sun and moist, eighty-six-degree, premonsoon heat. One produced Malaysian currency to pay the driver, the other emptied the trunk of their luggage. They were scuba divers' kit bags. Both had been diving the offshore reefs on behalf of the British magazine *Sport Diver*.

The man by the trunk could not handle all four bags, one each for clothes, one each for diving tackle. Before Suleiman could utter a word, Martin helped the diver by hefting one of the kit bags from the pavement to the curb. As he did so, the folded landing card went into one of the side pockets, of which all kit bags have an array.

"Thanks, mate," said the diver, and the pair of them headed for departure check-in to find their flight to Kuala Lumpur, with a connector to London.

Suleiman's instructions to the Malay driver were in English: a shipping agency in the heart of the docks. Here, at last, the travelers met someone waiting to receive them. Like the newcomers, he excited no interest by the wearing of ostentatious clothing or facial hair. Like them, he was *takfir*. He introduced himself as Mr. Lampong, and took them to a fifty-foot cabin cruiser, tricked out for game fishing, by the harbor wall. Within minutes, they were out of the harbor.

The cruiser steadied her speed at ten knots and turned northeast for Kudat, the access to the Sulu Sea and the terrorist hideout in Zamboanga Province in the Philippines.

It had been a grueling journey, with only catnaps on the airplanes. The rocking of the sea was seductive, the breeze after the sauna heat of Labuan refreshing. Both passengers fell asleep. The helmsman was from the Abu Sayyaf terror group; he knew his way—he was going home. The sun dropped, and the tropical darkness was not long behind. The cruiser motored on through the night, past the lights of Kudat, through the Balabac Strait and over the invisible border into Filipino waters.

Mr. Wei had finished his commission before schedule and was already heading home to his native China. For him, it could not have come too quickly. But at least he was on a Chinese vessel, eating good Chinese food rather than the rubbish the sea dacoits served in their camp up the creek.

What he had left behind he neither knew nor cared. Unlike the Abu Sayyaf killers or the two or three Indonesian fanatics who prayed on their knees, foreheads to the mat, five times a day, Wei Wing Li was a member of a Snakehead triad and prayed to nothing.

In fact, the results of his work were a to-the-rivet replica of the *Countess of Richmond,* fashioned from a ship of similar size, tonnage and dimensions. He never knew what the original ship had been called, nor what the new one would be. All that concerned him was the bulbous roll of high-denomination bills drawn from a Labuan bank against a line of credit arranged by the late

Mr. Tewfik al-Qur, formerly of Cairo, Peshawar and the morgue.

Unlike Mr. Wei, Captain McKendrick prayed. Not as often, he knew, as he ought to, but he had been raised a good Liverpool Irish Catholic; there was a figurine of the Blessed Virgin on the bridge just forward of the wheel, and a crucifix on the wall of his cabin. Before sailing, he always prayed for a good voyage, and on returning thanked his Lord for a safe return.

He did not need to pray as the Sabah pilot eased the *Countess* past the shoals and into her assigned berth by the quay at Kota Kinabalu, formerly the colonial port of Jesselton, where British traders, in the days before refrigeration and if they had acquired canned butter in the monthly drop-off, had to pour it onto the bread from a small jug.

Captain McKendrick ran his bandanna round his wet neck once again, and thanked the pilot. At last, he could close up all the doors and portholes and take relief in the air-conditioning. That, he reckoned, and a cold beer would do him nicely. The water ballast would be evacuated in the morning, and he could see his log cargo under the lights of the dock. With a good loading crew, he could be back at sea the evening of the next day.

The two young divers, having changed planes at Kuala Lumpur, were on a British Airways jet for London, and not being a dry airline the divers had consumed enough beer to send them into a deep sleep. The flight might be twelve hours, but they would be gaining seven on the time zones and touching down at Heathrow at dawn. The hard-shell suitcases were in the hold, but the dive bags were above their heads as they slept.

They contained fins, masks, wet suits, regulators and buoyancy-control jackets, with only the diving knives in the suitcases in the hold. One of the dive bags also contained an as-yet-undiscovered Malaysian landing card.

In a creek off the Zamboanga peninsula, working by floodlights from a platform hung over the stern, a skilled painter was affixing the last *D* to the name of the moored ship. From her mast fluttered a limp Red Ensign. On either side of her bow and round her stern was the name *Countess of Richmond*, and, on the stern only, the city *Liverpool* beneath the name. As the painter descended and the lights flickered out, the transformation was complete.

At dawn, a cruiser disguised as a game fisherman motored slowly up the creek. It brought the last two members of the new crew of the former *Java Star*, the ones who would take the ship on her—and their—last voyage.

The loading of the *Countess of Richmond* began at dawn, when the air was still cool and agreeable. Within three hours, it would return to its habitual sauna heat. The dockside cranes were not exactly ultramodern, but the stevedores knew their business, and chained cargo of rare timber swung on board and were stowed in the hold below by the crew that toiled and sweated down there.

In the heat of the midday, even the local Borneans had

to stop, and for four hours the old logging port slumbered in whatever shade it could find. The spring monsoon was only a month away, and already the humidity, never much less than ninety percent, was edging toward a hundred.

Captain McKendrick would have been happier at sea, but loading and the replacement of the deck covers was achieved at sundown, and the pilot would come aboard only in the morning to guide the freighter back to the open sea. It meant another night in the hothouse, so McKendrick sighed, and again found refuge in the air-conditioning belowdecks.

The local agent came bustling aboard with the pilot at six in the morning, and the last paperwork was signed. Then the *Countess* eased away into the South China Sea.

Like the *Java Star* before her, she turned northeast to round the tip of Borneo, then south through the Sulu Archipelago for Java, where the skipper believed six sea containers full of Eastern silks awaited him at Surabaya. He was not to know that there were not, nor ever had been, any silks at Surabaya.

The cruiser deposited its cargo of three at a ramshackle jetty halfway up the creek. Mr. Lampong led the way to a longhouse on stilts above the water, which served as a sleeping area and mess hall for the men who would depart on the mission that Martin knew as Stingray and Lampong as al-Isra. Others in the longhouse would be staying behind. It was their labors that had prepared the hijacked *Java Star* for sea.

These were a mix of Indonesians from Jemaat Islamiyah, the group who had planted the Bali bombs and others up the island chain, and Filipinos from Abu Sayyaf. The languages varied from local Tagalog to Javanese dialect, with an occasional muttered aside in Arabic from those farther west. One by one, Martin was able to identify the crew and the special task of each of them.

The engineer, navigator and radio operator were all Indonesians. Suleiman revealed that his expertise was photography. Whatever was going to happen, his job— before dying a martyr—would be to photograph the climax on a digital radio camera and transmit, via a laptop computer and sat phone, the entire data stream for transmission on the Al Jazeera TV network.

There was a teenager who looked Pakistani, yet Lampong addressed him in English. When he replied, the boy revealed he could only have been British born and raised but of Pakistani parentage. His accent was broad English North Country; Martin put it as coming from the Leeds/Bradford area. Martin could not work out what he was for, except possibly a cook.

That left three: Martin himself clearly granted his presence as the personal gift of Osama bin Laden; a genuine chemical engineer and presumably explosives expert; and the mission commander. But he was not present. They would all meet him later.

In the midmorning, the local commander, Lampong, took a call on his satellite phone. It was brief and guarded, but enough. The *Countess of Richmond* had left Kota Kinabalu and was at sea. She should be coming be-

tween Tawitawi and Jolo islands round sundown. The
speedboat crews that would intercept her still had
four hours before they needed to leave. Suleiman and
Martin had changed from their Western suits into
trousers, local flowered shirts and sandals, which were
provided. They were allowed down the steps into the
shallow water of the creek to wash before prayers and a
dinner of rice and fish.

All Martin could do was watch, understanding very little, and wait.

The two divers were lucky. Most of their fellow passengers were from Malaysia, and were diverted to the non-
UK passport channel, leaving the few British easy access
at immigration control. Being among the first down to
the luggage carousel, they could grab their valises and
head for the nothing-to-declare customs hall.

It might have been the shaven skulls, the stubble on
the chins or the brawny arms emerging from short-
sleeved flowered shirts on a bitter British March morning, but one of the customs officers beckoned them to
the examination bench.

"May I see your passports, please?"

It was a formality. They were in order.

"And where have you just arrived from?"

"Malaysia."

"Purpose of visit?"

One of the young men pointed at his dive bag. His ex-
pression indicated it was a pretty daft question, given
that the bags bore the logo of a famous scuba equipment

company. It is, however, a mistake to mock a customs officer. His face remained impassive, but he had in a long career intercepted quantities of exotic smoking or injecting material coming in from the Far East. He gestured to one of the dive bags.

There was nothing inside but the usual scuba gear. As he was zipping the bag back up, he ran his fingers into the side pockets. From one, he withdrew a folded card, looked at it and read it. "Where did you get this, sir?"

The diver was genuinely puzzled. "I don't know. I've never seen it before."

A few yards away, another customs man caught the rising tension, indicated by the exemplary courtesy, and moved closer.

"Would you remain here, please?" said the first officer, and walked through a door behind him. Those ample mirrors in customs halls are not for the vain to rearrange their makeup. They have one-way vision, and behind them are the duty shift of internal security—in the case of Britain, MI5.

Within minutes, both divers, with their luggage, were in separate interview rooms. The customs men went through the luggage, fin by fin, mask by mask and shirt by shirt. There was nothing illegal.

The man in plain clothes studied the now-unfolded card.

"It must have been put there by someone, but not by me," protested the diver.

By now, it was nine-thirty. Steve Hill was at his desk in

Vauxhall Cross when his private and very unlisted phone rang.

"To whom am I speaking?" asked a voice. Hill bristled.

"Perhaps I should ask the same question. I think you may have a wrong number," he replied.

The MI5 officer had read the text of the message stuffed into the diver's bag. He tended to believe the man's explanation. In which case . . .

"I am speaking from Heathrow, Terminal 3. The internal security office. We have intercepted a passenger from the Far East. Stuffed into his dive bag was a short handwritten message. Does 'Crowbar' mean anything to you?"

To Steve Hill, it was like a punch in the stomach. This was no wrong number; this was no crossed line. He identified himself by service and rank, asked that both men be detained and that he was on his way. Within five minutes, his car swept out of the underground garage, crossed Vauxhall Bridge and turned down Cromwell Road to Heathrow.

It was bad luck on the divers to have lost their whole morning, but after an hour's interrogation Steve Hill was sure they were just innocent dupes. He secured for them a full with-trimmings breakfast from the staff canteen, and asked them to rack their brains for a clue as to who had stuffed the folded note in the side pocket.

They went over everyone they had met since packing the bags. Finally one said, "Mark, do you remember that Arab-looking fella who helped you unload at the airport?"

"What Arab-looking fellow?" asked Hill.

They described the man as best they could. Black hair, black beard. Neatly trimmed. Dark eyes, olive skin. About forty-five, fit-looking. Dark suit. Hill had had the descriptions from the barber and the sailor of Ras al-Khaimah. It was Crowbar. He thanked them sincerely, and asked that they be given a chauffeured ride back to their Essex home.

When he called Gordon Phillips at Edzell and Marek Gumienny over breakfast in Washington, he could reveal the scrawl in his hand. It said simply: "If you love your country, get home and ring XXX XXXXXX. Just tell them Crowbar says it will be some kind of ship."

"Pull out all the stops," he told Edzell. "Just scour the world for a missing ship."

As with Captain Herrmann of the *Java Star*, Liam McKendrick had chosen to bring his vessel round the various headlands himself and hand over after clearing the strait between the islands of Tawitawi and Jolo. Ahead was the great expanse of the Celebes Sea, and the course directly south for Makassar Strait.

He had a crew of six: five Indians from Kerala, all Christians, loyal and efficient; and his first officer, a Gibraltarian. He had handed over the helm and gone below when the speedboats swept up from astern. As with the *Java Star*, the crew had no chance. Ten dacoits were over the rails in seconds and running for the bridge.

Mr. Lampong, in charge of the hijack, came at a more leisurely pace.

This time, there was no need for ceremony or threats of violence unless instructions were disobeyed. The only task the *Countess of Richmond* had to perform was to disappear, with her crew, and forever. Her valuable cargo, what had lured her to these waters in the first place, would be a total write-off, which was a pity but could not be helped.

The crew were simply marched to the taffrail and machine-gunned. Their bodies, jerking in protest at the unfairness of death, went straight over the rail. There was not even any need for weights or ballast to send them to the bottom. Lampong knew his sharks.

Liam McKendrick was the last to go, roaring his rage at the killers, calling Lampong a heathen pig. The Muslim fanatic did not like being called a pig, and made sure the Liverpudlian mariner was riddled but still alive when he hit the sea.

The Abu Sayyaf pirates had sunk enough ships to know where the sea cocks were. As the keelson began to flood below the cargo, the raiders left the *Countess* and bobbed on the water a few cables away until she reared on her stern, prow in the air, and slid backward, tumbling slowly to the bottom of the Celebes Sea. When she was gone, the killers turned and raced for home.

For the party in the longhouse of the Filipino creek, it was another brief call on a sat phone from Lampong out at sea that triggered the hour of departure. They filed down to the cruiser moored at the foot of the steps. As they went, Martin realized that the ones being left behind were not showing any sense of relief but only deep envy.

In a career in Special Forces, he had never actually met a suicide bomber before the act. Now he was surrounded by them, had become one of them.

At Forbes Castle, he had read copiously about the state of mind: the total conviction that the deed being done is for a truly holy cause, that it is automatically blessed by Allah Himself, that a guaranteed and immediate passage to paradise is ensured and that this sacrifice vastly outweighs any residual love of life.

He had also come to realize the level and depth of hatred that must be imbued in the *shahid* alongside the love of Allah. One half alone will not work. The hatred must be like a corrosive acid inside the soul, and he was surrounded by it.

He had seen it in the faces of the dacoits of Abu Sayyaf who relished every chance to kill a Westerner; he had watched it in the hearts of the Arabs as they prayed for a chance to kill as many Christians, Jews and secular or insufficient Muslims as possible in the act of death; most of all, he had seen the hatred in the eyes of al-Khattab and Lampong, precisely because they sullied themselves in order to pass unnoticed among the enemy.

As they chugged slowly farther up the creek, the jungle closing in on every side and beginning to shut out the sky above them, he studied his companions. They all shared the hate and the fanaticism. They all counted themselves more blessed than any other true believers on earth.

Martin was convinced that the men around him had no more clue than he exactly what the sacrifice would entail: where they would be going, to target what and with what weapon.

They only knew, because they had offered themselves to die and been accepted and carefully selected, that they were going to strike the Great Satan in a manner that would be spoken of for a hundred years. They, like the prophet so long ago, were going on a great journey to heaven itself—the journey called al-Isra.

Up ahead, the creek split. The chugging cruiser took the wider branch, and round a corner a moored vessel came into sight. She was facing downstream, ready to depart for the open sea. Her cargo was apparently stored in the six sea containers that occupied her foredeck. And she was called the *Countess of Richmond*.

For a moment, Martin toyed with the thought of escaping into the surrounding jungle. He had had weeks of jungle training in Belize, the SAS's tropical training school. But he realized as soon as the thought crossed his mind that it was hopeless. He would not make a mile without compass or machete, and the hunting party would have him within the hour. Then would come days of unspeakable agony, as the details of his mission were wrenched out of him. There was no point. He would have to wait for a better opportunity, if one ever came.

One by one, they climbed the ladder to the deck of the freighter: the engineer, navigator and radioman, all Indonesians; the chemist and photographer, both Arabs; the Pakistani from the UK with the flat northern accent, should anyone insist on speaking to the *Countess* by radio; and the Afghan, who could be taught to hold the wheel and steer a course. In all his training at Forbes, in all the hours of studying faces of known suspects, he had never seen any of them. When he reached the deck, the man who would command them all on their mission to eternal glory was there to meet them. Him, the ex-SAS man, he did recognize. From the rogues' gallery he had been shown at Castle Forbes, he knew he was staring at Yusef Ibrahim, deputy and right-hand man of al-Zarqawi, the butcher of Baghdad.

The face had been one of the "first division" in the gallery he had been shown at Castle Forbes. The man was short and stocky, as expected, and the stunted left arm hung by his side. He had fought in Afghanistan against the Soviets, and his left arm had stopped several shards of shrapnel during an air attack. Rather than accept a clean amputation, he preferred to let it hang, useless.

There had been rumors that he had died there. Not true. He had been patched up in the caves, then smuggled into Pakistan for more advanced surgery. After the Soviet evacuation, he had disappeared.

The man with the withered left arm reappeared after the 2003 coalition invasion of Iraq, having spent the missing time as chief of security in one of the AQ camps under Taliban rule.

For Mike Martin, there was a heart-stopping moment in case the man recognized Izmat Khan from those

Afghan days and wished to discuss it. But the mission commander just stared at him with featureless black-pebble eyes.

For twenty years, this man had killed and killed, and he loved it. In Iraq, as aide to Musab al-Zarqawi, he had hacked off heads on camera and loved it. He loved to hear them plead and scream. Martin gazed into the blank, manic eyes and gave the habitual greeting. Peace be unto you, Yusef Ibrahim, Butcher of Karbala.

CHAPTER 14

THE FORMER *Java Star* emerged from the hidden Filipino creek twelve hours after the destruction of the *Countess of Richmond*. She cleared the Moro Gulf, and headed into the Celebes Sea, heading south by southwest, to join the sea track the *Countess* would have taken though the Makassar Strait.

The Indonesian helmsman had the wheel, but beside him stood the British/Pakistani teenager and the Afghan, to whom he gave instruction on the keeping of a true course at sea.

Though neither of his pupils could be aware of it, counterterrorist agencies within the world of the merchant marine had known for years, and been perplexed by the times a ship in these waters had been hijacked, steered round in circles for several hours with her crew in the chain locker, then abandoned.

The reason was simply that just as the hijackers of 9/11 had achieved their practice in U.S. flying schools, the marine hijackers of the Far East have been practicing the handling of a large ship at sea. The Indonesian at the helm of the new *Countess* was one of these.

The engineer down below really had been a marine engineer before the ship he worked on had been hijacked by Abu Sayyaf. Rather than die, he had agreed to join the terrorists and become one of them.

The third Indonesian had learned all about ship-to-shore radio procedures while working in the harbormaster's office of a North Borneo trading port until he was radicalized in Islam and accepted into the ranks of Jemaat Islamiyah, later helping to plant the Bali disco bombs.

These were the only three of eight who needed technical knowledge of ships. The Arab chemist would eventually be in charge of cargo detonation; the man from the UAE, Suleiman, would take the data stream images that would rock the world; the Pakistani youth would, if need be, emulate the North Country voice of Captain McKendrick; and the Afghan would "spell" the helmsman at the wheel through the days of cruising that lay ahead.

By the end of March, spring had not even attempted to touch the Cascade range. It was still bitterly cold, and snow lay thick in the forest beyond the walls of the Cabin.

Inside, it was snug and warm. The enemy, despite TV

day and night, movies on DVD, music and board games, was boredom. As with lighthouse keepers, the men had not much to do, and the six-month term was a great test of the capacity of internal solitude and self-sufficiency.

Nevertheless, the guard detail could don skis or snowshoes and slog through the forest to keep fit and to get a break from the bunkhouse, eatery and game room. For the prisoner, immune to fraternization, the strain was that much greater.

Izmat Khan had listened to the president of the military court at Guantánamo pronounce him free to go, and was convinced Pul-i-Charki jail would not have held him for more than a year. When he was brought to this lonely wilderness—so far as he knew, forever—it was hard to hide the screaming rage inside.

So he donned the kapok-lined jacket they had issued him, let himself outside and paced up and down the walled enclosure. Ten paces long, five paces wide. He could do it with eyes shut and never bump into the concrete. The only variety was occasionally in the sky above.

Mostly, it was of heavy, leaden gray cloud, from which the snow drifted down. But earlier, in that period when the Christians decorated trees and sang songs, the skies had been freezing cold but blue.

Then he had seen eagles and ravens wheeling overhead. Smaller birds had fluttered to the top of the wall and looked down at him, perhaps wondering why he could not come and join them in freedom. But what he liked most to watch were the airplanes.

Some he knew were warplanes, though he had heard

of neither the Cascade range, where he was, nor Mc-Chord Air Force Base, fifty miles to the west. But he had seen American combat aircraft turning into their bombing runs over northern Afghanistan and he knew these were the same.

And there were the airliners. They were in different liveries, with varying designs on their tails, but he knew enough to know these were not national but company insignias. Except for the maple leaf. Some always had that leaf on the tail; they were always climbing, and they always came from the north.

North was easy to work out; to the west, he could see the sun set, and he prayed the opposite way, toward Mecca, far to the east. He suspected he was in the USA because the voices of his guards were clearly American. So why did airliners with different national insignias come from the north? It could only be because there was another land up there somewhere, a land where people prayed to a red leaf on a white ground. So he paced up and down, up and down, and wondered about the land of the red leaf. In fact, he was watching the Air Canada flights out of Vancouver.

In a sleazy dockside bar in Port of Spain, Trinidad, two merchant seamen were attacked by a local gang and left dead. Both had been skillfully knifed.

By the time the Trinidadian police arrived, the witnesses had acquired amnesia, and could recall only that there had been five attackers who had provoked the bar fight and that they were islanders. The police would never get further than that, and no arrests were ever made.

In fact, the killers were local lowlife, and they had nothing to do with Islamist terrorism. But the man who had paid them was a senior terrorist in the Jamaat al-Muslimeen, the principal Trinidadian group on the side of Al Qaeda.

Though still low profile across the Western media, JaM has been growing steadily for years, as have other groups right across the Caribbean basin. In an area known for its down-home Christian worship, Islam has been quietly growing with wholesale immigration from the Middle East, Central Asia and the Indian Subcontinent.

The money paid out by JaM for the killings came from a line of credit set up by the late Mr. Tewfik al-Qur, and the specific orders had come from an emissary of Dr. al-Khattab, who was still on the island.

No attempt had been made to steal the wallets of the dead men, so the Port of Spain police could quickly identify them as Venezuelan citizens and deck crew from a Venezuelan ship then in port.

Her master, Captain Pablo Montalban, was shocked and saddened to be informed of the loss of his crewmen, but he could not wait for too long in the harbor.

The details of shipping the bodies back to Caracas fell to the Venezuelan Embassy while Captain Montalban contacted his local agent for replacement sailors. The man asked around and got lucky. He came up with two polite and eager young Indians from Kerala who had worked their passage across the world, and who, even if they lacked naturalization papers, had perfectly good seamen's tickets.

They were taken on, joining the other four seamen who made up the crew, and the *Doña María* sailed only a day late.

Captain Montalban knew vaguely that most of India is Hindu, but he had no idea that there are also a hundred and fifty million Muslims. He was not aware that the radicalization of Indian Muslims has been just as vigorous as in Pakistan, or that Kerala, once the hotbed of communism, has been particularly receptive territory for Islamist extremism.

His two new crewmen had indeed worked their way from India as deckhands, but on orders and to gain experience. And finally the Catholic Venezuelan had no idea that though neither had suicide in mind, they were working with, and for, Jamaat al-Muslimeen. The two unfortunates in the bar had been killed precisely to put the two Indian matelots on his ship.

Marek Gumienny chose to fly the Atlantic when he heard the report from the Far East. But he brought with him a specialist in a different discipline.

"Arab experts have served their purpose, Steve," he told Hill before he flew. "Now we need people who know the world's merchant marine."

The man he brought was from America's Bureau of Customs and Border Protection, merchant marine division. Steve Hill came north from London accompanied by another of his colleagues; he came from the SIS's anti-terrorism desk, maritime section.

At Edzell, the two younger men met: Chuck Hemingway from New York and Sam Seymour from London. Both had heard of the other from the reading of papers and briefings within the West's antiterror community. They were told they had twelve hours to go into a huddle and come up with an evaluation of the threat and a game plan for coping with it. When they addressed Gumienny, Hill, Phillips and McDonald, Chuck Hemingway went first.

"This is not just a hunt; this is a search for a needle in a haystack. A hunt has a known target. All we have is something that floats. Maybe. Let me lay it on the line.

"There are forty-six thousand merchant ships plying their trade on the world's oceans as of now. Half of them are flying flags of convenience, which can be switched almost at the whim of the captain.

"Six-sevenths of the world's surface is covered by ocean, an area so vast that literally thousands of ships are out of sight of land or any other vessel at any given time.

"Eighty percent of the world's trade is still carried out by sea, and that means just under six billion tons. And there are four thousand viable merchant ports around the world.

"Finally, you want to find a vessel, but you don't know her type, size, tonnage, contours, age, ownership, stern flag, captain or name. To have a hope of tracing this vessel—we call them 'ghost ships'—we will need more than that, or a large dose of luck. Can you offer us either?"

There was a depressed silence.

"That's damn downbeat," said Marek Gumienny. "Sam, can you suggest a ray of hope?"

"Chuck and I agree there might be a way if we identify the kind of target the terrorists could be aiming for, then check out any ship heading toward that target and demand a gunpoint inspection of ship and cargo," said Seymour.

"We're all listening," said Hill. "What kind of target could they be most likely heading toward?"

"People in our line of business have been worried for years, and filing reports for years. The oceans are a terrorists' playground. The fact that Al Qaeda chose for its first huge spectacular an attack from the air was actually illogical. They only hoped to take out four floors of the World Trade Center towers, and even then they were incredibly lucky. All that time, the sea has been beckoning to them."

"Security of ports and harbors has been massively tightened," snapped Marek Gumienny. "I know, I have seen the budgets."

"With respect, sir, not enough. We know ship hijacking in the waters around Indonesia—that is, in all directions—has been steadily increasing since the turn of the millennium. Some has simply been to make money to fund terrorism's coffers. Other events at sea defy logic."

"Such as?"

"There have been ten cases of sea dacoits stealing tugs. Some have never been recovered. They have no value as resales because they are pretty noticeable and hard to disguise. What are they for? We think they could be used to tow a captured supertanker right into a busy international port like Singapore."

"And blow her up?" asked Hill.

"No need. Just sink her with her cargo hatches open. The port would be closed for a decade."

"Okay," said Marek Gumienny, "so . . . possible target number one. Take over a supertanker and use her to close down a commercial port. This is a spectacular? Sounds pretty mundane, except for the port in question . . . No casualties."

"It gets worse," said Chuck Hemingway. "There are other things that can be destroyed with a blocking ship, with vast damage to the world's economy. In his October 2004 video, bin Laden himself said he was switching to 'economic damage.'

"Nobody out there in the shopping malls or the gas stations realizes how the whole of world trade is now geared to just-in-time delivery. No one wants to store or stockpile anymore. The T-shirt made in China that sold in Dallas on Monday probably arrived at the docks the previous Friday. Same with gasoline.

"What about the Panama Canal? Or the Suez? Close them down and the whole global economy spins into chaos. You are talking damage in the hundreds of billions of dollars. There are ten other straits so narrow and so vital that sinking a really big freighter or tanker broadside would close them."

"All right," said Marek Gumienny. "Look, I have a president and the other five principals to report to. You, Steve, have a prime minister. We cannot just sit on this message from Crowbar. Nor can we simply burst into tears. We have to propose concrete measures. They will want to be active, to be seen to be doing something. So list the likelihoods, and suggest some countermeasures. Dammit, we are not without resources of self-defense."

Chuck Hemingway produced a paper that he and Seymour had worked on earlier.

"Okay, sir, we feel probability one is likely to be the taking over of a very large vessel—tanker, freighter, ore carrier—and her sinking in a narrow but vital shipping bottleneck. Measures to counter? Identify all such bottlenecks and post warships at either end. All entering vessels to be boarded by Marines."

"Christ," said Steve Hill, "that will cause chaos. It will be claimed we are acting as pirates. What about the owners of the host waters? Don't they have a say?"

"If the terrorists succeed, both the other ships and the coastal countries will be ruined. There need be no delays— the Marines can board without the freighter slowing down. And, frankly, the terrorists on board any ghost ship cannot permit boarding. They have to fire back, expose themselves and scuttle prematurely. I think the shipowners will see it our way."

"Probability two?" queried Steve Hill.

"Running the ghost ship, crammed with explosives, into a major facility, like an island of oil pipes or an oil rig, and blowing it to pieces. It causes astronomical eco-damage and economic ruin for years. Saddam Hussein did it to Kuwait, torching all their oil wells as the coalition moved in, so that he would leave them living off scorched earth. Countermeasure, same again. Identify and intercept every vessel even approaching the facility. Secure positive identification outside the ten-mile cordon sanitaire."

"We don't have enough warships," protested Steve Hill. "Every island, every seashore oil refiner, every offshore rig?"

"That is why the national owners have to share the cost burden. And it need not be a warship. If any interceptor vessel is fired on, the ghost ship is exposed, and may be sunk from the air, sir."

Marek Gumienny ran his hand over his forehead.

"Anything else?"

"There is a possible third," said Seymour. "The use of explosives to cause a terrible massacre of humans. In that case, the target would likely be a tourist facility crammed with holidaymakers by the seaside. It's a horrible prospect, reminiscent of the destruction of Halifax, Nova Scotia, in 1917, when an ammunition ship blew up in the heart of the inner harbor. It wiped the city off the map. It still rates as the biggest nonnuclear explosion in history."

"I have to report, Steve, and I am not going to enjoy it," he said as they shook hands on the tarmac. "By the way, if countermeasures are taken—and they will have to be—there is no way we can keep the media out of this. We can devise the best cover story we can to divert the bad guys' attention away from Colonel Martin. But, as you know, much as I take my hat off to him, you have to accept the reality. Chances are, he's history."

*   *   *

Major Larry Duval glanced out of flight dispersal into the Arizona sunshine and marveled, as he always did, at the sight of the F-15 Strike Eagle that awaited him. He had flown the F-15E version for ten years, and reckoned it had to be the love of his life.

His career postings included the F-111 Aardvark and the F-4G Wild Weasel, and they were both serious pieces of machinery that the U.S. Air Force granted him the privilege to fly, but the Eagle was for him, after twenty years as a USAF flier, the ace of them all.

The fighter he would be flying that day from Luke Air Force Base right up to Washington State was still being worked on. It crouched silently amid the teeming swarm of men and women in coveralls who crawled all over its burly frame, immune to love or lust, hate or fear. Larry Duval envied his Eagle; for all its myriad complexities, it could not feel anything. It could never be afraid.

The airplane being readied for this morning's air test had been at Luke AFB for fundamental overhaul and ground-up servicing. After such a period in the workshops, the rules stated she had to be given a test flight.

So the Strike Eagle waited in the bright spring sunshine of an Arizona morning; sixty-three feet long, eighteen high and forty across, weighing in at forty thousand pounds bone-dry, and eighty-one thousand pounds maximum takeoff weight. Larry Duval turned as his weapons systems officer, Captain Nicky Johns, strolled in from his own equipment checks. In the Eagle, the WSO, or Wizzo, rides in tandem behind the pilot, surrounded by millions of dollars' worth of avionics. On the long flight to McChord AFB, he would test them all.

The open utility drove up to the windows, and the two aircrew were driven the half mile to the waiting fighter. They spent ten minutes on their preflight checks, even though the chances their ground crew had missed something were extremely slim.

Once on board, they strapped themselves in, gave one last nod to the ground crew, who clambered down, headed back and left them in peace.

Larry Duval started the two powerful F100 engines, the canopy hissed down into its seals and the Eagle began to roll. It turned in to the light breeze down the runway, paused, received clearance and crouched for one last testing of the brakes. Then thirty-foot flames leaped from its twin afterburners, and Major Duval unleashed its full power.

A mile down the runway, at 185 knots, the wheels left the tarmac, and the Eagle was airborne. Wheels up, flaps up, throttles back to pull the engines out of gas-drinking afterburn mode and into military power setting. Duval set a climb rate of five thousand feet per minute, and from behind him his Wizzo gave him a compass heading for destination. At thirty thousand feet, in a pure blue sky, the Eagle leveled out, and pointed her nose north-west toward Seattle. Below, the Rockies were clothed in snow, and would stay with them all the way.

In the British Foreign Office, the final details for the transfer of the British government and its advisers to the

April G8 were almost complete. The entire delegation would fly in a chartered airliner from Heathrow to JFK, New York, there to be formally met by the U.S. secretary of state.

The other six, non-American delegations would fly in from six different capitals to JFK.

All the delegations would remain "air side" at the airport, a mile away from the nearest protesters outside its perimeter. The president was simply not going to allow what he called "loony tunes" to scream insults at his guest or harass them in any way. Repeats of Seattle and Genoa were not to be entertained.

Transfer out of JFK would be by an air bridge of helicopters that would deposit their cargoes into a second totally sealed environment. From there, they would simply stroll into the venue of the five-day conference and be sealed in luxury and privacy. It was simple and flawless.

"No one had ever thought of it before, but when you think about it it's brilliant," said one of the British diplomats. "Perhaps we should do it ourselves one day."

"The even better news," muttered an older and more experienced colleague, "is that after Gleneagles it won't be our turn for years. Let the others cope with the security headaches for a few years."

Marek Gumienny was not long getting back to Steve Hill. He had been escorted by the director of his own agency to the White House, and had explained to the six principals the deductions that had been drawn following

the receipt of a bizarre message from the unheard-of island of Labuan.

"They said much the same as before," Gumienny reported. "Whatever it is, wherever it is, find it and destroy it."

"The same with my government," said Steve Hill. "No
holds barred. Destroy on sight. And they want us to work
together on this."

"No problem. But, Steve, my people are convinced
the USA is likely to be the target, so our coastal protection takes precedence over everything else—Mideast,
Asia, Europe. We have top priority over all our assets—
satellites, warships, the lot. If we locate the ghost ship
anywhere away from our shores, okay, we'll divert assets
to destroy it."

The American director of national intelligence, John
Negroponte, authorized the CIA to inform their British
counterparts on a "for your eyes only" basis of the measures the States intended to take.

The defense strategy would be based on three stages:
aerial surveillance, identification of vessel and check it
out. Any unsatisfactory explanation, any unexplained diversion from course, would generate a physical intercept.
Any resistance would entail destruction at sea.

To establish a sea territory, a line was drawn to create a complete circle of three hundred miles' radius
round the island of Labuan. From the northern curve
of this circle, a line was drawn right across the Pacific
to Anchorage, on the south coast of Alaska. A second
line was drawn from the southern arc of the Indone-

sian circle east across the Pacific to the coast of Ecuador.

The enclosed area was most of the Pacific Ocean. It included the entire western seaboard of Canada and the USA and Mexico down to Ecuador, including the Panama Canal.

There was no need to announce it yet, the White House had decided, but it was intended to monitor every ship in that triangle steaming east to the American coast. Anything leaving the triangle or heading to Asia would be left alone. The rest would be identified and checked out.

Thanks to years of pressure by a few bodies often dubbed "cranky," there was one procedural ally. Major merchant marine shipping lines had agreed to file destination plans, as airliners file flight plans, as a matter of routine. Seventy percent of the vessels in the "check it out" zone would be on file, and the companies that owned them could contact their captains. Under the new rules, there was also an agreement that sea captains would always use specific words, known only to their owners, if they were secure. Failure to use the agreed-upon word could mean the captain was under duress.

It was seventy-two hours after the White House conference when the first KH-11 "Keyhole" satellite rolled onto its track in space and began to photograph the Indonesian circle. Its computers had been instructed to photograph, regardless of steaming direction, any merchant marine vessel within three hundred miles' radius of Labuan Island. Computers obey instructions, so it did. As the KH-11 began to photograph, the *Countess of Richmond,* heading due south through the Makassar Strait, was 310 miles south of Labuan. It was not photographed.

From London, the White House's obsession with an attack from the Pacific was only half the picture. The warnings from the Edzell conference had been submitted in the UK and the USA for further scrutiny, but the findings were broadly endorsed.

It took a long, personal call on the hotline between Downing Street and the White House to conclude a concordat on the two most vital narrows east of Malta. The agreement provided that the Royal Navy, in partnership with the Egyptians, would monitor the southern end of the Suez Canal to intercept all ships save the very smallest coming up from Asia.

The U.S. Navy's warships in the Persian Gulf, Arabian Sea and Indian Ocean would patrol the Straits of Hormuz. Here, the threat would only be from a huge vessel capable of sinking itself in the deepwater channel running down the center of the straits. The principal traffic here was of supertankers, entering empty from the south, coming back low in the water and full of crude after loading at any of the score of islands scattered off Iran, the UAE, Qatar, Bahrain, Saudi Arabia and Kuwait.

The good news for the Americans was that the companies owning such vessels are relatively few altogether, and ready to cooperate to prevent a disaster for all of them. Landing a party of U.S. Marines by Sea Stallion helicopter on the deck of a supertanker heading for the straits, but still three hundred miles short, and having a quick tour of the bridge, took very little time and did not slow the vessel at all.

As for threats number two and three, every government in Europe with a major seaport was warned of the possible existence of a ghost ship under the command of terrorists. It was up to Denmark to protect Copenhagen, Sweden to look after Stockholm and Göteborg, Germany to watch out for anything entering Hamburg or Kiel; France was warned to defend Brest and Marseille. British Navy airplanes out of Gibraltar started to patrol the narrows, the Pillars of Hercules, between the Rock and Morocco, to identify anything coming in from the Atlantic.

All the way over the Rockies, Major Duval had put the Eagle through its paces, and it had performed perfectly. Below him, the weather had changed.

The cloudless blue skies of Arizona betrayed first a few wisps of mare's tail cloud lines, which thickened as he left Nevada for Oregon. When he crossed the Columbia River into Washington, the cloud below him was solid from treetop height to twenty thousand feet, and moving down from the Canadian border to the north. At thirty thousand feet, he was still in clear blue sky, but the descent would involve a long haul through dense vapor. Two hundred miles out, he called McChord AFB and asked for a ground-controlled descent to landing.

McChord asked him to stay out to the east, turn inbound over Spokane and descend on instructions. The Eagle was in the left-hand turn toward McChord when what was about to become the USAF's most expensive wrench slipped out of where it had lain jammed between two hydraulic lines in the starboard engine. When the Eagle leveled out, the wrench fell into the blade of the turbofan.

The first result was a massive bang from somewhere deep in the guts of the starboard F100 as the compressor blades, sharp as cleavers and spinning close to the speed of sound, began to shear off. Each sheared blade jammed among the rest. In both cockpits, a blazing red light answered Nicky Johns's yelled "What the f—— was that?"

In front of him, Larry Duval was listening to something inside his head screaming, *Close it down.*

After years of flying, Duval's fingers were doing the job almost unbidden, flicking off one switch after another: fuel, electric circuits, hydraulic lines. But the starboard engine was blazing. The built-in fire extinguishers operated automatically but were too late. The starboard F100 was tearing itself to pieces in what is known as "catastrophic engine failure."

Behind Duval, the Wizzo was telling McChord: "Mayday, Mayday, Mayday. Starboard engine on fire . . ."

He was interrupted by another roar from behind him. Far from shutting down, fragments of the starboard engine had torn through the firewall and were attacking the port side. More red lights blazed. The second engine had caught fire also. With reduced fuel and one engine functioning, the Eagle with Duval piloting could have made it down. But with both engines dead, a modern fighter does not glide like fighters long ago; it plunges like a bullet.

Captain Johns would tell the inquiry later that his pilot's voice remained calm and level. He had switched the radio to TRANSMIT, so that the air traffic controller at McChord did not need to be informed; he was hearing it in real time.

"I have lost both engines," said the major. "Stand by to eject."

The Wizzo looked one last time at his instruments. Altitude: 24,000. Diving; dive steepening. Outside, the sun still shone, but the cloud bank was seething toward them. He glanced round over his shoulder. The Eagle was a torch, flaming from end to end. He heard the same calm voice up front: "Eject, eject."

Both men reached down for the handle beside their seats and pulled. That was all they needed to do. Modern ejection seats are so automated that even if the airman is unconscious, they will do everything for him.

Neither Larry Duval nor Nicky Johns actually saw their airplane die. With seconds to spare, their bodies were hurled upward through the shattering canopy and into the freezing stratosphere. The seat restrained their legs and arms so they would not flail and snap off. The seat protected their faces from the blast that could push their cheekbones through their skulls.

Both falling ejection seats stabilized with tiny drogues

and plunged toward the ground. In a second, they were lost in the cloud bank. Even when they were able to see through their visors, the two aircrew could only watch the wet, gray clouds rushing past them.

The seats sensed when they were near enough to the ground to release their charges. The restraining straps just flicked open, and the men, now separated by a mile from each other, fell out of their seats, which dropped into the landscape below.

The men's parachutes were also automatic. They, too, deployed, first with a small drogue to steady the falling men in the air, then with the main canopy. Each man felt the heaving jerk as a terminal velocity of 120 miles per hour slowed to around fourteen.

They began to feel the intense cold through their light nylon flight suits and G suits. They seemed to be in a weird, wet, gray limbo between heaven and hell until they crashed into the topmost branches of pine and spruce.

In the half darkness beneath the cloud bank, the major landed in a type of clearing, his fall cushioned by springy conifer branches lying flat on the ground. After several seconds dazed and winded, he released the main chute buckle at his midriff and stood up. Then he began to broadcast so the rescuers could get a fix on him.

Nicky Johns had also come down in trees, but not in a clearing; right in the thick of them. As he hit the branches, he was drenched in the snow that fell off them. He waited for the "hit," the ground, but it never came. Above him, in the freezing gloom, he could see that his parachute was caught in the trees. Below, he could make out the ground. Snow and pine needles, he thought, about fifteen feet down. He took a deep breath, hit the release buckle and fell.

With luck, he would have landed and stood up. In fact, he felt his left leg snap neatly at the shin as it slid between two stout branches under the snow. That told him that cold and shock would start to eat into his reserve without mercy. He, too, unhooked his transmitter and began to broadcast.

The Eagle had attempted to fly for a few seconds after its crew had ejected it. It turned its nose up, wallowed, tilted over, resumed its dive and, as it entered the cloud bank, simply blew up. The flames had reached the fuel tanks.

As the Eagle disintegrated, both its engines tore themselves from their housing and fell away. Twenty thousand feet below, each engine—five tons of blazing metal roaring down at five hundred miles per hour—hit the Cascades. One engine destroyed twenty trees. The other did more.

The CIA special ops officer who commanded the garrison at the Cabin took over two minutes to regain consciousness and pull himself off the floor of the chow room where he had been eating lunch. He was dazed and felt sick. He leaned against the wall of the log cabin amid the swirling dust and called out some names. He was answered with groans. Twenty minutes later, he had made his inventory. The two men playing pool in the game room were dead. Three others were injured. The lucky ones had been those outside on a hiking break. They had been a hundred yards away when the meteorite, as they thought, hit the Cabin. When they had confirmed that, of twelve CIA staffers, two were dead, three needed emergency hospitalization, the two hikers were fine and the other five badly shaken, they checked on the prisoner.

They would later be accused of being slow on the uptake, but the inquiry found in the end that they were justified in looking out for themselves first. A glance through the spy hole into the Afghan's room revealed there was too much light in there. When they burst in, the door from the living area to the walled exercise court was open. The room itself, being of reinforced concrete, had survived intact.

The wall of the compound was not so lucky. Concrete or not, the falling F100 jet engine had taken a five-foot chunk out of the wall before ricocheting into the garrison quarters. And the Afghan was gone.

CHAPTER 15

As THE GREAT AMERICAN sea trap closed around the Philippines, Borneo and eastern Indonesia, all the way across the Pacific to the U.S. coast, the *Countess of Richmond* slipped out of the Flores Sea, through the Lombok Strait between Bali and Lombok and into the Indian Ocean. Then she turned due west for Africa.

The distress call from the dying Eagle had been heard by at least three listeners. McChord AFB, of course, had it all on tape, because they had actually been talking to the crew. The Naval Air Station at Whidbey Island, north of McChord, also kept a listening watch on channel 16, and so did the U.S. Coast Guard unit up at Bellingham. Within seconds of the call, they were in contact, saying they were standing by to triangulate on the positions of the downed aircrew.

The days of pilots bobbing helplessly in a dinghy or lying in a forest waiting to be found are long gone. Modern aircrew have a life jacket with a state-of-the-art beacon, small but powerful, and a transmitter that permits voice communication.

The beacons were picked up at once, and the three listening posts had the men located within a few yards. Major Duval was down in the heart of the state park, and Captain Johns had fallen in a logging forest. Both were still closed for access due to the winter.

The cloud cover right on top of the trees would prevent extraction by helicopter, the fastest and the favored way. The cloud bank would force an old-fashioned rescue. Off-road vehicles or half-track vehicles would take the rescue parties in as near as possible; from there to the downed airman, it would be muscle and sweat all the way.

The enemy now was hypothermia, and in the case of Johns, with his broken leg, trauma. The sheriff of Whatcom County radioed to say he had deputies ready to move, and they would rendezvous in the small town of Glacier on the edge of the forest within thirty minutes. They were nearest to the Wizzo, Nicky Johns, with his broken leg. A number of the loggers lived around Glacier, and knew every logging road through the forest. The sheriff was given Johns's exact position within a few yards and set off.

To keep up the injured man's morale, McChord patched the sheriff right through to the communicator on the Wizzo's life jacket so that the sheriff could encourage the airman as they came nearer and nearer.

The Washington State Parks Service opted for Major Duval. They had experience to spare; every year, they had to pull out the occasional camper who slipped and fell. They knew every road through the park, and, where the roads ran out, every trail. They went in with snowmobiles and quad bikes. Since their man was not injured, a full stretcher would not be necessary.

But as the minutes ticked by, the body temperature of the airmen started slowly to drop, and faster with Johns, who could not move. The race was on to bring the two men gloves, boots, Space blankets and piping-hot soup before the cold beat them to it.

Nobody told the rescue parties—because nobody knew—that there was another man out in the wilderness that day, and he was very dangerous indeed.

The saving grace for the CIA team at the shattered Cabin was that their communications had survived the hit. The commander only had one number to call, but it was a good one. It went on a secure line to the desk of DDO Marek Gumienny at Langley. Three time zones east, just after four p.m., he took the call.

As he listened, he went very quiet. He did not rant or rave, even though he was being told of a major Company disaster. Before his junior colleague in the Cascade wilderness had finished, he was analyzing the catastrophe. In freezing temperatures, the two corpses might have to wait awhile. The three injured needed urgent CASE-VAC. And the fugitive had to be hunted down.

"Can a helo get in there to reach you?" he asked.

"No, sir, we have cloud right to the treetops, and threatening more snow."

"What is your nearest town with a track leading to it?"

"It's called Mazama. It's outside the wilderness, but there is a fair-weather track from the town to Hart's Pass. That's a mile away. No track from there to here."

"You are a cover research facility, understand? You have had a major accident. You need urgent help. Raise the sheriff at Mazama, and get him to come in there for you with anything he has got. Half-tracks, snowmobiles, off-roads—as near as possible. Skis, snowshoes and sleds for the last mile. Get those men to the hospital. Meanwhile, can you keep warm?"

"Yes, sir. Two rooms are shattered, but we have three sealed off. The central heating is down, but we are piling logs on the fire."

"Right. When the rescue party reaches you, lock everything down, smash all covert comms equipment, bring all codes with you, and come out with the injured."

"Sir?"

"Yes."

"What about the Afghan?"

"Leave him to me."

Marek Gumienny thought of the original letter John Negroponte had given him at the start of Operation Crowbar. Powers plenipotentiary. No limits. Time the Army earned its tax dollars. He rang the Pentagon.

Thanks to years in the Company, and the new spirit of information sharing, he had close contacts with the

Defense Intelligence Agency, and they, in turn, were best buddies with Special Forces. Twenty minutes later, he learned he might have had his first break of a very bad day.

No more than four miles from McChord Air Force Base is the Army's Fort Lewis. Though a huge Army camp, there is a corner off-limits to nonauthorized personnel, and this is the home of the First Special Forces Group, known to its few friends as Operational Detachment (OD) Alpha 143. The terminal 3 means a mountain company, or A team. Its ops commander was Senior Captain Michael Linnett.

When the unit adjutant took the call from the Pentagon, he could not be very helpful, even though he was speaking to a two-star general.

"Right now, sir, they are not on base. They are involved in a tactical exercise on the slopes of Mount Rainier."

The Washington-based general didn't know much about this mountain way down southeast of Tacoma in Pierce County.

"Can you get them back to base by helicopter, Lieutenant?"

"Yessir, I believe so. The cloud base is just high enough."

"Can you airlift them to a place called Mazama, close to Hart's Pass, on the edge of the wilderness?"

"I'll have to check that, sir." He would be back on the line in three minutes. The general held on.

"No, sir. The cloud up there is right on the treetops,

and snow pending. To get up there means going by truck."

"Well, get them there, by the fastest possible route. You say they are on maneuver?"

"Yessir."

"Do they have with them all they need to operate in the Pasayten Wilderness?"

"Everything for subzero rough-terrain operating, General."

"Live ammunition?"

"Yessir. This was for a simulated terrorist hunt in Mount Rainier National Park."

"Well, it ain't 'simulated' anymore, Lieutenant. Get the whole unit to Mazama sheriff's office. Check with a CIA spook called Olsen. Stay in contact with Alpha at all times, and report to me on any progress."

To save time, Captain Linnett, apprised of some kind of emergency while he was descending Mount Rainier, asked for exfiltration by air. Fort Lewis had its own Chinook troop carrier helicopter, which picked up the Alpha team from the empty visitor parking lot at the foot of the mountain thirty minutes later.

The Chinook took the team as far north as the snow clouds would allow and set them down on a small airfield west of Burlington. The truck had been heading there for an hour, and they arrived almost at the same time.

From Burlington, Highway 20 wound its path along the Skagit River and into the Cascades. It is closed in winter to all but official and specially equipped traffic; the SF truck was equipped for every kind of terrain, and a few not yet invented. But progress was slow. It took four hours until the exhausted driver crunched into the town of Mazama.

The CIA team was also exhausted, but at least their injured colleagues, doped with morphine, were in real ambulances heading south for a helicopter pickup and a final transfer to Tacoma General.

Olsen told Captain Linnett what he thought was enough. Linnett snapped that he was security cleared, and insisted on more.

"This fugitive, has he got arctic clothing and footwear?"

"No. Hiking boots, warm trousers, a light quilted jacket."

"No skies, snowshoes? Is he armed?"

"No, nothing like that."

"It's dark already. Does he have night-vision goggles? Anything to help him move?"

"No, certainly not. He was a prisoner in close confinement."

"He's toast," said Linnett. "In these temperatures, plowing through a meter of snow with no compass, going round in circles. We'll get him."

"There is just one thing. He's a mountain man. Born and raised in them."

"Round here?"

"No. In the Tora Bora. He's an Afghan."

Linnett stared in dumb amazement. He had fought in the Tora Bora. He had been in the first Afghan invasion when Coalition Special Forces, American and British, ranged through the Spin Gahr looking for a runaway party of Saudi Arabs, one of them six feet four inches tall. And he had been back to take part in Operation Anaconda. That had not gone well, either. Some good men had been lost on Anaconda. Linnett had a score to settle with Pashtun from the Tora Bora.

"Saddle up," he shouted, and the ODA climbed back in their truck. It would take them up the remainder of the track to Hart's Pass. After that, their transportation would go back three thousand years to the ski and the snowshoe.

As they left, the sheriff's radio brought the news both airmen had been found and brought out, very cold but alive. Both were in a hospital in Seattle. The news was good, but a bit too late for a man called Lemuel Wilson.

The Anglo-American investigators of the merchant marine who had taken over Operation Crowbar were still concentrating on threat number one, the idea that Al Qaeda might be planning to close down a vital world highway by blocking a narrow strait.

In that contingency, the size of the vessel was paramount. The cargo was immaterial, save only that venting oil would make the job of demolition divers almost impossible. Inquiries were flying across the world to identify every vessel of huge tonnage on the seas.

Clearly, the bigger the ships, the fewer there would be, and most would belong to respectable and gigantic companies. The principal five hundred ultralarge and very large crude carriers, the ULCCs and VLCCs, known to the public as "supertankers," were checked and found to be unattacked. Then the tonnages were lowered in integers of ten thousand tons fully loaded. When all vessels of fifty thousand tons and up were accounted for, the strait-blockage panic began to subside.

Lloyd's shipping list is probably still the world's most complete archive, and the Edzell team set up a direct line to Lloyd's, which was constantly in use. At Lloyd's advice, they concentrated on vessels flying flags of convenience and those registered in "dodge" ports or owned by suspect proprietors. Both Lloyd's and the Secret Intelligence Service's Anti-Terrorist (Marine) desk joined with the American CIA and Coast Guard in slapping a "no approach to coast" label on over two hundred vessels without their captains or owners being aware of it. But still nothing showed up to set the wind socks flying in the breeze.

Captain Linnett knew his mountains, and was aware that a man without specialized footwear, trying to progress through snow over ground riddled with unseen trees, roots, ditches, gullies and streams, would be lucky to make a heartbreaking half a mile per hour across country.

Such a man would probably stumble through the snow crust into a trickling rivulet, and, with wet feet, start to lose body core temperature at an alarming rate, leading to hypothermia and frostbit toes.

Olsen's message from Langley had left no room for doubt: Under no circumstances was the fugitive to reach

Canada, nor must he reach a functioning telephone. Just in case.

Linnett had few doubts. His target would wander in circles without a compass. He would stumble and fall at every second step. He could not see in the blackness under the tree canopy, where even the moon, had it not been hidden by twenty thousand feet of freezing cloud, could not penetrate.

True, the man had a five-hour head start; but even in a straight line, that would give him under three miles of ground covered. Special Forces men on skis could treble that, and if rocks and tree trunks forced the use of snow-shoes they could still do double the speed of the fugitive.

He was right about the skis. From the drop-off point of the truck at the final end of the track, he reached the wrecked CIA cabin in under an hour. He and his men examined it briefly to see if the fugitive had come back to rifle it for better equipment. There was no sign of that. The two bodies, rigid in the cold, were laid out, hands crossed on chests in the now freezing refectory, safe from roaming animals. They would have to wait for the cloud to lift and a helicopter to land.

There are twelve men in an A team; Linnett was the only officer, and his number two was a chief warrant officer. The other ten were all senior enlisted men, the lowest rank being staff sergeant.

They broke down into two engineers for demolition, two radio operators, two medics, a team sergeant with not one but two specialties, an intelligence sergeant and two snipers. While Linnett was inside the wrecked cabin, his team sergeant, who was an expert tracker, scouted the ground outside.

The threatening snow had not fallen; the area around the helipad and the front door, where the rescue team from Mazama had arrived, was a mush of snowshoe tracks. But from the shattered compound wall, a single trail of footprints led away due north.

Coincidental? thought Linnett. It was the one direction the fugitive must not take. It led to Canada, twenty-two miles away. But for the Afghan, forty-four hours of hiking. He would never make it, even if he could keep in a straight line. Anyway, the Alpha team would get him halfway there.

It took another hour to cover the next mile on snow-shoes. That was when they found the other cabin. No one had mentioned the other two or three cabins that were permitted in the Pasayten Wilderness because they predated the building prohibition. And this cabin had been broken into. The shattered triple glazing and the rock beside the gaping hole left no doubt.

Captain Linnett went in first, carbine forward, safety catch off. Round the edges of the shattered glass, two men gave cover. It took them less than a minute to ensure there was no one present, either in the cabin, the adjacent log-storage shed or the empty garage. But the signs were everywhere. He tried the light switch, but the power clearly came from a generator that the owner shut down behind the garage when not in residence. They relied on their flashlights.

Beside the deep fireplace in the main sitting area was a

box of matches and several long tapers, clearly for lighting the logs in the grate; also a bundle of candles in case the generator failed. The intruder had used both to find his way round. Captain Linnett turned to one of his comms sergeants.

"Raise the county sheriff, and find out who owns this place," he said. He began to explore. Nothing seemed to be smashed, but everything had been rifled.

"It's a surgeon from Seattle," reported the sergeant. "Vacations up here in the summer, closes it all down in the fall."

"Name and phone number. He must have left them with the sheriff's office."

When the sergeant had them, he was told to contact Fort Lewis, have them call the surgeon at his Seattle home and put him on a direct patch-through. A surgeon was a lucky break; surgeons have pagers in case of an emergency. This situation definitely rated.

The ghost ship never went near Surabaya. There was no consignment of expensive oriental silks to be taken aboard, and the apparent six sea containers on the *Countess of Richmond*'s foredeck were in place anyway.

She took the route south of Java, passed Christmas Island and headed out into the Indian Ocean. For Mike Martin, the onboard routines became a ritual.

The psychopath Ibrahim remained mainly in his cabin, and the good news was that most of the time he was violently ill. Of the remaining seven men, the engineer tended his engines, set at maximum speed regardless of fuel use. Where the *Countess* was going, she would need no fuel for a return journey.

For Martin, the twin enigmas remained unanswered. Where was she going, and what explosive power lay beneath her decks? No one seemed to know, with the possible exception of the chemical engineer. But he never spoke, and the subject was never raised.

The radio expert kept a listening watch and must have learned of a sea search taking place right across the Pacific and at the entrances to the Straits of Hormuz and the Suez Canal. He may have reported this to Ibrahim but made no mention of it to the rest.

The other five men took turns in the galley to turn out plate after plate of cold canned food, and took turns at the wheel. The navigator set the heading—always west, then south of due west to the Cape of Good Hope.

For the rest, they prayed five times a day, read the Koran yet again and stared at the sea.

Martin considered attempting to take over the ship. He had no weapon other than the chance to steal a kitchen knife, and he would have to kill seven men, of whom he had to presume that Ibrahim had one or more firearms. And the men were scattered from the engine room to the radio shack to the fo'c'sle. If and when they came close to a clear target on shore, he knew he would have to do it. But across the Indian Ocean, he bided his time.

He did not know whether his message in the dive bag had ever been found or was tossed with the bag into some attic unread; and he did not know he had triggered a global ship hunt.

"This is Dr. Berenson. Who am I speaking with?"

Michael Linnett took over the speakerphone from the sergeant and lied.

"I am with the sheriff's office at Mazama," he said. "Right now, I am in your cabin in the wilderness. I'm sorry I have to tell you there has been a break-in."

"Hell, no. Dammit, is there damage done?" the tiny voice speaking from Seattle asked.

"He broke in by smashing the main front window with a rock, Doctor. That seems to be the only structural damage. I just want to check on theft. Did you have any firearms here?"

"Absolutely not. I keep two hunting rifles and a shotgun, but I bring them out with me in the fall."

"Okay. Now, clothing. Do you have a closet with heavy winter clothing?"

"Sure. It's a walk-in, right beside the bedroom door."

Captain Linnett nodded to his team sergeant, who led the way by flashlight. The closet was spacious, full of winter kit.

"There should be my pair of arctic snow boots, quilted pants and a parka with zippered hood."

All gone.

"Any skis or snowshoes, Doctor?"

"Sure, both. In the same cupboard."

Also gone.

"Any weapons at all? Compass?"

The big bowie knife in its sheaf should have been hanging inside the closet door, and the compass and flashlight should have been in the drawers of the desk. They were all taken. That apart, the fugitive had ransacked the kitchen, but there had been no fresh food left there to rot. A newly opened—and emptied—can of baked beans and a can opener lay on the countertop with two empty cans of soda. There was an empty pickle jar that had been full of quarters, but no one knew that.

"Thanks, Doc. I'd get up here when the weather clears with a team for a new window, and file a claim for the loss."

The Alpha leader cut the connection, and looked round at his unit.

"Let's go," was all he said. He knew the cabin, and what the Afghan had taken shortened the odds, and maybe even now they could be against him. He put the fugitive, who must have spent over an hour in the cabin to Linnett's half hour, at two to three hours ahead, but now moving much faster.

Swallowing his pride, he decided to bring up some cavalry. He called a pause, and spoke to Fort Lewis again.

"Tell McChord I want a Spectre and I want it now. Engage all the authority you need—the Pentagon, if you have to. I want it over the Cascades and talking to me directly."

While waiting for their new ally to show up, the twelve men of Alpha 143 pressed on hard, pushing the pace. The sergeant tracker was at point, his flashlight picking up the marks of the snowshoes of the fugitive in the frozen snow. They were pushing the pace, but they were carrying much more equipment than the man ahead of them. Linnett estimated they had to be keeping up, but were they gaining? Then the snow started. It was a blessing and a curse. As the deceptively gentle flakes drifted down from the conifers around them, they covered the rocks and stumps, permitting another quick pause to switch from shoes to the faster skis. They also wiped out the trail.

Linnett needed a guiding hand from heaven, and it came just after midnight in the form of a Lockheed-Martin Hercules AC-130 gunship, circling at twenty thousand feet, above the cloud layer but looking straight through it.

Among the many toys that Special Forces are given to play with, the Spectre gunship is, from the viewpoint of the enemy on the ground, about as nasty as it gets.

The original Hercules transport plane was gutted and her innards replaced with a cockpit-to-tail array of technology designed to locate, target and kill an opponent on the ground. It is seventy-two million dollars' worth of pure bad news.

In its first "locate" role, it does not depend on daylight or dark, wind or rain, snow or hail. Mr. Raytheon had been kind enough to provide a synthetic aperture radar and infrared thermal imager that can pick out any figure in a landscape emitting body heat. Nor is the image a vague blur; it is clear enough to differentiate between a four-legged beast and a two-legged one. But it still could not work out the weirdness of Mr. Lemuel Wilson.

He, too, had a cabin, just outside the Pasayten Wilderness, on the lower slopes of Mount Robinson. Unlike the Seattle surgeon, Wilson prided himself on his capacity to overwinter up there, for he had no alternative metropolitan home.

So he survived without electricity, using a roaring log fire for heat and kerosene lamps for lighting. Each summer, he hunted game, and air-dried the meat strips for winter. He cut his own logs, and foraged for his tough mountain pony. But he had another hobby.

He had enough CB equipment, powered by a tiny generator, to spend his winter hours scanning the wave bands of the sheriff, emergency services and the public utilities. That was how he heard the reports of a two-man aircrew down in the wilderness and teams of professionals struggling toward the spot.

Lemuel Wilson was proud to call himself a concerned citizen. As so often, the authorities preferred the term "interfering busybody." Hardly had the two airmen broadcast their plight, and the authorities replied with their exact positions, than Lemuel Wilson had saddled up and ridden out. He intended to cross the southern half of the wilderness to reach the park and rescue Major Duval.

His band-scanning equipment was too cumbersome to bring along, so he never heard the two aviators were rescued anyway. But he did make human contact.

He did not see the man come at him. One second, he

was urging his pony through a deeper-than-usual snowdrift, the next a bank of snow came up to meet him. But the snowbank was a man in a space-age, quilted silver, two-piece suit.

There was nothing space age about the bowie knife, invented around the time of the Alamo and still very efficient. One arm round his neck dragged Wilson off his pony; as he crashed down, the blade entered his rib cage from the back and sliced open his heart.

A thermal imager is fine for detecting body heat, but Lemuel Wilson's corpse, dropped into a crevasse ten yards from where he died, lost its heat fast. By the time the Hercules AC-130 Spectre began its circling mission high above the Cascades thirty minutes later, Lemuel Wilson did not show up at all.

"This is Spectre-Echo-Foxtrot calling Team Alpha. Do you read me, Alpha?"

"Strength-Five," reported Captain Linnett. "We are twelve on skis down here. Can you see us?"

"Smile nicely and I'll take your picture," said the infrared operator four miles above them.

"Comedy comes later," said Linnett. "About three miles due north of us is a fugitive. Single man, heading north on skis. Confirm?"

There was a pause—a long pause.

"Negative. No such image," said the voice in the sky.

"There must be," argued Linnett. "He is up ahead of us somewhere."

The last of the maple and tamarack was well behind them. They emerged from the forest to a bare scree, always climbing north, and the snow fell straight on them without being filtered by branches. Way behind, in the darkness, stood Mount Lago and Monument Peak. Linnett's men were looking like spectral figures, white zombies in a white landscape. If he was having trouble, so was the Afghan. There was only one explanation for the no-image scenario: the Afghan had taken shelter in a cave or snow hole. The overhang would mask the escaping heat. So Linnett was closing on him. The skis were sliding easily across the shoulder of the mountain, and there was more forest up ahead.

The Spectre fixed his position to within a yard. Twelve miles to the Canadian border. Five hours to dawn, or for what passed for dawn in this land of snow, peaks, rocks and trees.

Linnett gave it another hour. The Spectre circled and watched but saw nothing to report.

"Check again," asked Captain Linnett. He was beginning to think something had gone wrong. Had the Afghan died up here? Possible, and that would explain the absence of a heat signature. Crouching in a cave? Possible, but he would die in there or come out and run. And then . . .

Izmat Khan, urging the feisty but tired pony off the scree and into the forest, had actually lengthened his lead. The compass told him he was still going north, the angle of the pony beneath him that he was climbing.

"I am scanning an arc subtending ninety degrees with you at the point," said the imager operator. "Right up to the border. In that arc, I can see eight animals. Four

deer; two black bear, who are very faint because they are
hibernating under deep cover; what looks like a maraud-
ing mountain lion; and a single moose ambling north.
About four miles ahead of you."

The surgeon's arctic clothing was simply too good.
The pony was sweating as it neared exhaustion and
showed up clearly, but the man on top of it, leaning forward along its neck to urge it onward, was so well
muffled he blended with the animal.

"Sir," said one of the engineer sergeants, "I'm from
Minnesota."

"Save your problems for the chaplain," snapped
Linnett.

"What I mean, sir," said the snow-caked face beside
him, "is that moose do not move up into the mountains
in weather like this. They come down to the valley to forage for lichen. It can't be a moose."

Linnett called a halt. It was welcomed. He stared at
the falling snow ahead. He had not the faintest idea how
the man had done it. Another isolated cabin, maybe,
with an overwintering idiot with a stable. Somehow, the
Afghan had gotten himself a pony and was riding away
from him.

Four miles ahead, back in deep forest, Izmat Khan,
who had ambushed Lemuel Wilson, was himself ambushed. The mountain lion was old, a bit slow for deer,
but cunning and very hungry. It came down from a
ledge between two trees, and the pony would have
smelled it but for its own exhaustion.

The first thing the Afghan knew, something fast and

tawny had hit the pony, and the pony was going down sideways. The rider had time to grab Wilson's rifle from the sleeve alongside the pommel and go backward over the rump. He landed, turned, aimed and fired.

He had been lucky the mountain lion had gone for the pony and not himself, but he had lost his mount. The animal was still alive, but ripped round the head and shoulders by claws with 135 pounds of angry muscle behind them. The pony was not going to get up. He used a second bullet to finish its misery. The pony crumpled, lying half across the body of the mountain lion. It did not matter to the Afghan, but the torso and front legs of the mountain lion were under the pony.

He unhitched the snowshoes from behind the saddle, fitted them over his boots, shouldered the rifle, checked the compass and moved forward. A hundred yards ahead of him was a large rock overhang. He paused under it for a brief respite from the snow. He did not know it but it masked his escaping heat.

"Take out the moose," said Captain Linnett. "I think it's a *horse* with the fugitive on it."

The operator studied his image again.

"You're right," he said. "I can see six legs. He's paused for a rest. Next circuit, down he goes."

The "destroy" part of the Spectre's role is provided by three systems. Heaviest is the 105mm M102 howitzer, which is so powerful that using it on a single human being would be a tad excessive.

Next comes the 40mm Bofors cannon, derived, long ago, from the Swedish antiaircraft weapon, a fast repeater with enough muscle to rip buildings or tanks to fragments. The Spectre crew, told their target was a man on a horse, chose the GAU-12/U Gatling gun. This horror fires eighteen hundred rounds per minute, and each round is a 25mm—one-inch diameter—slug, one of which will pull a human body apart. So intense is the fire of the rotating five-barrel gun that if used on a football field for thirty seconds, nothing much bigger than a mouse would be left alive. And that mouse would die of shock.

The maximum altitude for the GAU-12/U is twelve thousand feet, so the circling Spectre dropped to ten thousand feet, locked on its target and fired for ten seconds, loosing off three hundred rounds at the body of the pony in the forest.

"There's nothing left," remarked the imager operator. "Man and beast, both gone."

"Thank you, Echo-Foxtrot," said Linnett. "We'll take over now."

The Spectre, mission accomplished, returned to Mc-Chord AFB.

The snow stopped, the skis hissed over the new powder, making the sort of progress that skis ought to make with a skilled athlete on them, and the Alpha team came across the remains of the pony. Few fragments were bigger than a man's arm, but they were definitely horse, not human. Except the bits with tawny fur.

Linnett spent ten minutes looking for pieces of arctic clothing, boots, snowshoes, bowie knife, femurs, skull or beard.

The skis were lying there, but one was broken. That had happened when the pony fell. There was a sheepskin sleeve but no rifle. No snowshoes. No Afghan.

Two hours to dawn, and it had become a race. One man on snowshoes, twelve on skis. All exhausted, all desperate. The Alpha team had their Global Positioning System, or GPS. As the sky lightened fractionally in the east, the team sergeant murmured, "Border half a mile."

They arrived twenty minutes later on a bluff overlooking a valley that ran from their left to right. Below was a logging road that constituted the Canadian border. Right across from them was another bluff, with a clearing containing a cluster of log cabins, a facility for Canadian lumberjacks when the timber concessions resumed after the snows.

Linnett crouched, steadied his forearms and studied the landscape through binoculars. Nothing moved. The light increased.

Unbidden, his snipers eased their weapons from the sleeves that had housed them throughout the mission, fixed their scopes, inserted one shell each and lay down to stare across the gulf through their scopes.

By the norms of soldiering, snipers are a strange breed. They never get near the men they kill, yet they see them with a clarity and an apparent proximity greater than anyone else. With hand-to-hand combat almost extinct, most men die not by the hand of the enemy but by his computer. They are blown away by a missile fired a continent away or from somewhere under the sea.

They are destroyed by a smart bomb loosed by an aircraft so high they neither saw nor heard it. They died because someone fired a shell from two counties away. At the nearest, their killers, crouching behind a machine gun in a swooping helicopter, see them only as vague shapes, running, hiding, trying to fire back. But not as real humans.

The sniper sees the enemy like that. Lying in total silence, utterly immobile, he sees his target as a man with three days' stubble, a man who stretches and yawns, who spoons beans out of a can, unzips his fly or simply stands and stares at a lens a mile away that he cannot see. And then he dies. Snipers are special—inside the head.

They also live in a private world. So total does the obsession with accuracy become that they lapse into a silence peopled only by the weights of projectile heads, the power of various powder loads, how much a bullet will wind-drift, how far it will drop over various distances, whether yet another tiny improvement can be made to the rifle.

Like all specialists, they have their passions for rival pieces of equipment. Some snipers like a really tiny bullet, like the Remington M700 .308, a slug so small that it has to be sheathed in a detachable sleeve to go down the barrel at all.

Others stay with the M21, the sniper version of the M14 standard combat rifle. Heaviest of all is the Barrett "Light Fifty," a monster that sends a bullet like a human forefinger over a mile with enough speed times weight to cause a human body to explode.

Lying prone at Captain Linnett's feet was his leading

sniper, Master Sergeant Peter Bearpaw. He was a half-blood Santee Sioux with a Hispanic mother. He came from the slums of Detroit, and the Army was his life. He had high cheekbones, and eyes that sloped like a wolf's. And he was the best marksman in the Green Berets.

What he cradled as he squinted across the valley was the .408 Cheyenne by CheyTac of Idaho. It was a more recent development than the others, but with over three thousand rounds on the range it had become his weapon of choice. It was a bolt-action rifle, which he appreciated because the total lockdown of a closed bolt gave that tiny extra stability at the moment of detonation.

He had inserted the single slug—very long and slim—and he had burnished and buffed the nose tip to eradicate the tiniest vibration in flight. Along the top of the breech ran a Leatherwood ×24 scope.

"I have him, Captain," he whispered.

The binoculars had missed the fugitive, but the scope had found him. Set among the cabins across the valley, walled on three sides by timber, with a single, glass-paneled door, was a phone booth.

"Tall, long shaggy hair, bushy black beard?"

"Roger that."

"What's he doing?"

"He is in a phone booth, sir."

Izmat Khan had had little concourse with his fellow inmates at Guantánamo, but one with whom he had spent many months in the same solitary confinement block had been a Jordanian who had fought in Bosnia in the midnineties before returning to become a trainer in the AQ camps. He was hardline.

As security slackened around the Christmas period, they found they could whisper from one cell to another. If you ever get out of here, the Jordanian told him, I have a friend. We were in the camps together. He is safe, he will help a true believer. Mention my name.

There was a name. And a phone number, though Izmat Khan did not know where its owner lived. He was not quite sure of the complexities of subscriber trunk dialing, for which he actually had enough quarters; but, worse, he did not know the overseas code for dialing out of Canada. So he punched in a quarter and asked for the operator.

"What number are you trying, caller?" said the unseen Canadian telephone operator.

Slowly, in halting English, he read out the figures he had so painstakingly memorized.

"That is a UK number," said the operator. "Are you using U.S. quarters?"

"Yes."

"That's acceptable. Put in eight of them, and I will connect you. When you hear the pips, put in more if you wish to continue the call."

"Have you acquired the target?" asked Linnett.

"Yes, sir."

"Take the shot."

"He's in Canada, sir."

"Take the shot, Sergeant."

Peter Bearpaw took a slow, calm breath, held it inside

and squeezed. The range was a still-air 2,100 yards on his range finder, well over a mile.

Izmat Khan was pushing quarters into the slot. He was not looking up. The glass front of the booth disintegrated into pinpricks, and the bullet took away the occiput from the rest of his head.

The operator was as patient as she could be. The man down in the logging camp had inserted only two quarters, then apparently left the booth and left the handset hanging. Finally, she had no choice but to hang up on him and cancel the call.

Because of the sensitivity of the cross-border shot, no official report was ever made.

Captain Linnett reported to his commanding officer, who told Marek Gumienny in Washington. Nothing more was heard.

The body was found in the thaw when the lumberjacks returned. The hanging phone was disconnected. The coroner could do little but record an open verdict. The man wore U.S. clothing, but in the border country that was not odd. He had no ID; no one recognized him locally.

Unofficially, most people around the coroner's office presumed the man had been victim of a tragic stray shot from a deer hunter, another death from careless shooting or ricochet. He was buried in an unmarked grave.

Because no one south of the border wanted to make waves, it was never thought to ask what number the fugitive had asked for. To even make the inquiry would give away the source of the shot. So it was not made.

In fact, the number he wanted was that of a small apartment off-campus near Aston University in Birmingham. It was the home of Dr. Ali Aziz al-Khattab, and the phone was on intercept by Britain's MI5. All they waited for was enough evidence to justify a raid and an arrest. They would get it a month later. But that morning the Afghan was trying to call the only man west of Suez who knew the name of the ghost ship.

CHAPTER 16

AFTER TWO WEEKS, enthusiasm for the hunt for a seemingly nonexistent ghost ship was starting to fade, and the mood came from Washington.

How much time, trouble and treasure could be expended on a vague scrawl on a boarding card stuffed into a dive bag on an island no one had ever heard of? Marek Gumienny had flown to London to confer with Steve Hill when the SIS expert in maritime terrorism, Sam Seymour, called up from the Ipswich HQ for Lloyd's shipping list and made matters worse. He had changed his mind. Hill ordered him to London to explain.

"With hindsight," said Seymour, "the option of Al Qaeda seeking to use a huge blocking ship to close down a vital sea highway to wreck global trade was always the likeliest option. But it was never the only one."

"What makes you think it was the wrong way to go?" asked Marek Gumienny.

"Because, sir, every single vessel in the world big enough to achieve that has been checked out. They are all safe. That leaves options two and three, which are almost interchangeable but with different targets. I think we should now look at option three: mass murder in a seashore city. Bin Laden's public switch to economic targets could have been a hoax, or he has changed his mind."

"Okay, Sam, convince me. Steve and I both have political masters demanding results or our heads. What kind of ship if not a blocking vessel?"

"For threat number three, we do not look at the ship so much as the cargo. It need not be large so long as it is absolutely deadly. Lloyd's have a hazardous cargo division—obviously, it changes the premium."

"Ammunition ship?" asked Hill. "Another Halifax wipeout?"

"According to the boffins, military ordnance simply does not explode like that anymore. The modern stuff needs huge provocation to go off inside the hull. You'd get worse from an exploding fireworks factory, but it would not begin to deserve the term 'spectacular,' as in 9/11. The Bhopal chemical leak was far worse, and that was dioxin, a deadly weed killer."

"So, a tanker truck driving dioxin up Park Avenue, and completing the job with Semtex," suggested Hill.

"But these chemicals are closely guarded inside their manufacturing and storage base," objected Gumienny. "How do they get the cargo with no one noticing?"

"And we were specifically told a ship would be the carrier," said Seymour. "Any hijacking of such a cargo would bring immediate retaliation."

"Except in some parts of the Third World that are virtually lawless," said Gumienny.

"But these ultralethal toxins are not made in such places anymore, not even for labor-cost savings, sir."

"So, we are back to a ship?" said Hill. "Another exploding oil tanker?"

"Crude oil does not explode," Seymour pointed out. "When the *Torrey Canyon* was ripped open off the French coast, it took phosphorus bombs to persuade the oil to ignite and burn off. A vented oil tanker will only cause ecodamage, not mass murder. But a quite small gas tanker could do it. Liquid gas, massively concentrated for transportation."

"Natural gas, liquid form?" asked Gumienny. He was trying to think how many ports in the USA imported concentrates of gas for industrial power, and the number was becoming unsettling. But surely these docking facilities were miles from massed humanity.

"Liquid natural gas, known as LNG, is hard to ignite," Seymour countered. "It is stored at minus 256 Fahrenheit in special double-hulled vessels. Even if you took one over, the stuff would have to leak into the atmosphere for hours before it became combustible. But according to the eggheads, there is one that frightens the hell out of them. LPG. Liquid petroleum gas.

"It is so awful that a quite small tanker, if torched within ten minutes of catastrophic rupture, would unleash the power of thirty Hiroshima bombs, the biggest nonnuclear explosion on this planet."

There was total silence in the room above the Thames. Steve Hill rose, strolled to the window and looked down at the river flowing past in the April sunshine.

"In laymen's language, what have you come here to say, Sam?"

"I think we have been looking for the wrong ship in the wrong ocean. Our only break is that this is a tiny and very specialist market. But the biggest importer of LPG is the USA. I know there is a mood in Washington that all this may be a wild-goose chase. I think we should go the last mile. The USA can check out every LPG tanker expected in her waters, and not just from the Far East. And stop them until boarded. From Lloyd's, I can check out every other LPG cargo worldwide, from any point on the compass."

Marek Gumienny took the next flight back to Washington. He had conferences to attend and work to do. As he flew out of Heathrow, the *Countess of Richmond* came round Cape Agulhas, South Africa, and entered the Atlantic.

She had made good speed, and her navigator, one of the three Indonesians, estimated the Agulhas Current and the north-running Benguela Current would give her an extra day, and plenty of time to reach her intended destination.

Farther out into the seas off the Cape, and on into the Atlantic, other ships were moving from the Indian

Ocean to head for Europe or North America. Some were huge ore carriers, others general cargo ships bringing the ever-increasing amount of Asian manufactures to both Western continents as marketers "outsourced" manufacturing to the low-cost workshops of the East. Others still were supertankers too big even for the Suez Canal, their computers following the hundred-fathom line from the east to the west while their crews played cards.

They were all noted. High above, out of sight and mind, the satellites drifted across inner space, their cameras relaying back to Washington every line of their structure and the names on their sterns. More, under recent legislation they all carried transponders emitting their individual call sign to the listening ears. Each identification was checked out, and that included the *Countess of Richmond,* vouched for by Lloyd's and Siebart and Abercrombie as being a Liverpool-registered small freighter bringing a legitimate cargo on a foreseen route from Surabaya to Baltimore. For the USA, there was no point in probing deeper; she was thousands of miles from the American coast.

Within hours of the return of Marek Gumienny to Washington, changes were made to the U.S. precautions. In the Pacific, the check-out-and-examine cordon was extended to a thousand-mile band off the coast. A similar cordon was established in the Atlantic from Labrador to Puerto Rico, and across the Caribbean Sea to the Yucatán Peninsula in Mexico.

Without fuss or announcement, the emphasis abandoned the giant tankers and freighters, which by then had all been checked, and looked hard at the scores of smaller tankers that ply the seas from Venezuela to the Saint Lawrence River. Every EP-3 Orion available was pressed into coastal patrol, flying over hundreds of thousands of square miles of tropical and subtropical sea looking for small tankers, and especially for those bearing gas.

American industry cooperated to the full, supplying details of every cargo expected, where and when due. The data from industry was cross-indexed with the sightings at sea, and they all checked out. Gas tankers were permitted to arrive and dock, but only after taking on board a posse of U.S. Navy, Marine or Coast Guard personnel to escort them in, under guard, from a point two hundred miles out.

The *Doña María* was back in Port of Spain when the two terrorists she harbored in her crew saw the signal they had been briefed to expect. As instructed, when they saw it they acted.

The Republic of Trinidad and Tobago is a major supplier of petrochemical products across a wide spectrum to the United States. The *Doña María* was berthed at the offshore island, the tank farm where tankers large and small could approach, take cargo on board and leave without ever approaching the city itself.

The *Doña María* was one of the smaller tankers, a member of that fleet of vessels that service the islands whose facilities neither need nor can accommodate the giants. The big vessels are wont to bring in the Venezuelan crude, which is refined down to its various "fractions" at the onshore refinery, then piped out to the island for loading into the tankers.

Along with two other small tankers, the *Doña María* was at a specially remote section of the tank farm. Her cargo after all was liquefied petroleum gas, and no one wanted to be too close during the loading. It was late afternoon when she was finished and Captain Montalban prepared her for sea.

There were still two hours of tropical daylight left when she slipped her mooring lines and eased away from the jetty. A mile offshore, she passed close to a rigid inflatable launch in which four men sat with fishing rods. It was the awaited sign.

The two Indians left their posts, ran below to their lockers and returned with handguns. One went amidships, where the scuppers were closest to the water and the men would board.

The other went to the bridge, and pointed his gun straight at the temple of Captain Montalban.

"Do nothing, please, Captain," he said with great courtesy. "There is no need to slow down. My friends will board in a few minutes. Do not attempt to broadcast or I will have to shoot you."

The captain was simply too amazed to fail to obey. As he recovered, he glanced at the radio at one side of the bridge, but the Indian caught his glance and shook his head. At that, all resistance was snuffed out. Minutes later, the four terrorists were aboard and opposition became futile.

The last man out of the inflatable slashed it with a carving knife and it sank in the wake when the painter was released. The other three men had already hefted their canvas grips and stepped over the spaghetti mix of pipes, tubes and tank hatches that define a tanker's foredeck as they made their way aft.

They appeared on the bridge seconds later: two Algerians and two Moroccans, the ones Dr. al-Khattab had sent over a month earlier. They spoke only Moorish Arabic, but the two Indians, still courteous, translated. The four South American crewmen were to be summoned to the foredeck, and would wait there. A new course would be calculated and adhered to.

An hour after dark, the four crewmen were coldly murdered and tossed overboard after a length of chain from the forward locker had been secured to each body's ankle. If Captain Montalban had had any spirit to resist left in him, that was the end of it. The executions were very mechanical; the two Algerians had, back at home, been in the GIA—the Armed Islamic Group—and had slaughtered hundreds of helpless *fellahim,* outback farmers whose mass murder was simply a way of sending a message to the government in Algiers. Men, women, children, the sick and the old, they had killed them all many times, so four crewmen was just a formality.

Through the night the *Doña María* steamed north, but no longer toward her scheduled destination of Puerto Rico. To her port side was the expanse of the Caribbean basin, unbroken all the way to Mexico. To her starboard side, quite close, were the two island chains called the Windward and the Leeward, whose warm seas are often thought of only as vacation destinations but are alive with hundreds of small tramps and tankers that keep the islands supplied and alive for the tourists.

Into this blizzard of coastal freighters and islands, the *Doña María* would disappear, and remain so, until she was logged overdue at Puerto Rico.

When the *Countess of Richmond* reached the doldrums, the sea calmed, and Yusef Ibrahim emerged from his cabin. He was pale, and drained by nausea, but the hate-filled black eyes were the same as he gave his orders. The crew brought out from its storage place in the engine room a twenty-foot inflatable speedboat. When it was fully rigid, it was suspended from the two davits above the stern.

It took six men, sweating and grunting, to bring up the one-hundred-horsepower outboard engine from below and fix it to the rear of the speedboat. Then it was winched down to the gentle swell beneath the stern.

Fuel tanks were lowered and hooked up. After several false starts, the engine coughed to life. The Indonesian navigator was at the helm, and he took the speedboat away for a fast circle round the *Countess.*

Finally, the other six men descended down a ship's ladder over the gunwales to join him, leaving only the crippled killer at the helm. It was evident this was a dress rehearsal.

The point of the exercise was to allow the cameraman, Suleiman, to be taken three hundred yards from the freighter, turn and photograph her with his fully digital equipment. When linked through his laptop to the Mini-M sat phone, his images could be transmitted to another Web site on the other side of the world for recording and broadcast.

Mike Martin knew what he was watching. For terrorism, the Internet and cyberspace have become must-have propaganda weapons. Every atrocity that can be broadcast on the news is good; every atrocity that can be seen by millions of Muslim youths in seventy countries is gold dust. This is where the recruits come from—actually seeing it happen and lusting to imitate.

At Forbes Castle, Martin had watched the video recordings out of Iraq, with the suicide bombers grinning into the lens before driving away to die on camera. In such cases, the cameraman survived; in the case of the circling speedboat, it was clear that the target would have to be monitored visually as well, and filming would continue until the boat and its seven men were wiped out. Only Ibrahim, it seemed, would stay at the helm.

But he could not know when and where, or what horror lay inside the sea containers. He considered a possible idea to be first back on the *Countess,* cast the inflatable adrift, kill Ibrahim and take over the freighter. But there was no such chance. The speedboat was much faster, and the six men would be swarming over the rail in seconds.

When the exercise was over, the speedboat was swung empty from the davits, where it looked like any other ship's dinghy, the engineer increased power and the *Countess* headed northwest to skirt the coast of Senegal.

Recovered from his nausea, Yusef Ibrahim spent more time on the bridge or in the wardroom, where the crew ate together. The atmosphere was already hypertense, and his presence made it more so.

All eight men on board had made their decision to die *shahid*, a martyr. But that did not prevent the waiting and the boredom tearing at their nerves. Only constant prayer and the obsessive reading of the Koran enabled them to stay calm and true to the belief in what they were doing.

No one but the explosives engineer and Ibrahim knew what lay beneath the steel containers that covered the foredeck of the *Countess of Richmond* from just in front of the bridge almost to the forepeak. And only Ibrahim appeared to know the eventual destination and planned target. The other seven had to take on trust the pledges that their glory would be everlasting.

Martin realized within hours of the mission commander's presence among them that he was constantly the object of Ibrahim's blank and crazy stare. He would not have been human if the phenomenon had not rattled him.

Disquieting questions began to haunt him. Had Ibrahim after all seen Izmat Khan in Afghanistan? Was he about to be asked some questions he simply could not answer? Had he slipped up, even by a few words, in the relentless reciting of the prayers? Would Ibrahim test him by asking to recite passages he had not studied?

He was, in fact, part right, part wrong. The Jordanian psychopath across the mess table had never seen Izmat Khan, though he had heard of the legendary Taliban fighter. And there had been no mistakes in his prayers. He simply hated the Pashtun for his reputation in combat, something he had never acquired. Out of his hatred was born a desire that the Aghan should, after all, be a traitor, so that he could be unmasked and killed.

But he kept his rage under control for one of the oldest reasons in the world. He was afraid of the mountain man; and even though he carried a handgun in a saraband under his robe, and had sworn to die, he could not suppress his awe of the man from the Tora Bora. So he brooded, stared, waited and kept his own counsel.

For a second time, the West's search for the ghost ship—if it even existed—had run into complete frustration. Steve Hill was being bombarded with requirements for information—anything—to appease the frustration that went right up to Downing Street.

The controller, Middle East, could offer no resolution to the four questions that were raining down upon him from the British premier and the U.S. president. Does this ship exist at all? If so, what is it, where is it and which city is its target? The daily conferences were becoming purgatory.

The chief of the SIS, never known or greeted by anything other than "C," was steely in his silences. After Peshawar, all the superior authorities had agreed there was a terrorist spectacular in preparation. But the world of smoke and mirrors is not a forgiving place for those who fail their political masters.

Since the discovery at customs of the scrawled message on the folded landing card, there had been no sign of life from Crowbar. Was he dead or alive? No one knew, and some were ceasing to care. It had been nearly four weeks, and with each passing day the mood was swinging to the view that he was now past tense.

Some muttered that he had done his job, been caught and killed, but had been the cause of the plot being abandoned. Only Hill counseled caution, and a continued search for the source of a still-unfound threat. In some gloom, he motored to Ipswich to talk to Sam Seymour and the two eggheads in the hazardous-cargo office of Lloyd's List, who were helping him go through every possibility, however bizarre.

"You used a pretty hair-raising phrase in London, Sam. 'Thirty times the Hiroshima bomb.' How on earth can a small tanker be worse than the entire Manhattan Project?"

Sam Seymour was exhausted. At thirty-two, he could see a promising career in British Intelligence coming to a polite sidelining to the archives of the Central Registry, even though he had been saddled with a job that was looking every day more impossible to fulfill.

"With an atomic bomb, Steve, the damage comes in four waves. The flash is so searingly bright it can cauterize the cornea of a watcher unless he has black-lens shields. Then comes the heat, so bad it causes everything in its path to self-incinerate. The shock wave knocks down buildings miles away, and the gamma radiation is long term, causing carcinoma and malformations. With the LPG explosion, forget three of them—this explosion is all heat.

"But it is a heat so fierce that it will cause steel to run like honey and concrete to crumble to dust. You've heard of the 'fuel-air bomb'? It is so powerful it makes napalm seem mild, yet they both have the same source: petroleum.

"LPG is heavier than air. When transported, it is not, like LNG, kept at an amazingly low temperature; it is kept under pressure. Hence, the double-hulled skins of LPG tankers. If a tanker is ruptured, the LPG will gush out, quite invisible, and mix with the air. It is heavier than air, so it will swirl round the place it came from, forming one enormous fuel-air bomb. Ignite that and the entire cargo will explode in flame, terrible flame, rising quickly to five thousand degrees centigrade. Then it will start to roll. It creates its own wind. It will roll outward from the source, a roaring tide of flame, consuming everything in its path until it has completely consumed itself. Then it gutters like a fading candle and dies."

"How far will the fireball roll?" asked Hill.

"Well, according to my newfound boffin friends, a small tanker of, say, eight thousand tons, fully vented and ignited, would consume everything, and extinguish all human life, within a five-kilometer radius. One last thing, I said it creates its own wind. It sucks in the air from periphery to center, to feed itself, so even humans in a protective shell five klicks away from the epicenter will die of asphyxia."

Steve Hill had a mental image of a city cluttered round its harbor after such a horror exploded there. Not even the outer suburbs would survive.

"Are these tankers being checked out?"

"Every one. Large and small, right down to tiny. The hazardous-cargo team here is only two guys, but they're good. As a matter of fact, they are down to the last handful of LPG tankers.

"As for the general freighters, the sheer numbers mean that we had to cut off at those under ten thousand tons. Except when they enter the American forbidden zone along each seaboard. Then the Yanks spot them and investigate.

"For the rest, every major port in the world has been apprised that Western intelligence thinks there may be a hijacked ghost ship on the high seas, and they must take their own precautions. But, frankly, any port likely to be targeted by Al Qaeda for massacre would be in a Western, developed country; not Lagos, Dakar; not Muslim, Hindu, Buddhist. That leaves our non-American list of possible ports at under three hundred."

There was a tap on the door, and a head came round. Pink-cheeked, very young, name of Conrad Phipps.

"Just got the last one in, Sam. *Wilhelmina Santos*, out of Caracas, bringing LPG to Galveston, confirms she is okay, Americans prepared to board her."

"That's it?" asked Hill. "Every LPG tanker in the world accounted for?"

"It's a small menu, Steve," said Seymour.

"Still, it looks as if the LPG tanker idea was a blind alley," said Hill. He rose to leave, and return to London.

"There is one thing that worries me, Mr. Hill," said the cargo egghead.

"It's Steve," said Hill. The SIS has always maintained the tradition of first names, from the highest to the humblest, with the sole exception of the chief himself. The informality underwrites the one-team ethos.

"Well, three months ago an LPG tanker was lost with all hands."

"So?"

"No one actually saw her go down. Her captain came on the radio in high distress to say he had a catastrophic engine-room fire, and did not think he could save his ship. Then . . . nothing. She was the *Java Star*."

"Any traces?" asked Seymour.

"Well, yes. Traces. Before the captain went off the air, he gave his exact position. First on the scene was a refrigerator ship coming up from the south. Her captain reported self-inflating dinghies, life belts and various flotsam at the spot. No sign of survivors. Captain and crew have never been heard from since."

"Tragic, but so what?" asked Hill.

"It was where it happened, sir. Er . . . Steve. In the Celebes Sea. Two hundred miles from a place called Labuan Island."

"Oh, shit," said Steve Hill, and left for London.

While Hill was driving, the *Countess of Richmond* crossed the equator. She was heading north by northwest, and only her navigator knew exactly where. He was going for a spot eight hundred miles west of the Azores and twelve hundred miles east of the American coast. If extended due west, her track would bring her to Baltimore, at the top of the vastly populated Chesapeake Bay.

Some of those on board the *Countess* began their early preparations for the entry into paradise. This involved the shaving of all body hair, and the writing of the last testaments of faith. These testaments were done into the camera lens, and were read aloud by each writer.

The Afghan read his as well, but he chose to speak in Pashto. Yusef Ibrahim, from his time in Afghanistan, had learned only a few words of the language, and he strained to understand, but even if he had been fluent he could not have faulted the testament.

The man from the Tora Bora spoke of the destruction of his family by an American rocket, and his joy at soon seeing them again while bringing justice at last to the Great Satan. As he spoke, he realized that none of this was ever going to reach any shore in physical form. It would all have to be transmitted by Suleiman by data stream before he, too, died, and his equipment died with him. What no one seemed to know was how they would die, and what justice would be visited upon the USA— the exceptions being the explosives expert and Ibrahim himself. But they revealed nothing.

Given that the entire crew was surviving on cold canned food, no one noticed that a steel carving knife with a seven-inch blade was missing from the galley.

When he was unobserved Martin was quietly honing its blade with the whetstone in the knife drawer to a razor-edge. He thought of using the dead of night to drop over the stern to slash the dinghy but rejected the idea.

He was with the four men who slept in bunks in the fo'c'sle. There was always a helmsman at the wheel, which was right next to the access point for going over the stern on a rope. The radioman practically lived in his tiny communications shack behind the bridge, and the engineer was always down in his engine room, below the bridge at the stern. Any of them could stick their head outside and see him.

And the damage would be spotted. A saboteur would be known about at once. The loss of the dinghy would be a setback, but not enough to abort the mission. And there might be time to patch the damage. He dropped the idea, but kept the rag-sheathed knife strapped to the small of his back. Each spell at the bridge, he tried to work out which port they were going to and what was inside the sea containers that he might be able to sabotage. Neither answer surfaced, and the *Countess* steamed north by northwest.

The global hunt switched and narrowed. All the marine giants, all the tankers and all the gas ships had been checked and verified. All the ID transponders conformed to their required transmissions; all the courses conformed to their predicted routes; three thousand captains had personally spoken to their head offices and agents, giving date of birth and other personal background details, so that even if the captains were under duress no hijackers could know whether they were lying or not.

The USA, her Navy, Marines and Coast Guard stretched to the limits without furlough or time off, was boarding and escorting in every cargo vessel seeking berth in a major port. This was causing economic inconvenience, but nothing big enough to inflict real damage to the biggest economy on earth.

Following the tip from Ipswich, the origins and ownership of the *Java Star* were checked with a fine-tooth comb. Because she was small, her owning company concealed itself behind a "shell" company lodged with a bank that turned out to be a brass plate in a Far Eastern tax haven. The Borneo refinery that had provided the cargo was legitimate, but knew little about the ship itself. The freighter's builders were traced—she had had six owners in her lifetime—and they provided plans. A sister ship was found, and swarmed over by Americans with tape measures. Computer imaging produced an exact replica of the *Java Star*, but not the ship itself.

The government whose flag of convenience she flew when last seen was visited in force. But it was a Polynesian atoll republic, and the checkers were soon satisfied that the gas tanker had never even been there.

The Western world needed answers to three questions: Was the *Java Star* really dead? If not, where was she now? And what was her new name? The KH-11 satellites were instructed to narrow their search to something resembling the *Java Star.*

During the first week of April, the joint operation at Edzell air base in Scotland stood down. There was no more it could do that was not now being done far more officially by the main Western intel-gathering agencies.

Michael McDonald returned with relief to his native Washington. He stayed with the hunt for the ghost ship, but out of Langley. Part of the CIA's mission was to reinterrogate any detainee in any of its covert detention centers who might, before capture, have heard a whisper of a project called al-Isra. And they called in every source they had out in the shadowy world of Islamist terrorism. There were no takers. The very phrase referring to the magical journey through the night to great enlightenment seemed to have been born and died with an Egyptian terror financier who went off a balcony in Peshawar in October.

With regret, Colonel Mike Martin was presumed to have been lost on mission. He had clearly done what he could, and if the *Java Star,* or another floating bomb, was discovered heading for the USA, he would be deemed to have succeeded. But no one expected to see him again. It had simply been too long since his last sign of life in a diver's bag on Labuan.

Three days before the G8 meeting, patience finally ran out—and at the highest level—with the global search based on the British tip-off. Marek Gumienny, at his desk in Langley, called Steve Hill on a secure line with the news.

"Steve, I'm sorry. I'm sorry for you, and even more so for your man Mike Martin. But the conviction here is that he's gone, and, with the biggest trawl of global shipping ever attempted, he must have been wrong."

"And Sam Seymour's theory?" asked Hill.

"Same thing. No dice. We have checked out just about every goddamn tanker on the planet, all categories. About fifty left to locate and identify, then it's over. Whatever this al-Isra phrase meant, either we'll never find out, or it means nothing, or it has been long discontinued. Hold on . . . I'll kill the other line."

In a moment, he came back on. "There's a ship overdue. Left Trinidad for Puerto Rico four days ago. Due yesterday. Never showed. Won't answer."

"What kind of ship?" asked Hill.

"A tanker. Three thousand tons. Look, she may have foundered. But we're checking now."

"What was she carrying?" asked Hill.

"Liquefied petroleum gas," was the answer.

It was a KH-11 "Keyhole" satellite that found her six hours after the complaint from Puerto Rico to head office of the oil company owners of the refinery, based in Houston, was turned into a major alarm.

Sweeping through the eastern Caribbean with its cameras and listening sensors checking on a five-hundred-mile-wide swath of sea and islands, the Keyhole heard a transponder signal from far below, and its computer confirmed it was from the missing *Doña María*.

The intelligence went instantly to a variety of agencies, which was why Marek Gumienny was interrupted in his phone call to London. Others in the loop were SOCOM headquarters at Tampa, Florida, the U.S. Navy and the Coast Guard. All were given the exact grid reference of the missing vessel.

In not switching off the transponder, the hijackers were either being very stupid or hoping to get very lucky. But they were only following orders. With the transponder emitting, they gave away their name and position. With it switched off, they became immediately suspect as a possible rogue ship.

The small LPG tanker was still being navigated and steered by a terrified Captain Montalban, four days without sleep, stealing only a few catnaps before being kicked awake again. She had slipped past Puerto Rico in the darkness, passing west of the Turks and Caicos, and lost herself for a while in the cluster of seven hundred islands that make up the Bahamas.

When the Keyhole found her, she was steaming due west just south of Bimini, the westernmost island of the archipelago.

At Tampa, her course was plotted and extended forward. It went straight into the open mouth of the port of Miami, a waterway that leads to the heart of the city.

Within ten minutes, the small tanker was attracting real company. A P-3 Orion sub hunter, aloft from the Naval Air Station at Key West, found her, dropped to a few thousand feet and began to circle, filming her from every angle. She appeared on a wall-sized plasma screen in the near darkness of the ops room at Tampa, almost life-sized.

"Jesus, would you look at that," murmured an operator to no one in particular.

While the freighter was at sea, someone had gone over the stern with a brush and white paint and daubed a crossbar over the letter *i* in *María*. It attempted to rechristen her the *Doña Marta,* but the white smear was simply too crude to dupe any onlooker for more than a few seconds.

There are two Coast Guard cutters operating out of Charleston, South Carolina, both Hamilton class, and both were at sea. They are the 717 USCG *Mellon* and her sister ship, the *Morgenthau*. The *Mellon* was closer, and turned toward the hijacked fugitive, moved from optimum cruising speed to flanking speed. Her navigator rapidly plotted her intercept at ninety minutes, just before sundown.

The term "cutter" hardly does the *Mellon* justice; she can perform like a small destroyer, at 150 meters in length and 3,300 tons deadweight. As she raced through the early-April Atlantic swell, her crew ran to prepare her armament—just in case. The missing tanker was already rated as "likely hostile."

The *Mellon*'s weaponry is not to be trifled with. Lightest of her three systems is the six-barrel 20mm Gatling gun, which pumps out such a blizzard of ordnance that it is used as an antimissile weapon. In theory, even an incoming missile would be torn apart when flying through such a hail of bullets. But the Phalanx gun does not have to be used against missiles; it can tear almost anything apart, but it needs to be fairly close.

She also carries two Bushmaster 25mm cannons, not as rapid, but heavier, and enough to give a small tanker a completely spoiled day. And she has her deck-mounted Oto Melara 76mm rapid-fire cannon. By the time the *Doña María* became a speck on the horizon, all three systems were crewed and ready, and the men crouching over what so far they had used only in training would have been more than saintly if they did not harbor a sneaking lust to use them in real action.

With the Orion above them, filing everything in real time and passing the images to Tampa, the *Mellon* curved round the stern of the tanker and came abreast of her, throttling back just two hundred yards off the beam. Then the *Mellon* called on the *Doña María* with her loudspeaker.

"Unidentified tanker, this is United States Coast Guard vessel *Mellon*. Heave to. I say again, heave to. We are coming aboard."

Powerful binoculars could pick up the figure at the helm holding the wheel, and two other figures flanking him. There was no response. The tanker did not slow down. The message was repeated.

After the third message, the captain gave the order for a single shell to be fired into the sea ahead of the tanker's bow. As water erupted over the forepeak, soaking the tarpaulins with which someone had vainly tried to hide the network of pipes and tubes that betray any tanker's

real purpose, those on the bridge of the *Doña María* must have got the message. Still, she did not slow down.

Then two figures appeared from the door of the stern-castle, just behind the bridge. One had an M60 machine gun slung round his neck. It was a futile gesture, and sealed the tanker's fate. He was clearly North African, and clearly visible in the setting sun. He loosed off a short burst of gunfire that went over the top of the *Mellon,* then took a bullet in the chest from one of the four M16 carbines being aimed at him from the deck of the *Mellon.*

That was the end of negotiations. As the Algerian's body slumped backward, and the steel door through which he had stepped slammed shut, the captain of the *Mellon* asked for permission to sink the runaway. But permission was denied. The message from the base was unequivocal.

"Pull away from her. Make distance now, and make it fast. She's a floating bomb. Resume station a mile from the tanker."

Regretfully, the *Mellon* turned away, powering up to maximum speed and leaving the tanker alone to her fate. The two F-16 Falcons were already airborne, and three minutes distant.

There is a squadron at Pensacola Air Force Base, on the Florida panhandle, that maintains a five-minutes-to-scramble standby readiness round the clock. Its primary use is against drug smugglers, airborne and sometimes seaborne, trying to slip into Florida and neighboring states with mostly cocaine.

They came out of the sunset in a clear, darkling sky, locked on to the tanker west of Bimini and armed their Maverick missiles. Each pilot's visual display showed him the SMART . . . MISSILES . . . LOCK on the target, and the death of the tanker was very mechanical, very precise, very devoid of emotion.

There was a clipped command from the element leader, and both Mavericks left their housing beneath the fighters and followed their noses. Seconds later, two warheads involving some 135 kilograms of unpleasantness hit the tanker.

Even though the *Doña María*'s cargo was not air-mixed for maximum power, the detonations of the Mavericks deep inside her petrol jelly were enough.

From a mile away, the crew of the *Mellon* watched the *Doña María* burn and were duly impressed. They felt the heat wash over their faces and smelled the stench of concentrated gasoline on fire. It was quick. There was nothing left to smolder on the surface. The forward and stern ends of the tanker went down as two separate pieces of molten junk. The last of her heavier fuel oil flickered for five minutes, then the sea claimed it all.

Just as Ali Aziz al-Khattab had intended.

Within an hour, the president of the USA was interrupted at a state banquet with a brief, whispered message. He nodded, demanded a full verbal report at eight the next morning in the Oval Office and returned to his soup.

At five minutes before eight, the director of the CIA,

with Mark Gumienny at his side, were shown into the Oval Office. Gumienny had been there twice before, and it still impressed the hell out of him. The president and the other five of the six principals were there.

The formalities were brief. Marek Gumienny was asked to report on the progress and termination of a lengthy exercise in counterterrorism known as Crowbar.

He kept it short, aware that the man sitting under the round window overlooking the Rose Garden, with its six-inch bulletproof glass, loathed long explanations. The rule of thumb was always "Fifteen minutes, and then shut up." Marek Gumienny telescoped the complexities of Crowbar into twelve.

There was silence when he finished.

"So, the tip from the Brits turned out to be right?" said the vice president.

"Yes, sir. The agent they slipped inside Al Qaeda, a very brave officer whom I had the privilege of meeting last fall, must be presumed dead. If not, he would have shown sign of life by now. But he got the message out. The terror weapon was indeed a ship."

"I had no idea cargoes that dangerous were being carried around the world on a daily basis," marveled the secretary of state in the ensuing silence.

"Nor I," said the president. "Now, regarding the G8 conference, what is your advice to me?"

The secretary of defense glanced at the director of National Security and nodded. They had clearly prepared their joint advice to go ahead.

"Mr. President, we have every reason to believe the

terrorist threat to this country, notably, the city of Miami, was destroyed last night. The peril is over. Regarding the G8, during the entire conference you will be under the protection of the U.S. Navy, and the Navy has pledged its word that no harm will come to you. Our advice, therefore, is that you go ahead to your G8 with an easy mind!"

"Why, then, that's what I shall surely do," said the president of the USA.

CHAPTER 17

DAVID GUNDLACH RECKONED he had the best job in the world. Second best, anyway. To have that fourth gold stripe on the sleeve or epaulette and be the captain of the vessel would be even better, but he happily settled for first officer.

On an April evening, he stood at the starboard wing of the huge bridge and looked down at the swarming humanity on the dock of the new Brooklyn Terminal two hundred feet below him. The borough of Brooklyn was not above him; from the height of a twenty-three-story building, he was looking down on most of it.

Pier 12 on Buttermilk Channel, being inaugurated that very evening, is not a small dock, but this liner took up all of it. At 1,132 feet long, 135 feet in the beam and drawing thirty-nine feet so that that whole channel had had to be deepened for her, she was the biggest passenger liner afloat by a large margin. The more First Officer Gundlach, on his first crossing since his promotion, looked at her, the more magnificent she seemed.

Far below, and away in the direction of the streets beyond the terminal buildings, he could make out the banners of the frustrated and angry demonstrators. New York's police had with great effectiveness simply cordoned off the entire terminal. Harbor police boats skimmed and swerved round the terminal to ensure that no protesters in boats could come near.

Even if the protesters had been able to approach at sea level, it would have done them no good. The steel hull of the liner simply towered above the waterline, its lowest ports more than fifty feet up. So those passengers boarding that evening could do so in complete privacy.

Not that they were of interest to the protesters. So far, the liner was simply taking on board the lowly ones: stenographers, secretaries, junior diplomats, special advisers and all the human ants without whom the great and good of the world could apparently not discuss hunger, poverty, security, trade barriers, defense and alliances.

As the notion of security crossed his mind, David Gundlach frowned. He and his fellow officers had spent the day escorting scores of American Secret Service men over every inch of the ship. They all looked the same; they all scowled in concentration, they all jabbered into their sleeves where the mikes were hidden and they all got their answers in earpieces, without which they felt naked. Gundlach finally concluded they were professionally paranoid—and they found nothing amiss.

The backgrounds of the twelve hundred crew had been vetted, and not a shred of evidence had been found against any of them. The Grand Duplex apartment set aside for the U.S. president and First Lady was already sealed and guarded by the Secret Service, having been given an inch-by-inch search. Only after seeing it for the first time did David Gundlach realize the enveloping cocoon that must surround this president at all times.

He checked his watch. Two hours to completion of boarding of the three thousand passengers before the eight heads of state or government were due to arrive. Like the diplomats in London, he was admiring of the simplicity of chartering the biggest and most luxurious liner in the world to host the biggest and most prestigious conference in the world; and to do so during a five-day crossing of the Atlantic from New York to Southampton.

The ruse confounded all the forces that habitually sought to bring chaos to the G8 conference every year. Better than a mountain, better than an island, with accommodation for forty-two hundred souls, the *Queen Mary 2* was untouchable.

Gundlach would stand beside his captain as the typhoon hooters sounded their deep bass A note to bid farewell to New York. He would give the required power settings from her four "Mermaid pod" motors, and the captain, using only a tiny joystick on the control console, would ease her out into the East River and turn her toward the waiting Atlantic. So delicate were her controls, and so versatile her two aft pods that swivel through 360 degrees, that she needed no tugs to bring her out of the terminal.

Far to the east, the *Countess of Richmond* was passing the Canary Islands, to her starboard. The holiday islands, where so many Europeans sought to leave the snow and sleet of their winter homes to find December sunshine off the African coast, were out of view. But the tip of Mount Teide could be seen on the horizon with binoculars.

She had two days before her rendezvous with history. The Indonesian navigator had instructed his compatriot in the engine room to cut power to SLOW AHEAD, and she was moving at a walking pace through the gentle swell of the April evening.

The tip of Mount Teide dropped out of sight, and the helmsman eased her a few more degrees to port where, sixteen hundred miles away, lay the American coast. From high in space, she was spotted yet again; and again, when consulted, the computers read her transponder, checked the records, noted her harmless position so far out at sea and repeated her clearance: "Legitimate trader, no danger."

The first government party to arrive was the prime minister of Japan and his entourage. As agreed, they had flown into Kennedy direct from Tokyo. Staying air side, out of sight and sound of the demonstrators, the party had transferred to the passenger cabins of a small fleet of helicopters, which lifted them straight out of Jamaica Bay and brought them to Brooklyn.

The landing zone was inside the perimeter of the great halls and sheds that made up the new terminal. From the Japanese passengers' point of view, the protesters beyond the barriers, mouthing silently whatever point it was they wished to make, simply dropped out of sight. As the rotor blades slowed to a gentle twirl, the delegation was greeted by ship's officers, and conducted along the covered tunnel to the entrance in the side of the hull, and from there to one of the Royal Suites.

The helicopters left for Kennedy to collect the Canadians, who had just arrived.

David Gundlach remained on the bridge, fifty yards from side to side, with huge panoramic windows looking forward out over the sea. Even though the bridge was two hundred feet in the air, the wipers in front of each window revealed that when the bow of the *Queen* hit the sixty-foot midwinter Atlantic waves, spray would still drench the bridge.

But this crossing, so went the forecasts, would be gentle, with a slow swell and light winds. The liner would be taking the southern great circle route, always more popular with guests because of its milder weather and calmer sea. This would bring her in an arc sweeping across the Atlantic at its shortest point, and, at its southernmost, just north of the Azores.

The Russians, French, Germans and Italians succeeded each other in smooth sequence, and dusk fell as the British, owners of the *Queen Mary 2,* took the last flights of the helicopter shuttle.

The U.S. president, who would be hosting the first

dinner just after eight p.m., came in his customary dark blue White House helicopter at six on the dot. A Marine band on the dock struck up "Hail to the Chief" as he strode into the hull and the steel doors closed, shutting out the outside world. At six thirty, the last mooring ropes were cast off, and the *Queen*, dressed overall and lit like a floating city, eased out into the East River.

Those people on smaller vessels in the river and along the roads round the harbor watched her go and waved. High above them, behind toughened plate glass, the state and government heads of the eight richest nations in the world waved back. The brilliantly illuminated Statue of Liberty slid by, the islands dropped away and the *Queen* sedately increased her power.

Either side, her two escorting missile cruisers of the U.S. Navy's Atlantic Fleet took up position several cables away and announced themselves to the captain. To port was the USS *Leyte Gulf* and to starboard the USS *Monterey*. In accordance with the courtesies of the sea, he acknowledged their presence and thanked them. Then he left the bridge to change for dinner. David Gundlach had the helm and the command.

There would be no escorting submarine, for this was not a carrier group, and the submarine was absent for two reasons. No nation possessed the kind of submarine that could evade the missile cruiser's detect-and-sink capacity, and the *Queen* was so fast that no submarine could keep up with her.

As the lights of Long Island dropped away, First Officer Gundlach increased the power to optimum cruise. The four Mermaid pods, pounding out 157,000 horsepower between them, could push the *Queen* to thirty knots, if needed. Normal cruising speed is twenty-five knots, and the escorts had to move to maximum cruise to keep up.

Overhead, the aerial escort appeared: one U.S. Navy EC2 Hawkeye, with radarscopes that could illuminate the surface of the Atlantic for five hundred miles in any direction around the convoy, and an EA-6B Prowler, capable of jamming any offensive weapons system that might dare to lock on to the convoy and destroying it with HARM missiles.

The air cover would be refueled and replaced at end of shift out of the USA until its mission could be relieved by identical cover coming out of the U.S.-leased base in the Azores. That, in turn, would continue until it could be replaced by cover out of the UK. Nothing had been unforeseen.

The dinner was a triumphant success. The statesmen beamed, the wives sparkled, the cuisine, it was agreed, was superb and the crystal glittered as it was filled with vintage wines.

Following the example of the American president, the more so as the other delegations had long flights behind them, the diners broke early and retired for the night.

The conference met in full plenum the following morning. The Royal Court Theatre had been transformed to accommodate all eight delegations, with, sitting behind the principals, the small army of minions that each seemed to need.

The second night was as the first, save that the host was the British prime minister in the two-hundred-seat Queen's Grill. Those of less eminence spread themselves through the huge Britannia Restaurant or the various pubs and bars that also serve food. The younger element, freed from their diplomatic labors, favored the Ballroom after dinner, or the G32 Nightclub.

High above them, all the lights were dimmed on the sweeping bridge where David Gundlach presided through the night hours. Spread out in front of him, just beneath the forward windows, was the array of plasma screens that described every system in the ship.

Foremost among these was the ship's radar, casting its gaze twenty-five miles in all directions. He could see the blips made by the two cruisers either side of him, and, beyond them, those of other vessels going about their business.

He also had at his disposal an Automatic Identification System, or AIS, which would read the transponder of any ship for miles around, and a cross-checking computer based on Lloyd's records that would identify not just who she was but her known route and cargo, and her radio channel.

Either side of the *Queen*, also on darkened bridges, the radar men of the two cruisers pored over their screens with the same task. Their duty was to ensure nothing remotely threatening got near the huge monster thundering between them. Even for a harmless and checked-out freighter, the closeness limit was three kilometers. On the second night, there was nothing nearer than ten.

The picture created by the E2C Hawkeye was inevitably bigger because of its altitude. The image was like an immense circular torch beam moving across the Atlantic from west to east. But the great majority of what it saw was miles away and nowhere near the convoy. What it could do was create a ten-mile-wide corridor thrusting forward of the moving ships, and tell the cruisers what lay ahead of them. For the purpose of realism, it chose a limit on this projection as well. The limit was twenty-five miles, or one hour's cruising.

Just before eleven on the third night, the Hawkeye posted a low-level warning.

"There is a small freighter twenty-five miles ahead, two miles south of intended track. It seems to be motionless in the water."

The *Countess of Richmond* was not quite motionless. Her engines were set to MIDSHIPS, so that her propellers idled in the water. But there was a four-knot current that gave her just enough "way" to keep her nose into the flow, and that meant toward the west.

The inflatable speedboat was in the water, tethered to her port side with a rope ladder running down from the rail to the sea. Four men were already in it, bobbing on the current beside the hull of the freighter.

The other four were on the bridge. Ibrahim held the wheel, staring at the horizon, seeking the first glimmer of the approaching lights.

The Indonesian radio expert was adjusting the transmitting microphone for strength and clarity. Beside him stood the Pakistani teenager born and raised in a suburb of the Yorkshire city of Leeds. The fourth was the Afghan. When the radioman was satisfied, he nodded at the boy, who nodded back and took a stool beside the ship's console, waiting for the call.

The call came from the cruiser, plunging through the sea six cable lengths to the starboard of the *Queen*. David Gundlach heard it loud and clear, as did all on the night watch. The channel used was the common wavelength for ships in the North Atlantic. The voice had the drawl of the Deep South.

"*Countess of Richmond, Countess of Richmond,* this is U.S. Navy cruiser *Monterey.* Do you read me?"

The voice that came back was slightly distorted by less-than-state-of-the-art radio equipment aboard the old freighter. And the voice had the flat vowels of Lancashire, or maybe Yorkshire.

"Oh, aye, *Monterey, Countess* 'ere."

"You appear to be hove to. State your situation."

"*Countess o' Richmond.* 'Aving a bit of overheating"— *click click*—"prop shaft"—static—"repairing as fast as we can."

There was a brief silence from the bridge of the cruiser. Then . . .

"Say again, *Countess of Richmond.* I repeat, say again."

The reply came back, and the accent was thicker than ever. On the bridge of the *Queen,* the first officer had the blip entering his radar screen slightly south of dead ahead and fifty minutes away. Another display gave all the details of the *Countess of Richmond,* including confirmation her transponder was genuine and the signal from it accurate. He cut into the radio exchange.

"*Monterey,* this is *Queen Mary 2.* Let me try."

David Gundlach was born and raised in the Wirral County of Cheshire, not fifty miles from Liverpool. The voice from the *Countess* he put at either Yorkshire or Lancashire, next door to his native Cheshire.

"*Countess of Richmond,* this is *Queen Mary 2.* I read you have an overheat of main bearing in the prop shaft, and you are carrying out repairs at sea. Confirm."

"Aye, that's reet. 'Ope to be finished in another hour," said the voice on the speaker.

"*Countess,* give your details, please. Port of registry, port of departure, destination, cargo."

"*Queen Moory,* we're registered in Liverpool, eight thousand tons, general cargo freighter, coming from Java with brocades and oriental timber, heading for Baltimore."

Gundlach ran his eye down the screened information provided by the head office of McKendrick Shipping in Liverpool, brokers Siebart and Abercrombie in London and insurers Lloyd's. All accurate.

"Who am I speaking to, please?" he asked.

"This is Captain McKendrick. 'Oo are you?"

"First Officer David Gundlach speaking."

The *Monterey,* following the exchange with difficulty, came back.

"*Monterey, Queen.* Do you want to alter course?"

Gundlach consulted the displays. The bridge computer was guiding the *Queen* along the preplanned track, and would adjust for any change of sea, wind, current or waves. To divert would mean going to manual, or resetting the program, and then returning to original course. He would pass the hove-to freighter in forty-one minutes, and he would be two miles, or three kilometers, to his starboard.

"No need, *Monterey*. We'll be past her in forty minutes. Over two miles of sea between us."

Formatting on the *Queen*, the *Monterey* would be less than that, but there was still ample room. High above, the Hawkeye and the EA-6B scanned the helpless freighter for any sign of missile lock-on, or any electronic activity at all. There was none, but they would keep watching until the *Countess* was well behind the convoy. Two other ships were also in the no-entry alley, but much farther ahead, and would be asked to divert, left and right.

"Roger that," said the *Monterey*.

It had all been heard on the bridge of the *Countess*. Ibrahim nodded that they should leave him. The radio engineer and the youth scuttled down the ladder to the speedboat, and all six in the inflatable waited for the Afghan.

Still convinced that the crazed Jordanian would reengage the engine and attempt to ram one of the oncoming vessels, Martin knew he could not leave the *Countess of Richmond*. His only hope was to take her over after killing the crew.

He went down the rope ladder backward. In the thwarts, Suleiman was setting up his digital photography equipment. A rope trailed from the rail of the *Countess*; one of the Indonesians stood near the speedboat's bow, gripping the rope and holding her against the flow of the current running past the ship's side.

Martin held the ladder fast, turned, reached down and slashed the gray, rock-hard fabric over a six-foot length. The act was so fast and so unexpected that for two or three seconds no one reacted, save the sea itself. The escaping air made a low roar, and, with six on board, that side of the inflatable dipped downward and began to ship water.

Leaning farther out, Martin slashed at the retaining rope. He missed, but cut open the forearm of the Indonesian. Then the men reacted. But the Indonesian released his grip, and the sea took them.

There were vengeful hands reaching out at him, but the sinking speedboat dropped astern. The weight of the great outboard pulled down the rear end, and more salt water rushed in. The wreckage cleared the stern of the freighter and went away into the blackness of the Atlantic night. Somewhere down current, it simply sank, dragged down by the outboard. In the gleam of the ship's stern light, Martin saw waving hands in the water, and then they, too, were gone. No one can swim against four knots. He went back up the ladder.

At that moment, Ibrahim jerked one of the three controls the explosives expert had left him. As Martin climbed, there was a series of sharp cracks as tiny charges went off.

When Mr. Wei had built the gallery masquerading as six sea containers along the deck of the *Java Star* from bridge to bow, he had created the roof, or "lid," over the empty space beneath using a single sheet of steel held down by four strongpoints.

To these, the explosives man had fitted shaped charges, and linked all four to wires, taking power from the ship's engines. When they blew, the sheet metal lid of the cavern beneath lifted upward several feet. The power of the charges was asymmetric, so one side of the sheet rose higher than the other.

Martin was at the top of the rope ladder, knife clenched in teeth, when the charges blew. He crouched there as the huge sheet of steel slid sideways into the sea. He put the knife away, and entered the bridge.

The Al Qaeda killer was standing at the wheel, staring ahead through the glass. On the horizon, bearing down at twenty-five knots, was a floating city, seventeen decks and 150,000 tons of lights, steel and people. Right beneath the bridge, the gallery was open to the stars. For the first time, Martin realized its purpose. Not to contain something; to hide something.

The clouds moved away from the half-moon, and the entire foredeck of the onetime *Java Star* gleamed in its light. For the first time, Martin realized this was not a general freighter containing explosives; it was a tanker. Running away from the bridge was the cat's cradle of pipes, tubes, spigots and hydrant wheels that gave away her purpose in life.

Evenly spaced down the deck toward the forepeak were six circular steel disks—the venting hatches—above each of the cargo tanks beneath the deck.

"You should have stayed on the boat, Afghan," said Ibrahim.

"There was no room, my brother. Suleiman almost fell overboard. I stayed on the ladder. Then they were gone. Now I will die here with you, *inshallah*."

Ibrahim seemed appeased. He glanced at the ship's clock, and pulled his second lever. The flexes ran from the control down to the ship's batteries, took their power and went forward into the gallery where the explosives man, entering through the secret door, had worked during his month at sea.

Six more charges detonated. The six hatches blew away from above the tanks. What followed was invisible to the naked eye. Had it been possible to see, six vertical columns rose like volcanoes from the domes as the cargo began to vent. The rising vapor cloud reached a hundred feet, lost its impetus, and gravity took over. The unseen cloud, mixing furiously with the night air, fell back to the sea and began to roll outward, away from the source, in all directions.

Martin had lost, and he knew it. He was too late, and he knew that, too. He knew enough to realize what a floating bomb he had been riding since the Philippines, and that what was pouring out of the six missing hatches was invisible death that could not now be controlled.

He had always presumed the *Countess of Richmond*, now become again the *Java Star,* was going to drive herself into some inner harbor and detonate what lay below her decks.

He had presumed she was going to ram something of value as she blew herself up. For thirty days, he had waited in vain for a chance to kill seven men and take over her command. No such chance had appeared.

Now, too late, he realized the *Java Star* was not going to deliver a bomb; she *was* the bomb. And with her cargo venting fast, she did not need to move an inch. The oncoming liner had to pass only within three kilometers of her to be consumed.

He had heard the interchange on the bridge between the Pakistani boy and the deck officer of the *Queen Mary 2.* He knew too late the *Java Star* would not engage engines. The escorting cruisers would never allow that, but she did not need to.

There was a third control by Ibrahim's right hand, a button to be hammered downward. Martin followed the flexes to a Very pistol, a flare gun, mounted just forward of the bridge windows. One flare, one single spark . . .

Through the windows, the city of lights was over the horizon. Fifteen miles, thirty minutes cruising, optimum time for maximum fuel-air mixture.

Martin's glance flicked to the radio speaker on the console. A last chance to shout a warning. His right hand slid down toward the slit in his robe, inside which was his knife strapped to his thigh.

The Jordanian caught the glance and the movement.

He had not survived Afghanistan, a Jordanian jail and the relentless American hunt for him in Iraq without developing the instincts of a wild animal.

Something told him that despite the fraternal language, the Afghan was not his friend. The raw hatred charged the atmosphere on the tiny bridge like a silent scream.

Martin's hand slipped inside his robe for the knife. Ibrahim was first; the gun had been underneath the map on the chart table. It was pointing straight at Martin's chest. The distance to cross was twelve feet. Ten too many.

A soldier is trained to estimate chances, and do it fast. Martin had spent much of his life doing that. On the bridge of the *Countess of Richmond,* enveloped in her own death cloud, there were only two: go for the man, or go for the button. There would be no surviving either.

Some words came into his mind, words from long ago, in a schoolboy's poem: "To every man upon this earth / Death cometh soon or late . . ." And he recalled Ahmad Shah Massoud, the Lion of the Panjshir, talking by the campfire.

"We are all sentenced to die, Angleez. But only a warrior blessed of Allah may be allowed to choose how!" Colonel Mike Martin made his choice. . . .

Ibrahim saw him coming; he knew the flicker in the eyes of a man about to die. The killer screamed and fired. The charging man took the bullet in the chest, and began to die. But beyond pain and shock, there is always willpower, just enough for another second of life.

At the end of that second, both men and ship were consumed in a rose pink eternity.

*   *   *

David Gundlach stared in stunned amazement. Fifteen miles ahead, where the world's largest liner would have been in thirty-five minutes, a huge volcano of flame erupted out of the sea. From the other three men on the night watch came cries of "What the hell was that?"

"*Monterey* to *Queen Mary 2*. Divert to port. I say, divert to port. We are investigating."

To his right, Gundlach saw the U.S. cruiser move up to attack speed and head for the flames. Even as he watched, they began to flicker and die upon the water. It was clear the *Countess of Richmond* had sustained some terrible accident. His job was to stay clear; if there were men in the water, the *Monterey* would find them. But it was still wise to summon his captain. When the ship's master arrived on the bridge, his first officer explained what he had seen. They were now a full eighteen miles from the estimated spot, and heading away fast.

To port, the USS *Leyte Gulf* stayed with them. The *Monterey* was heading straight for the fireball miles up ahead. The captain agreed that in the unlikely event of survivors, the *Monterey* should search for them.

As the two men watched from the safety of their bridge, the flames began to flicker and die. The last blotches of flame upon the sea would be the remnants of the vanished ship's fuel oil. All the hypervolatile cargo was gone before the *Monterey* reached the spot.

The captain of the Cunarder ordered that the computers resume course for Southampton.

EPILOGUE

THERE WAS AN INQUIRY. Of course. It took almost two years. These things are never done in a few hours, except on television.

One team took the real *Java Star*: from the laying of her keel to the moment she steamed out of Brunei loaded with LPG, destination Fremantle, western Australia.

It was confirmed by independent witnesses with no reason to lie that Captain Herrmann was in charge, and that all was well. She was seen by two other captains rounding the northeastern tip of Borneo Island shortly after that. Precisely because of her cargo, both ships' masters noted she was well away from them, and logged her name.

The single recording of her captain's last Mayday message was played to a Norwegian psychiatrist, who confirmed that the voice was a fellow Norwegian speaking good English, but that he seemed to be speaking under duress.

The captain of the fruit ship that had noted her given position and diverted to the spot was traced and interviewed. He repeated what he had heard and seen. But experts in fire at sea reckoned that if the fire in the *Java*

Star's engine room was so catastrophic that Captain Herrmann could not save her, it must have ignited her cargo eventually. In which case, there would be no fabric-tented life rafts left floating on the water where she sank.

Filipino commandos carried out a raid, supported by U.S. helicopter gunships, on the Zamboanga peninsula, ostensibly on Abu Sayyaf bases. They trawled, and brought back two jungle-dwelling Huq trackers who occasionally worked for the terrorists but were not prepared to face a firing squad for them.

They reported they had seen a medium tanker in a narrow creek in the heart of the jungle being worked on by men with oxyacetylene torches.

The *Java Star* team entered its report within a year. It declared the *Java Star* had not been sunk by an onboard fire but had been hijacked intact; and, further, that a lot of trouble had been gone to in order to persuade the marine world that she no longer existed when, in fact, she did. The entire crew was presumed dead already, and this had to be confirmed.

Because of need-to-know, all the arms of the inquiry were working on the various facets without knowing why. They were told—and believed—that it was an insurance investigation.

Another team followed the fortunes of the real *Countess of Richmond*. They proceeded from the offices of Siebart and Abercrombie in Crutched Friars, City of London, to Liverpool, and checked out the family and crew. They confirmed all was in good order when the *Countess* unloaded her Jaguars at Singapore. Captain

McKendrick had run into a friend from Liverpool on the docks, and they shared a few beers before he sailed. And he telephoned home.

Independent witnesses confirmed she was still in the command of her lawful captain when she took on valuable timber at Kinabalu.

But an on-the-spot visit to Surabaya, Java, revealed she never even stopped there to take on her second-part cargo of Asian silk. Yet Siebart and Abercrombie in London had received confirmation from the shippers that she had. So it was forged.

A likeness of "Mr. Lampong" was created, and Indonesian homeland security recognized a suspected but never proven financial supporter of Jemaat Islamiyah. A search was mounted, but the terrorist had vanished into the human tides of Southeast Asia.

The team concluded that the *Countess of Richmond* had been boarded and hijacked in the Celebes Sea. With all her papers, ID radio codes and transponder stolen, she would have been sunk with all hands. Next of kin were advised.

The clincher came from Dr. Ali Aziz al-Khattab. The wiretaps on his phones revealed he was booking a departure to the Middle East. After a conference at Thames House, home of MI5, it was decided that enough was enough. The Birmingham police and Special Branch took down the apartment door of the Kuwaiti academic when the listeners confirmed he was in the bath, and he was escorted away in a bathrobe.

But al-Khattab was clever. A total strip search of his apartment, car and office, cell phone and laptop, revealed not one incriminating detail about him.

He smiled blandly, and his lawyer protested, through the statutory twenty-eight days allowed to the British police for holding a suspect without preferring a formal charge. His smile faded when, as he stepped out of Her Majesty's Belmarsh Prison, he was rearrested, this time on an extradition warrant lodged by the government of the United Arab Emirates.

Under this legislation, there is no limit of time. Al-Khattab went straight back to his cell. This time, his lawyer lodged a vigorous appeal against extradition. As a Kuwaiti, al-Khattab was not even a citizen of the UAE, but that wasn't the point.

The Counter-Terrorist Center at Dubai had amazingly come into possession of a sheaf of photos. These showed al-Khattab conferring closely with a known Al Qaeda courier, a dhow captain, already under surveillance. Others showed him arriving at, and leaving, a villa in the outback of Ras al-Khaimah, known to be a terrorist hideaway. The London judge was impressed, and granted the extradition.

Al-Khattab appealed . . . and lost again. Faced with the dubious charms of HMP Belmarsh or an athletic interrogation by UAE Special Forces at their desert base in the Gulf, he asked to stay as a guest of Queen Elizabeth.

That posed a problem. The British explained they had nothing to hold him on, let alone try and convict him.

He was halfway to Heathrow Airport when he struck his deal and began to talk.

Once started, he caused CIA guests who sat in on the sessions to report back that it was like watching the Boulder Dam give way. He blew away over one hundred AQ agents who until then had been lily-whites, unknown to Anglo-American intelligence, and twenty-four sleeping bank accounts.

When the interrogators mentioned the AQ project code-named al-Isra, the Kuwaiti was stunned into silence. He had no idea anyone knew. Then he started to talk again.

He confirmed everything London and Washington already knew or suspected, then added more. He could identify all the eight men aboard the *Countess of Richmond* on her final voyage, except the three Indonesians.

He knew the origins and parentage of the teenager of Pakistani derivation who, born and raised in the English county of Yorkshire, could speak in place of Captain McKendrick on the ship's radio and fool First Officer David Gundlach.

And he admitted the *Doña María* and the men on board her had been a deliberate sacrifice, though unaware of it themselves; a mere diversion lest there be any hesitation, for any reason, in sending the American president to sea on a liner.

Gently, the interrogators brought the subject round to an Afghan whom they knew al-Khattab had interrogated in the UAE villa. In fact, they did not know it at all; they suspected it, but al-Khattab hardly hesitated.

He confirmed the arrival of the mysterious Taliban

commander in Ras al-Khaimah after a daring and bloody escape from custody outside Kabul. He claimed these details had been carefully checked by AQ sympathizers in Kabul and authenticated.

He admitted he had been instructed by Ayman al-Zawahiri himself to go to the Gulf and question the fugitive for as long as it took. And he revealed that it was the sheikh, no less, who had verified the Afghan's identity on the basis of a conversation years earlier in a hospital cave in the Tora Bora.

It was the sheikh who permitted the Afghan the privilege of joining al-Isra, and he, al-Khattab, had dispatched the man to Malaysia with others.

It gave his Anglo-American interrogators exquisite pleasure to wreck what was left of his life by telling him who the Afghan really was.

In a final detail, a handwriting expert confirmed that the hand of the missing colonel and the person who had scrawled the message thrust into the dive bag at Labuan Island were one and the same.

The Crowbar committee finally agreed that Mike Martin had boarded the *Countess of Richmond*, still posing as a terrorist, somewhere after Labuan, and that there was not a shred of evidence that he had been able to get off in time.

Theories as to why the *Countess* blew up forty minutes prematurely were left open in the file.

It is customary in the UK that seven years are required to elapse before a person missing without trace can be legally presumed dead and a certificate issued.

But when the interrogation of Dr. al-Khattab reached its conclusion, the coroner for the City of Westminster, London, was entertained to a very discreet dinner in a private room at Brooks's Club, St. James's Street. There were only three others present, and they explained many things to the coroner once the stewards had left them alone.

The following week, the coroner issued a certificate of death to an academic from the School of Oriental and African Studies, a Dr. Terry Martin, in respect of his late brother, Colonel Mike Martin of the Parachute Regiment, who had vanished without trace eighteen months earlier.

On the grounds of the headquarters of the SAS Regiment outside the town of Hereford stands a rather odd-looking structure known simply as the Clock Tower. The tower was dismantled piece by piece when the regiment moved several years ago from its old base to the newer premises. Then it was reconstructed.

Predictably, it has a clock at the top, but the points of interest are the four faces of the tower on which are inscribed the names of all SAS men killed in combat.

Shortly after the issuance of the death certificate, a memorial service was held at the foot of the Clock Tower. There were a dozen men in uniform, and ten in civilian clothes, and two women. One of these was the director-general of MI5, the Security Service, and the other the dead man's ex-wife.

The missing-in-action status had needed a bit of persuasion, but the pressure came from very high indeed, and when apprised of all the known facts the director, Special Forces, and the commanding officer of the regiment had agreed that the status was justified. Colonel Mike Martin was certainly not the first, nor would he be the last, SAS man to be lost in a faraway place and never recovered.

Across the border to the west, the sun was dipping across the Black Mountains of Wales on a bleak February day when the brief ceremony was held. At the end, the chaplain spoke the habitual words from the Gospel according to John: "Greater love hath no man than this, that a man lay down his life for his friends."

Only those grouped round the Clock Tower knew that Mike Martin, Parachute Regiment and SAS colonel, retired, had done this for four thousand complete strangers, none of whom ever knew he existed.

SIGNET

DANIEL SILVA

PRINCE OF FIRE

Now Gabriel Allon is back in Venice, when a terrible
explosion in Rome leads to a disturbing personal
revelation: the existence of a dossier in the hands of
terrorists that strips away his secrets, and lays bare
his history. Hastily recalled home to Israel, drawn
once more into the heart of a service he had once
forsaken, Allon finds himself stalking an elusive
master terrorist across a landscape drenched in
generations of blood, along a trail that keeps turning
in upon itself, until, finally, he can no longer be
certain who is stalking whom. And when at last the
inevitable showdown comes, it's not Gabriel alone
who is threatened with destruction—for it is not his
history alone that has been laid bare.

"Those in the know are calling Daniel Silva the new
John le Carré. Those who are reading him can't put
him down." —*Chicago Sun-Times*

"A first-rate thriller." —*Rocky Mountain News*

Available wherever books are sold or at
penguin.com